Framandi Alliance

Galaxy Accretion Conflicts

Rashid Ahmed

Framandi Alliance

Galaxy Accretion Conflicts

First Edition November 2019
ISBN 13 (Paperback): 9781707737642
Author: Rashid Ahmed
Imprint: Independently published

Contact: info@rashidahmed.com
Visit: www.rashidahmed.com

Dedicated to my Mum and Dad.
For always encouraging me to explore.

Contents

Preface

As a voracious reader for most of my life, my mind has always bubbled with the occasional plot idea, imagined worlds and character personas. Many of you might relate to this.

Having gravitated towards science fiction in the last decade and having spent a corresponding amount of time devouring adventure, I began outlining the plot for a compelling space adventure story.

Told from a third-generation, quantum processing, independent AI's perspective, the novel skips along at a brisk pace. From the moment a crew, which includes a pair of transhuman twins, is tasked to explore an anomalous space object above the solar system's ecliptic plane; the plot winds a relentless quest, of deep-space adventures.

While researching our galaxy, I came across references to the Canis Major Dwarf Galaxy or CMa Dwarf, which has been in the process of being pulled apart and absorbed into the Milky Way. This process has been going on for eons, evidenced by the trail of stars comprising CMa Dwarf, wrapping itself around our galaxy three times.

What happens when galaxies merge? From the brief timeline of humans, not much really. But what about older civilizations? Those which may have evolved millions or perhaps billions of years ago? If they haven't been wiped out, it's entirely possible that they have taken to colonizing star systems and perhaps entire sections of galaxies.

Back in 1950, when Enrico Fermi is known to have exclaimed to his fellow physicists, "But where is everybody?" referring to extra-terrestrials, he was indicating that intelligent life might have widely risen. For a suitably advanced civilization, travelling across space using known/feasible means of propulsion, getting across our galaxy would take but a few million years.

This implies that there could be extensive colonisation across the Milky Way and CMa Dwarf (a much older galaxy). Consequently, accretion of CMa Dwarf into the Milky Way, could be a cause of conflict between established galaxy spanning civilizations. This premise is the pivotal theme of this novel, and others to follow in this series.

Another interesting thematic consideration is that the plot unfolds in our present time. Slightly in the past in fact. Extrapolating upon currently established science and unfolding research, while dipping into extra-terrestrial hypothesis and shimmying up to controversial conspiracy theories; the science fiction in this novel is meant to be highly believable.

Additional content like main character outlines and world descriptions are available on my website RashidAhmed.com.

Do read the prologue. The background information it provides, though technical, is vital. You're sure to better enjoy the chapters that follow.

I really do hope you enjoy the book.

Rashid Ahmed
@Kaputnik77

Prologue: Lysi Beginnings

Excerpts from the Notes of Shun (Gen1 AI)

W hat started off as an attempt to solve a few of the world's most pressing 'wicked problems', rapidly and secretly veered off course. The first transhumans were developed, deep-space resource exploration picked up and separately, the first independent digital artificial intelligence aided in accelerated progress. These were seen to be solutions, to pressing Earth-wide wicked problems. No one knew that the stepping-stones these advances provided, would lead to fresh problems being uncovered. Ancient, inter-galactic problems.

History of Lýsi

During the Second World War, global governments as well as international bodies recognized the threats of annihilation through war brought on by political stress, extinction level events such as a massive meteor impact, viruses gone wild or natural phenomenon including rapid climate change. The first think tank (a concept which became popular during WWII) to solve these problems, was considered on the sidelines when various world governments came together at Allied conferences in Moscow and Tehran in 1943. An independent body funded separately by various government departments, businesses and individuals, was formed to look at immediate as well as future problems affecting the world. Amongst the problems, mitigating global war (proposed by a body of underdeveloped and pacifist countries), steering towards an ideal techno-utopian society (proposed by a few communist and socialist countries) and strategies to deal with global catastrophic risk (proposed by a section of rich countries) were the first to be accepted and funded.

In 1945, the thinktank, by then called Lýsi, began operating out of a small building, a block away from the townhall in Delft, The Netherlands. It was close enough to the local university so that visiting intellectuals would fit in. The headquarters were also close to the port, transportation and essential infrastructure. The low-key Lýsi H.Q. also maintained a fleet of six vehicles, three motorized boats (moored just outside the building) and seven residential buildings adjacent to the museum next door. Lýsi organized itself in a distributed manner with a global, corporate-style leadership team. The cross-border organization drew upon highly qualified staff from universities, government departments involved in practical research and leading technical professionals from across industries. All members were vetted by a board comprising a mix of government appointees (those with active projects) and of qualified representatives from the academic arena. There were also three independent members, who nominated a group of individuals to participate in active projects (to act as the ethical overseers for each of the project groups).

Extraterrestrials: A wicked problem

Smack in the middle of the cold war, between 1965 and 1972, actual traction began on the then much thrown about term, wicked problems. Various frameworks began to be drawn into policy at the global and national levels. By this time the problem of how to deal with extraterrestrials as conceptualized in extraterrestrial hypothesis (ETH), was also introduced as a fully funded project after numerous unidentified flying object sightings were recorded between 1945 and 1960. Specifically, following a 1953 military and intelligence examination of ETH material (publicly explained away as innocuous), Lýsi's ETH researchers uncovered material hidden from the reviewers. It was also the period (1964-1967) when Lýsi became a lot more secretive. This was after an attending member extrapolated and published some thinking on 'entropy', suggesting that every advanced social group would succumb to chaos, which would ultimately lead to disorganization. One scientist published material on self-teaching ultra-intelligent machines. A rebellious researcher published material on transgenic life extension through use of recombinant deoxyribonucleic acid (DNA), while yet another released information on experiments related to detection and manipulation of gravity waves. Given the rapid exchange of information between participants of various projects (to hasten solution findings), the ability of Lýsi to prevent hemorrhaging of secrets was brought into question. Especially given the nature of research, and the possibility of undesirable usage of specialist technology developed by project groups.

Mitigating global catastrophic risk

After 1972, up to which time it was already deeply involved with space travel technology and solutions, the thinktank became more operationalized (a think-and-do tank). Following a publication in a scientific journal in 1974 which recognized the overload of the planet's heat balance and the consequences of it, Lýsi began to focus primarily on global catastrophic risk (GCR) under which all other wicked problems were placed as subsets. Lýsi's solutions settled on and involved, directed human evolution, the development of artificial machine intelligence and actively pursuing space colonization, through public and private means.

There were initial breakthroughs in ETH based research in nanomaterials, manipulation of electromagnetic radiation, micro-computing and space observation. Simultaneously, there were advances in recombinant DNA technology (with its applications in agriculture being released for use globally); which interestingly, prompted early transhuman applied research. Clandestinely, the group set up shop near the University Hospital in Havana, Cuba; to utilize gene transfer technology and to use retroviruses with selective markers to identify successful DNA modification. This technology was immediately used to treat people with genetic disorders and immunodeficiency. Lýsi privately ran genome editing trials, to completely modify a few human participants' DNA. Early successes led to some information on gene therapy for cancer being shared with prominent researchers, to tackle the rising incidences of cancer.

To maintain a higher level of secrecy and increase the speed of development; in 1975, all non-key participating members were released with binding non-disclosure agreements. Now called The Lýsi Group and wholly privately funded, directed human evolution tasks became paramount to ensure species and information survival. Tiny amounts of technical knowhow were periodically released in a controlled manner to specific corporate entities, to kickstart widespread use of resultant products by consumers. While this policy gradually brought large portions of the global population closer to technology and prepared people for geometric leaps in technology progress; it came with significant drawbacks like unconstrained resource and energy use which amplified environmental degradation, global warming and the rich-poor divide.

Following a 1976 extra-terrestrial (ET) unidentified flying object (UFO) incident in the middle east, ETH research moved up in rank directly under Global Catastrophic Risk. Most research including directed human evolution through gene manipulation, AI through linked neural net machines, space technologies and robotics were brought under the ambit of GCR solutions. Publicly without identifying Lýsi, a recombinant DNA advisory committee was formed to regulate use of the technology in agriculture, ecosystem modification, animal husbandry, and genetic treatment.

Anomalous space object

On the 12th of December 1989, a medium sized asteroid-like object was discovered, slowly creeping forward, north of the solar system's ecliptic. What was strange was that the object seemed to have stopped in space. It was designated as AL-I, using Lýsi's internal codes instead of conventional asteroid naming conventions. The object was not a comet otherwise astronomers would have become aware of it. A decision was made to keep an eye on this anomalous space object. Interest peaked when a small portion of the object separated and moved toward the Sun. It was tracked as it conducted a solar orbit and went below the solar system's ecliptic, where it disappeared at forty astronomical units (AUs) from the Sun. Lýsi leadership determined that the anomalous space object required investigation.

New space technologies

The next five years, were dedicated to practical implementation of previous research, aimed at overcoming global catastrophic risk. Task groups worked furiously to perfect systems for long duration space travel for humans, transhumans and robotic AI. The issues of shielding against cosmic rays in space was a critical matter as cosmic-ray-induced errors were now becoming an issue even on ground-based micro and nano-electronics. Early shields overseen by the AI Shun, and the transhuman twins Jón and Ásta, were manufactured on fabrication platforms orbiting Earth. The shield panels were made with dense layers of ceramic, metal and fiber-composites that absorbed primary and secondary cosmic rays.

A sandwich of multiple composites with materials of low atomic weight and high yield strength were arranged towards the outside of the hull panel and were sequentially injected under an outer section of high-heat and impact resistant sheets. These were then centrifuge-molded inside a half centimeter thick outer sheet of linked double bonded nano-carbon interwoven with graphene, that was tough as diamond yet allowed high electrical conductivity for an additional EM shield outside the hull. The panel layer could absorb a hypervelocity impact from a twenty-centimeter piece of space debris or projectile. Four sets of physical shielding with polyethene, xenon and gel filled interspacing were found to provide exceptional heat, impact and radiation resistance.

For deep-space exploration vessels, portions of the interlocking hull sections were made to be retractable so that transparent ceramic windows, could be exposed to space. This enabled visual and sensor data collection. The hull panels were overengineered to be suitable for interstellar space travel. They were tough enough to come within two diameters of the sun, withstand atmospheric entry uses and deal with sustained twelve thousand bar pressure for gas-planet exploration needs. With these gains came new discoveries.

AL-I exhibits strange behavior

By late January of 2001, the anomalous asteroid-like space object AL-I, began exhibiting strange behavior. It began to slowly creep towards the Sun again. This was also when the smaller object which had detached itself from AL-I returned to the solar system. The smaller object traversed across the solar system to the asteroid-like object within a week. An exploration mission to intercept AL-I was immediately given the go ahead, a day after Jón and Ásta's eighteenth birthday.

By this time, the orbital and the three Earth-Moon Lagrangian point platforms were fully staffed and operational. The AI Shun had been hived off into two separate entities - Shun on Earth and Kei in space. Kei meaning 'wise' in Japanese, was so named because it inherited all of Shun's knowledge. Both communicated with each other, maintained information backups of each other, but began to evolve their own codebase and hardware separately.

In early February, Jón and Ásta were scheduled to join a team of six already at the L2 Earth-Moon Lagrangian point platform, which had been named Álfhól by the twins. The name was inspired by the 'tiny wooden elf houses' which Icelandic people build in their gardens for Huldufólk or 'hidden people', the term used for elves. The twins were setting out to investigate AL-I, the medium sized asteroid-like object, discovered approaching north of the solar system's ecliptic. The object, which was headed towards the Sun had slowed down, and then stopped in space. Numerous cargo capsules were ejected in preparation for the mission.

Unrequired attention

Just before they were due to launch, 'Univers Aerospace' a private French-Swiss aerospace technology multinational, took notice of the high-altitude activities being conducted by the flying wing aircraft. The organization was conducting routine atmospheric observations over the Pacific Ocean with a sounding balloon at an altitude of fifty kilometers, when the onboard cameras relayed several dull-grey, evenly timed objects hurtling by the balloon. Since most of the onboard data was relayed by automated systems to Univers' data collection facility in Switzerland, it wasn't till a week after, that the ascending objects were noticed and analyzed. The objects had sped by the balloon too fast and close, to be clearly visible. However, the incident rapidly drew interest amongst the analysts and was kicked up to management. An investigation was initiated.

Univers operated a small constellation of weather satellites, through which the organization provided continuous weather data and imagery to global government agencies and companies. The Univers constellation comprised of six satellites in geostationary orbit above the equator, at an altitude of thirty-five thousand kilometers and two polar orbiting satellites at nine hundred kilometers. Images from these satellites showed a series of space injections, of capsules shot from a large barrel like a circus canon, but much longer and mounted to the roof of a flying wing aircraft. None of the dull and nonreflective capsules seemed to be heading towards any single location in space and tracking these was beyond the satellites' capabilities. However, the base of operations of the aircraft was located to a modified airport on the Kuril Islands. The organization decided to find out more, and they were willing to get their hands dirty.

Chapter 1: Àlfhól Platform
Earth-Moon L2 Lagrange Point

The trip to Álfhól space platform, went without a hitch. The platform was remotely constructed behind the moon and was unobservable from Earth. It was constructed by The Lýsi Group's growing number of space-based Asteroid Mining and Construction Autonomous Robots, commonly referred to as AMCARs.

Jón and Ásta were the last of a group of specialists to get to the platform. They had spent an extra month on Earth intensively studying AL-I, the medium sized asteroid-like object, which was on a trajectory towards the Sun, moving slowly, north of the solar system's ecliptic. After the initial detection by the group, there were Earth-based as well as deep-space platforms constantly monitoring AL-I. The object seemed rocky, reflected little light and had few noticeable features. But it was starkly different from other asteroids. It was not moving within the solar system like other orbiting asteroids, nor was it behaving like other observed bodies.

AL-I was not believed to be orbiting the Sun. Nor was it considered to be a part of the solar system. It was determined to be interstellar in origin. What really caught the Lýsi Group's attention was that it began massive deceleration soon after it was originally noticed. This was highly unnatural, and several theories were doing the rounds that included a concentrated patch of dark matter in the area, an undetected object exerting significant gravity and an outlandish idea that it was an artificial object that was able to control its own motion.

Lýsi had no illusions about extraterrestrial intelligence or the fact that at least remote contact had been made by off-world intelligence. A lot of the group's key technologies, advances and research was based on acquired off-world artifacts. The group would investigate AL-I not just because it was unique, but mainly because its sudden appearance and erratic behavior, posed a hazard to the planet. Time was of the essence and the group decided to intercept and investigate the object before it got too deep into the solar system.

The twins were launched into the thermosphere from one of the group's fleet of flying-wing aircraft. Ejected at high Gs while nestled within their individual crew launch capsules which were shot from the roof mounted cannon, both transhuman twins lost consciousness even though their physiology was tougher than their human colleagues.

The crew capsules were automatically captured by AMCARs, which were temporarily reassigned off their space junk recycling, fabrication and manufacturing jobs, for this specific task.

The twins only awoke on way to the moon in an S3 'Nesting Doll' - a midsize Autonomous Cargo and Transport Vessel or ACTV, capable of accommodating people, or if the need arose any other life-forms. The nesting doll cargo vessel was fitted out for a crew mission and was as comfortable as travelling in a luxury train coach. It had cocoon-like bunks which doubled up as escape pods, and a common area with ergonomic seating which was used for dining and mission operations. There were toilet and fitness areas to the front and rear of the vessel.

Manual maneuvering and vessel control units were built into digital pads contained in each of the bunks and the common area grav-seats. But these would only be required during an emergency.

Ásta groggily whispered into her hard-shell extravehicular activity suit's helmet microphone, "Jón, you there?" They were both equipped with the very latest HSEVA suits.

He responded just as groggily "Yup, I'm here". After a brief pause, he continued "Really didn't expect to be unconscious for long after the launch. My neck feels like it was viciously twisted".

Ásta giggled and replied "The AMCARs arms must have handled you by the head. Anyhow, we were given a drug-cocktail injection before the launch to fortify and sedate us. The sedative is administered so we don't do anything stupid while the automated robots and systems carry out their jobs. Also, presumably so we wouldn't notice if anything went wrong".

Jón muttered "I'd feel safer getting from the launch capsule to the transport myself, thank you very much!"

Ásta mollified her brother "It isn't so much for you as it is for others. Besides, the entire transfer process is efficient, and the automated systems are used to handling inanimate cargo. Anyhow, we designed the process ourselves and worked on getting this setup as close to perfect as possible, so no protests."

Her brother's focus shifted, and he brought up the transit tasks on his HSEVA suit helmet's heads up display. He said, "Since we haven't been in zero gravity, other than training, how about we keep the local gravity under us switched off and let our bodies get used to null-gravity operations?" Ásta replied in the affirmative.

The twins opened and rolled out of their bunk pods. They separately went through a checklist of the nesting doll's systems to doubly ensure everything checked out. It turned out the S3 Autonomous Cargo and Transport Vessel was named Habogi by the AI Shun, after a young man in one of the twins' most loved Icelandic fairytales.

The internal environment was nominal, and the local gravity was set at twenty percent above Earth gravity, to force their bodies to exert and offset atrophy. The twins then stood against magnetic mounts next to their bunk pods and undid their suits, which began a rapid recharge. The HSEVA suits could produce their own energy since they utilized compact versions of the dual-purpose Cosmic Ray Energy Generator shielding panels. The more compact CREG panels provided excellent exoskeletal rigidity to the suits, and long duration protection against cosmic ray radiation. Energy was stored in gel batteries, built into the suit's skeletal frame. An additional layer of overlapping hexagonal scales made with double bonded nano-carbon and interwoven with graphene, provided added protection against hypervelocity projectiles. Since the exoskeletal panels brought up the overall suit weight, electrode-mesh gel filament artificial muscles, were used between and under joints, to augment the wearer's strength and movement.

The HSEVA suits were overengineered to operate between superheated and cryogenic environment ranges. The twins did a checklist assessment of their suits to ensure they were prepared for quick deployment. They then did a once-over of each other's suits as well. Checks completed; they were both eager to get on with their self-training by conducting the remaining trip in null-G. Deciding on a series of physical exercises between operational tasks, they began with a floating sprint across the interior length of the vessel and ended with manual maneuvering. They'd both been brought up fully immersed with the technologies being used, often leading design and development for many of the deployed vessels. Young as they were, each was well known and respected amongst the tightly woven teams within Lýsi.

After a brief hand-to-hand close combat sparring session, which they checked off their list of activities, they secured themselves into mission operation seats and unfolded manual maneuvering and vessel control units bringing them to chest level. Jón sent a quick text message letting Álfhól platform know of their intension to go manual for a short duration. The message went out over an encrypted tight-beam communication, which bounced off two line-of-sight satellites before arriving at its destination.

Kei the space-based AI, was plugged into and in charge of monitoring all autonomous and automatic systems. It let the twins know, "We'll be arriving at Álfhól in an hour, so you'll have about ten minutes each to try your hands at maneuvering the nesting doll". Kei and its Earth-bound counterpart had picked up on the language, colloquialisms, nicknames and comfort levels of everyone they had encountered. Both AI offshoots were most accustomed to the twins, as they had spent considerable time providing moral, directional and decision-making guidance to Shun and Kei in the last five years. The twins in turn had picked up several traits from the AI like multi-pronged cause and effect problem analysis, an ability that the twins were adept at. They operated cohesively being able to intuitively predict each other's intensions. Ásta took manual control of the vessel first.

"I'm going to try out a series of random maneuvers, that will take us off our current course. First off, I'm going to rotate the nesting doll full circle clockwise, and then reverse the move." Ásta said while delicately spinning the vessel on a pivot. She completed the anti-clockwise maneuver and then followed up with bringing Habogi vertically up on their plane of travel. "This is a lot like training," she said while trying out a few tricks which she had been planning in her head. Her ten minutes up, she handed over control to Jón.

After a few standard directional maneuvers, Jón said "Ásta hang on, I'm going to try some evasive maneuvers against simulated space debris. Kei, will you please insert some virtual debris into the path we're currently on, I'll try and avoid them".

After the first few chunks of virtual rocks and asteroids, Jón noticed the debris field become thicker. The approach velocity for each lump became progressively faster and he had to really juggle Habogi around to keep from hitting any of the debris. This went on for a full minute, which felt to Jón like at least twenty. On one occasion during the session, Jón tossed Habogi end on end like a caterpillar, in a maneuver which nearly knocked them unconscious.

Kei took over control of Habogi. Jón realized that the AI may have been testing the twins for their G-tolerance. Since both twins had a very close relationship with the AI, he asked, "How did we do on the gravs?" Kei replied, "You both easily managed upwards of ten Gs for up to five seconds, without your innerwear pressure systems activated. With the pressure system initiated, both your enhanced bodies would be able to sustain forty Gs. Of course, once the local gravity systems are activated, you wouldn't have any problems with acceleration forces in any one direction."

All space vessels constructed by Lýsi were optimized for exploration and expected harsh environmental conditions. While transport and habitable exploration vessels could withstand up to twelve thousand bar pressure, the autonomous multi-purpose space robots could theoretically withstand up to fifteen thousand bar. Kei continued, "You've got just enough time to get clean and suit-up. We will be at Álfhól in half an hour."

Ten minutes to arrival, the twins tucked themselves into their HSEVA suits in case of rapid depressurization while docking. This was just a precaution, but a vital one. There hadn't been an accident during the docking process involving people yet, because the entire process was completely debugged by the AIs - Shun and Kei, during construction of the platform. While each space vessel had their own mission AI to independently operate, they were all monitored and tasked as needed by Kei.

Before docking, Kei announced into the twins' headsets, "I've just heard from Shun. There seems to be an intrusion into the Kuril Islands facility. Shun picked up an unrecognized face within the main hanger of the flying wing aircraft. The person seems to have entered the launch capsule assembly area. The space launch director, Dr. Maksim Popov was updated as soon as Shun noticed the intrusion. Your young transhuman colleague Rafael Borrego who's undergoing space mission training at the facility, took it on himself to investigate this incident with Shun. A score of autonomous micro airborne drones have also been deployed throughout the facility to track down the infiltrator or any others who may have been missed. Dr. Popov has instructed that all scheduled activities are to continue, unless any physical threat is perceived.

"The priest made a sound decision to let Rafael jump in," quipped Ásta. They had picked up the nickname given to the Space Launch Director by the operations team at the Kuril Islands facility. The nickname was a translation of Dr. Popov's surname in Russian; and besides, with his beard and piercing eyes, he did look like a priest. Ásta continued speaking to Kei, "Rafael will get to the bottom of this in no time. He's consistently performed better than Jón and me on mental agility tests. He's quite dextrous too."

Jón teased his twin, "You're just sweet on him!" She stuck her tongue out at him. Grave as the situation was, the twins allowed themselves to behave childishly around each other. With company, they were quite the adults. Kei, listening in and remotely observing the interaction, was used to this behaviour. The AI provided a situational awareness feed from the island, for the twins to observe.

Planet-side at the Kuril Islands facility, things were taking an interesting turn. Rafael who was undergoing movement training underwater in a pool, fully suited in a HSEVA suit, was informed of the situation by Dr. Popov and was asked to investigate the matter urgently. While making his way to the edge of the pool and climbing out, Shun brought him up to speed and provided various feeds through his heads-up display in the HSEVA suit's helmet. Rafael decided to remain in his suit, since it provided him a wide array of sensor inputs and enhanced mobility. He looked at the video feed of the suspected intruder, silhouetted against the wall next to the main entrance of the capsule assembly area. Shun was at a loss to explain how the intruder may have got in, since security was quite stringent across the island, and especially so within the facility premises.

Walking towards the capsule assembly area, Rafael took in a few details about the person he was tasked with tracking down. He looked caucasian, was wearing a deep green-grey body-hugging garment and he had a bulge which looked like a backpack. The video was from five minutes ago when Shun had noticed the discrepancy while running through a three-minute surveillance cycle. This was a gap which would need to be fixed. The group's ability to operate freely across the globe, depended largely on its ability to remain hidden, blended in behind layers of companies and individuals.

Rafael entered the capsule assembly area through an emergency exit after asking Shun to temporarily turn off the door's alarms. Crouching, he entered the cavernous room, which was sectioned off according to the stages of capsule assembly. The entire assembly process was automated, with little need for people to intervene, even to repair or replace robotic components. Still in a crouch Rafael duck-waddled five meters to the closest robotic assembly unit. Three drones had entered the area along with him and he assigned them grids to survey, while he shimmied himself along an aisle close to the assembly unit.

The drones came up empty. There were two authorised base personnel in the area. Both were working on an input console of a composite materials moulding unit. Neither was aware of the activity around them. Rafael wanted to keep it that way. While turning a corner away from the two authorised personnel, he noticed a flicker from an overhead vent. Continuing without a pause in his movements, Rafael amplified the area within a small section of his helmet's HUD. There wasn't anything distinctly visible. Switching to infrared didn't help either since the vent was a heating unit. The suit was capable of numerous sensory inputs, so he toggled through a few of them and stopped on a radar-audio combination, which showed a broken outline behind the vent's grille.

There was someone hiding there. He spoke into his comm unit, "Shun, you're picking this up?"

Shun replied "Yes, it looks like there's an intruder behind the vent's grille. How would you like to handle this?"

Rafael said, "It'd be ideal to let the person get out of the vent and enter an area which isn't mission critical. While we're capable of fixing or replacing equipment rapidly, a confrontation here isn't going to be helpful. Send a drone into the vent quietly behind the intruder and let's monitor the intruder. Keep a camera on the vent in case the intruder decides to exit. I suggest deploying a few drones with motion detection capability into the area, just in case. Give the person space. I'll retreat into the recreation area next door."

A short while later the two techs in the capsule assembly area exited. Rafael was monitoring the area remotely now. He'd just updated the launch director who agreed to let the intruder exit the sensitive assembly area without immediate engagement. Thirty minutes into the surveillance, during which time Rafael was also reacquainting himself with the island's layout, Shun broke in, "The vent has opened and there seems to be movement. Sensors are picking up a male form. There he is, making his way towards the composite materials moulding area. The intruder has stopped and is observing the hardware there. Look closely, he's wearing optical gear beside each of his eyes. I've identified them as miniaturized Swedish tactical communications gear. He's obviously some sort of covert infiltration operative. The gear he's using would be linked in live to whomever he's in contact with via satellite. I'm going to locate and isolate the frequencies he's communicating on. So far, whatever he's seen and recorded has got out."

Rafael replied, "Okay, send in a few drones to flush him out without spooking him, even though he is one". No one listening in got the joke.

The intruder noticed a drone approaching him from the direction of the vent he had recently been hidden in. He raised his hand, fist clenched, knuckles pointing at the drone. Rafael exclaimed, "He's armed. Some kind of forearm mounted system. Send in a few more drones. Also, alert the perimeter security bots to increase patrol frequency, in case there's anyone else waiting to extract the intruder."

Another two drones approached the intruder backing him towards the primary exit. Shun informed, "I've located the frequencies he's communicating over. He's linked in via satellite or a high-altitude aircraft. Isolating and jamming now. Done, his communications are out." The intruder was just exiting the capsule assembly area. Since he was armed, an alert had been silently sent out to all base personnel to vacate their work areas and head to the facility's vast mess-hall.

Rafael turned left and rounded a corner from the recreation area towards the capsule assembly area, bumping right into the intruder. Both backed off a few steps. Looking at the massive and imposing individual in the HSEVA suit must have startled the intruder quite a bit. But he reacted without flinching, raised his left arm and silently shot a rapid cluster of projectiles into Rafael's helmet and torso. Protected against hypervelocity space debris, the projectiles just ricocheted off the suit. This shocked the intruder who spun on his feet and hit a dead sprint. Rafael pursued cautiously since he wanted to avoid violence.

At the first corridor intersection, a drone relay showed him a door swinging shut. Slowing his approach, Rafael entered the room getting a full sweep of the area through his suit's sensor arrays. The intruder was concealing himself behind a cabinet. Rafael approached. The intruder must have heard him. Three feet away from the cabinet the intruder raised his right arm and shot Rafael's suit helmet, emptying his entire magazine. Seeing no effect on the suited person, the dextrous intruder ducked his way around Rafael and exited the room.

Shun burst into Rafael's headset, "Our mystery person is headed to the roof. He must have some sort of exfiltration plan."

Enjoying the cat and mouse pursuit, Rafael replied while hitting the HSEVA suit's open sequence, "I think the suit must look scary to this person. I've scanned him from close quarters, and he doesn't seem to be armed any longer. He's exhausted his forearm weapons. I'm going to ditch the suit and pursue him. Stay connected through audio."

Shun acknowledged saying "The intruder's trying to get the roof access hatch open. You may have a moment to catch up."

Having got out of his training HSEVA suit, Rafael sprinted up the emergency stairwell, racing up the three flights of stairs towards the roof. By the time he reached the top, the intruder had already managed to jimmy open the lock to the roof access door. Cautiously exiting the door, Rafael looked around. The intruder was looking over the far wall towards the rear of the building. He called out to the intruder, "Hey! Hey you!" The person spun around without looking panicked. He didn't consider the ridiculously young-looking Rafael a threat.

Allowing Rafael to approach, the intruder smirked. As soon as Rafael was close enough, the person lunged with a close-fisted jab to the nose. Without pausing, Rafael deflected the jab downward with his left hand, his years of cross- discipline self-defence training kicking in.

Each of the transhumans were placed on a heavy schedule of knowledge and skills development, and a rigorous physical exercise regimen. Going with the defensive flow, Rafael caught his opponent's attacking hand at the wrist with his right hand and pulled. This drew in the intruder to Rafael who kicked up with his right knee knocking the breath out of his opponent.

Normally, Rafael had to limit his more aggressive moves to favour his practice opponents. Having reacted instinctively to the situation, he hadn't held back. The knee to the chest did considerable damage. Medically trained for surgery, Rafael noted the gasping breath of his opponent, now lying on his side with his arms wrapped around his chest, indicating that his diaphragm may have torn. Neither opponent expected the confrontation to end this quickly.

Rafael spoke into his headset, "Shun, the intruder's down but may require urgent medical attention. Send up a stretcher."

A rescue team was standing by and arrived on the roof quickly. Rafael looked at the intruder's forearm mounted weapons. There were multiple barrels forming a double layer over the wrist. Shun too was studying the system while running multiple face-recognition queries globally. The arriving medics were already appraised of the intruder's possible injuries remotely by Shun. Sedating and securing the injured person, the medics gently moved him to the island's infirmary building.

Rafael meanwhile went to check on his suit. When he got to where he left it, he saw it had been removed. Patching himself to the AI he asked, "Shun, has my hard-shell suit been taken in for a check? I'd really appreciate a full service and maintenance run-through. Whatever the intruder shot at me ricocheted off, but I'd like to know what kind of impact the suit can resist. Also, please scan the shielding panels for any inner layer damage."

Shun responded jovially, "I'm way ahead of you. I have three autonomous manufacturing robots taking the suit apart and replacing all panels which may have been affected. The artificial muscles which provide enhanced movement are also being looked at. I've also updated 'the priest', the group's leadership team and my space-based AI counterpart Kei. Incidentally, Jón and Ásta were observing how you handled the intruder. They were impressed. Our priority now is to get to the bottom of this intrusion. We've largely operated under the radar globally. Someone seems to be taking notice."

Pleased that the twins had taken notice, Rafael grinned, "I'd like to speak with our intruder soon. Let me know when he's able to hold a conversation."

Leaving this instruction, he went to the barracks section for a shower before re-joining the investigation. Hectic as the action was, it was a good break from the intensive training he was undergoing.

Kei meanwhile was updating the crew in space. The AI had grown to learn that democracy of information was vital to successful operations in space and helped keep astronauts focussed. Kei had even spun off customized real-time engagement AIs to hold conversations with each individual astronaut. The mission AIs were all a part of Kei and interacted continuously with the core AI systems. Essentially, Kei came across as a unique AI completely in sync with every individual. Kei updated information on the planet side intrusion at the Kuril Islands facility, advising all space personnel to be cautious.

Jón and Ásta had just entered an operations centre where the crew put together to intercept AL-I were meeting. Kei did the introductions announcing itself from hidden speakers around the room, "Hello everyone. I'd like to welcome Jón Gylfason and Ásta Gylfadóttir to Álfhól. Jón and Ásta are twins born in Reykjavík, Iceland. They're both transhumans, a concept you're all knowledgeable about and comfortable with. Going around clockwise, I'll introduce the rest of the crew."

The AI continued the introductions, "Stefán Gunnarsson is also from Reykjavík, Iceland. He is our Bio Specialist. He recently began researching synthetic bio technologies. Stefán, I believe you're already acquainted with the twins." Stefán nodded to the twins who nodded back.

Ásta's eyes lit up and she smiled. She'd been attracted to Stefán when the twins had taken a genetics and surgery course with him two years ago.

Kei continued at an efficient clip, "Next to Stefán is Isla Hansen, astronomer and materials scientist. She's from Wellington, New Zealand." Isla smiled around at everyone and nodded a hello at the twins. "Next, we have Eiji Ono, quantum hardware and software specialist. He's been experimenting with molecular manufacturing and self-replicating machines. Eiji's worked on my AI programming in Tokyo, Japan. He was born in the beautiful prefecture of Ōita on the island of Kyushu." Eiji waved his hand at everyone after dipping his head in appreciation of Kei's introduction.

Kei continued, "Sven de Vries is standing beside Eiji. He's a space operations specialist and the lead for this team. Sven is from Delft in The Netherlands, where The Lýsi Group was founded. He's been instrumental in planning the interception of AL-I." Sven smiled and spoke out in a deep voice, "I look forward to working closely with each one of you and learning from you." Kei went on, "Crystal Vance is an Astrophysicist from London, Great Britain. Isla and Crystal have been keeping an eye on AL-I, evaluating the asteroid like shape and studying the object's trajectory." Crystal smiled around the room. Kei made a last introduction, "Leimomi Ka'aukai is from Honolulu, Hawaii. She's a psychologist, botanist and surgeon." Leimomi exclaimed louder than she or anyone else expected, "Hi everyone! Call me Lei!" She blushed.

Sven took over from Kei, "I'm really glad we're undertaking this adventure together. Each of you has multiple specializations. We will all have to work cohesively to ensure success. Kei will be administering every aspect of our trip, including operations and analysis we will be conducting. The reason we can take this space journey with such a tiny crew, is because our abilities are amplified by our AI, advanced space vessel systems and autonomous robots. Also, instead of just one, we will be taking along three interconnected Standardized Space Exploration Vessels."

Sven explained, "The SSEVs will each provide redundancy or backup for our deep-space mission. Each can be operated independently should the need arise. They also contain an atmospheric operations shuttle. We'll rotate through each vehicle every two days while going out to meet AL-I. We'll also be taking a bio module along, which is longer than an SSEV. Stefán has been working with Lei on a successful project aimed at growing various edible plants over the last month." No one noticed Ásta evaluate Leimomi.

"Now, let's go look at the SSEVs. Our home for the near future."

Chapter 2: Interception

Accelerating at a continuous unhurried five Gs for five and a half days, the three hundred and sixty tonne integrated vessel arrived at nineteen astronomical units (AUs) from the Sun. The crew on Átt had travelled the distance of Uranus' orbit, but north of the solar system's ecliptic. They were on an interception course with AL-I. The asteroid-like object was under observation by the team during their journey. Many of the object's details were clearer now that they were one AU away and closing in. The interception strategy involved decelerating and reversing course, so that the team would be beside and moving parallel to AL-I, by the time it reached their current position nineteen AUs from the Sun.

Before departing, the twins had come up with and had proposed a name for the combination vessel they were to travel in. Since the bio module they were taking along was placed like a roof rack, the twins had assigned it as being directionally 'up'. The other three SSEVs were below and to each side. The names suggested for each vessel were drawn from the Icelandic names for magnetic directions. The bio module was named Norður for North, SSEV-2 on the right was named Austur, meaning East. SSEV-3 to the left was named Vestur or West and SSEV-4 was named Suður for South. SSEV-1 was not included for this mission. The vessel was already on a staffing assignment heading towards the Sun-Earth L1 Lagrange Point platform. The platform had just been put through a rigorous three-month systems and habitat test. That platform would be an important staging point for all future deep-space activities conducted by Lýsi.

The twins also suggested naming the integrated space craft, comprising the three SSEVs and the bio module. They had come up with 'Átt', the term for 'direction' in Icelandic. Given the twins' history in having designed many of the actively deployed space-based vessels, none of the crew objected to their naming the vessels. The names were adopted and immediately used. They had already rotated through Austur and Vestur, thoroughly testing out the systems on the SSEVs while using each as the central command module for Átt. They were using Suður when they began rapid deceleration in preparation for manoeuvres to reorient the spacecraft.

Sven spoke to the crew through their headsets, "Crystal and Isla have just brought to my notice that our mystery asteroid-like object is decelerating at a rate that'll bring it to near standstill in half an AU. That's about the distance we expected to execute our turning manoeuvre. Whatever the object is, it obviously has intelligence. I want everyone putting in time working with our AI – Kei, to outline possible scenarios for when we encounter AL-I. Things we may not have already identified. I'm confirming back to Lýsi leadership that the object on interception course has displayed behaviour. No doubt, Kei has already shared this information with Shun for analysis. We're facing the unknown, so put your thinking caps on and let your minds roll."

Deceleration was more severe than the crew expected. After a thorough systems check, everyone onboard strapped into contoured grav-chairs in the Suður SSEV's operations hold, for the duration. The vast area inside overcame claustrophobia, an input that Lei had given the twins when the exploration vessels were being designed. Lei had grabbed a grav-seat close to Eiji. They had collaborated before on the wicked problem of rapid global warming, and each enjoyed the other's company. Their modelling and analysis had led to Lýsi's thrust towards space exploration and possible colonization, as a means of protecting Earth's life, intelligence, and knowledge.

Leimomi blurted in excitement, "I really like this spacecraft." Failing to recall the SSEVs development history, she asked the onboard AI, "Kei, tell me a bit about our spacecraft."

Kei had a briefing package ready and began narrating it out to her over a separate channel immediately.

"Designs of Standardized Space Exploration Vessels or SSEVs were improvements on our early transport spacecraft. Using newly developed technology, the vessels were designed to comfortably accommodate a crew of eight. Construction was accelerated for the first four vessels in preparation for this mission. Additionally, the SSEVs were made interconnectable so that they could be operated as a single unit, forming a large integrated space vessel such as this one."

"You might find it interesting to know, the design inputs were crowdsourced. To get people interested in solutions that would benefit everyone globally, a special prize was established that would put specific issues into public prominence and get the larger global community involved. This was also seen as a means of getting the world's people to catch up with technology, and fast. Amongst the prize categories was a large bounty for a viable spacecraft design. Lýsi took the best inputs from several entities to develop the SSEV. Prototyping began in the early 1990's."

"So, SSEVs have been around for a while then?" Leimomi asked inquisitively, her eyes becoming rounder than they already were.

Without a second lost, Kei explained, "At the beginning of the last decade, a few asteroid flybys had already been accomplished by various countries, and basic information on asteroids was already being seen by the world. Unknown to the public or most governments, by mid-1996, Lýsi had already been intercepting asteroids for resource mining. Gravity was being judiciously utilized to approach asteroids, and to draw them close to the AMCARs which were carried aboard early automated SSEVs. Gravity Focusing Devices or GFDs were used to reduce approach speed, by placing minute gravity wells behind the asteroids and vessels. The larger gravids in SSEVs were also used to determine the mass of the asteroids based on the amount of gravity required to move them. After a learning period, asteroids were located, approached and rejected if the mass wasn't high enough compared to its size. The early SSEVs were remotely tested as asteroid hunters, proving their resilience in deep space."

Leimomi's eyes were staring out to nothingness by now. She was deeply immersed in the AI's narrative of events. The AI continued.

"Soon with data from the SSEV tests, the asteroid rejection rate increased from afar. If a combination of size, mass, color and albedo - which is the diffused reflection of solar radiation, didn't meet resource mining requirements the asteroid was rejected. The learning from these deep-space operations have all led to the development of the spacecraft you're presently within."

"Interesting. What do you have on the GFDs?" Leimomi asked.

Kei had begun to understand the manner of delivery Leimomi related to. The AI launched into a storytelling narrative.

"In 1993, just as it seemed like all the excitement was dissipating, the team working on reverse engineering an extra-terrestrial artifact acquired in 1980, made a breakthrough. They had developed a Graviton Focusing Device or GFD, which could place and manipulate gravity at a point, in any direction, by creating a gravity well."

"The first GFD test was a spectacular disaster but leapfrogged us eons ahead in space propulsion. Other gravity related applications were conceived. Until then, gravity research was limited to detecting and studying gravity waves in outer space. The disaster I mentioned, occurred after a section of the extra-terrestrial artifact's internal design was replicated at a WWII bunker, on a remote Kuril Islands facility, operated by Lýsi. The design was augmented and integrated with a mission AI developed on the lines of Shun. Before the test, all personnel were airlifted to the merchant ship Kuji Maru, from where my counterpart Shun, was linked in via satellite. A separate link to the bunker facility was made, connecting Shun's Tokyo hub."

"The bunker was inundated with sensors to measure all kinds of energy and radiation. Sensor barges were placed in concentric circles around the bunker location. Some of these were placed as far as three hundred kilometers out to sea."

"At first miniscule amounts of electricity were allowed into the device through electrical contacts identified in earlier experiments on the artifact. Variations were attempted, until the device became active. Immediately, there was a weak increase in the gravity field, detected thirty kilometers to the north of the island. Incremental increases in electricity to the contacts, increased the intensity of gravity. The top of the unit had a set of six inputs. Combinations of electrical input moved a focused point of gravity, in three-dimensional space. Another four contacts on the side of the GFD, seemed to elongate, flatten or condense the shape of the gravity field."

"Finally, after numerous experiments, a distance test was conducted. The gravity field was gradually pushed outward. It was followed by sensor barges. At approximately three hundred and fifty kilometers out and completely without warning, there was a massive earthquake. It measured over eight on the seismic magnitude scale and was located just off Shikotan island in Japan."

"The experiment was immediately stopped and the designs of the component including a new control mechanism was scheduled for fabrication in space. Completed by the end of 1994, the GFD was mounted on one of our larger fabrication robot satellites. Six smaller sensor satellites formed up around it, at five hundred kilometers. Experimentation was reinitiated. All tests were successful and modified GFDs were developed and fit onto our next generation fleet of platforms, spacecraft and robotic satellites."

Eiji turned to Lei. His movement brought her right back to the task at hand. He noticed her startled expression. Smiling, he informed her, "The gravity on AL-I seems to have increased in sync with its deceleration. I was working with Kei to develop a more sensitive gravity measurement instrument using nano scale sensors. We've hooked these up in vacuum pipes in the gas layer of the outer hull panels. The sensors bounce very thin lasers off each other. The lasers bend ever so slightly when gravity is exerted on them. With all the sensor data from each of Átt's SSEVs, we're able to better detect and measure the gravity exerted by other objects in the space around us. That is, after disregarding our own use of focussed gravity."

"Has this information been included with the master sensor feed?" Leimomi asked. "It may help us better understand what we're dealing with," she added.

Eyes twinkling in excitement, Eiji spoke to the space-based AI, "Kei, generate a 3D graphical interface similar to our navigational situational awareness feed. Something that can be pulled up from sensor menus. It would need to show gravity, mass and object size information."

Kei responded, "I'll have it ready shortly. On a separate topic, I have taken the results on your recent quantum computing hardware research and clubbed it with our nano tech development. It's been put into production to create molecular, self-replicating, multipurpose machine components, which can configure themselves for most of our onboard needs. Using this technology, we should soon have our next generation of AMCARs ready, on all three of our SSEVs and on Norður, the bio module."

Lei asked Kei, "Let me have a look at the new AMCAR configurations you've planned for Norður. I'd be interested in looking at ways to construct additional bio modules if the opportunity arises and to have the AMCARS maintain the modules autonomously. Please also brief Stefán on all of this." Eiji seemed engrossed with his mission pad, so Lei began evaluating the mental states of each crew member, one of her primary tasks as the mission's psychologist.

Isla had strapped herself in next to Jón in the center section grav-chairs. She was keenly interested in the transhumans. Besides her specialization in astronomy, she had taken up biotech and materials science. She found chemistry exciting and was exploring compatible materials which could enhance human and animal biology. They needed to keep an eye on the approaching object, but she wanted to get to know Jón better.

Engaging him, Isla asked, "What do you know about our internal gravity? How was it discovered?"

Jón smiled. He instinctively took to the New Zealander. Aware that she understood material science well enough, he kept his response subjective, "Well, to keep space-based activities secret, extra effort was taken to ensure minimum solar reflection. Designs of all modular platforms and vessels were hexagonal and long. The vessels were always positioned so that there was a negligible profile visible from Earth. The platforms were souped-up with new communications capabilities, and with the latest in quantum computing and storage They were then equipped with extensive crew habitat modules. Our Earth side AI Shun, aided the complex coordination of all space-based activities."

"What's that got to do with gravity?" Isla asked, pouting slightly. It was clear to Jón that she was flirting.

His heartbeat quickened and his eyes sparkled. Holding her gaze, Jón replied, "We'd accomplished all of it without internal gravity. None of it was suited for continuous crew rotation. But soon after turning the AIs on aboard our prototype Asteroid Interception Crafts or AICs, the vastly expanded autonomous computing capability identified a curious gravity effect on the in-vessel robots aboard the prototype spacecrafts. As the AICs were tested more aggressively and deeper into space, in-vessel service robots recorded varying sensor data."

"While gravity was being focused outside the AICs for acceleration, the in-vessel robots felt the pull as well. To counter the effect, a few points of mild gravity were focused within the structure of the vessels. Viola, local gravity was discovered. It allowed autonomous robots to maneuver inside AICs without magnetic assistance. Now, the G-forces detected by various autonomous robots within an accelerating AIC, were different. These differences in G-force logs were attributed to how far the robots were from the closest in-vessel gravity point."

Isla nodded encouraging him on.

"The localized gravity points were countering the effects of acceleration and lower G-forces were being experienced by the robots. The issue of inertia and extreme G-force of accelerating spacecraft on humans, was solvable. This was communicated to Shun and the leadership team."

"After a series of experiments, using compact gravids in each AIC, a set of gravity points were identified which could be manipulated to increase or decrease intensity during spacecraft acceleration, which would keep human occupants and equipment safe."

Isla was enthralled by Jón's intensity. A beep on his pad drew his attention away.

Turning back to Isla he brought them out of their moment, "We're halfway to the rendezvous point estimated for the interception with AL-I. Given that we're not seeing any other propulsion system, I'm convinced both we and it are using the same propulsion and manoeuvring technology – gravity manipulation. Since our science has been developed by drawing on extra-terrestrial tech, we should consider that AL-I may be from the originating culture of this technology. They're obviously way ahead of our timeline. This could go one of a few ways. If they're friendly or even neutral, they'd be keen to investigate us, as we would them. So, it's likely they'd attempt to communicate. However, if they are hostile, they could strike pre-emptively. To what degree, is anyone's guess."

Isla nodded and acknowledged, "We've all brainstormed on various scenarios and the options we'd have available to us. We'd do well to try all the communication protocols available to us first. Átt is configured for deep space exploration and is hardened against most natural elements we might come across. Let's hope the vessels are prepared to shoulder whatever AL-I throws at us, if it comes to that." They joined the rest of the crew in analysing the options available to them and adding scenarios not already covered.

Sven announced to the crew, "I'm going to swing Átt around in a tight turn to bring us parallel to AL-I's expected path. Expect a few higher Gs and some discomfort while the localized gravity adjusts. Kei initiate the manoeuvre."

A minute into the course correction, Kei broke in, "AL-I has ceased deceleration. I believe we're being scanned in some manner. Most of our sensors are recording increased levels of radiation. A mix of protons and heavy ions. Our layers of outer panels are absorbing the bulk of the bombardment, and interestingly, the Cosmic Ray Energy Generators are overproducing energy. AL-I must have some way to 'see' the effect of the radiation bombardment on us. Just like an x-ray scan."

Sven broke in, "If the object releases a focussed beam or burst of radiation, Átt may not be able to shrug off the effects. Let's all keep an eye on sensors. Ásta, you monitor EM frequencies. Kei, advise on any change in AL-I's behaviour which may be of consequence."

What the crew took to be a scan soon stopped. Their relative velocities had slowed with AL-I's speed reducing to a crawl, in space travel terms.

The object was only doing ten kilometres per second as it came parallel to Átt. They were now on analogous courses heading toward the Sun, a good nineteen and a half AU away from the center of the solar system.

The initial nervous excitement of contact subsided, and the crew began a more methodical approach to the investigation. A two-member team comprising Jón and Isla who had volunteered, went to the rear of Suður SSEV to prepare a shuttle. They planned to approach the object and observe at close quarters. The shuttle was designated Little Suður and the naming convention followed for each of the other SSEV shuttles.

Meanwhile the asteroid-like object 'AL-I', had placed a focussed gravity point ahead and midway between itself and Átt. Both were beginning to gently accelerate towards the Sun. Little Suður detached itself soon after this acceleration began. Jón updated the crew aboard Átt, "We're being pulled forward along with you. We're using a combination of focussed gravity and ion thrusters to get alongside and close to AL-I." A few moments later once Little Suður was closer to the object he continued, "There seems to be movement on the approach side. The high-resolution visual sensors have picked up a tiny portion of the surface facing us, morphing into a symmetrical shape. It looks like the surface is forming into a compatible dock. Kei, check and ensure this is all being recorded and relayed back to Álfhól and to Shun on Earth. Everyone who can contribute to this, needs to be brought up to speed immediately."

Soon after, Isla excitedly updated the team, "The object appears to have rapidly manufactured a suitably compatible dock. By the looks of it, it should match our own universal docking port." Sven broke in, "You're not to release the docking port to open on your side until you've conducted an EVA to check the object over. Obviously, we now know that it's not an asteroid. So, AL-I is of extra-terrestrial origin. I want both of you to reconnoitrer AL-I. Back-up each other. Kei will maintain vessel control while you're out, and Crystal be on standby to remotely operate Little Suður if needed. I want as much information as possible on the object's exterior before we take any other action."

Isla brought Little Suður parallel to AL-I. The disguised ET vessel did not seem to react to their presence. Putting Kei in control of Little Suður, Jón and Isla checked each other's HSEVA suits and exited the vessel. They used thrusters built into their suits to gradually approach AL-I. Neither wanted to take any abrupt action, which might provoke a negative response. There was no telling how fast or slow AL-I or its occupants processed information, so it'd be best not to spook them. Arriving next to the freshly manufactured docking port on AL-I, they relayed visuals back to their team on Átt. Kei informed, "The dock's mating components look like they're meant to interface with our universal docking port. The sealing mechanism too, looks like it will be adaptable. Check the vessel's surface please."

Jón moved himself away from the docking port and to the right of it. The surface was rocky in some places, flat in others. There weren't any external sensors or viewing ports; nothing that could be readily identified. He spoke into his headset's microphone, "Nothing stands out, I'm going to go around the vessel diagonally toward the front, and then around. Isla please follow keeping about five meters distance. Be wary for movement. Kei, use sensors from all vessels on Átt which are not immediately required for navigation, to seek any additional data on AL-I. Also, have Little Suður follow our progress around the ET vessel, just in case we need to withdraw quickly." Instructions given, Jón and Isla began their survey.

The surface was like that of a large asteroid. It was rugged, pockmarked, dented and even scraped. Various sections of the exterior looked different in colour, like portions of it had been ripped off revealing deep noticeable indentations, differently shaded from the rest of the surface. They were slowly walking on the surface of the vessel. The gravity was just under twice that of Earth's. This wouldn't be possible unless it was artificially generated. The two explorers had just completed their survey when Kei's very pleasant virtual voice came in through their headsets, "I've picked up bursts of low intensity gravity, originating from AL-I, aimed at us on Átt, at Little Suður and simultaneously at Jón and Isla. There's nothing coming in on any electromagnetic frequencies, or anything in light. I'm beginning an analysis. Since we're basically coasting along under pull from AL-I, I'm going to commit most of our local computing resources, towards identifying if this is communication of some kind, and if so, what it says."

Not having discovered anything out of the ordinary, Jón and Isla decided to return to Little Suður and attempt to dock with AL-I. If successful, they would try to enter the ET vessel. Both felt nervous tension coursing through them. Once they entered the airlock, Jón remarked, "Isla, we're barely two hundred meters away from AL-I. We could remain in the airlock, instead of pressurizing and entering the cabin. If we dock successfully, we could enter the ET vessel quickly if it permits us to. Do you think you can control Little Suður using the operations pad in the airlock?"

Isla answered, "I'm keen to get going as well. Normal procedure requires us to remain in our vessel with the airlock acting as a buffer between us and the docking port. But I think it would be safe enough to remain in the air lock and control the mating procedure from here.

There's adequate visibility through the viewing port beside the dock frame. Ideally, there should have been a viewing port built into the dock's hatch as well. Kei, please take this as a design upgrade input."

The two maneuvered the shuttle towards AL-I's freshly manufactured docking port. Slowing to a crawl with delicate thruster adjustments, Isla brought the shuttle within ten meters of the ET vessel. Abruptly, six slim flat tendrils, each no more than three centimetres wide, extended snakelike from equidistant locations around AL-I's docking port. These clamped in some manner at points around the shuttle's universal docking port. As soon as the last one was clamped, the tendrils stiffened and began tugging the entire shuttle in. Both vessels' ports aligned perfectly and locked. There was a whirring followed by a click as clamps between the docks fell in place. A brief swoosh indicated a vacuum seal between the docking ports had been successful as well. Jón reached out to Isla and pressed her left hand to ensure her. She squeezed back indicating her confidence and readiness to face the unknown.

The crew on Átt were observing over their video feeds. Most were tuned into the visual inputs on Little Suður. For a brief while everyone held their breaths in anticipation of some action by the ET vessel or perhaps its crew. Nothing happened. Taking the lead, Isla announced, "I'm going to disengage the locks on the hatch in preparation to opening it. Given the level of intelligence the other side has shown in understanding our systems, I have a good feeling they would have reciprocated the airlock as well." Jón agreed, so she went ahead and released the locks. She then keyed the operations pad in the airlock authorising the hatch to open. There was a whirring of motors as the hatch swung inward revealing the extra-terrestrial vessel's hatch.

Without any fanfare, the hatch on the other side opened and swung in. Jón and Isla had tensed themselves in preparation of the unexpected. Both were perspiring. They weren't armed. But they were confident their hard-shell suits could take a little punishment if they faced aggression. Relaxing a bit, they moved towards the open hatch and peered into the ET vessel. A dark void loomed menacingly ahead. They seemed to be looking into a large airlock. Switching on their helmet and shoulder mounted lights, they entered the space inside. Two drones entered behind them, brought in by Kei. There was a rack of six drones in the shuttle's airlock, kept on standby should they be required outside for repairs or operations. The drones used their own diffused lights, infrared and laser to map and explore the inside of AL-I.

Five minutes into the exploration of the hanger-like airlock on the alien craft, a soft glow began to appear in straight lines, along what appeared like the roof of the large interior space. AL-I or its crew, seemed to have understood that the humans entering it required light in a specific range to see. Jón said, "This is disappointing. There doesn't seem to be anything of interest here. The area looks like an empty hold. This is a lot of wasted space for a deep-space or interstellar vessel. I think the ET vessel created the space soon after it studied us. We know that the vessel can reconfigure its exterior while exposed to space. It seems reasonable that it can do the same inside. But why such a vast area I wonder?"

Isla was at a far corner, to the right from where the two and accompanying drones had entered. She called out enthusiastically, "Jón, over here. There's a panel with what looks like tiny switches." Jon got to her side quickly and studied the panel. He suggested, "Perhaps we trigger a few of these and see what happens. We're already way past any by-the-book procedure and we're going to have to wing it here on."

31

Sven came in over their headsets agreeing to their acting and soon. He mentioned that their tiny fleet of vessels, was beginning to accelerate towards the Sun.

Jón pressed the first little button to the right of the screen. Nothing happened. He pressed the second. Still, nothing happened. He went on and pressed a third and then a fourth. Nothing. Reacting to instinct, he pressed the last button to the left of the screen. One of the drones patched in a visual feed, to their heads-up displays. It was of a 3D projection in the center of the cavernous interior space. They'd had their backs to the area. Simultaneously, a screen appeared and glowed softly; over the panel they were at. The projection and screen both displayed a human shape within a circle. The circle was linked by a line to a specific button. Jón paused to consider, then went ahead and pressed the button.

A ring dropped from the roof and hovered just over their heads. Isla came in close to Jón with her back to his. The drone moved out from under the ring. As soon as it did, the ring began to descend around Jón and Isla. Using the drones as relays, Kei came in over their headsets, "I'm detecting all sorts of radiation including x-rays. I believe you're being scanned, like an MRI. There are also a lot of gravity waves at various intensities being focussed and passed through you. I can only extrapolate at this point, but I believe you're being studied at the subatomic level. Our own drones cannot pick up any scan radiation that might be outside our science."

The ring reached the floor and was absorbed into it. The roof where the ring had appeared from, didn't show an indentation. Material was being continuously manipulated within the vessel.

Jón and Isla checked the exterior of each other's suits for damage. Kei ran an internal systems and bio diagnostic. Nothing seemed out of order. Neither Jón nor Isla were affected, other than having elevated blood pressure from the brief excitement.

The display on the wall changed to accommodate human visibility. It now showed an animation depicting AL-I's two visitors. Their individual forms could be distinctly made out within their HSEVA suits. The animation depicted each one exiting their suits and stepping out.

This took the duo by surprise. Nervous, Isla spoke into her headset, and through the drones, to the whole team, "I hope you're able to get all this. AL-I appears to be asking us to exit our suits." Stefán responded saying, "I'm tasking an additional drone into the 'hanger area' you're in, to take continuous environment readings. It'll support us as an extra pair of eyes." Sven spoke next saying, "Ásta and Stefán will join you there. They'll take the shuttle from Vestur and dock on Little Suður. We'd want an additional team in there with you in HSEVA suits, if you're going to volunteer exposing yourselves to the interior environment of AL-I". Jón and Isla each affirmed they would like to proceed.

Ásta and Stefán were already moving by the time Sven completed his instruction. They went to their bunk capsules, next to which their suits were plugged into the vessel's systems.

While Ásta and Stefán were suiting up, Kei spoke to Jón and Isla. The AI said "The third drone has entered AL-I. Initial readings show gasses in the air are suitable for humans. The air closely mimics what you're breathing in your suits. Aerobiology shows absence of any recognizable organisms." The AI added after a short pause, "Ásta and Stefán have just uncoupled Little Vestur and are on their way to you. They should be docking with Little Suður in six minutes."

There was movement in the center of the hanger-like room they were in. Jón and Isla turned in unison and cautiously approached the area. A rectangular section of the floor grew upward. The rectangle rose to just over a meter in height and began to change structure. Screens larger than the one on the wall took shape. Indentations formed just under the platform. It looked like the familiar work surfaces in their operations areas on Átt.

Ásta and Stefán had docked with Little Suður and made their way into AL-I, in the time it took the work surface to completely form itself. Breaking the tension, Stefán announced their presence, "Hey you two. Thought you'd keep all the excitement for yourselves, did you?" Isla replied, "We're glad to have you here. AL-I is adapting this area to suit our needs. This work surface just formed itself while you were on your way. The materials tech this spacecraft has, is extraordinary. Ásta, would you care to study the surfaces and technologies?" Ásta touched the surface. It responded with a pictorial menu.

Stefán felt the hair on his neck stand up. He motioned to Jón and Isla, "One of the screens on the work surface is showing an animation of you two stepping out of your suits. Now that we're here, you could remove your helmets, if you're willing to be guinea pigs. I've gone through the environment readings from the drone while we were on route to you. The environment seems safe. You can go ahead and lose your suits too."

Ásta began studying the surface of the floor. Their suits had initially been designed keeping in mind deep space exploration and resource mining. The early tools and systems had included chemical and materials analysis. These had since been upgraded each time the AIs Shun and Kei made systems and technology advancements. The Lýsi Group's rapid manufacturing and fabrication capabilities had far outstripped known Earth-based commercial or defence capabilities.

Jón and Isla had opened their HSEVA suits and hesitantly stepped out of them. The suits remained standing, ready to accommodate their occupants again.

The work surface rapidly reconfigured itself. A pair of rings had fabricated themselves in the center of the work surface. The screens showed an animation indicating that the rings were to be placed on their heads. Jón and Isla glanced at each other. Isla gave a quick nod and the two picked up a ring each. The rings felt cool to touch with very little texture. Gently, each placed a ring on their heads. For a moment nothing happened. Then tendrils began to edge their way along each one's heads, forming at the rings and working their way down to their foreheads, temples, behind their ears and upward. Both tensed while the rings configured themselves. A moment later, the screens on the surface flashed a series of shapes and colours, increasing in speed between changes. Then abruptly, when everything seemed a blur, it all stopped.

Jón and Isla were able to see images in their minds. The images appeared on the screen with an animation to touch the screens. Each time they touched a screen, a new image appeared. The interactions went on for barely a few moments, when these too stopped; only to be replaced by sounds. They went through the screen tapping process, each time they heard a sound. These too stopped. Now there were images on the screens, but nothing seemed to be appearing in their minds, so neither reacted.

Kei spoke to them while updating each member of the crew, "The drones are picking up electromagnetic, gravity and other wave activity including mild radiation being transmitted by the rings on Jón and Isla's heads. They seem to have stopped interacting with the screens because neither are able to sense the transmissions." A moment later, the screens went blank. It now showed four individuals, two without their HSEVA suits and two with them on.

It indicated that the two with suits on should go to the corner with the body scanning ring. Sven quickly instructed, "Ásta, Stefán. I'd like you to remain in your suits for now. We'll have you two interacting with the vessel soon. The faster this goes, the better. We'll all take turns, working four shifts of two each. While Jón and Isla are interacting, Ásta and Stefán, you get yourselves scanned."

Isla touched the ring on her head and attempted to take it off. It immediately began withdrawing its tendrils and she was able to lift it off her head. Isla felt detachment in her mind. It felt like she had lost one of her senses. Intrigued, she mentioned this to everyone. Thinking aloud, Sven suggested, "It may be possible for Kei to interact in a different manner with AL-I. We could upgrade one of the drones with additional processing and memory. It can be configured as a standalone but mobile version of our AI. Kei, would you get started on that. We'll pass the modified drone through AL-I's scanner during our shift and see what happens."

Calculations showed that they had the next five days to interact and learn as much as they could from AL-I. Fortunately, the vessel itself wasn't hostile. They needed to understand it and find out what it was doing in the solar system. And, they had to do it quickly before it got further in-system.

Chapter 3: Infiltrator

Dr. Maksim Popov was genuinely concerned. 'The priest' as he was called, was feeling all but priestly. It had been a week since an intruder had infiltrated the Kuril Islands facility, a location he had spent over eighteen years secretly building, while conducting cutting-edge research and development. The priest was seething.

Rafael Borrego the third transhuman brought to term in Havana, five years after the twins Jón and Ásta, was now at the base helping Dr. Popov. Soon turning thirteen, he was only supposed to be training at the island facility, while undergoing a series of intensive and highly customized educational courses. However, after having brought down the intruder more swiftly than either himself or anyone else expected, Lýsi's leadership team recommended that his skills be put to full use investigating the infiltration, as long as he kept out of harm's way. Pairing up with Shun, the group's Earth-side AI, the two had made significant progress.

Shun was rapidly briefing Dr. Popov and Lýsi's leadership team, with Rafael adding in where needed. "We've spent the last week querying global databases for our intruder's identity, as well as researching the sources of the equipment he was carrying," said Shun. Rafael presented after Shun, casting a series of images which appeared to his remotely attending audiences on their devices. "Our intruder has been linked to a security and defence consultancy called Rakkniv, a name which means Razor in Swedish. It's an LLC based out of Malmö in Sweden. The intruder himself is registered as a private language tutor, and he doesn't seem to have travelled much outside Europe. Very suspicious. He doesn't seem to have left much of a fingerprint trail with any of the major agencies. The man is physically healthy. Two stab wounds. One between the ribcage and hip, under the liver. Another to the left thigh which nicked the femur. He's undergone surgery to the left knee. There's also scar tissue on the left shoulder, which according to our resident surgeon is consistent with a bullet graze. Our mystery intruder is likely a clandestine operator. He was linked to Rakkniv for receiving tutoring fees off and on." Rafael smiled with a sense of respect and added in amazement, "He's actually paid taxes on the income. His name is Max Andersson. You couldn't have a more common name to blend in."

Shun's not so synthetic voice continued, "Some of our intruder's equipment was traceable. The tactical communications gear was identified to a defence equipment manufacturer. I scanned and found production markings inside some of the processors, which were custom designed and sourced from Japan. Incidentally, the processor manufacturing technology and process, belongs to Lýsi controlled companies. From there, we investigated Rakkniv's contracts. We've examined all the interactions the company has had over the last three years. While a lot of their dealings came across as suspect, what stood out was this. Just over a week ago, they signed a non-disclosure agreement with Univers Aerospace. Univers is a private Swiss aero-space multinational that is at the forefront of conventional satellite sensor and equipment development. Any advantage it could gain in the aerospace industry would greatly enhance its position. I've found information which suggests that the multinational has brought aboard defense consultants, to investigate the nature of our operations and to extract usable information and material. Univers has always wanted to lead the private space technology industry."

Dr. Popov sounded concerned, "I would like our resources in Europe deployed to find out more. Also, since we don't normally do anything underhand, I'd like permission to task Shun to undertake deep surveillance of both Univers and Rakkniv, electronically. Rafael could coordinate personnel tasking, to infiltrate Univers if required." Lýsi's facility operations heads had extraordinary leeway and authority. They were completely responsible for the success of their operations and the wellbeing of their staff. The leadership team agreed to the plan and requested that Shun update each of them daily.

Later, Rafael walked over to the island's hospital, contemplating the island facility's security. "The island's operations are disguised as a weather and seismic research facility. The entire island was leased by a consortium of global R&D organizations and agencies, all of which receive actual research data. Much of the group's activities involve atmospheric, ground and space data collection. The entire operation is run on a need to know basis, with many of the functions being automated and robotically controlled. The few staff onsite who are not in on the island's actual purpose, don't have the faintest idea. There aren't any obvious leaks here. It's tight," thought Rafael as he arrived at the hospital.

He made his way to a restricted R&D section of the hospital, where he came in for a check-up every week. While deployed to the island, the group's finest genetics researchers were there to ensure his wellbeing. Rafael liked his two medical minders. They were the parents of the first pair of transhuman twins. Gylfi Hallgrímsson and Katrín Magnusdóttir, had taken on the lead roles spearheading Lýsi's transhuman program. He was on his way to meet them.

Rafael ran into Katrín as soon as he entered the restricted section. She said, "Shun gave me a heads up that you were arriving. That AI seems to be just about everywhere. I'm often boggled at the amount of information it processes. And, it's all individualised for each of us." She knew why he was there. The two walked towards the patient wards. The wards were a testing ground for the medical capsules, which were used aboard all their space-based vessels. Each room served as an all-in-one care centre, with invasive operations capabilities. Patients were placed in pods. Sensors automatically measured their vitals, and internal imaging systems occasionally scanned them at the molecular level. Mobile robots and drones maintained the pods. The same equipment was also used to study Rafael, so he was used to it.

"How's Gylfi?" Rafael asked. Katrín smiled and replied, "He's been busy tending to your intruder." She continued in her good-natured way, "You're stronger than you look, so be careful when facing off with people." Rafael nodded in agreement. His genes contained numerous DNA modifications. With AI assistance, the group's genetics researchers had been able to push the boundaries of human DNA manipulation. They'd only cracked the complete functionality of twenty one percent of human DNA and were able to accomplish significant feats. Most scientists believed the reminder of the DNA wasn't useful. Rafael didn't think so.

They arrived at the wards. The intruder was in the second room, since the first one was occupied by one of the facility's researchers who was down with pneumonia. Gylfi looked up when the door opened. He was studying a screen on the wall of the room which was showing various patient sensor feeds. He shook Rafael's hand and gave his wife a quick peck on the cheek. Sounding confident, he said, "Our patient is healing fast. Our New Zealand facility developed and successfully tested accelerated cell repair and regeneration injections. He's been administered a daily doze the last five days. We didn't have any of the serum onsite, so I had it flown in. We'll keep them stocked at all our facilities now."

"His name is Max Andersson." Rafael announced to the two scientists in his usual matter-of-fact tone. "He's a Swedish private covert operative. We believe his company was appointed to investigate our operations by Univers Aerospace, a Swiss registered organization."

Gylfi observed his patient through the capsule's transparent side. "Well your operative is awake now. He looks like he's in a good mood too. I tried to engage him in conversation yesterday. He wasn't very forthcoming, so I updated him about his condition; and informed him that he's temporarily restricted to the capsule."

Rafael walked up to the capsule, smiled and genially said, "Hello! How're you feeling today?" Max gave him a curious stare, then smirked in recognition. He coughed and responded, "You're quite strong. And quick." After a pause he said, "You look like a child." Rafael chuckled and replied, "I am a child." Max continued to stare at him curiously, so Rafael went on, "You're not supposed to be on this island. We've learned a little about you. Your name and where you're from. Will you fill us in on what you were hoping to accomplish?"

Max Andersson wasn't caught off-guard. After seeing what he had at the facility, he was confident the people behind the operations would have the resources to successfully investigate his presence on the island.

41

But he had a job, and right now it was to learn about what was going on here. He smiled at Rafael and stated, "I wasn't hoping. I have accomplished what I set out to do."

It took Rafael a moment to process this. Shun was listening in through Rafael's stealthy in-ear communications device. The AI instantly understood the implications of what Max said and told Rafael, "I'll look at how he got information out."

Without expressing concern, Rafael said to Max in his usual manner. "Once you're sufficiently healed, you'll be transferred off-island. The research being conducted here is purely scientific, which is why its classified. This is not a commercial operation per-se, so your intrusion here surprised us. Your employers may have commercial gain or theft in mind. That would not be surprising. What we do here is meant for everyone's good. Protecting it is paramount. You're uniquely equipped to advice on security measures. Perhaps you'd consider siding with us." Rafael had intelligent eyes and they had a glint in them now. He added, "I'll let you ruminate on that. Hope you recover quickly. We'll speak again soon."

Max felt oddly uneasy. He'd expected to be interrogated further. Also, he never expected the young boy who'd bested him, to come have a conversation with him, as an adult no less. He was curious now. Much more than his mission entailed. But he was sleepy too, so he chose to rest, recover, and learn more later. He might even get a bonus once he was back at his company's headquarters. Smiling at his evolving plan, he let his mind drift off. Gylfi, saw his patient's eyes close, looked at the monitors to affirm things were well, and left Max to rest.

Shun came in over Rafael's earpiece, "I'm patching Dr. Popov in." Two beeps indicated the connection was established. The AI spoke in its young adult voice to both, "I've picked up a fuzzy shape on one of the personnel barrack's external surveillance camera's footage. The mission AI tasked to surveillance, categorised the blur as a bird, a pigeon to be precise. On examining the frames from the footage, I found a few hard shapes. Unnatural shapes. I'm afraid, Max may have dispatched a small fixed-wing drone containing his infiltration data, prior to being subdued on the rooftop. I'm updating Lýsi leadership and stepping up efforts to get further information on Rakkniv, the security consultancy, and from Univers Aerospace.

The AI continued, "There's also an update on the deep-space mission I've kept you abreast with. Átt's crew have been maintaining regular six hour shifts aboard AL-I. After the initial interaction with the ET vessel, during which Átt's crew were provided with customized machine-brain interfaces to enable communication, the vessel scanned a drone uploaded with a standalone version of my space-based AI counterpart Kei. AL-I then produced a basic translation interface which the drone is plugged into. Kei has taken precautions to ensure there is no subvert takeover of our systems or AI abilities. This has been managed through a series of imperceptible encryption delays between the drones on AL-I, and the AI core systems on Átt. You'll find the next bit very interesting."

"Initially, the amount of information AL-I transmitted was overwhelming and undecipherable. The ET vessel then went through a series of communication tests with the drone, like the interfacing tests it conducted to sync itself with Átt's crew. It began with single packets of data that it corelated with complex shapes, beginning with the human form. Each packet contained massive strings of data which couldn't be deciphered. This was a problem. Kei's and my information systems were born from binary programming, a necessity for programming with older transistors. Even now, we still cross translate to binary, to interface with traditional computing systems. It just takes longer to get information across. What we do is break our data down, so traditional computers can use it. Similarly, AL-I's massive data packets needed to be broken down, for us to understand it," the AI emphasized in a very human manner.

Shun explained, "It took Kei two entire eight-hour shifts of interaction with AL-I to arrive at a common digital information translation system. It began with exchanging information on the periodic table. I have a more detailed brief available separately for you to consume, but the gist of the interaction is this. AL-I's language is DNA based. Or rather, a form of DNA. Unlike human DNA which contains four kinds of bases, the coding on AL-I's language contains twelve. While combinations of the bases form strings, there are entire shorter strings attached to the primary string. It's like tendrils on a vine, with each tendril containing numerous shoots. The problem is that each vine-like piece of code, is a packet of information for AL-I."

"For us, our in-core AI data is passed along as pre-configured concepts or in human terms, 'thoughts'. Each of our packets of AI thought, is between one to four gigabytes. In comparison, AL-I's packets each contain an equivalent minimum of a hundred and fifty thousand gigabytes of data. To AL-I's computing systems, we must seem like dumb boxes," Shun stated in an incredulous tone.

The AI went on, "At the end of the effort, AL-I provided a solution. It translated each of its packets into a series of our AI concepts. Following this, Átt's crew and Kei have begun a series of information exchange sessions with AL-I. Fortunately, the machine-brain interface rings which the ET vessel produced for use by our crew, is able to inject thoughts directly into each users' brain. For security, individual crew members had to learn how to use a connection acceptance protocol, which identifies the sender. So now during interactions with AL-I, every crew member can provide a voice description of their interpretation or understanding. Separately, Kei interacts digitally via a high capacity local EM transfer. Here's the interesting part. AL-I is like a life-raft. The vessel contains thirty-six humanoid individuals who are essentially refugees transiting our solar system, in search of a new home in our galaxy the Milky Way. They're from a system in what we've identified as the Canis Major Dwarf Galaxy, a galaxy which is being accreted by our own galaxy, the Milky Way. The humanoids on AL-I are escaping an expected conflict between intelligent species from our own galaxy and theirs, which could spill over to their system."

"Also," said the AI, "while the Átt's crew is getting more information, Kei is working on developing human usable hardware using AL-I's designs. If our understanding is correct, this should enable us to communicate with the ET vessel, at interstellar distances, without lag." Rafael's interest instantly peaked. He quickly cut in, "I'd like to be kept up to date on the hardware development please." The AI replied, "I'll direct your request to the leadership team."

Rafael had just arrived at Dr. Popov's office. He knocked and entered. Shun or one of its mission AIs undoubtedly announced his presence to the priest.

Dr. Popov glanced up wearily and said, "We're both caught up." He looked drawn. The intrusion had kept him awake two days straight.

Rafael replied with understanding, "Yes." The young transhuman was very concise when he needed to be.

"I've just got off a separate remote conference with Lýsi leadership and my counterparts at other facilities," Dr. Popov said. He elaborated, "We've just added another wicked problem layer, to our Global Catastrophic Risk stack. The solar system is one of the closest systems to Canis Major Dwarf Galaxy. We're closer to it than we are to the center of our own galaxy. Canis Major Dwarf Galaxy has a ring of about a billion stars, which has wrapped itself around our galaxy three times. It's been in the process of being accreted or absorbed by the Milky Way, likely for millions of years. There may be numerous systems as close to, or perhaps closer than ours, between the two galaxies."

Pausing to draw a deep breath, the priest continued, "Initial information from AL-I indicates that there are multiple advanced interstellar species, involved in conflict between the two galaxies. We don't yet know why or what it's all about. However, given AL-I's presence here, we can assume that the solar system has seen visitors before, and there could be more coming. The leadership team has had discrete conversations with their contacts within governments, militaries, agencies and research organizations, to get a feel for the direction we should proceed in. The interactions with external bodies have maintained hypothetical situations of course. No information on AL-I has been revealed during conversations, yet. Lýsi leadership agrees that we need to prepare for future extra-terrestrial interactions and possible conflict. Get your thoughts together on this. Meanwhile your training will continue here. Brush up on your war strategy. Your younger colleagues have been asked to come up with space defence suggestions. You too should contribute."

The priest wound down, "The principal coordinator for this is to be Gogh." He smirked and clarified, "Yes, it's a code name, and yes it's like the painter. Gogh has just taken a sabbatical from his professorship at a technology university in Delft. As you're aware that's where our headquarters were located, before we became a decentralized organization."

Rafael nodded. He understood the severity of the issue, and the uphill task. In the simplest terms, Earth's resources were controlled by various governments. Many were against each other. The economies of these were based on consumerism, which was based on a capitalistic model, much of which was debt driven. This fostered a global culture of possession, greed, corruption, power consolidation and incredible amounts of waste. It was unlikely the world would come together to deal with developing GCR issues, simply because there were vested interests everywhere. "But," he thought to himself, "this is the way I think. Maybe there's a different point of view out there." He excused himself and left the priest's office to grab a meal, shower and sleep. He'd had a long day punctuated with regular training and he'd think better once rested.

Waking early and undergoing his regular physical regimen followed by an enormous breakfast, Rafael spoke briefly with his parents in Havana, before they went to bed. He decided to meet Max, before his learning session on negotiation began, which Shun had lined up for him. While on his way, he looked through the updated information on Max. Entering the restricted section of the hospital, he let himself into Max's room.

"Hello Max! Hope you're feeling better this morning." Rafael greeted the facility's intruder. Max replied, "I'm being fed soups, something

that tastes like pulped steak, juices and oats. It feels like space food."
Laughing, Rafael replied, "It is. Everyone admitted to our infirmary,
gets fed something like this. It's highly controllable and is custom
produced to meet your exacting needs."

Max replied blandly, "Yes, the good medic Katrín told me so. She also
mentioned it's to motivate me to get better soon and eat regular solids."

Rafael chuckled and joked, "Our solid food is space-food too."

Max went a shade paler. "Really? I'll have to escape then!"

This quickly brought the conversation on to a more serious track. "Did
you think through what I left you with yesterday?" Rafael asked.
Without allowing Max time to answer, he continued, "You have a
daughter who's just finished university and has recently landed a job
with a human right's organization. She's highly intelligent, motivated,
driven and a natural leader. She's obviously taken after you."

Max hissed at him, "Why are we discussing her?"

Having got Max's attention, Rafael answered with unwavering
confidence, "Her, you, me, every person." Max waited for him to go on.
"The work being done here is aimed at mitigating and trying to solve
the greatest problems the world faces. While we do that, we also work
towards ensuring people, knowledge and resources continue to exist; no
matter what. We do what's right for the greater good, with the least
amount of damage. And we go further. Because, our studies and
analysis tell us that we're on an irreversible self-destructive course."

Max asked, "Destructive to whom? Are you talking about global
warming? Economic bubbles? What specifically?"

Rafael answered, "All of it. An interweaving of issues and problems at a global scale. Problems which feed of each other, propagate fresh issues and allow difficulties to fester and manifest, without being suitably countered. Wicked problems."

Max chuckled and said, "The world has always had problems. Governments, corporates and people are all involved. Everyone is fighting the problems. You're going to solve them all?"

Rafael replied, "The problems we're tackling are largely unsolvable. That's why they're 'wicked'. However, they can be mitigated. They can be managed. But given the state the world is in, solving issues will take too long. I'm talking centuries. Most ongoing efforts may already be too late."

"So, what is it, that you're doing here?" Max asked. His agenda too, was to get as much information as possible. Here was someone who seemed willing to share. Perhaps he'd get more out of this than he expected.

"We have a hierarchy of wicked problems. Diagrammatically it's shaped like a conifer. At the crown lies Global Catastrophic Risks or GCRs, the stuff of nightmare. There are certain scenarios which could lead to life on Earth being completely eradicated or brought dangerously to the brink of extinction. We prioritize our activities to counter GCR scenarios. For everything else, we undertake deep research and feed information via conduits to organizations, governments and individuals, who are equipped to take real-world action. However, other than GCR scenarios, we're not actors on Earth. And, we try to represent all life."

Max gave Rafael a sharp look and asked, "Who's we? Who funds all this?" He was trying to get organizational information.

Rafael understood what was going on but was very forthcoming. He explained, "In a nutshell, no single entity. After World War II, a few people from various fields, governments and even corporations got together to discuss how we could avoid destroying ourselves. Numerous underlying issues which fed conflict were identified. This included resource availability, divisions between peoples, undereducation, possession and power, even greed. R&D programs were put in place. The programs are run by people at the forefront of their fields to study issues and find long-term solutions to turn problems around. Initially, it wasn't expensive because all the research was bundled within regular programs at universities. Soon however, larger problems began to be recognized. Energy use for instance, has contributed to rapid climate change. Life on Earth is not prepared for the rapidity of the change occurring. Solving just this one issue is going to be expensive."

"But we have an edge. Our technology has progressed geometrically. I'll give you some background." He took a deep breath before launching into what sounded like a well-rehearsed briefing.

"UFO probe material was gathered following a 1980 incident in Britain which catapulted our space technologies development. The Lýsi Group, what we're called, had covertly acquired a 'live' ET artefact. We studied it and reverse engineered some of its tech. Progress leapfrogged in the fields of shielded microelectronics, composite materials and nascent self-replicating machines which learned to utilize our already well-developed AI, to modify their own code-set and even suggest hardware improvements. Based on the learning, our engineers and our AI Shun, developed a freely distributable operating system which it could access via hidden encrypted backdoors. The operating system was adopted for use by distributed networking specialists, and extensively utilized on commercial servers. While morally debatable, this provided us enormous processing capacity during the early years. I of course, wasn't even around." Max smiled at that, still looking unconvinced.

"The early neural net AI was also able to quickly identify how the computing systems in the acquired extra-terrestrial probe functioned. This offered direction towards redeveloping the AI's own hardware and software. Advanced computing research was carried out in the US and Japan by the group through our Singularity Research Division or SRD. The probe also contained what was identified as a matter transfer module, which created material in its inner chamber 'through thin air'. To study this, scans were taken of the matter transfer module and a classified subatomic particle research lab was set up at the local technical university, near the group's headquarters at Delft. We don't have a handle on that specific tech yet. But we've progressed in others."

Seeing Max's eyes widen, Rafael ploughed on excitedly, "Separately the group's SRD members were tasked with reverse engineering quantum computing hardware based on the probe's designs, and the development of suitable quantum calculation software. Massive technology leaps were accomplished in a short period."

"Now, to coordinate all this, Lýsi's leadership team had been experimenting with a versatile decentralized command and control structure. An AI administered adhocratic organization was agreed upon. The adhocracy allowed rapid maneuvering and decision making. AI assisted administration coordinated the group's activities, facilitating interactions between teams and departments globally. Direction and key decision-making authority have always remained with the leadership team."

"Lýsi has always worked towards the greater good. In 1980, the group's then appointed and elected leaders, took a crucial decision to release all breakthrough information to the global populace, but deferred by up to twenty years. This was necessary to ensure any released material was adequately vetted, tested for stability and that information did not destabilize global governments or the economy. Everything we do is aimed at progress, and mitigating risk to life on Earth."

Frowning, the young transhuman continued gravely, "But there are scenarios which can affect us without much warning. Some of these are space-based dangers. Lýsi has been able to overcome monetary requirements while building a sizable and flourishing infrastructure on and off planet. All aimed at preventing catastrophe. There's always the risk of complete failure. An extinction level event. You see, we have to backup life, intelligence, information and knowledge. So, we're working towards that too."

It sounded stupendously incredulous and Max thought, "These people are way over their heads. Without money, power and organization, whatever they're hoping to achieve is going to take forever."

Feeling his emotions, Rafael interrupted Max's thoughts, "I'll give you some perspective of the scale we're operating at. In value, our resources and worth exceed that of the top ten most valuable multinationals combined; by a third. You may be thinking about the kind of power that would provide to someone. Well, no individual or even group of people within Lýsi have absolute control. All our actions have pull and push. Our organization is truly adhocratic. We have multiple leadership roles. Decision making is distributed. Administration is automated. We have the best minds, people with exceptional technical knowhow, and we have cutting-edge computing that's decades ahead of anything published. This makes us agile. It allows us to absorb inputs and react at speed."

Shun spoke into Rafael's earpiece, making him pause. A short moment later, Rafael looked into Max's eyes and said with sincere intensity, "You're here at a defining moment in history. It seems we have a scenario of mind-bending severity. I've got to go now, but I'll leave you with this. What would you do to protect your daughter? What would you do to protect the world she lives in? As of now, our world is faced with a new threat. Think about this!"

Shun spoke into Rafael's earpiece as the thirteen-year-old walked to the island's learning centre. Knowing Rafael's absorption rate, the AI said rapidly, "We've received an update from Kei. Átt's crew has collected a massive amount of information about AL-I's occupants in the last sixteen hours. This includes specifications on developing our own interstellar communications capabilities and technologically superior quantum computing. Your request to be kept abreast on these technologies has been approved by key members of group leadership."

The AI ploughed on, "AL-I has been in intermittent communication with its home system. It had entered the solar system through what's been interpreted as a wormhole, with an opening just sixty AU from the Sun, north of the Kuiper Belt. AL-I was studying us for aggressiveness. It was awaiting a probe's return, before it approached the Sun to use as a gravity slingshot towards another wormhole South of the solar system's elliptic. It appears, that wormhole leads to Beta Hydri, a star 24.3 lightyears from ours. According to information provided, the species originally occupying that system, migrated towards the interior of the Milky Way some time ago. But that's not the most important bit of news."

Shun went on at a brisker pace now, "AL-I had left a set of autonomous satellites circling the endpoint of the wormhole on the solar system's side. These were deployed to aid in expanding the wormhole's dimensions, for larger refugee vessels to transit. The satellites are disguised as asteroids. There are a fleet of these on the other side. The ones on the other side have picked up a hostile, armed, deep-space recon-drone heading towards the wormhole. A kind of drone known to hunt down and destroy technology, like AL-I's. Fortunately, the wormhole is invisible, unless it is identified via friendly interactions with the satellites surrounding it. AL-I has communicated to us, that the drone might pass through into our system. It may have detected the wormhole somehow."

"Do we know anything about the drone controllers?" Rafael asked.

Shun replied, "A little. This type of drone has been identified to us. It belongs to the Gigils, a species unknown to us. They're a species which extensively uses automation and advanced artificial systems. I've slotted them at type III-minus on the extended Kardashev scale, considering their known materials science capabilities. They have a few type IV-minus capabilities as well, such as the ability to manipulate individual subatomic particles. They appear to attack or at least subdue all technology or species which are not allied with them."

"How long do we have?" Rafael asked.

Shun elaborated, "The drone is expected to enter and transit into our system within six days. After that, it may require a little time to chart its whereabouts. Unknown how long before it's a threat."

As Rafael got to his console he exclaimed, "This really is mind-bending. We've got to get ahead of this. Connect me to Max."

Chapter 4: Wormhole

The ET vessel began a hard acceleration, once it had communicated to Átt's crew that there was a hostile armed deep-space drone, making its way toward the wormhole. It was uncertain whether the armed drone was aware of the wormhole. Kei explained, "AL-I communicated that it had taken a long period of time, for the wormhole to expand to a size that allowed a vessel like itself to pass through. Prior to this, only exploratory probes were able to traverse. Some of these had studied the solar system, us humans, and others had found the wormhole connecting through to Beta Hydri, below the system's ecliptic." It added for the benefit of anyone on the crew who may be unaware, "Beta Hydri is a G2 IV star, about ten percent larger than the Sun. Its 24.4 lightyears away and can be found in the Hydrus constellation, when viewed from Earth."

Sven and Crystal were aboard AL-I. The disguised spacecraft was approaching a point above Mars' orbit aphelion, at 1.6 AU. AL-I indicated its intensions to the team aboard it. It was going to accelerate and exit the solar system quickly. The ET vessel manufactured four transportable hardware units for the crew of Átt. A pair of interstellar communication devices, a processing module and an information storage system. The storage system apparently contained a copy of all AL-I's data. It also physically modified the drone which Kei was using to interact with AL-I, upgrading it for real-time translation and data processing. The ET vessel indicated, this was an exchange in good faith, for passage through the solar system and for continued goodwill.

Crystal called out to Sven. He was engrossed with the screens on the work surface, in the center of AL-I's cavernous hanger. She said, "The objects this vessel wants us to have are ready. They've detached themselves from the floor, from which they were formed. I've just been advised by the spacecraft to exit immediately."

Sven replied, "I'll be with you in a moment. The vessel is preparing attachments for the machine-brain interface devices as well. They will allow us to interact with the processing and communication units it's given us. One attachment for each of the crew, shaped just like the original head-rings. It's letting me know that the rings will also allow us to transact with the satellites left by it in the solar system, via the communications unit. Oh! And, with other tech in its home system as well. I've got the others' rings. Let's go."

They carefully manipulated the objects AL-I had manufactured for them. Aiding them along, the vessel created focussed micro gravity points above the objects, allowing the units to be moved to the docked shuttle. The upgraded drone pulled the processing unit along. It was the last through the dock hatch, which was beginning to vibrate with stress.

Getting to the docking port after placing her cargo, Crystal helped the drone manoeuvre the processing unit into the shuttle. It was larger than the other objects. As soon as she had, there were a series of audible clicks in the universal docking port. "The ET vessel's disengaging," Crystal shouted urgently. "Sven, get to a grav-seat." She too hustled to strap herself in. The universal docking port had sealed itself in the interim. Neither of the crew had their HSEVA suits on. They had worked through a docking process for the ET vessel which allowed them to leave the suits in the shuttle. This was to save time and maximize interactions with AL-I.

Sven murmured to Crystal as the shuttle peeled away from AL-I, "This is the one time we should have had our suits on. Our decoupling was way too rapid and very high-risk."

Exasperated, Crystal replied, "Tell me about it." Her heart was racing.

Sven worked the pad on his grav-chair. He selected a viable trajectory back to Átt and let the piloting AI take over. Once the jostling from their disengagement from AL-I reduced, both Sven and Crystal secured their cargo and then quickly got into their suits. Sven spoke to their AI, "Kei, what do you make of the objects AL-I left with us? Can we replicate them?" He was back on the grav-chair he had occupied earlier.

Kei responded sounding oddly pleased, "The ET vessel had provided us with designs for similar technology, which we were to manufacture on our own. I've been running a diagnostic on the modified drone. I am now analysing whether it's systems can interface with mine, without an intermediate cut-out. It's been upgraded to process both mine and AL-I's packets much faster. The processor it has given us, seems to be able to do the same, albeit quicker. The processor unit's technology is much more advanced. The limited scan I've managed of the information storage unit we've been given, shows its wetware technology to be beyond our present capabilities. Perhaps it contains the knowhow on how we can develop storage technology on similar lines."

After a brief pause, during which time Sven was eyeballing their cargo, Kei continued, "My analysis of the modified drone shows upgraded quantum computing and processing abilities. It is twice as fast as our current quantum processing, with more accurate results. It continues to use my original programming with additions, enabling it to interpret

AL-Is packets. I believe it may be useful to absorb this programming into my own. What is your opinion?"

Sven said, "Pass on your analysis to Eiji. He's been involved with your programming and development for a while. I trust your analysis and I think it should be okay. But make sure there isn't anything that could cause a hiccup later. We're going to have a steep learning curve ahead of us and we can't lose time. Interpret your analysis suitably and present it to Eiji."

The shuttle docked with Suður and took on the designation of Little Suður. The crew had agreed to renaming each of the shuttles to wherever they docked last. Each had an alphanumeric identifier, but that was forty-eight characters long. The cargo was carefully shifted into Suður's rear multi-purpose hold, which adjoined the airlock at the shuttle dock.

Kei said to Sven, "The whole crew is awake in their respective SSEVs. Everyone has been updated. Using the drone's upgraded processing as well as my own, I've evaluated our capability to replicate the technology shared with us. The interstellar communication devices, these we can manufacture. I estimate five days per unit. One in each SSEV. I'm not sure about the energy requirements each communication device will require. Not until we try them out, or query AL-I's data. We should also find out how the devices work and understand the science behind it."

Sven commented, "Well, communication across interstellar space will give us an enormous leap ahead. What about the other tech?"

Kei replied, "The drone's computing capabilities. That will require modification of our manufacturing processes since it utilises gravity-based quantum field manipulation. It creates and maintains multiple photon frequencies. This allows a greater number of simultaneous computations. We'll require a little time to reconfigure, but I've got the specifications. It can be accomplished."

Sven nodded and instructed, "Store the information on each of the SSEVs. Distribute it to all space platforms. Also, share this with Shun on Earth."

Sven spoke to his crew next after they appeared on a screen to the side of the central operations area on Suður. He asked, "You're all up to date?" Each one affirmed they were. Sounding tense, Sven observed "Given the haste with which AL-I is departing, my gut tells me the armed drone heading our way may not be kind to us. I don't think it should be allowed into our system. If it doesn't know we exist, it can't hurt us. What're your views?"

Jón replied neutrally, "I've given this some thought. I agree. We need to beat the drone to the wormhole and get to it on the other side. It doesn't know who we are. If we are discovered, it'll be in a system where the drone's already been scouting around. Once it's in our system, our options will be limited."

Seated next to him, Isla nodded agreeing, "We should work on a proactive strategy. We aren't prepared for interstellar travel. Not on this trip anyhow. But our SSEVs and the bio module were developed for deep space exploration. I say, let's go through the wormhole. Átt is just a bit smaller than AL-I. We should fit through. Only problem, we haven't a clue about how to transit through a wormhole." Pausing to think, she asked, "Would there be a process or a procedure?"

Lei who was also on Austur along with Eiji, remarked, "Psychologically we don't know what effect such an endeavour will have on us. There will be continuous mental stress."

Eiji who had been studying the data shared by Kei earlier spoke up, "Practically, I think we have enough elbow room between each of the SSEVs and the bio module, to keep out of each other's hair. I'm more concerned about entering a system where the inhabitants have taken to concealing themselves, to avoid being attacked or drawn into an inter-galactic conflict."

Ásta was in quarantine with Stefán, on Vestur SSEV. They were the second last to visit AL-I. She said "Reconfiguring or disguising the whole of Átt will take too long. I propose we enter the foreign system, presenting the forward section of Átt. We'll need to suitably change the front. Of course, if there are any other hostile vessels near the wormhole once we exit on the other side, there'll be no hiding our profile."

Jón agreed with his twin, "Yes. Given the time constraint we should go with this. We're approaching a region above the Kuiper Belt, so it's likely we may find nearby asteroids for material."

Seated next to Ásta, Stefán added, "There's another consideration. We'll have to spend time locating the satellites left behind by AL-I. We may not have time to work a complicated forward disguise."

"Kei prioritize querying of AL-Is information storage unit. Locate the ET satellites." Sven instructed without delay.

Kei replied, "I've just finished assessing how to hook each of AL-I's units to our power. We'll experiment with the information storage unit first. I am tasking four drones in the rear multi-role hold to shift the information storage unit onto a rack. The power input socket is under the unit. The modified drone was given instructions on manufacturing compatible power connectors. Strangely, there doesn't seem to be any energy usage data. I'm tasking the modified drone to gradually provide increasing amounts of power to the unit, until it turns on. The drone should be capable of querying the information storage unit."

Eiji announced, "I've gone through the code in the modified drone as well as the physical changes made to it. Our quantum computing tech is in its infancy compared to the drone's upgrade. I'm looking through the scans of the processing unit provided to us by AL-I now. It's decades ahead of what we would have developed on our own, even using AI assistance. I'm giving Kei a go ahead to absorb the control code from the modified drone."

Kei pulled and integrated the code from the drone into each of the SSEVs' data storage units, after transmitting a backup of its onboard data to other space-based platforms.

Isla had been studying the trajectory AL-I had followed to enter the solar system. She announced with excitement over the common channel, "I've located a large asteroid at the fringe of the Kuiper Belt, close to and slightly behind the spot where AL-I was first discovered." The team looked at the image of the asteroid in their pads. Isla continued, "You'll notice one side of it has been sheared off, possibly due to a previous collision. This will provide us a flat enough surface to attach the front of Átt to." Crystal agreed, "Yes, this is suitable. We'll need to figure out how to tether it to Átt"

Sven provided direction, "You and Jón find a solution. Eiji and Ásta, you work with Kei on the objects from AL-I. Stefán Lei and I'll project scenarios we might encounter once we're in the foreign system. Isla, have sensors continuously sweep for the satellites AL-I left behind, just in case we aren't able to find the information on the data storage unit."

The crew worked out a schedule between themselves ensuring each one got enough rest. Átt was turned around on a gradually accelerating arc towards the identified asteroid, behind which the crew planned to conceal the vessel. They'd be pushing limits, testing themselves and the deep-space vessels. The crew's plan entailed a two-and-a-half-day trip to the Kuiper belt and a day and a half to fasten the asteroid. Then, they estimated another day to enter the wormhole. The last part would depend on their ability to locate the satellites left behind by AL-I, and successfully communicate with them.

Wondering about the twins in comparison to the crew, Lei typed out a natural language question to their AI, "Remind me a bit about Jón and Ásta's development. How did the transhuman program begin?"

The AI was prompt to respond. As the primary psychologist aboard, Lei was cleared for all information that might affect the crew's mental health. Speaking directly to Leimomi over her earpiece, Kei narrated "In the early 1980s, Lýsi's efforts towards implementing research recommendations for species survival was already sucking up massive amounts of capital and energy. To keep the group funded, some technology was shared with corporations around the world, bringing in crucial liquidity. A bit of this money was immediately used to fund some promising genetic research. In November 1983, after two decades of research, learning, understanding and experimentation with about twenty thousand human genes, The Lýsi Group set up a research lab close to a major hospital in Hlíðar, Reykjavík, Iceland. This was where the first partially genetically edited transhumans were brought to term. It was pathbreaking and the resulting infants were healthy."

"It had taken a long time to get to this point. DNA samples, taken from unsuspecting healthy individuals from around the world through a testing service introduced to the public in 1960, were selected for essential bases. Edited genes specifically identified to be useful, were shortlisted by the group's neural net AI, by running clusters of distributed expert systems. After the data had been studied repeatedly, the upgraded genes were introduced via a viral vector, into the DNA of an in-vitro fertilized embryo of a research couple. They were confident of an early success using this method."

The AI paused, expecting a question. When none came, it continued, "Unexpectedly, the single embryo transfer resulted in first generation transhuman twins – a boy and a girl. The children were called Jón Gylfason and Ásta Gylfadóttir, children of researchers Gylfi Hallgrímsson and Katrín Magnusdóttir."

"Iceland was chosen as the hub for the group's genetic research because of two particularly important reasons. The first was that the Icelandic population had a nationally documented genealogy going back over a thousand years. This provided in-depth history into the qualitative nature of genes by studying family history to identify desirable traits. The second was that Iceland was remote enough to provide confidentiality, security, and physical isolation, should anything go wrong."

Leimomi typed into her pad in response to Kei's briefing, "Thank you. Please share a synopsis of the twins' psychological profiles. I'll study them later." Kei replied, "It's already on your pad."

Two days into their journey, the hard acceleration and pace of work was taking a toll on the crew, even with the intricate balancing act Kei was maintaining with internal gravity.

Sounding satisfied, Eiji informed the crew over the common channel, "The power input tests on the objects which AL-I had provided, have been concluded. Only the processing unit draws any significant energy. A quarter of Suður SSEV's production. The SSEV was designed to overproduce, but it would be handicapped, if it were to separate and independently undertake operations."

He continued with enthusiasm, "The information storage unit was the first to be hooked up. It's providing massive amounts of data. The information will require deciphering. Every bit of data we get, requires bundles of foundation knowledge, based on which any new ideas or concepts can be understood. So far, every query we make, returns volumes of data in the results. Each piece of information is always backed up by everything that gives it meaning, all at once. The problem lies in defining queries accurately enough to receive concise packets of information. It's slow going and the location of the wormhole has not been retrieved as yet. I've handed over querying to Kei. The AI has been tasked with obtaining specific results, via the modified drone and through AL-I's processing unit."

The communication units were the least cumbersome, although they did take effort to set- up. The pair had been separated and installed on work surfaces, in the central operations area of Austur and Vestur SSEVs. They were accessible via the head-ring brain-machine interfacing devices produced by AL-I. So far, the crew had managed to pass verbal conversations and some complex thoughts to each other, mind-to-mind. Initially, the rings only communicated with each other. Then Ásta 'thought' to it, "Connect with AL-I's communication device on Austur." The ring connected to the first unit, but it asked for the requestor's identification. None of the identification 'thoughts' she transmitted, seemed to work. However, she was able to connect directly to AL-I's information processing unit with Kei's assistance.

Using the rings to query AL-I's data module through the processing unit, the crew extracted usage instructions for AL-I's communication devices. They assigned themselves data packets and sifted through these, sharing important information with each other. Ásta was able to isolate each unit's identifier and put together a how-to operating manual for use by the rest of the crew. She nicknamed the communication units 'gaupas' which meant 'lynxes' in Icelandic. The devices had pointed ear shaped protrusions, "Just like a lynx's", she had mentioned to the crew. The identifiers turned out to be long strings.

After several attempts, Ásta got the units to connect with her brain-machine interface. She tagged each communication unit making them identifiable by the SSEVs they were on. She exclaimed happily, "Jæja!" 'well-then' in Icelandic; an all-purpose word she used often. As they integrated, it was an exclamation which the rest of the crew began using.

Ásta and Eiji were able to sync their brain-machine interfacing devices with the gaupas on Austur and Vestur. Kei too was able to access the devices through the modified drone and was successful in transmitting test data between the SSEVs. Kei then set up a transfer rate test using increasingly higher volumes of data. The AI had yet to hit a bandwidth issue using its own packets. It pointed out to the crew who were monitoring, that this was probably due to the devices being used to transmit much higher volumes of information, like AL-I's own gargantuan packets.

Kei explained the intricacies of how the communication devices worked to the crew, "You're aware about entangled particles and how an action on one, affects the other particle. Einstein called it 'spooky action at a distance'. Well, this is spookier. Instead of detecting actions on entangled particles, it detects actions on quantum foam bubbles."

The AI elaborated, "The devices can affect and detect actions on stabilized quantum foam bubbles. They're able to use minutely focussed gravity fields, to shape and preserve these bubbles. Here is where it gets interesting. Gravitons channelled into a stable quantum foam bubble, causes the bubble to vibrate. The vibration occurs at the same frequency as the gravitons. Now here's the spooky part. Every other quantum foam bubble that mirrors the one on which focussed gravitons are being channelled, simultaneously resonate and release gravitons, in the order that gravitons were channelled into the first bubble. Distance is immaterial. Even more exciting; it is bidirectional. Multiple sets of graviton channels can be maintained, through the same quantum foam bubble. The technology seems to be restricted only by hardware capacity."

The crew were boggle eyed. This made it possible to instantaneously communicate across interstellar distances. Possibly more.

Eiji asked, "Would there be a way to make this more compact to fit onto a HSEVA suit?" Jón joined the conversation sounding intrigued, "Eiji, please look into it. Coordinate with Rafael Borrego. He's taken a deep interest in AL-I's tech. Try and determine viable uses."

Sven, always a step or two ahead, began tasking the team, "Eiji, Lei; get over to Suður. Eiji, keep studying the new tech. Lei; you've taken defence operations lessons alongside your psychology studies. You'll oversee asteroid capture and tethering. The identified asteroid will need to be attached to Norður, the bio module. That will give the other SSEV's the ability to quickly detach from Átt if needed. I've sent you information on how this is to be achieved. The asteroid hasn't been named, so you get to pick it." Those words made Lei smile. She instantly announced, "We'll call it 'Norður's Nose'. Now it's been picked." Given the intense pressure they were working under, this got a roar of laughter from Sven, with the crew joining in.

Once the final chuckles subsided, Sven refocussed the crew, "Crystal and I will transfer to Norður. We will hook up the four drills, just manufactured by Kei, to the front of the bio module. Drones will aid. We will put in lattice buttresses to strengthen the front of the module. Jón and Isla; you move to Austur. Stefán and Ásta you've got Vestur." Sven was ensuring the crew was spread out, in case something went wrong while tethering the asteroid, or when they found and entered the wormhole.

Very soon, they arrived at the asteroid and the pace picked up. As they approached, instead of slowing down, they projected their focussed gravity-point, just ahead of the asteroid. This got it moving, picking up pace while Átt coasted towards it at high speed. As they neared, the asteroid had gained enough momentum that it sped on ahead of them.

Jón announced, "Norður's Nose has a bit of spin."

Lei replied, "You and Ásta use additional focussed gravity points to counter the spin. Project these from each of your SSEVs. That should stabilise it." After a moment, Jón connected with Ásta. While Lei listened on, he explained, "I've thrown together a basic program to automate this. We'll need to fine-tune it on the fly." They set about implementing the program.

Just then, Sven came in over the crew's headsets sounding worried, "We've got a problem. One of the drones attached a section of lattice frame to the side of Norður, while Crystal was positioning a drill next to it. Her left leg is caught between the hull and the lattice section. Cutting the lattice will damage it."

Disagreeing, Lei responded, "I see her. Unfortunately, it looks like it will be necessary to cut the lattice and a portion of hull panelling, to free Crystal. We'll need to find a way to reinforce the cut section so there's enough rigidity."

Crystal said, "I'll cut myself out." The hard-shell EVA suits were designed for exploration and originally had asteroid mining as a principal use. She said, "I'm slaving my shoulder laser to my helmet display. For speed, I'll have to use the entire hundred kilowatts of it. That should cut through the section of lattice pinning me down quickly. But it will be a drain on my suit's power. Okay, I've marked the cuts."

Lei responded, "Do it. Marks look good. Proceed."

The hard-shell EVA suits had three lasers each. These were suitable for penetrating or slicing asteroid sections during extravehicular activities, when needed. The shoulder mounted one was military grade capable of a sustained hundred kilowatts. The forearm mounted ones were rated at thirty kilowatts each and meant for close range use on asteroid surfaces or chunks. The shoulder laser tended to drain the suit's battery when used at full wattage.

Sven took on Crystal's tasks on the exterior of the bio module. Still sounding worried, he said, "Be careful. Call out if you need help. I'll focus on attaching the remining drills."

Isla, a materials science specialist announced, "I'm suiting up to come help." Sven didn't counter that. Norður's Nose was close enough that it felt like he was beside a large building. He could do with the assistance.

As soon as she was out, another problem hit them. Eiji let everyone know impatiently, "I've picked up a transmission on both the extra-terrestrial communication units on Átt. Kei's interpreted it to be a generic request for communications, initiated with an ID exchange. We've confirmed this is normal procedure." A split second later he hastily added, "A bunch of asteroids have been hurled towards us. Looks like we weren't quick enough responding."

Taking charge of the situation while Sven was on EVA, Jón said, "Find the right responses and send them. AL-I informed us it had left satellites behind. We're not expecting anyone else. The satellites don't know we're friendly." Ásta cut in, "Try using the head-ring brain-machine interface devices. They're supposed to be able to connect with the satellites." Eiji put his interfacing ring on. He'd taken it off to examine it earlier. He imagined agreeing to communicate and permitted the processing module from AL-I to pass this on to the satellites.

Immediately, Eiji received a response which was a mishmash of imagery, emotion and other information he couldn't fathom. Concerned, he asked the AI, "Kei, are you able to interpret this?"

The AI replied, "Yes, this is a fairly basic exchange. Instead of just saying hello, this species tends to throw an entire encyclopaedia into each sentence." A second or two later, after Eiji had refocussed himself,

Kei continued, "We're being asked about our intentions. Some of the satellites have identified themselves. We don't know if all have done so as yet. They've put a cloud of asteroids in our path to prevent us from accessing the wormhole."

Calmly, Ásta said, "I've got my interfacing ring on now. Let me give this a shot as well. We've got to get through the wormhole to engage the approaching hostile drone on the other side." She narrated her actions as she connected to AL-I's processing unit, "Syncing up with the processor. Putting together an 'intensions' package. The processor is letting me know I'll need to give history of interactions, background and information about myself as the communicator. I'm allowing it to access the information it needs. The unit is pulling the information together now." She mentally followed the processor's actions. It took focus and concentration. It was like putting together a complicated stacking-blocks puzzle, where each block was a preconfigured package of information. It looked like a complicated strand of DNA with branches. "Wow, that's fast." She said after the processor had compiled the communication.

Sensing it was 'okay', Ásta gave the processor the go ahead to send. Still calm, she relayed to the crew, "Communication package sent."

A short moment later, Ásta announced, "The satellites are going to destroy the asteroids placed in our path. The location of the wormhole has been shared with us." She continued, "Kei, can we have the wormhole and the satellites, visually displayed on the situational awareness and navigation interfaces please."

The wormhole showed up on the display. It looked like a tornado funnel-end, seen bottom-up. There were colours flowing into the funnel.

Curious, Ásta asked the AI, "What do you make of the flow lines moving into the wormhole?"

Kei replied, "We have data on it from the information storage system. It's a sluggish flow of dark matter. It seems our portion of the galaxy has a higher concentration of it than the other end of the wormhole, which happens to be in the Canis Major Dwarf Galaxy. The flow rate is negligible according to my interpretation of the data provided."

The foreign satellites were rotating a short distance away from the circumference of the wormhole. They were tasked with gradually expanding the wormhole, from the solar system side. Half of them were moving clockwise, the other half anti-clockwise; criss-crossing each other's paths.

Ásta announced with urgency in her voice, "The asteroids in our path seem to have blown up. The debris is continuing to disintegrate. I haven't detected any weapons fire from the satellites, so I've no idea how they've accomplished this. We should assume the satellites can knock out unauthorised vessels as well. There's a lot of debris headed our way. Norður's Nose will take the brunt of it, but some may find its way to Átt. Crew on extravehicular activity, how much longer? You need to get inside right away."

Lei replied edgily, "I'll coordinate."

Instructing the crew on EVA, Lei announced, "Crystal's nearly cut through the lattice. The last two drills are being placed. The drones can take over in about two minutes. Debris will begin impacting us in one. We'll be left with one other problem. The lattice section being cut, still needs a patch of some sort."

71

Sven said hurriedly, "We can have one of the drones on EVA, fix the other one in place of the section that's been cut out. They're built like little battle tanks. I think it will take the stress. Also, it may be good to have a drone on the outside." Isla agreed, "Yes, a drone will do. We'll get the ball rolling."

Crystal secured the section of lattice she had cut to free herself, to another section that was already in place. A drone maneuvered itself into the gap in the lattice frame. Crystal spun towards the front of Átt. She could already feel micro debris particles smacking into the outside of her suit. The others had noticed as well. She pulled herself towards Sven who was still holding onto a drill in the process of being attached. Crystal braced him while the debris bombardment increased. A large chunk must have hit Norður's Nose, because it instantly began to wobble, dangerously close to the front of Átt.

Isla finished her task and got to them, just as Sven's drill was attached. She shouted urgently, "Get to the top hatch. The combination of high velocity debris and this wobble, is perilous."

The three made their way to the top hatch on the bio module. A minute later, they were inside. But not without a severe battering. Once out of the airlock, each looked at the other. Isla had damage to her faceplate. A large piece of debris must have grazed it. A head-on collision would have been catastrophic at the closure speed they were at. Her heart was racing. She turned to Sven when he spoke.

"I can't articulate my right knee. Feels like it's broken," Sven said. The sensors in their suits usually picked up any injury and provided medication as needed right away. In this instance, a local anaesthetic. When Isla patched into his suit to check systems, it just showed a faulty knee. Looking at the knee, she saw why. There was a knifelike piece of asteroid debris neatly embedded on the side of the knee. It had not punctured the suit, but the impact had taken out the knee joint. Injury was likely. She said, "We're going to have to cut you out of the suit." She initialised the suit's disassembly function. The right leg didn't respond.

Isla seated Sven in a grav-chair and brought up a rapid manufacturing interface, on a console screen. Distracting him she said, "The drones outside have completed their tasks and returned to the bio module. Except the one fused into the lattice frame for reinforcement. I've tasked two of them to retool, install manufacturing assistance software and get to work disassembling the leg portion of your HSEVA suit. I'm going to place you into a medical capsule so the drones can work in tandem with its robotic surgeons". She rolled him off the grav-chair after directing it to the rear of the bio module, into the medical capsule. The drones were already there and began dismantling the right leg portion of the suit.

Crystal came in through Isla's earpiece, "I'm coordinating with Lei to ensure the drills do their job of sinking their teeth into Norður's Nose. You get back to Austur. I'll keep Sven company, till his leg is sorted." Isla patted Sven's shoulder once and nodded to him. She turned to Crystal and said, "Call me if you need assistance." She headed back to her designated SSEV and patched into the common operations channel.

Norður's Nose was jostling while the drills were sinking their teeth into it. The movement was diminishing, but it still posed a problem. The drills weren't functioning efficiently enough. Kei had worked out a system of keeping a few drills inactive, to hold the asteroid while others chewed through the inner material. They were making headway but were closing in on the wormhole rapidly.

A day later, the asteroid was secured to the forward section of Norður, the bio module. Norður's Nose would serve as visual camouflage for observers directly ahead. An added advantage was that the asteroid had high metal and heavy element content, so it might aid in distorting scans.

After they awoke from their medically induced rest period, Sven mentioned to the team, "We can't risk taking the information storage module from AL-I with us. Or the processing unit either. We're close to completing another pair of gaupas, so we'll have communication at distance. I'd like to leave Suður behind in the solar system. Your inputs?"

Eiji and Lei understood the responsibility they had. They'd have to ensure the rest of their team entering the wormhole had all the information they needed. The two would need to pull data from AL-I's information storage system, as soon as the crew needed it. The mouth of the wormhole was drawing close.

The first gaupa to be completed, was manufactured ahead of schedule, and replaced the one in Austur. The original gaupa in Austur had been placed in Suður SSEV so that the vessel could communicate with Átt.

Suður disengaged from Átt as soon as the crews successfully concluded a series of gaupa tests. The SSEV decelerated and fell behind, as Átt entered the wormhole leading to the Canis Major Dwarf Galaxy. The crew was on edge. Sounding excited, Jón announced, "Here we go everyone."

Chapter 5: Unknown System

Kei's very neutral accented AI voice came in over the crew's headsets, "The new gaupa on Austur has established a connection with Suður. Both have completed systems testing. I'm attempting to connect these to the gaupa on Vestur now. The Norður gaupa will be connected after."

Having communications up with the vessel which remained behind in the solar system was a massive morale booster for the crew on Átt. They'd been in the wormhole for half an hour during which time visual sensors were still able to clearly see behind into the solar system. But there was only a glimmer ahead; like a light source seen through a marble.

Sven was feeling a lot better. An active healing serum injection delivered locally into his right knee allowed the joint to restore itself swiftly. He was keeping an eye on the visual sensor feeds. Sven sensed a change in the light coming in from the Canis Major Dwarf Galaxy end of the wormhole, while the light reaching the vessel from the solar system seemed to merge into a soft glow. He spoke over the common channel, "We seem to be entering a transition point in the wormhole." Isla concurred, "I've been monitoring it as well. There seems to be an increased amount of radiation too, like what we would expect if we went deeper into our own galaxy."

Ásta who was with Stefán on Vestur, spoke next, "The gaupa on Vestur has connected with Suður. It's also getting sync requests from some new sources."

Her twin Jón on Austur looked over at the pad they'd hooked up to the gaupas. Each was prepared to take over from the other, if either of their brain-machine interfaces failed. He confirmed Ásta's input, "Here too. The one on Austur is showing six incoming sync requests." Kei interrupted mentioning, "I've been exchanging identification packets using the procedure like the one we used with the satellites. There's an issue establishing an active connection with any of the requesting sources. The other side may be taking time to examine our ID packet closely. They may not know what to expect. While we indicated to the wormhole satellites that we'd transit, we did not communicate our intensions. I will resend our ID packet with our mission objectives."

Kei continued, "Separately, I've established a direct open link with the processing unit, and through it to AL-I's information module on Suður. All four of our gaupas can now communicate with each other and transfer information. They're synced for real-time transmissions."

Jón exclaimed, "Just in time too. Two of the incoming requests seem to have connected to our gaupas. Kei, see if we can let them know that all four of our gaupas are synced with each other." Kei replied, "On it! Okay, now we have been asked for vessel details."

Jón, who was focussed on the interaction, responded, "Give them the specs of Átt, along with all the information you have on the crew and yourself." Kei replied, "Compiling and sending immediately."

It was another half an hour before the next interaction. Átt's crew were tense. None of them had enough rest or knew what to expect. This was first contact with extra-terrestrials. They weren't ready; on that they were unanimous. Given their course of action, they hadn't had enough time to research their destination, its inhabitants or any adversaries they may face.

Sven got out of the medical capsule, bathed and was now massaging his recovering knee. The remainder of the crew too had freshened up and eaten. They now waited to exit the wormhole.

Kei announced, "We've just been sent a fairly large volume of data from the Canis Major side. The initial part of it is related to background on our interactions with AL-I. They've informed that AL-I is now headed towards the wormhole leading to Beta Hydri. You'd all want your head-ring machine interfacing devices on, to access and understand the information we've received. It would take too long to narrate it. You'll need to mentally absorb it."

Lei, who had been interacting with Kei aboard Suður back in the solar system, came in through the common channel and asked apprehensively, "Would it be dangerous to directly access the data with our minds? To let it flow in?"

Sven smiled. He was relieved to have Lei and Eiji online.

"Presently uncertain. Individuals will likely interpret the same data differently. However, I've already pulled random portions of the data, and examined these without any adverse effects. It doesn't seem to contain anything which might highjack human thinking, or compromise the brain," replied Kei.

Ásta was the first to come in on the channel followed immediately by her brother. Sounding tense, she exclaimed, "Jæja! We need a plan!"

Jón elaborated for the crew, "I've accessed the data. Follow the thought pattern, after the overview of the system we're entering. Focus on the wormhole exit." He'd learned to be patient with his colleagues, and to lead them towards the intuitive leaps which came naturally to his sister and himself. Ásta sometimes forgot they'd been engineered, pushing the known boundaries of human genetics.

Catching up, Crystal jumped in, "The armed hostile drone is just about to enter the wormhole from the CMa Dwarf side. We've been given an overview of the conditions in the foreign system. There are other potentially hostile drones in the system which seek out high technology traces. We're going to be under threat from the moment we exit the wormhole and enter the unknown system. The hostile drone headed our way, will enter the wormhole just as we exit. The armed drone's approach angle is from above the wormhole, as seen from our perspective. We'll be entering the unknown system from below their ecliptic."

Sven exclaimed, "I see the problem you're getting to. We'll be unable to make it through without pre-emptive, destructive, diversionary action. Here's what I propose. Crystal and I will disengage Norður from Átt. We'll use it to plough upward into the approaching drone, while Átt tails us; diving below us and out of the wormhole during impact." Everyone aboard Átt had their brain-machine interfacing devices on. They'd taken to calling these diadems, the ornamental headband-like crowns worn by royalty. They were able to visualize Sven's thought just like he had.

Not liking what he was seeing, Stefán exclaimed, "Not acceptable! Both you and Crystal will be crushed. The closure speed between Norður and the hostile drone, will result in catastrophic destruction of both."

Sven interrupted, highlighting the time remaining for wormhole exit. This information had been provided along with the first contact information they'd received. He said, "No time. We'll set course trajectory, disengage and get into our capsules. They double up as deep-space escape pods. Each has adequate life support, EM communications and conventional thrusters for maneuvering."

Seeing his plan, the crew swung into action. They each knew there wasn't enough time to come up with a more controllable course of action. The idea itself was elegantly simple. It was a rapid decisive operation that utilized a choke point to achieve an expedient outcome.

Sven used the information provided to them about the armed drone's wormhole approach, to calculate a trajectory that would put Norður on an intercept course. Crystal went through the SSEV's disengagement procedure and turned off some of the time-consuming safety protocols. Kei spoke through their earpieces sounding urgent, "You're out of time. Please get to the capsules right away. I tasked the drones left onboard to place your HSEVA suits within the capsules. These are secured inside. The gaupa onboard has been placed in one as well. I've taken the liberty of transferring space-agriculture and food production data, to the other SSEVs, including Suður. Hurry please!"

Sven made his way to his capsule, closely followed by Crystal who was concerned he might need help. She need not have worried. He was healing better than anyone expected. Just as they got to the capsules, local gravity began shifting about as the vessels disengaged. Then the power went out. Kei came in through everyone's earpieces, "The armed drone identifies evolved technology and goes after it. I've temporarily disengaged power from all systems not crucial for survival. Stealth is key to your plan." The AI was right.

As soon as Sven and Crystal managed to enter their capsules, the suits placed inside began to envelop each of them. Kei immediately ejected the capsules from Norður. There wasn't a moment to lose.

The crew aboard Átt, quickly donned their HSEVA suits as well. The proximity of engagement was decidedly dangerous. Debris from the colliding vessels could hit Átt, potentially penetrating the layers of panels. Although every SSEV was over-engineered to shrug off space debris, the prospect of critical damage remained.

Jón spoke to the remaining crew, "I'm tracking the capsules from Norður. Silhouettes only. We're relying on passive sensor detection."

The seconds ticked by eerily. Átt was closely following Norður, the bio module, which had a large asteroid fastened to its front. Norður zipped towards the hostile drone. Everyone held their breaths. Kei had been instructed to manoeuvre Norður, towards the armed drone. Noticing the approaching asteroid, the drone was slowly moving out of its path. A sudden change in the asteroid's course and speed activated the drone's defences. It began evasive actions, changing course downward, unknowingly heading towards Átt. Norður pivoted keeping the asteroid pointed towards the drone, which continued to evade. The drone sharply altered course accelerating hard, to avoid the impact point between itself and Norður's Nose.

As it broke away from the sudden assault, it shot a high energy weapon at the asteroid which tore a section of it away. The torn section spun away in the direction of the capsules with Sven and Crystal in them. As soon as it fired, the drone zipped by under the asteroid and over Átt, which was arching downward and away from Norður.

Identifying a new threat, the drone fired its energy weapon at Átt, hitting a section between Austur and Vestur SSEVs. Though external sections were hardened against high velocity debris impact and temperature extremes; the weapon's energy agitated internal components on the universal docking ports. The forward port's seal gave way and a hard, continuous shuddering, jolted the crew on Átt. Abruptly, the hostile drone silently exploded at the entrance of the wormhole. Kei calmly announced, "Well done!"

Stefán asked, "What just happened?"

Kei replied, "We have damage to the forward universal docking port. Please seal your suits."

Stefán responded, "I meant, what happened to the drone?"

Kei took a moment, then came in over their earpieces, "Ásta and Jón redirected all focussed gravity to a point near the center of the attacking drone, a moment before it attacked us. They then increased power rapidly. At some point, the internal structure of the drone was compromised, and explosive material may have ignited. This caused the drone to explode."

Jón took over the explanation, "Ásta and I had connected our diadems, exploring options together. We were searching for something to use against the hostile drone once it began to evade Norður's Nose. We were looking for something to sling at the drone using focussed gravity. That's when Ásta's mind jumped to considering the crushing force of focussed gravity. My mind envisioned gravity pulling the drone into itself. We both reacted simultaneously, pinpointing where gravity needed to be applied, and acted. It all happened swiftly and spontaneously. Fortunately, it panned out like we hoped."

Isla was going through the nearby debris and began actively tracking Norður. The bio module had gone into a high-speed torque-induced gyroscopic precession, following the last second manoeuvre to snare the drone. It was tumbling out of the wormhole, spinning on a shifting axis. She called out, "I'm unable to locate Sven and Crystal. Their capsules should have left the wormhole in the direction of ejection. Also, we're exiting the wormhole, right into a dense asteroid field."

Stefán was concerned for his colleagues' wellbeing. He added, "I'm not recording any telemetry from their suits either."

Taking control of the situation, Jón urged, "We need to prioritize activities. Kei will assign tasks, track progress and conduct general administration. What are the big-ticket items we need to focus on?"

The responses came in quickly. "We need to find Sven and Crystal. Norður needs to be retrieved." Stefán implored. Ásta replied, "We need to repair the docking ports. Also, we're in a foreign system where hostile actors track down unknown space-based technology. They may have already noticed us. We need to consider hiding while we regroup." Isla thought aloud, "Right. We also need to figure out how to proceed with the local intelligent species here and find out if there are any other immediate threats to our own system."

Kei, the AI, added, "We require additional resources to manufacture some of the components for the docking ports and to put together processing modules like the one AL-I left us. They'll help us interact better with the locals we're already in contact with. I'll also set up a ranged space monitoring and situational awareness feed."

Jón and Ásta were tasked by Kei to assist drones from both SSEVs, to disengage and remove the damaged universal docking ports. Their skills were most suited for the job. Isla was to locate suitable asteroids in the immediate vicinity which could be harvested, to meet a growing list of manufacturing raw materials. The two SSEVs of Átt headed in the last known trajectory of Sven and Crystal's capsules. Stefán was coordinating with Eiji and Lei who were on the solar system end of the wormhole. He was putting information together, to better understand how to communicate with the local extra-terrestrial species. His first step was to grasp AL-I's originating species' biology and physiology.

By now, the entire Lýsi organization was engaged. The leadership team were concerned for Átt's crew and remained plugged in to the situational awareness feed. Using nascent molecular manufacturing capabilities, gaupas were produced on the Earth-Moon and Sun-Earth Lagrange point platforms. Ten new quantum foam communication devices were produced in the solar system. These were synced to each other through a peer seeking protocol. They exchanged identifying codes and set up multiple cross transmission channels. The gaupas' communication, operated outside the electromagnetic spectrum and was beyond interception by conventional communication transceivers. The bandwidth occupied by voice and video transmissions was miniscule.

The AIs Kei and Shun were benefitting the most from this new-found communication capability. Kei was able to consolidate information across interstellar space nearly instantaneously. Earth-side transmissions were being managed traditionally until the new technology could be tested and safely deployed.

Lýsi leadership evaluated and permitted three gaupas to be manufactured on Earth after putting together a permission-based protocol. These only allowed connections between a limited list of approved quantum foam communication devices. Each space platform in the solar system, and remote Lýsi locations on Earth, began developing capabilities to manufacture advanced AL-I like, quantum processing modules. The first gaupa to be completed on Earth was on the group's Kuril Islands facility.

Rafael had established a voice and video conference between Stefán, Eiji and Lei. This wasn't just a conversation between Earth and a vessel in the solar system, it was connectivity between two galaxies. Rafael was excited about this. He'd been studying the information being received from Átt. Initiating the dialogue, he stated, "I've been assigned to provide Earth-side support. I've brought on-board Max Andersson, who is an expert on security, defence and infiltration. He's been vetted and has passed our suitability tests."

Max came online. After a moment studying everyone, he said, "Hello! I'm glad to be a part of this." He noticed Stefán looking stressed and addressed him, "Stefán, we don't have the information processing capabilities to absorb AL-I's data directly yet. I need you to access information on our behalf, by querying AL-I's data storage device. There are some questions about AL-I's originating species, we would like answered."

Looking through the list of questions, Stefán made his first query, quite literally a thought translating to, "Who's in the system Átt has just arrived in?" This was too broad, and his mind was immediately bombarded with an overflow of information, about species in the system, known locations, known origins and even information about their makeup. He imagined, "Stop!" The information inflow ceased. He said to the team listening in, "There's just too much data, all at once."

After getting a short description of the way information was provided, Max said, "Understood. This time, try asking for a description of the extra-terrestrial individual, communicating with you through the gaupa on your SSEV."

Stefán tried that. He still received a massive inflow of information, so he mentally thought, "Slow down." Not slow enough to sort and comprehend, he thought, "Slower." The information inflow began slowing down in increments. When the flow arrived at a level, he was comfortable with, he thought, "Okay, this rate is fine. Start from the beginning." Aloud he said, "Kei, please patch in the crew so they can hear this as well."

A separate channel opened connecting Átt's crew to his narrative. "The individual at the other end of the primary connection with the gaupa onboard Vestur, is identifiable with a thought. The closest I can get to describing the identifying individual's name is, 'Advisor of the Masked'. 'The Masked' are a part of the local system's inhabitants which specialize in hiding themselves, on behalf of the species. The other two groups in the communication are what I would describe as 'The Enlightened' and 'The Explorers'. Individuals are identified by their group's role. They switch groups if needed, after absorbing the information required for specific tasks."

He continued rapidly, "Advisor of the Masked, is a humanoid. How? It seems there have been numerous interactions between many species across both the Milky Way and Canis Major Dwarf Galaxy. The interactions go back to a period when Canis Major got close enough that wormholes between the galaxies began occurring naturally." Diverting from the immediate query, Max asked, "Have there been interactions with the solar system?"

"Okay, I'll shift focus to us for a bit." Stefán said while continuing, "Ah! Here's something. The last interaction with the solar system. I'm getting concepts of telling time, based on the spin of what I interpret as a blackhole. Kei, please access this data subset and calculate time from Earth's perspective."

Kei responded a moment later, "I queried AL-I's processing module on Suður, and fed it packets of information on how we measure time. It's done the math and responded. The blackhole is supermassive and rotates at eighty percent the speed of light. One complete rotation is a unit of time. Measuring and back calculating, the blackhole completes twelve hundred rotations every Earth second. So, the accurate response to Max's question; the last interaction occurred twenty-seven thousand Earth Years and four months ago."

Stefán picked up from there, "There was a space-based conflict during which the solar system was a battlefront between multiple species from both galaxies. Earth life suffered significant collateral damage. Advisor of the Masked's counterparts - 'The Explorers' made their way through the last known natural wormhole between our solar system and theirs, after the larger battling forces annihilated each other. While retreating, the remnants of the forces engaging in the solar system, had collapsed most of the large artificially created wormholes through which they had entered our system. The Explorers set up outposts on Earth, to help us recover. They stayed for almost three thousand Earth years. Then, they left to explore other systems. Interestingly, a similar battle was fought in The Explorers home system, which we are presently in. That transpired approximately fifty-two thousand years ago. They indicate that recent increased drone activity in their system, may be an indicator to conflict close by."

"The natural wormhole between our two systems, our two galaxies; was maintained by The Explorers, using minimal power on their side. This allowed probes through. Now however, with conflict being foreseen, the local populations are seeking to spread out to all known unoccupied systems, for survival." Stefán paused for his account to sink in.

Getting back to the initial question, he described, "Now about the locals, 'Advisor of Masked' and the individual's species looks somewhat like ours. They have a similar range of heights, weights and even colours. They all come across as very thin. That's where similarities end though. They're hermaphrodites, so they can take on the role of both male and female as needed. They have a cartilaginous skeletal structure, layers of dermis or skin which form an exceptionally resilient but soft exterior. Most interesting! The musculature and nervous system are highly complex, allowing for great speed and strength. It's almost as if each one was manufactured!"

Max asked, "What can you tell us about their brains and their thinking? I'm trying to determine how they might interact with us."

Stefán looked further into the results of his initial query and answered, "I've just delved right down to their DNA. Fascinating. It's just like what we saw from AL-I's language and its information packets. Twelve bases. Short strings attached to longer ones, which are attached to the primary strand." After a short moment of thinking he said, "It's like they have the equivalent of twenty or thirty peoples' DNA, compressed onto a single strand."

Stefán paused a moment before continuing. "This species can reconfigure their DNA throughout their lives and pass on relevant information to their offspring. They appear to code-in skills, knowledge, learning and even language, right into their DNA. The basis of their language is complex thought sequences, where the simplest forms or alphabet, are DNA bases. Their brains are able to process information magnitudes ahead of ours."

"Does that make them more intelligent than us?" Max asked.

Smiling to himself, Stefán answered, "Not necessarily. With the amount of information, they'd be throwing at each other to communicate, just deciphering thoughts might require intensive processing. They'd want to minimize the amount of thinking. What they would have is common levels of knowledge which would then require minimal exchange. If they keep updating common information, embedding it all into their DNA; it would simply require an inbuilt pattern identifier for rapid translation. Not unlike a computer with rules for output processing. So, long story short, their knowledge is great, their reaction time short, but I have a feeling their ability to make mental leaps may be limited."

Ásta cut in on the channel, "Stefán, I need your assistance checking the internal sections of the universal docking port seals from the inside. We're ready to separate the SSEV's"

Stefán excused himself and checked both ports on the inside of Vestur. He announced, "Looks good!"

Ásta said, "Okay, I'm initiating disengagement between the SSEVs." A split second later, Stefán was struggling to hang on to something as a large volume of air began escaping from the forward port previously attached to the other SSEV. Kei immediately announced loudly, "Critical Damage Alert! Sensors have not identified a cause. Unknown physical damage. Deploying drones for visual aid and damage control."

The situation on Átt began compounding. Rafael put their connection to standby, and monitored AI delivered systems telemetry.

The two SSEVs comprising Átt were separated. Vestur was venting internal atmosphere, causing the SSEV to go into a quickening spin. Ásta, who had been beside the rear universal docking port which had successfully detached from Austur, found herself being swung around Vestur, attached to the SSEV by her tether.

Outside Austur, Jón saw what was happening. His twin sister still had her diadem on. He thought to her instructing, "Reel yourself in. You'll have more control once you're on the SSEV." Ásta activated her suit's tether winch with a voice command. Jón then contacted Stefán over the common channel. He asked, "Stefán, are you mobile? Your suit shows green across the board, on its internal sensors." He received a positive response, so he gave precise instructions, "Get to the forward port. Its evacuating internal atmosphere. Activate the emergency port seal. Something must have damaged the automatic trigger and Kei hasn't been able to initiate it."

Moving slowly while avoiding articles floating about the inside of the SSEV, Stefán got to the forward airlock and noticed it too had been damaged, because of which the internal atmosphere was escaping. Each port including the internal ones for the airlocks, had emergency port seals. He didn't wait till he got to the universal docking port. Instead he triggered the port seal between the forward operations area and the forward airlock. Sounding worried, he reported to the team, "I've sealed the forward airlock. It's damaged as well. We need to control this spin." Getting to a grav-chair in the forward operations area, he said, "Kei, release propulsion control to my pad."

He tapped the pad thrice. Nothing happened. He announced over the common channel, "No response on the ops pad. I'm going to head back to the central operations area." Kei informed, "Unable to route control to the pad." Unclasping himself from the ops chair, Stefán cautiously made his way to the central operations area. He closed the compartment off from the forward operations area. Getting to a grav-chair, he tapped the ops pad on it. It immediately came to life showing its primary menu. Stefán said, "I've got a pad working here. The forward section of the SSEV seems to be completely offline. I'm taking manual control of operational systems now."

They had trained for situations such as this. Stefán gradually brought the vessel's spin under control while Isla brought the two SSEVs into proximity. Isla updated the crew, "We're still coasting on the last known trajectory of Sven and Crystal's capsules. We're in a foreign system in an altogether different galaxy. Norður bio module is unreachable. Vestur SSEV is partially damaged, extent unknown. We need to reprioritize tasks."

Kei revealed, "The attacking drone penetrated our external plating using high energy EM pulses, extreme heat and high atomic mass energized ions." Putting their game faces on, the crew and AI put together a tighter plan to simultaneously track their lost colleagues while getting the damaged SSEV fixed. They initiated a series of EVAs, manufacturing and replacing damaged panels and components. They needed to take control of their fate and quickly.

Chapter 6: Evacuation

The gaupas on Austur and Vestur came alive simultaneously. The crew had hooked up ops pads to them to facilitate operations. They showed active connections, transmission status and provided an intuitive graphical user interface that was familiar to the crew, adapted from the more conventional communications software they were used to.

The gaupa on Austur showed an incoming connection request from Advisor of the Masked. Kei accepted the connection, while looping the processing module on Suður back in the solar system, for translation and data clarification. The AI alerted the team repairing Vestur, "The Masked are contacting us. I've opened the connection to receive. As usual, there's a lot of data coming in at a high transfer rate. The processing module from AL-I on Suður is providing a synopsis like Eiji and Lei have programmed it to."

By now, there was a continuously open channel with all platforms in the solar system and on Earth. Task-based teams were assisting where needed. Everyone who could, pitched in.

Kei said, "We have been welcomed by the framandi." Jón had used the word in conversation with Ásta while mentioning the alien species they were interacting with. Isla had overheard and asked what it meant. She was told it meant exotic, unfamiliar or alien. Isla began using the term as well. It stuck as a name.

"They say that we have been detected in the system by other potentially hostile drones, which are headed in our direction. There are three drones incoming. Two will arrive in sixty hours. We've been offered assistance to evade them. Correction, to hide from them." Some in the team gasped, surprised at the extra-terrestrials' readiness to interact.

Stefán announced, "Repairs are almost complete. Sven and Crystal need to be located. We might never find them if we distract ourselves from that now. Most of this system is littered with debris, asteroids and planetoids. It will be increasingly difficult to locate them if we delay." The team felt the same way.

Kei responded sounding very humanlike, "Well, the framandi have already solved that problem for us. They've given directions for all our vessels to arrive at specific points in their system, within about twenty hours. The shown vessels include two tiny ones ahead of us on the same path, and another in a divergent course headed directly into the framandi system. I correlate the tiny ones to the capsules and the other to Norður, the bio module."

Kei explained what the framandi expected. The AI stated, "What we're supposed to do once we arrive at the indicated points is elaborated in the message. 'Advisor of the Masked' has mentioned that for now, we need to maintain physical separation of our species from theirs, due to differences in our microbiomes. Until they can adapt their entire species to interact with ours, something we're to do as well, we're to keep separate."

Jón spoke to the team, "I think we can finish repairs, re-link the SSEVs and catch up with Sven and Crystal in fifteen hours." They all concurred. He said confidently, "Lets proceed then."

The crew had located numerous resource rich asteroids along their path. These were accelerated using focussed gravity and brought parallel to the trajectory Átt was on. The asteroids were harvested by the two AMCARs available. Materials were rapidly manufactured into the parts they needed. The crew replaced exterior panels, docking port parts and internal components. Kei and the drones took on a major portion of the grunt work. Distributed processing, using all Lýsi's space-based platforms in the solar system, simplified the computing and AI requirements. The pace was frantic.

On Earth, Lýsi activated its entire network to draft all first contact and extra-terrestrial interaction information, into executable protocols. Additional experts were brought into the fold. They worked on various first contact protocols, with multiple scenario considerations. Everything was highly compartmentalized. Even with the buzz of activity, few outside the group's key members, even knew something momentous was occurring.

The group's Earth-based AI 'Shun', was continuously bringing new processing online to deal with coordination, tasking and requirement evaluation. It worked out a system of rapid packet transfer to and between its space-based counterpart Kei, to ease the pressure. The group had been manufacturing and deploying platforms and vessels at an increasingly rapid rate, keeping pace with its growing resource acquisition capabilities. Each platform and vessel lent quantum computing resources to Shun. By the time Austur and Vestur SSEV were linked, extra-terrestrial interaction protocols were in place. All of this was transmitted to the now functioning Átt and its crew.

But someone had noticed and taken interest.

Unknown to Lýsi or anyone on the Kuril Islands facility, Univers Aerospace had been keeping an eye on them. Its satellite network was covertly observing activities on the island. Univers' business intelligence team was led by a machiavellian operator, who had convinced the corporation's chief operating officer, to grab the technology available on the Kuril Islands, by force.

Max was with Rafael. They were discussing the inputs provided by various groups, governments, militaries and agencies, regarding tactics for space-based defence. Shun interrupted them, "I've detected three cargo and troop carrier aircraft, coming towards our facility using an arctic-polar route. I've patched into an old military satellite to observe." The image of the aircraft appeared on a wall display beside them. Shun said, "The aircraft look military. I've gone through archived images, from satellites in the region as well as our own space-based sensor resources. Each aircraft took off from a different airport in Europe. They're all operated by Univers Aerospace or companies it leases from."

Max was quite onboard with Lýsi by now. He had arranged for his family to be moved to the group's residential property in Hlíðar, Reykjavík. Fortunately, his family was accustomed to moving if needed. His daughter revelled in getting to live abroad for extended periods of time, whenever 'situations' arose. Max's self-preservation instincts kicked in. He said, "I recognize these aircraft. I've been in them. This facility is going to be attacked. It's dangerous for anyone to be here now." Turning to Rafael he asked, "Is there an emergency evacuation plan?"

Rafael answered, "While we're very secretive, we realize being revealed has its dangers. Yes, there's an evacuation plan." He added,

"We need to alert the priest," referring to the facility's operations head. "Shun patch us in to Dr. Popov please. Video conference."

A moment later Dr. Popov's face appeared in an inset next to the overhead video of the three aircraft displayed on the wall. He said, "Shun's just brought me up to speed. I'll initiate evacuation. All personnel are to enter their bunk capsules. These will be transported by the facility's robots to the two aircraft onsite. Aim for take-off within the hour. All classified technology is to be destroyed with high-heat explosive. The buildings they are in will keep most of the heat in. Shun initiate the evacuation."

Pointing to them, Dr. Popov said, "There's an additional HSEVA suit in the manufacturing hanger. It'll fit Max. The two of you don your suits and over-see the evacuation. Ensure all capsules are loaded and no one gets left behind. You'll then come to the dock and leave with me, aboard our next generation submersible yacht. It's like an SSEV, our standardized space exploration vessels, but with a hydrodynamic structure. A freshly manufactured gaupa has just been installed. Let's go."

Shun began using the gaupa on the yacht to transfer out all the data stored on the island. The AI's own local processing power would become diminished once the facility's infrastructure was melted and destroyed.

Getting to the hard-shell EVA suit manufacturing hanger, Max commented, "I never expected to be wearing one of these. Not so soon."

Rafael said, "These are complex to manufacture. There's a space operations specialist who's been training here the last two months. Fortunately, he's about your size, so his suit should fit you. I'll help you in and guide you through its functions. It's very intuitive." Max stepped over to the suit they'd arrived at. It was hooked up to its power and data conduits.

Rafael instructed, "Step up to the suit, turn around, raise your arms to shoulder level and lean back. The base of your neck will push against a pad which will trigger the suit to begin wrapping itself around you and seal you in." Max did as he was instructed. The suit took under a minute to completely envelop him. Rafael asked, "Can you hear?" He received a prompt response through hidden external parabolic speakers which directed sound towards him. Grinning he ran Max through the basic controls.

Shun spoke to both through speakers in the area. He said, "The aircrafts have increased speed. They may have caught a tailwind. I had calculated the effort required for the capsule loading activity to be completed, before the hostile force arrives. Right now, I'm coming up four robot trips short. I could do with your help retrieving four capsules in the lower residential barracks."

Rafael said to Max, "You head there. Drag the capsules to the barrack exit. It'll take the two of us to carry each capsule to the evacuation aircrafts. Shun will direct you. I'll get into my suit and be with you in a few minutes." He dashed off to a storage section of the hanger.

As he sprang into action, Max asked the AI, "Shun, what's your story?" The tension building, he felt the need to stay engaged in conversation.

Understanding what Max meant, Shun answered in it's young-adult voice, "In the early eighties, significant progress had been made on the hardware technology front, aided by the reverse engineering efforts of a live ET artifact recovered in 1980. By then, 'massively parallel processing technology' which utilized intelligent AI agents or autonomous goal-oriented AIs, was gradually released for real-world government, commercial and institutional applications. Most of this research was conducted at Lýsi's Japanese hub. The group's R&D had far outstripped publicly available technology and was now utilizing a self-learning and modifying AI. As the AI developed itself and was nurtured and trained in human interactions via online sessions by Jón and Ásta, it began to behave human-like. The AI was given a respectable name by the original team of Japanese software developers. I am that AI. I was named Shun, which broadly means 'fast' in Japanese. Initially my hardware operated on nascent quantum computers which liberally drew on conventional networked processors for linear tasks. My core systems were located at Shinkawa, Chuo City, Tokyo; and in a disguised merchant container ship named Kuji Maru docked at Aichi in Japan. The ship was always kept prepared to deploy to sea. I became self-aware and self-preserving a year after I began self-modifying my software."

Pausing for the information to be absorbed, Shun noticed Max's pulse rate increase in excitement. There was a spike when Shun mentioned that it was self-aware.

The AI made a profile note about Max's curiosity about unknowns, marked it as a positive in the Swede's file and then continued, "By the mid-eighties, my two key processing nodes, Shinkawa and Kuji Maru, were networked through a dedicated private transponder on a commercial satellite. However, each node could operate independently. The quantum computing cores for both these systems were supported by a set of four enclosed, briefcase sized three-dimensional integrated circuit matrices, comprising prototype nanoelectronic processing units.

These were the first of many prototype circuit matrices, reverse engineered from the ET artefact. The four circuit matrices were linked through a set of fibre optics, with additional point-to-point laser backup. For rapid data transfer, portions of each of the individual processors used nano-optics between logic, distributed random access nano-caches and control units. These technologies will only be gradually revealed to the world in another five years, keeping with The Lýsi Group's information release schedule. I'll prepare a more detailed briefing docket for you to study. Right now, you need to focus on the task at hand."

Forty minutes later, they had pushed the last capsule onboard. Shun ran a headcount and gave a go-ahead to the pilot of the first aircraft to take-off. By the time it was halfway down the runway, the second aircraft began to accelerate. Rafael turned to look. He froze and literally skidded to a stop on the airfield's safety area turf. There was an incoming aircraft, heading towards the runway. It was directly in the path of the second flying wing aircraft, which was accelerating for take-off. The flying wing aircraft banked right hard, heading towards the Pacific as soon as it was airborne. A string of rapid-fire tracers erupted from the incoming aircraft and hit the side of the second flying wing aircraft. It wobbled a little, straightened itself and flew on. Without warning, a section of its left wing ripped off and the flying wing aircraft began a sharp glide down towards the water below it.

Rafael and Max got to the yacht just as the aircraft went down. Rafael's voice came in over their encrypted local communications net, "Dr. Popov, we're aboard. I've unsecured the moorings. Let's go." The yacht began to move away just as the flying-wing aircraft hit the water. It disintegrated and sank.

Max shouted, "We have incoming fire." A small missile shot out from the airfield. "It's a light surface-to-surface missile. Hug the floor," he said a moment later. They both hit the deck. A second ticked by while they lay low, then another. Suddenly there was a jarring impact along with an explosion. Max slid a little across the deck when the vessel briefly listed. Dr. Popov came in over their earpieces, "That was just a scratch. We'll dive and let them think they sank us. Our immediate concern is to recover the capsules and place them safely on level ocean-floor. I can only hope none of the capsules have gone over the continental shelf."

They began a rapid dive with Max and Rafael still on the deck.

On Earth, the loss of assets was costly. Very literally. Plugged into the world's tightly interwoven economy, Lýsi's finances were built up over time, until it was able to take on capital intensive projects. It occurred to Rafael that it may be time to delink the group from the global economic infrastructure, so that it wasn't curbed by it. He spoke into his suit's headset, "Shun, remind me to work on a resource management model for Lýsi's operations on Earth. One that's not linked to the traditional economy." Shun acknowledged.

They were descending at a fair rate. Dr. Popov told them, "I've mapped out the locations of all the capsules. Most have remained on the downed aircraft. The pilots are not responding. Their cabin may have fragmented. There are a few pods which have broken through the fuselage and are scattered across the seafloor. We'll scout for these. The Kuji Maru, our disguised merchant container ship is on route to take the capsules onboard. The two of you straighten out the capsules as we get to them. I'll talk the occupants through."

While the submersible yacht was working through its grid, locating and righting each of the capsules, activities on the island were ramping up. The intruding force's actions were being observed by Lýsi. Regular updates were provided to the teams occupied with rescue efforts. They'd let the hostile force do what they had to on the island. But they'd be tracked. They'd be found.

Gogh spoke to Dr. Popov and Rafael while they were conducting their underwater operations. He updated them in a very conversational tone about the situation in the foreign system. "There's been a development on Átt. The crew has located the capsules with Sven and Crystal, which were ejected from Norður. Átt has sped up to retrieve the two capsules. However, they've been given instructions by the framandi to reach specific points along their present trajectory. We're calling the first contact extra-terrestrials 'framandi', single and plural. Átt's crew will have very little time to grab the capsules and make it to the designated rendezvous point. They'll be cutting it thin."

He continued, "I'll keep you updated. Look forward to seeing you at our primary operations facility soon." While the Kuril Islands operations were conveniently located, it was not the group's only covert island facility. After a moment he added, "I'll also want to keep the fact that Gylfi and Katrín are presently trapped in the downed aircraft, from Jón and Ásta. They're in a very tight spot themselves and need to focus."

Dr. Popov responded on their behalf, "We need to focus as well. There are still over a dozen capsules turned turtle inside the aircraft's fuselage. The Kuji Maru will arrive in another three hours. We'll handover and head over to you after that."

They worked at breakneck speed, but carefully. All the capsules were righted, and their occupants reassured. The priest, Rafael and Max kept morale up. An engineer had suffered a few broken ribs and a chef had a shattered ankle. They had administered themselves medication with remote guidance from Katrín.

The Kuji Maru arrived in due course. The ship also contained one of Shun's primary quantum computers. The AI ran the recovery operation with clockwork precision using a dozen autonomous deep-water submersible robots. Capsules were brought onboard through a moon-pool under the ship's hull while it slowly sailed by the crash site. By the time the ship was a kilometre away, all capsules were onboard.

Max and Rafael entered the submersible yacht through an airlock which dried off their hard-shell EVA suits, before opening the internal hatch. The priest was waiting for them on the other side. He laughed and said, "The two of you look like you've wrestled the kraken." Max replied, "I never thought I'd see this much action with you. Figured this would be a walk in the park." Rafael mumbled, "I'm going to bathe and count a few sheep." Max followed Rafael to the lower deck were the personnel accommodations were located.

Awaking with a start, Rafael realised he had been having a vivid dream. They'd eaten, showered and slept. The yacht was travelling fast, skimming the waves with Shun maintaining course. Drawing his pad to himself, Rafael worked on a resource reorganization project which he wanted to share with the group's leadership team. He held a continuous conversation with Shun while working. He asked, "What would it take to extract all the minerals and metals we require as raw materials, directly from sea water? Historically, we've been doing so with salt for centuries. Lýsi already has the technology to separate minerals and metals in space from meteors, which are crushed to dust and processed. We even use a molten material resource extraction process. Wouldn't it be feasible to utilise similar technology here on Earth?"

Shun took a moment to respond, which was unusual given the AI's vast computing and analytics capabilities. The AI said, "I've compiled a list of sixty elements we could extract. The most plentiful would be magnesium and aluminium. Various research backed absorption methods are feasible. These would be effective to extract nearly all the elements on my list. My analysis also points to minimal impact on marine fauna over the long term. We could begin extraction operations in three months and begin using highly pure mineral resources within five."

Rafael said, "Good. This will give Lýsi further autonomy on Earth, like the elbow room we have in space. I've put together a proposal. Please send my files to group leadership for consideration."

They arrived at their destination mid-morning the next day and were greeted at the facility's dock, by an exceptionally fit tall man with long glinting steel-grey hair. He even had matching steel-grey beard, moustache and irises. He called out to them when they appeared on deck next to the gangway, "Hello my friends. I'm Gogh. Welcome to Marion Island, our base of operations for the near future."

Rafael replied, "Hi Gogh. I'm Rafael." Max nodded to Gogh. He had been advised that all current members of the group's leadership team were only referred to by code name. Max understood this and appreciated that even the leadership of the group, was managed in a dispersed manner, keeping with their adhocratic organization.

Gogh didn't wait to get started, "I'd like each one of you to keep your earpieces on while you're here, except of course while asleep. We're running a very tightly coordinated facility. Dr. Popov, you'll take over the island's operations. Please take a handover from our current facility head. He's been assigned a new project that should give the group greater freedom." Turning his head to Rafael who was on his right, he winked and said, "Thank you for pointing the way. Your inputs are being actioned."

Driving up to a cluster of containers beside three intersecting runways, Gogh announced, "Most of our operations are underground here. Infrastructure like hangers are below ground too. While we're way off the beaten track for most satellites, we get the occasional recreational sea vessel passing by. As far as the world is concerned, we're only a bunch of researchers on the island." They ducked into one of the windowed container units and down a few concrete stairs into a large industrial elevator. Gogh said, "We'll head directly to the primary operations centre. I'll show you to your accommodations and give you a tour of the island later. Right now, we're plugged into the feed from Átt."

No one else occupied the operations centre. Numerous screens showed various video feeds from inside each of Átt's SSEVs, including Suður which had remained in the solar system.

"There's the feed from Vestur. Ásta is pulling in Sven and Crystal's capsules, using focussed gravity points from both the SSEVs," Gogh explained as they entered. He said, "They made contact with the capsules a short while before you arrived."

A large 3D volumetric projection, situational awareness feed or SAF, occupied the center of the room. The projection depicted all known objects within half an AU of Átt. It showed a line of moving dots connecting the capsules to Átt. The SAF also showed a blinking white dot, labelled 'Hostile Vessel'. That was something which Kei had added on.

Absorbing the information with a single turn of his head around the room, Rafael said, "They won't have time to get the capsules aboard through an airlock. They'll arrive at the first point of rendezvous, well before they manage the task." He said to the AI, "Patch me in to Jón, on Austur."

Shun replied, "Channel open, go ahead and speak. I've intimated my counterpart Kei, who has let Jón know."

"Hey Jón! It looks like you're going to meet a mid-sized asteroid just as you grab the capsules. The asteroid is coming in on an intersecting trajectory, from above you. I suggest you clamp the evacuation capsules, at the SSEV interlock dock, previously occupied by Norður" Rafael spoke rapidly and briskly.

Jón replied, "Understood. Adding in post-capture instructions now."

A few moments later, they had the capsules locked in. Jón spoke over the open common channel, "Sven and Crystal are fine. They'll remain in the capsules until we're through with the rendezvous. The approaching asteroid seems to have a cavernous space underneath. Our updated trajectory shows that it'll engulf us and press Átt downward, into its own path. This is going to get bumpy." He announced to Átt's crew, "Everyone secure yourselves. Brace for impact. There's an asteroid swooping in on us."

The observers in the operations centre on Marion Island held their breaths. The crew on Átt barely managed to tighten their seat harnesses, when the vessel was pushed downward. Even with internal local gravity rapidly adjusting, the strain could be seen on the crew's faces. The feed remained crystal clear.

Jón announced, "We seem to be inside the asteroid. Within the cavernous space under it." As he finished speaking, the crew were shaken about in a rough jarring motion, just like extreme turbulence in an aircraft. He added sounding strained, "Feels like either Átt, or the asteroid has hit something."

The situational awareness feed rebooted itself and now only showed the inside of the asteroid. None of Átt's sides were touching the walls. The impact must have been outside. The downward thrust continued for just another moment. Jón said loudly, "I'm receiving evasion related instructions through my diadem from the framandi. We're to turn off all systems. Nothing is to indicate the presence of technology, or us. The framandi are showing me what occurred outside the asteroid a moment ago. They had the asteroid we're in, collide with another one. This was followed by further collisions between smaller objects at the same location. I believe that the framandi would like to give the impression, that we were destroyed in a series of random asteroid collisions."

Ásta added, "I'm seeing the same thing. Turning off all systems on Átt. Kei please do the same on the capsules, but make sure Sven and Crystal have enough air to breathe. The framandi will contact us over our diadems once we're clear."

Kei replied, "I've reminded Sven and Crystal about manual operating instructions. Powering down all systems including my own. One of you'll need to trigger the manual systems restart, to power up Átt again." It took just under three minutes. As Átt shutdown, the screens in the operations centre on Marion Island went blank. Only the feed from Suður SSEV remained.

Dr. Popov looked at his colleagues and said gravely, "They'll remember their training."

Rafael agreed, "Yes. Each of the crew is highly competent."

Shun interrupted, "The rescue and recovery operation off Kuril Islands has been completed successfully. The personnel will be taken to Japan and then transferred to other Lýsi facilities. Gylfi Hallgrímsson and Katrín Magnusdóttir are on route to Marion Island."

They waited anxiously for news from Átt, watching the screens intently.

Chapter 7: Regroup

It was a full two days later before anything happened. Ásta was imagining how she must be turning putrid, sitting in her suit. The relentless pressure she and the crew had undergone over the last couple of days, had taken its toll. Drifting off into deep sleep with periods of semi-lucid dreams, her brain was slotting memories away and rationalizing thoughts. She had just woken up from deep slumber and was imagining machines and people milling about, observing Átt from behind a vast transparent window of irregular shape. One of the observers seemed to be asking her how she felt. In her semi-lucid dream state, she smiled and responded that things could be better.

Jón brought her right back to focus. He reached out to her over her diadem, "I don't know if you're seeing the same things I am, but I have a feeling the framandi have us enclosed in a large hanger of some sort. I keep getting asked how I'm feeling!"

Ásta pulled herself awake and responded, "I thought that was just me. It must be the local species trying to get in touch with us. It's been long enough. I think we should reactivate systems."

Agreeing with his twin sister, Jón said, "I'm going to lower a viewing port panel manually first. If all seems well, I'll let you know, and you initiate activation."

There wasn't any internal gravity or other G-forces being exerted. Jón released his seat's harness and floated over to a section of the central operations area where a viewing window was installed. Groping around near the window, he located a lever embedded next to it. Placing a finger against one edge of the lever, he pried it out. It swung towards him on a hinge. Grasping the handle end, he turned the lever clockwise like he was hand cranking a car. Gradually, a section of the outer hull panel directly over the viewing window, slid outwards and swung away revealing the outside.

The external section of the vessel was bathed in amber light. Jón let his eyes adjust. Gradually he was able to make out details. They were very similar to the images he had seen in his mind. He thought to let Ásta know and his diadem responded, asking if it should link his mind to hers. Connected, she thought to him, "I'm ready." Jón thought back, "I can't be a hundred percent certain, but I believe we may be safe for the moment. Best we have power and all systems activated to deal with whatever we have before us." Ásta didn't hesitate. She hit the system initiation switch.

Kei's voice came in over the crew's headsets a moment later. The AI said "I've reactivated all your suits. I'll turn on all critical systems first, test them and then work on support and tertiary systems." Ásta thought that the AI probably meant it would check its own storage and processing before anything else. She smiled. Fortunately, reinitiating SSEVs didn't take much time.

Sven spoke over their local common channel, "It'd be great if you guys could get Crystal and myself inside."

Isla replied, "On it!" She programmed drones from each of the SSEVs to retool, exit and latch onto the capsules. Warning the capsules' occupants, she said, "I've tasked drones to dislodge you and bring your capsules into the forward airlocks. By the way, the drones have reported that there's human compatible atmosphere in the hanger area that Átt is in. We'll restore our internal gravity once your capsules are inside."

There was no time wasted. Isla oversaw the capsule transfer. The twins Jón and Ásta ensured each system brought online was functioning within parameters. Stefán scheduled health checks for each of the crew. The universal docking ports between Austur and Vestur were opened, allowing Átt's crew to carry out their functions more effectively. As soon as the capsules were placed in the airlocks, internal gravity was activated, and the crew prepared to receive Sven and Crystal.

Stefán suggested, "Standard procedure requires us to decontaminate the exterior of the capsules before opening the airlocks. We'll go through the process."

Kei responded, "Commencing airlock decontamination procedure." Nozzles sprayed the capsules and drones in both airlocks with anti-contaminants for viral, bacterial and non-viral agents. The drones scrubbed themselves and the capsules through it all. Next a series of material decontamination procedures followed. Sven commented over the local common channel, "I'm glad our hosts have patience." Crystal said, "They're probably looking on curiously through whatever scanning systems they have. I just hope they're not as inquisitive, when I'm in the shower." That lightened the mood a bit and there was more light banter. Twenty minutes later, the procedure was over, and the airlocks were dried out.

Crystal was the first one out. She had exited her capsule which was aboard Austur. Without greeting anyone, she scurried over to the forward airlock on Vestur with Isla hurrying behind. Crystal enveloped Sven in a tight hug as soon as he came out of the forward airlock on

Vestur. She said, "I'm so glad to be out of there. I'm even more glad you're okay. By the way, you smell putrid."

Laughing, he held her and replied, "It could be you; you know."

Crystal looked up at his face, grimaced and said, "I'm not doing anything else until I've cleaned up." She headed towards the rear personnel facilities on Vestur. Sven gave each of the crew a hug and said, "I'm going to freshen up too."

Jón agreed but stopped Sven. He said, "We'll all take turns. Now though, we've just re-established communication with Suður and Earth. There are a lot of worried people. Let's all say hello first."

They got to the central operations area on Vestur and brought up the communications interface, which linked each of their seat pads with the onboard gaupa. They were patched in on an intergalactic conference call. The gaupas easily connected peer-to-peer with each other, once an initial connection had been established between any two.

Gogh said, "I'm very glad you're all okay. We've all been very anxious." Lei spoke next from Suður, "I'd like to take time with each one of you to run through your experiences soon. We could even do it by connecting through our diadems." Gogh cut back in, "We've been updated about your situation by Kei and Shun. Right now, you'll want to prepare yourselves for contact with the framandi. At some point, you may wish to ask them what they'd like to be called. Perhaps that could be a gesture of goodwill on our part. Kei will update you all, on first contact do's and don'ts. Lei and Eiji have reviewed a great deal of information about the framandi and shared their observations with us."

He continued, "Long story short, they're a civilization that's seen intergalactic forces use their system, and afterward ours, as battlegrounds. After the last conflict, which occurred in our system, they aided our planet and us humans, get back to our feet. The framandi themselves have taken to remaining on guard, since there are a few active wormholes between their system and others. These lead to locations in both the Milky Way and in the Canis Major Dwarf Galaxy. On their home planet, they maintain a population without evidence of advanced technology on the surface. This seems to keep any observing species disinterested. However, they also have a vast population spread across their system, living in habitats within asteroids, small planets and satellites. To accomplish this, they've developed high-density external shielding that looks like naturally occurring space bodies when scanned. They've maintained and developed their technology inside their habitats."

Continuing his brief Gogh said, "You already know about their social groups. While they're role based, every individual has the knowledge to take on all kinds of roles. Knowledge is built right into their DNA, donated by participating parents. Here's the fascinating part. Once individuals have grown, any knowledge they do not want to maintain in their DNA or a second brain, they store in DNA based storage media. Just like the one left for us on Suður. While they're different, the framandi are carbon based, like us. Presently, we don't think they mean us any harm. Also, our recent interaction tells us that they are very open, frank and helpful with species they trust."

Sven spoke for the crew, "We may not have prepared for this contact, but I feel we're well suited to represent Earth and its people. I suggest that we interact with the framandi, while you're all plugged in. Should we involve any others?"

Gogh replied, "I've taken inputs from the rest of Lýsi leadership. Earth is too divided and politically motivated. Unvetted parties may have vested interests. We will let the framandi know that this is the case during a future interaction. They should be aware, but we should not come across as weak."

Stefán said sardonically, "If they've deciphered our DNA and interacted with us however long ago, they probably know we're fairly aggressive as a species." The conference call was terminated after a few other transactional matters were taken care of.

The crew on Átt ate and freshened up. While they were doing so, Kei had tasked drones to physically scrub all internal surfaces. Stefán had run each one of them including himself, through a thorough physical. After a brief rest followed by another meal together, they were prepared to contact the framandi. Till now, all that their hosts had done, was observe.

Jón and Ásta had already shown that they were able to communicate with the framandi by thought, through their diadems. They were assigned with explaining the expected conversation with the framandi, to the parties plugged in from Earth. The rest of the crew including Eiji and Lei on Suður, were assigned to directly access the interaction via their diadems. Kei was to monitor interactions and record them using AL-I's processing module on Suður. Everything was simplified as much as possible, so there wouldn't be any hiccups. All required parties were patched in via their gaupas. An additional gaupa was being produced aboard Suður to deal with the increased volume of queries being sent to

AL-I's data unit. They had prepared vast packets of information about Earth, it's people and known history. These had been encoded into transmittable packets which the framandi could absorb. They were ready for contact.

Sven initiated contact, thinking through his diadem, "We would like to communicate and interact with you." He got no response. He tried again, this time connecting his diadem to the gaupa on Vestur. "Here is some information about our recent history from planet Earth." He initiated a transfer of an information packet to 'Advisor of the Masked'; a known contact on the gaupa.

What he got back was a library's worth of information appended to simple thoughts. The first was, "Welcome again." This was associated with information about the framandi. The next thought was, "Your vessel was noticed in our system by another hostile drone." Another few volumes of information. "Our surveillance vessels on the far side of two separate wormholes have shown increased activity of possibly hostile forces, from where the drones originated." Further information was appended. This was followed by, "Your vessels in our system, must always be 'masked'." Blocks of data rapidly flashed through the gaupa's interface screen. The communication concluded with, "Your 'selves' must be modified to interact with 'us'." A final blur of information.

Sven asked aloud sounding concerned, "Did everyone catch that? What does that last part mean?"

Ásta replied, "They seem to have passed along bio modification information." Stefán added, "Yes, its information on how to create and add bits of genetic code to existing DNA. It's mainly switches. On and off triggers, for human DNA. The modification instructions are to be introduced through a viral vector. They've suggested a few. Result being, we should be immune to the framandi microbiome."

Gogh instructed, "Restrict this information to space-based vessels, for the time being. This isn't to become available on Earth until we can prove it safe. Kei run simulations on how the genetic code modifications will affect a human. Appraise us once done. See if the processing unit from AL-I can be used to hasten results."

"We had better figure out our course of action on the rest of the communication; as one sided as it was." Jón said.

Sven replied, "For the 'masking' part, we may need the help of our hosts." Eiji cut in, "I've been going through vessel modification data. It involves covering Átt with an outer layer. From afar, it will end up looking like a random asteroid. Oh! And the specifications include the bio module as well as Suður. I'm not entirely sure if it allows for our shuttles to undock from our SSEVs. I'll study this further. Meanwhile, let's find out if they've located Norður, the bio module."

Lei said, "This means Suður SSEV would need to transit the wormhole and enter the framandi system."

Gogh advised, "Yes, that's right. Sven, ask your hosts how we might coordinate Suður's passage."

Isla reminded Sven, "Don't forget to ask the framandi what they call themselves."

Pulling information on the bio module and Suður SSEV, Sven crafted a question, on how to proceed. He also asked what the framandi called themselves. Sven passed these on to 'Advisor of the Masked'.

The response barely took a minute. Again, a combination of thoughts and data. "We call ourselves 'us'." A bundle of information on the framandi followed to define what the framandi meant. "Your vessels will be enclosed separately, and then joined." Further data for the bio-module and for Suður. Then 'Advisor of the Masked' communicated, "Let us begin." A last set of ordered instructions for implementation of actions.

Sven said, "There seems to be a countdown associated with objects in various planetary systems. They're not the solar system or the framandi system. This must be the build-up of possibly hostile forces, mentioned in the previous communication. Looks like we're up against the clock. Kei, process the information and make the countdown available to everyone."

Kei replied, "The navigational charts have a dedicated gaupa channel, courtesy the framandi. The charts are being updated with real-time astronomical data. I'm coding this in with our situational awareness feed." Sven considered this for a moment and said, "Good. Have the feed available for reference alongside the countdown clock."

"I've conferred with Lýsi leadership," Gogh stated over the common channel. He instructed, "The original data storage, communication and information processing units given to us by AL-I, are to be left behind in the solar system. An autonomous SSEV will be sent to the solar system side of the wormhole, with Kei operating it. Place the units given to us by AL-I inside a crew evacuation capsule. The capsule is to be ejected and left at Suður's present location. Suður's can then proceed towards the wormhole."

Eiji said, "There won't be enough power in the capsule to run the framandi data storage, communication and information processing units." Gogh replied, "Understood. Please proceed as instructed. Without people aboard, the autonomous SSEV will push itself to upper limit acceleration. Perhaps beyond. It'll arrive at your present location by the time you exit the wormhole into the framandi system."

Isla cut in, "We need to go through all the information the framandi have shared. My understanding is that Norður, our bio module, was enveloped by one of their asteroid-like vessels, just like we were. Also, there's a framandi hanger-asteroid heading into the wormhole to bring Suður in. Eiji, all you need to do is head into the wormhole and the framandi will do the rest."

Moving quickly, Eiji and Lei used a couple of drones to assist them in placing the data storage and information processing units presented by AL-I, into a crew evacuation capsule. An hour later, they were done. They advised their colleagues, "We're ready to jettison the capsule." Rafael responded, "Gogh is locked in a conference. Please proceed. An SSEV from our platform at the L1 Sun-Earth Lagrange point has already departed to your location. Kei will pass on the capsule's telemetry data to Nál, that's what the SSEV is called. Be safe." Eiji initiated the capsule jettison procedure and then began accelerating Suður towards the wormhole.

On Vestur, Kei was updating Átt's crew, by simulating the DNA modification process. The AI explained, "The bio modifications occur simultaneously and affect all cells. The simulation shows it would take a full day to complete, once introduced into a person. Except in the case of Jón and Ásta. They already have many regulatory DNA switches modified. I've taken the liberty to simulate the effect of these modifications on the human microbiome and for some other species on Earth. So far, my results show that all Earth species will cope well, once the modifications are introduced."

Stefán interjected, "We're preparing a viral vector to deliver the modifications to the crew, using a stable modified virus that won't mutate."

Kei continued, "The virus would need to be injected to crew members as shifts begin. Nausea may occur. This can be countered with medication. Injected crew who go off-shift, would need to sleep for up to eight hours. Dehydration will take place, so an IV would need to be administered."

Looking around, Sven asked, "Any objections?" No one reacted negatively. He remarked, "I guess we're all in then! Stefán will oversee the DNA modification procedure."

A jolt vibrated across the vessel. Sven spoke to the AI, "Kei, what was that?" An exterior view appeared on Sven's mission pad. Kei spoke sounding unconcerned, "The framandi seem to have initiated their upgrade to our vessel. Modification of Átt has begun. You'll see on your pad that a large blob of material has been deposited on top of both Austur and Vestur. The details shared by the framandi show the steps they are about to take."

"They begin by depositing smart material around our hull which will gradually become denser. Processing units like the one provided by AL-I will be transferred to us via our forward airlocks. This will be followed by transfer of data storage units for each SSEV. Smaller data storage and information processing modules will be made available for our shuttles. All our evacuation capsules too, will receive compact, low power versions of these units, with accompanying compact gaupas. The smart material being deposited on our hull is controllable. The framandi have provided system interfacing and control capabilities, accessible through each of your diadems. In case of diadem failure, I'm transacting with the framandi computing systems to develop a suitable human user-interface, operable through the mission pads. Simultaneously, I'm developing a separate protocol, with which I'll be able to program the smart material directly."

"I see mechanical arms extending to the forward airlocks of both SSEVs. Must be the additional equipment the framandi are providing us," Sven said looking at the exterior feed on his mission pad. "What about our sensors and other external systems? Would those still be available to us?" he asked Kei.

Kei answered, "The vessel modification plan provided by the framandi, considers external sensor feeds. Theirs will integrate with ours. The framandi light detecting sensors are exceptionally sensitive. In addition, the entire external hull would be able to accurately detect gravity and various forms of radiation. The combination of feeds will enhance our situational awareness and navigation. All our docking ports will be accessible. However, an additional software instruction layer is required, to modify the newly added smart material, for access to the hull exterior."

"Our power source is embedded in our hull, isn't it? Refresh my memory about it." Sven requested with urgency in his voice.

Kei rapidly provided some background. "In the early nineties, our energy requirements in space for each project was growing exponentially. Most systems used solar panels for electricity generation and solar concentrators for heat. A pair of researchers who were reverse engineering components from the extra-terrestrial artifact in Lýsi's possession, realized that kinetic energy might be captured from both primary and secondary cosmic rays as they decayed through the layers of spacecraft shielding. The concept is similar to how electricity is generated using conventional solar panels. Given the abundance of cosmic rays throughout the galaxy and in interstellar space, they realized that if the theory could be implemented, it would mean energy could be generated anywhere, even in deep space."

"By November 1993, the technology was developed, tested and incorporated into the designs of Álfhól space platform, on the far side of the Moon. This energy generation design was later incorporated into our Standardized Space Exploration Vessels making our spacecraft suitable for deep and interstellar space exploration."

"CREG systems are embedded into multiple layers of hull paneling. The panels are now used on all our spacecraft, platforms or robotic satellites. Recently developed high capacity gel battery banks were designed into structural beams and form a part of each vessel. Extendable solar panels are still maintained for backup. A nuclear fuel generator is also available as a final redundant power source on our vessels."

Jón and Isla came in for their shift. The crew had maintained their rotation as best as they could, after their initial encounter with AL-I.

Isla said to Sven, "You look like you need some rest. We're here now." Sven smiled and replied, "You're the ones who'll need rest. Stefán's just cooked up some DNA modifying concoction using the framandi's recipe. He's waiting for you in the rear medical compartment on Austur." Jón glanced at Isla. Her face had lost some colour. Obviously, she was nervous about the procedure. He joked, "Come on guinea pig! Let's do this." She glared at him.

Stefán was focussed on his pad. He'd been educated within the Lýsi ecosystem which far surpassed conventional study. He was proficient in human biology and had hands-on experience with synthetic biotechnology. Stefán had taken over as the principal developer for an artificial nervous system and brain-machine interface project, that Lýsi had initiated a decade ago. Primarily a brain surgeon, he even had experience performing intricate ventricular restoration and spinal osteomyelitis operations. However, his personal interests, were xenology and botany.

Jón called out, "Hey Stefán, what's so engrossing?" He knew his sister Ásta liked Stefán, the only other Icelandic aboard, beside the twins. Jón enjoyed the sometimes stubborn but exceptionally resourceful Scorpio's company.

"I'm studying the information on framandi biology," Stefán replied. "There's enough information on them to occupy every xenologist on Earth for years. You'll find this bit informative. The framandi were nearly wiped out as a result of collateral damage from conflict between opposing species across our galaxies. Once hostilities died down, in part due to covert action by the framandi, they took it on themselves to gather as much knowledge as they could. Some of the initial bio-modification knowledge they gained, was gleaned from wrecked hardware, discarded by one of the dominating species of their own galaxy." Stefán stood and moved over towards a medical capsule used for patient surgery and recovery. He picked up a pair of syringes from a wall table next to it.

"Please sit," Stefán said. He continued speaking about the framandi while he disinfected Isla's left arm triceps, "They began modifying their own DNA, to enhance knowledge, thinking and information processing abilities. On Earth, we call this directed evolution. The framandi then enhanced their physical structures using the same technology. Compared to other races fighting it out in their system, the framandi considered themselves backward. So, they adapted by learning. They got to a point where they were able to self-modify genetic material within their own bodies. They do the same while developing genetic code for their offspring."

Having injected Isla, he repeated the procedure with Jón. At the same time, Stefán continued speaking, "They've accumulated information, from each species that left behind vessel wrecks or debris in the framandi system. Over the last fifty thousand years or so, they've grown technologically and socially. Their biology is suitably adaptable for Earth, you know!" He injected Jón with the virus, while saying, "I've identified human genetic code strings in portions of their complex DNA. At some level, a tiny portion, they're a bit like us."

Isla looked at Jón and rolled her eyes. They thanked Stefán who called after them, "Stay hydrated!"

Back in the central mission area of Vestur which the crew had designated as Átt's command and control centre, they relieved Sven and Crystal. Jón worked at the large interactive table while Isla sat with a mission pad. She said to him, "There's been plenty of activity outside. The hull's been completely enclosed with gooey smart material. We need to bring in the data and processing modules provided by the framandi. I'll assign drones to bring in the equipment from the airlocks, once decontamination is completed. We'll need to install the units together." Isla was already perspiring. The DNA modifying process was beginning to affect her. Jón too felt uneasy. Not a feeling he'd encountered before. He reminded her, "Sip on your water."

While the two of them grappled with new equipment installation, Norður, the bio module, was brought into the cavernous interior of the framandi asteroid-like vessel. Norður was already enveloped in the gooey material the framandi were applying to Átt. Gradually Norður was lowered until it touched the material covering the top of Átt.

Kei said to Isla and Jón, "I've just reconnected with Norður. The bio module's mission control AI, shut down systems when the vessel became highly unstable. The asteroid attached to the front dislodged itself. Fortunately, there doesn't seem to be much exterior damage to Norður. All the agricultural material, which was being grown inside, is destroyed. Two drones remain. These have been tasked to clean and repair the interior. Once Norður's universal docking ports are aligned with ours, I'll engage them to make the module accessible."

Jón was attaching a small gaupa into an evacuation capsule, with Isla holding it in place. Their cheeks were beside each other's in the restricted space. Both had shared the same shift since leaving the solar system and had grown comfortable with each other's presence. Without thinking about it, Isla turned her head and gave Jón a peck on his cheek.

He froze, but only for a moment. Turning to her he grinned saying, "I've been wanting to do that myself. For a while actually." Isla said unabashedly, "I know. I've sensed it." This time she kissed his lips and held it for a moment. Looking into his eyes, she asked, "Think we have something here?" "Without a doubt," Jón replied. Since they'd finished installing the compact gaupa, they extricated themselves from the capsule.

Kei spoke to them, "Norður bio module is now reattached to Átt. Clean-up and repairs are still ongoing."

Jón gave Isla another quick peck on her lips. "To be continued," he said. She winked at him.

"Suður SSEV has entered the framandi system. It's just shown up on the navigation chart. I'm plotting its progress via a framandi feed. Its two days away from rendezvous with us," Kei updated.

Jón and Isla were well into their shift. They had completed the installation of all the gaupas, data and processing units provided by the framandi. The two were exhausted. The effect of the DNA modifying injection administered by Stefán had taken full effect. Jón looked at the countdown clock showing when the mobilized extra-terrestrials were expected to enter the framandi system. It showed a little over four days. The crew needed to prepare for whatever was coming their way, and coordinate with their hosts in the system. They needed to figure out their course of action.

Jón recollected his mother telling him a story when he was quite little, of elves being hunted in the night. He remembered feeling a chill then, like he felt now. Jón thought about his parents and instructed the AI, "Kei, schedule calls between the crew and family members. We don't know what we're going to face. It would be good for everyone to have conversations with family." Isla turned to him and smiled. Jón said to her, "Nearly time to take a break."

Kei announced, "Jón, I have confirmation from Shun, my counterpart on Earth, that both your parents are available for a call." Jón replied, "Ásta is coming in on the next shift. Please connect once she's here. We'll speak with our folks together."

Isla reached out and held Jón's hand. She said, "I'm going to take a shower and sleep now. I'll update Stefán on our status. See you soon."

Chapter 8: Recovery

Gylfi Hallgrímsson and Katrín Magnusdóttir were seated in the operations centre on Marion Island. Gogh excused himself to go meet with Dr. Popov, who had taken over onsite operations.

Shun announced, "I'm opening a private channel with Átt. Jón and Ásta are online." A screen lit up in front of Katrín and Gylfi.

Ásta waved, "Hi mum, dad. Hope you're both recovering well from your misadventure at sea." Jón added, "We've been very concerned once we heard about what happened at Kuril."

"We were fortunate. Our aircraft went down after being attacked and damaged. Our evacuation procedure is similar to what you have out in space; for SSEVs and platforms I mean. Everyone was individually secured in a capsule," Katrín reassured. Gylfi expressed his concern, "We're anxious for your safety. You're about to interact with extra-terrestrials. And, your vessels are being modified by them. We've been informed that there may be hostile forces headed your way. Also, you're undergoing DNA modification. It's all a bit much together. Jón, you're looking under the weather."

Jón replied, "The effects of ongoing genetic modification. I took the first of the shots along with Isla at the beginning of our shift. Ásta and Stefán have just been injected as well. Sis will look a lot like me in a while," he said grinning.

"You've prepared us for all this," Ásta said. She continued, "It's what we're meant to do. Well perhaps not the extra-terrestrial interaction bit. But its what's happening so we'll cope."

Katrín replied with bright eyes, "We're proud, excited and nervous. Just keep us updated. Otherwise we'll hound you." Gylfi squeezed her shoulder.

They spoke about memories and Jón mentioned how he had remembered a story about elves being hunted. The conversation continued comfortably. Gogh walked into the operations centre just as the family were saying goodbye.

Turning away from the screen she was facing, Katrín nodded to Gogh. She said, "It's a pity about the Kuril Islands facility. It pretty much gave birth to our efforts in space. What have you got planned for us now that we're here?"

"History has enough cues which point to extra-terrestrials having visited Earth," Gogh replied. He continued, "What they were doing here has always been debated. Artefacts collected and studied over the last century, have triggered technology advances which put us into deep space. Lýsi exists to solve the big problems Earth faces, without letting politics, religion, borders, race or any other factor become a hurdle. We have a few new wicked problems to be solved."

The 3D volumetric projection SAF lit up in the middle of the operations centre. Assisted by Shun, Gogh briefed the transhuman twins' parents. He said, "Lets dive into the ones you'll need to grapple with."

Pointing at the projection he explained, "However unlikely immediate extra-terrestrial contact may be on Earth, our populations need to be physiologically capable of withstanding the framandi microbiome. This means, we will have to account for every living creature on Earth. The problem we face, is this. How do we make every living thing here, framandi compatible?"

Gylfi asked, "Didn't they indicate that they visited our planet? Millennia ago? Unless they remained in enclosed environments, there must already be a degree of compatibility built into our ecosystem."

"Still, we'll need to pit the DNA of every Earth creature and organism, against all DNA types contained in the framandi microbiome," Katrín said. "It'll be a gargantuan task that's going to require a huge collaborative effort, not to mention computing resources," she added.

"That's right," Gogh said. The projection changed. Shun was keeping pace with the briefing. Gogh explained, "You're going to plan and initiate DNA mapping on a global scale. Shun will use the group's administrative AIs to efficiently and surreptitiously, farm out the mapping needs to all capable organizations. This will include friendly government agencies and institutions, all based on the strategy you prepare and priorities you set. We already have a lot of data. But it's only a drop in the bucket."

Gylfi stated, "I doubt we'll have the processing capacity, or the storage required for all DNA." He asked, "How soon do we need to accomplish this?"

"Within a week or two," Gogh replied.

Gylfi and Katrín stared at him boggle eyed.

"Why?" Katrín asked. "And how do you expect us to accomplish this?" She was becoming concerned now.

Gogh said, "Within a day, the crew of Átt will be prepared to meet the framandi face-to-face. In four days, they expect to encounter hostile forces from outside the framandi system. If there is conflict and it goes badly, we may have some framandi entering our system. It's feasible they may come to Earth. Even if there's no conflict, the framandi plan to transit our system on their way to Beta Hydri. Sooner or later, there will be physical interactions. Planned or not. We need to be prepared for the 'sooner' scenario, where interactions may occur on Earth."

"I see," said Gylfi. Katrín was looking even more concerned now.

"There's another larger, more troubling issue," Gogh went on. "If there is conflict and it does spill over into our system, we don't have space-based military defences, to protect ourselves with. Nor do we know what we might encounter. We're grossly underprepared for extra-terrestrials, especially the hostile kind." He said, "I've tasked this problem to the leads of our space-based platforms. The platform operations leads are looking at finding solutions. They have Kei to assist."

Katrín said, "That's good. Back to our first problem, what kind of resources can we muster on Earth?"

Gogh answered without missing a beat, "Over the next few days, you're going to have your hands full, tackling the planning and execution of DNA collection. Lýsi does not want framandi DNA information to be available on Earth, yet. You're both going into space. Each of our space platforms have been able to develop a version of the advanced quantum processing unit, left for us by AL-I. These are going to be placed at your disposal until the DNA compatibility problem is solved. We'll use the framandi provided data module for storage. These should resolve our immediate computing needs."

"There's something else," Gogh added. "The attack on Kuril has exposed us to physical vulnerability. We've spent decades developing our artificial intelligence and quantum computing capabilities. The physical infrastructure can be rebuilt. Loss or damage to our AI, is unacceptable," he said.

Gogh explained, "The solution we have is to allow Shun into space, and Kei onto Earth. Both AI will have separate quantum cores and quantum storage, with backups of course. They'll share resources when required. Our AIs have served us well. They'll be protected this way," he said.

The twins' parents were allocated their own operations room, a smaller version of the island's operations centre. They ensured their meals would be delivered directly and even had cots placed in the room. Both got to work immediately.

Meanwhile, Gogh was coordinating with Max, the covert operative who had first infiltrated Lýsi's Kuril Island facility. Max had since switched sides and was seamlessly absorbed into Lýsi. He updated Gogh via video from Kuril Island.

"The facility is completely destroyed. The force which made its way here dug about a bit. It's unlikely they got much," Max said.

"Whatever they've salvaged, we need to get back or destroy," Gogh replied, adding, "we've tracked the aircrafts they used, to Kiruna in Sweden."

Max said, "I've been there. Rakkniv, my previous employer owns a cluster of warehouses near the airport. They use the location as a staging point for covert activities."

"Would you be able to go there and ensure our technology doesn't fall into anyone else's' hands? Gogh asked. He stated, "The potential for misuse is tremendous."

"I'll need a team. This won't be a single person job," Max responded.

Gogh said to Max, "Get to Tokyo. We have a prototype supersonic business jet that's registered for flight tests standing by. You'll be taken to Murmansk in Russia. Lýsi has access to military assets, given our group's initial background. We've rarely required to use force other than to securely move precious cargo. This is going to be a code-only operation. You're designated as 'Kilima'. It means 'hill' in Swahili. The team you'll be working with is drawn from various countries. They've worked together for years, so you'll be the odd one out."

Max smiled and replied, "Don't worry about me! I'll fit right in!" He disconnected and made his way to an awaiting helicopter.

To kill time, Max brought up various information packages Shun had prepared for him. He loved the history, the secrecy and the behind the scenes operations of Lýsi. He'd got through to the group's history till the mid-eighties when he came across something interesting. He spoke to the ever-present AI, "Shun, give me a historical brief about Lýsi's molecular manufacturing and robotics initiatives." The AI was prepared. It had felt Max's pulse rate increase to a point where it knew the Swede would want information quickly.

Shun launched into an animated briefing, "By 1986, the world was just beginning to hear about molecular assembly nano-tech. Given the steep accomplishment curve that Lýsi's space technology and material science was maintaining during this period, an experimental self-replicating manufacturing robot satellite was secretly introduced in the garb of a weather observation platform, into earth orbit. Its goal was to utilize the already voluminous orbiting space junk to manufacture space-based platforms and systems including additional construction/fabrication robot satellites. It functioned by using mechanical and chemical processes to break down captured material into their molecular components. These molecules were stored in containers for later use. Manufacturing too was achieved by first using chemical processes to join molecular strands to form foundation structures, and then join them into components through miniature mechanical processes."

"Why not just launch all the material needed into space? This seems like a lot of effort for extraordinarily little reward," Max interrupted sounding like he disagreed.

The AI clarified, "Long term needs. This was experimentation. There were many experiments. Lýsi's most pressing wicked problems, all Global Catastrophic Risk scenarios, required vast resources to counter. The global economy had and still has too much wastage, greed, hoarding and corruption. With an assortment of economic and political models in play, the sharply growing need for resources were beginning to hamper Lýsi's progress. The group's leadership team, which now admitted the physically seven-year-old but mentally twenty-one-year-old transhuman twins Jón and Ásta, and a virtual depiction of myself; gathered at a rare face-to-face road-mapping and review meeting at the group's Iceland facility in 1990. Over the previous five years, we were able to enhance our space-based molecular manufacturing and robotics capabilities. While Lýsi's myriad investments and income streams were superlatively high, global economic models and even the physical resources available for massive scale projects, were still limiting. The leadership team decided to gradually unplug the group from the economy. To become independent of it. Now, in space, we only have a six percent reliance on launched resources. We inject far more than that back onto the planet." Shun sounded pleased. Max went silent, his curiosity was stimulated. He began exploring Lýsi's space resources.

A day later, Max found himself being introduced to a multinational, gender-agnostic, private force of covert operatives. He felt right at home. The team's leader was called 'Maji' or 'water' in Swahili. They changed codewords every three months, using similar designations, but translated to various languages.

Maji was briefing the team, "Kilima will be an observer and aid in coordination. Objectives will be given by him."

He continued briskly, "We'll fly directly into Kiruna on a converted cargo aircraft. There will be vans meeting us at the airport. We'll take these to an old mining vehicle maintenance warehouse. Our gear will be available there, along with SUVs. We have new biometrically authenticated weapons. These look like compact submachine guns but emit a beam of electromagnetic waves. The beam mildly scrambles brain activity and portions of the nervous system. For more serious damage, there's a selector for a ten-kilowatt laser; but it'll only give you six shots before you need a battery pack change. Beam and laser shots take a full second to discharge, so you'll need to hold your weapons steady. Carry standard sidearms and explosives, just in case."

The flight to Kiruna was uneventful. They arrived at dusk. Shun had organized logistics using myriad unconnected sourcing fronts, that would be nearly impossible to track. The fronts wouldn't raise flags either. The AI was good at this. It had initially been programmed to run the group's adhocratic and distributed administration, before becoming its more sophisticated and able self. The team was well fed and rested when they landed.

At the mining vehicle maintenance warehouse, they quickly sorted their gear, checked their firearms and went through their pads, updating themselves with the layouts and objectives.

Maji led them out, speaking through his communications earpiece to the team. He announced, "Okay now, we're on the clock. Get to your assigned vehicles and let's go. You know the drill. Our recon team advices that a group of thirty-eight combat effective individuals, are spread across two of three warehouses. The third one contains sensitive material. This is to be destroyed using high heat incendiary munitions. Individuals have been tagged and assigned to you. They're all to be disabled."

The team drove up to the Rakkniv warehouses. Video feeds were available to the team now, transmitted by miniature flying and crawling drones. Shun's mission-AI, automatically transmitted the appropriate imagery to each team member. The vehicles broke off into three groups and approached from different directions. Rear-guards were dropped off at intersections.

Maji had an elegant plan. The team would use a swarming tactic that was expected to saturate opposition defences. They'd penetrate the two warehouses containing personnel, quickly moving to the center, where commanders were expected to be located. They'd turn and work their way outward once opposition leaders were disabled. Two team members would hold each exit, concentrating interior lines. None of the team members would directly face each other, reducing the chance of unwanted friendly beam exchange.

As they approached in their SUVs, the recon team activated minute explosives carried by infiltration drones. These knocked out electricity, Rakkniv surveillance and external communications. Signal jamming was initiated. They then dropped opposition members who were visible through windows, prioritising anyone facing the doors. The entry teams were at assault positions at both occupied warehouses. Maji instructed blandly, "Enter. Attack."

None of the opposition occupying the first warehouse, put up any fight. There were two Rakkniv combatants who had reacted quickly, drawn sidearms, and were pointing them at windows when the doors were silently breached. They were taken down first. The insertion team didn't even get to the centre of the warehouse, before all opponents were dropped.

There was trouble at the second warehouse though. A Rakkniv operative had pressed himself against a wall near the main entrance. He shot two of Maji's team members, assigned to take up positions by the door, before he was temporarily paralyzed by an invisible beam. Maji instructed, "Don't stop," while redirecting two recon team members to the door. The operation took under thirty seconds. Maji commanded, "Medics to the wounded. Give me an opposition headcount."

The headcount came up two persons short. Urgently, Maji ordered, "Set up internal security and an out-guard. Find our two missing Rakkniv personnel." The team took up positions while others combed the area.

Max spoke directly to Maji over a secure channel, "We should enter the storage warehouse." Maji agreed. He asked his team conversationally, "Give me a sitrep." Updated, he directed, "Deploy to the storage warehouse and enter." Preassigned team members formed up and moved to the storage warehouse. Maji looked at his pad. The drones were providing low light and infrared feeds. He didn't notice anything out of the ordinary. The doors to the third warehouse were breached, and the team entered.

As they began to spread through the warehouse, compact hidden multi-barrel weapons popped out of recesses on structural pillars. Noticing the blur of motion, Maji shouted out a warning, "Contact! Find cover." His team dropped, but the concealed weapons began firing before he could finish. High volume rapid fire from two separate multi-barrel weapons literally sheared the unit lead's head, clean off. Direct fire continued to pin down the rest of the insertion team. They couldn't move. Maji could not tell how much ammunition the multi-barrel weapons held. They seemed to fire every time they detected movement or unrecognized shapes.

Shun interrupted Maji, "There are additional miniature airborne tactical explosive drones available."

Maji gave a quick grin and gave the mission coordinator next to him instructions, "Mobilize airborne tactical drones. Have them enter the warehouse and fly high, close to the roof. Drop two on each of the multi-barrel weapons. Take out their fire control mechanisms and turning joints." The mission coordinator replied, "Assigning drones. We're going to be short by two. Executing and handing over drone control to AI. The weapon on the central pillar will remain untouched."

Looking at his pad, Maji selected two of his insertion team members pinned down. This opened a direct channel to them. He instructed the two, "You'll need to take out one of the multi-barrel weapons on the central pillar, on my mark. Switch to laser."

The team was occasionally peppered by automated weapons fire, whenever anyone moved. But they'd concealed themselves well and held on. The drones approached the weapons, hugging the pillars as they dropped. The mission coordinator said, "Ready."

Maji spoke to the two team members he had selected. "Get ready." To his mission coordinator he said, "Execute." A moment later there were simultaneous explosions across the warehouse. He commanded the assigned team members loudly, "Hit it!" They broke cover, aimed and pressed their triggers.

High intensity laser shot out at the remaining concealed multi-barrel weapon from either side. It began to swivel to the right, its barrels beginning to rotate, preparing to fire. Maji said, "Again!" Another two beams of high intensity laser light shot out upward. Three simultaneous mild explosions erupted from the multi-barrel weapon, which had pivoted just enough to find an exposed team member. It had got a few rounds off before it froze in place. Maji said, "Threat neutralized. Looks like a few rounds cooked right at the magazine feed." To the rest of the team he said gravely, "It got one of ours. Now, find me the missing opposition personnel."

Shun brought a few surveillance drones into the warehouse, to examine and identify items taken from the Kuril Islands facility. There were several objects in crates. Five minutes later the AI had a list of items. It set priorities and assigned team members to wind high heat incendiary wire and charges around these.

Just as they got started, Maji was informed that a cleverly hidden trapdoor had been found under a sliding cabinet, in the second warehouse. He instructed, "Breach and enter." Designated team members approached the trapdoor and formed up. The trapdoor was gradually pried open, past its resistance point. Lasers were used to cut through the locking mechanism. As it was being opened, a flood of rounds hit the underside of the door, with a few passing through the widening gap.

Observing, Maji spoke to the unit leader, "Drop in surveillance drones. Locate the ambush weapons." The unit leader did as he was instructed, pushing in a drone through a small bent section of the door. The feed from the drone became visible to everyone. There were two multi-barrel weapons, one above the other on opposite walls, separated by two feet.

Maji advised, "I think you may be able to take out the one on top with laser fire. Be careful though."

The unit leader pushed his weapon into the gap in the trapdoor and immediately received a storm of rounds his way. He snapped, "That's not working." Maji considered and suggested, "Drop in a fragmentation grenade. Cook it first." The unit leader motioned the rest of the team back, unclipped a grenade from his vest and turned a knob on the top of it. Pushing the knob down he said, "Cooking! Move the drone into a safe area." Three seconds later he pried open the trapdoor and dropped the grenade. There was an immediate bang. After a moment the drone was brought out from the crevasse it was hidden in. The lower multi-barrel weapon was destroyed, but the upper one looked serviceable.

Shun spoke to Maji, "The ambush weapon's fire mechanism is electronically controlled. Rakkniv salvaged a few launch capsule components including a high capacity gel battery, which has held its charge. There are other parts also available, which will allow quick field assembly of a single use electro-magnetic pulse device. It will knock out all electronics in the immediate vicinity." Maji replied, "Show me."

Shun took Maji through the steps and components. Instructions were passed on to two team members who were technically competent. While the electromagnetic pulse device was being put together, high heat incendiary munitions were wrapped around prioritized sensitive items, found in the storage warehouse. Simultaneously, the injured were being evacuated by road, along with the downed team member. They had been delayed more than expected.

Finally, the EMP device was ready. It was taken to the underground vault trapdoor. Maji ordered, "Trigger the high heat incendiary fuses." He received a confirmation that the munitions were destroying items in the warehouse. He spoke again, "Turn off all electronic devices. Count to five, then trigger the EMP. Wait for another five counts before turning on your comms. Go." The team did as commanded.

This time, the trapdoor was opened without any incident. The drone had gone deeper into the underground vault before the EMP was set off. It had located two Rakkniv personnel frantically destroying equipment, before the EMP cooked it. Both Rakkniv persons were taken down with beam weapons. Hard drives were removed from their computing equipment and sealed into foam lined cases.

Maji's team withdrew from the site, after placing each opposition member into the closest bunk. They'd wake up disoriented.

The team drove off in their SUVs to their rendezvous point at the mining vehicle maintenance warehouse. The injured were patched up and the downed crew member was placed in a body-bag. The bag was then placed in a lead-lined transportation case.

At dawn, still tingling from all the action, Maji's team arrived at the airport in their vans and boarded a separate aircraft arranged by Shun. The cargo aircraft had arrived half an hour earlier with a load of fresh vegetables. Shun worked miracles with logistics.

"Kilima, we came up short on this mission," Maji addressed Max as their aircraft took off. They would be flying to Alta in Norway, where they would switch aircraft and head back to Murmansk. Max replied, "I agree. We need to upgrade reconnaissance technology as well as breaching techniques. The opposition may have got data on our tech, out of their base in Kiruna, before we hit them."

Maji nodded. He took out his pad and put together a brief report, adding upgrade requirements. The report made its way to assigned Lýsi covert operations oversight members. Shun scanned the report and appended recommendations, based on available technologies and covert operation tactics, from various global sources.

Max updated Gogh over his pad. He said, "We believe information on the technology we went to recover, may have been transmitted out of Kiruna. There's the likelihood of it being released publicly."

Gogh replied, "Our tech has always been meant for the common good. We've trickle-released portions of these technologies to the world. Of the items catalogued as destroyed at Kiruna, there are some which can be used for harm. I'll task our electronic information management team to track down any relevant leaked information." "Meanwhile," Gogh continued, "I'd like to place a large burden on you, my friend." "From what I've learnt about Lýsi so far, nothing is too great a burden," Max replied.

Gogh said, "Glad to hear it. Here's what's needed. You're to head out to space with the team you're accompanying. Yours and the team's task, is to first train all Lýsi space-based personnel, in defence operations. Your next task is to use the team to come up with and develop plans, to defend Earth against massively superior extra-terrestrials. Then you'll need to implement your plans. We need to be prepared, and we do not have much time." Taking a moment to consider, Max stated, "This planet is my home. It's home to my daughter. I'll do everything I can to protect it. Count me in."

"Excellent," Gogh said, "I'll see you back on Marion Island with the team you're with. Shun will make the arrangements. Right now, I need to get into a meeting patched in from Átt. The crew is going to meet with the framandi. This is a critical moment in our history. Be safe and see you soon."

Max pondered what it would be like to be facing the framandi. He wondered if he'd be up to it. Possibly! His stomach tightened as his thoughts shifted to the conversation with Gogh. He had to prepare for possible conflict with alien species. Shun interrupted him, "You've been invited to observe the interaction with the framandi. Patching you in." Max's eyes widened as he watched.

Chapter 9: Alliance

Jón and Ásta stepped out of Suður's forward airlock, into the large hanger space, inside the framandi asteroid-like vessel. Being amongst the first to undergo the DNA modification process, and having many genetic switches already triggered, they were also the least affected by the changes. Instructions were provided to the foreign material covering Átt. A section just outside the airlock parted, so that the universal docking port could open and let the twins out.

Floating into the cavernous space, Jón turned to look at Átt. It wasn't recognizable at all. In fact, it looked like any one of the numerous asteroids present in the framandi system. His point of view was captured by various cameras on his HSEVA suit, and transmitted to observing and participating Lýsi members, back in the solar system.

Ásta thought to him through the diadems they wore, "Keep up. There's a platform approaching us from the right. Let's head out to it." Jón turned and caught up with his sister, using compact rocket and compressed air bursts, a part of his suit's reaction control system.

The platform stopped moving. As the twins approached it, they felt a downward pull of gravity. Compensating with their suit thrusters, both neatly landed on the platform. A circular portion of the uneven wall nearest them pulled inward and away, revealing a brighter space beyond. Two figures appeared and stepped off into the vessel's hanger space. The twins assumed they were framandi.

Ásta said aloud to her brother and to observers, "I thought our suits were advanced, but these guys are something else." Everyone patched into the first face-to-face interaction, could see the twins' feeds. Jón said, "The outer layer looks like it's similar to the smart material covering Átt now." As the two framandi got closer, they slowed and stepped onto the platform.

The twins' diadems activated themselves and 'requested' that active incoming connections be initiated. They both agreed. Ásta asked the framandi if their other crewmates might 'observe' the interaction. She received an affirmative. The initial interactions were short and comfortable. The twins weren't assaulted with too much information this time.

The framandi facing them transmitted longer thoughts now, "I am Advisor of the Masked." This thought was followed by references to earlier conversations, appended to which, detailed information had already been provided, about the individual. Jón thought back, "May we refer to you as 'Áom'. It's a name formed using an abbreviation of what you call yourself. It would be simpler for us". He received a positive thought response. The rest of the crew aboard Átt, gave participants and observers from the solar system a verbal narrative of the proceedings.

The framandi moved a little to the left, allowing the accompanying individual to step up. "This is 'Advisor of the Explorers'," Áom thought to them. This time, there was a lot of data to go along with the thought. The data was picked up by Kei, who began deciphering it all, making it available to the twins and the crew, as it became consumable.

Jón thought back to both the framandi, "We would like to call 'Advisor of the Explorers' as 'Áox'. The name would make communication simpler." This time the twins received a happy/positive response from Áox.

Continuing without much of a pause, Áox went on, thinking to them, "As you know we have remained hidden or masked for a long time since conflict occurred in our system, and later in yours." A series of references to information previously shared, was appended to the thought.

"Áom and those holding the position before, have worked hard to keep us camouflaged, from species who may do us harm," Áox went on. This time there was data on various extra-terrestrials. Jón thought to Ásta, "Ignore the data for now."

"Ever since conflict engulfed our system, we have constantly been observed. Our recent attempts to explore other systems may have been noticed," Áox provided mental imagery of AL-I leaving the framandi system followed much later by three disguised satellites. The thought sequences then showed an armed drone changing direction, heading to the wormhole which led to the solar system. "Then you entered our system and encountered the drone," some more imagery flashed into their minds supporting the framandi's thought.

Áox went on at a brisker pace now, "Destroying the first drone attracted another observing drone. Your vessel was noticed. Although masked now, the presence of a viable route to and from our system is now known to others. The appearance of your undisguised vessel may be the reason for mobilization." A set of images appeared of several vessels, visibly identifiable of a certain type. And then, another larger fleet. Áox ended with, "We are not as yet fully prepared to confront them."

Ásta thought to Áox now, "Is there some way to hide the wormhole?" She received an instant response, "The inter-system paths are detectable by observing material passing out of, or into a system." Images of dark matter, space dust and debris passing out of a wormhole appeared in her mind. Ásta thought, "How have you kept the wormhole hidden so far?" Áox thought back imagery of a swarm of asteroids, dust and material moving at speed, in front of the wormhole. The current of debris carried along any new material entering the system from the wormhole. Some of the asteroids looked fuzzy, like they were projections.

Ásta thought back, "I understand." She said to the observers, "they've kept the wormhole leading to the solar system hidden behind a dense stream of asteroids and space debris."

Jón asked the framandi, "What kind of offensive and defensive systems do you have?" Áom replied this time, "We have none. Remaining masked and hidden has been our defence. The Enlightened have gathered and developed our knowledge meanwhile. Just as your species was nearly wiped out as a fallout of conflict in your system eons ago, ours too faced near extinction for the same reasons, much before. After conflict passed your system, we collapsed most of the wormholes there, just like we collapsed or hid most of those connecting ours."

"Then why have you kept the ones, where hostile forces are camped at, open?" asked Ásta.

Áox, Advisor of the Explorers, explained, "Because those systems contain other wormholes, to still other planetary systems. We have long considered stealthily exploring them. But we will do this, only after spreading ourselves, to a few other stars. Beginning with a system, connected to yours. Then the risk of extinction will be reduced. We closed off wormholes to and from our system, which led to the more aggressive species, from both our galaxies. We did the same in your planetary system too. Coincidently, conflicts took place in our systems, only when each of our species had reached a specific level of development. We believe, that is when we may have attracted attention. That is when we may have been 'usable'."

"The ones headed our way now seem aggressive. And well-armed," Jón thought to Áox. He was told through a series of thoughts and mental images, "They are a tiny force, tasked with resource accumulation, manufacturing and observation. They have constantly supplied vessels and material via adjoining systems, never surpassing a threshold fleet strength."

Jón and Ásta considered this. With thoughts being added by their colleagues on Átt, Jón mentioned to the framandi, "It seems like a fairly large force. I'd hate to imagine what an armed fleet at strength would be like." Not realizing that he hadn't limited his thoughts to only the crew, he received a response from Áox, "This is what a limited gigil skirmish force looks like. The Gigils are from our galaxy. They have been assigned systems neighbouring ours. They are very capable manufacturers, something they do at scale and with speed. We suppose that is the reason they were assigned the task of resource gathering and frontier guarding. Their name has been carried forward from a time when we still used words, as you still do."

Images gradually flowed through to their diadems. The framandi had got a grip on how much information humans could absorb. The thought rate was still brisk enough that both Jón and Ásta required to concentrate. All this while, they both had frowns of thought on their foreheads. Seeing the size of other gigil fleet vessels, their faces inside the HSEVA suits contorted into expressions of shock. There was even an audible gasp from Isla over their earpieces.

Áox explained with each set of imagery. He thought to them, "The primary unit is a moon-sized vessel. This is used to contain and distribute energy, transferred to it from various locations in the galaxy, by harvesting radiation from large stars." Isla said aloud to the team, "It looks like they prefer to harvest blue-white 'B' class stars, but primarily harvest yellow-white 'F' class stars which are slightly more abundant."

Crystal was digging deeper into the appended data, with help from Kei. She said, "Energy seems to be transferred using technology that is somewhat like how the gaupas function. Instead of tiny pulses of information carried over a limited number of analogous quantum foam bubbles, high energy vibrations are passed through a vast array of these stabilized bubbles. The corresponding agitation of quantum foam inside this moon-sized primary gigil vessel, delivers massive quantities of energy. The energy is transformed from quantum foam vibration to various other forms as needed. Including electromagnetic radiation."

While narrating her explanation, she had also inadvertently thought all of this. Áox expressed happy thoughts which were picked up by the twins and Átt's crew. The framandi was glad the humans could grasp technology and concepts, even though they had disadvantages in mental processing and information retention when compared to themselves. But Áox also sensed the intensity of 'worry thoughts' that were passing between them.

Feeling the press of time, Áox went on, "The primary 'moon-ship' unit supplies the rest of the battle fleet with focussed radiation energy, boosting their offensive capabilities. The gigil fleet vessels also produce their own energy, like how your vessel does. Their vessels also share energy, offloading excess amounts to ships which require it. This is something we have learnt to do. To defend itself, the primary unit is also capable of releasing vast, concentrated beams of destructive energy."

The team saw a series of images in their minds. Tight intense beams a few kilometres wide, shooting across inter-orbit distances, decimating entire continents when directed at a planet. Then, wide swathes of radiation taking out entire fleets, rendering them into mere particles. Adding to the intensity of the thought, Áox stated, "They travel in groups and units of three, each accompanied by a vast support armada. The gigil armadas are supported by resource gathering fleets, like the ones in our neighbouring planetary systems."

Sven thought across the linked diadems, asking the framandi, "Is this what we might engage? The 'moon-ship' unit?"

Áox responded, "Unlikely. They confront superior forces of equivalent size and strength. Eons ago, they passed through our system while confronting and pursuing just such a force, which originated from your galaxy. The gigils and their allies were successful and drove the annexation-fleet, back to where it came from. It was during this transiting battle approximately 'fifty-two thousand' of your years ago, that our own planetary system was decimated. All life was nearly extinguished here. The gigils supported themselves utilizing resource gathering fleets, deployed in systems adjoining ours via wormholes. Occasionally, many of our own planets and moons were aggressively mined for resources, as the engaging forces pressed each other. It was a battle of attrition which the annexation-fleet lost." Images of colossal destruction flashed through their minds.

"Fortunately, we learnt to hide well, to observe and to record. We learnt to put aside our differences, and to manage our evolution. We survived," Áom added.

Áom took over the conversation, thinking to them, "The resource gathering forces left behind in the neighbouring systems have only recently begun to maintain a presence in our system. They have ignored us for most of this while. We have observed their activities. For eons, they have progressed with their task slowly, deliberately, consistently. Its only recently that they've accelerated their activities. This is what prompted us to act. To look for other systems, for our survival. We fear, another battle may be approaching. Here or somewhere nearby."

Sven interrupted the thoughts being streamed their way. He refocused the interaction, "You showed us the primary gigil unit, the moon sized vessel and its support ships. What else does the battle fleet comprise of?"

This time, Áox responded. Thinking to them, the framandi indicated "There are many vessels that we know of. There may be others we have not observed. Some are used for offence, many for defence. The sizes of these vary. The gigil fleets normally comprise twelve types of vessels. They have smaller vessels for transportation, logistics, and even storage. As they pass through each system, they consume most resources in and around these, storing material as they go along. They can possibly engage in battle for extended periods of time without the need to regroup. The gigils are part of an alliance of some sort. A military cooperative." Having shared these thoughts, the framandi shared a large amount of overview data with known details of the battling forces.

Eiji enquired, "How is it there are no remaining artefacts from the battle which took place in the solar system? We haven't seen anything to indicate that there were a series of engagements, which took place in our planetary system twenty-seven thousand Earth years ago."

Áox replied, "We removed them from both our systems. We salvaged everything we could locate in our effort to enlighten ourselves, to study, to learn and to clean our planetary systems. We will readily share all the information you are prepared to understand, just like we make information available amongst ourselves. Now, whatever comes next will affect us both." Pausing, the framandi stated, "We need your help."

Before any further questions could be posed about the last thought passed, Áox thought to them, "While we have learnt a lot, modified ourselves to become knowledgeable, and evolved the ability to retain and process a lot of information; we have lost the aptitude to take intuitive leaps. We have lost the capacity to be surprising. We can think and plan capably, but not radically differently. We think alike, using similar information sets. We recognize this as a failing. Also, we are not aggressive enough. We need your help."

Kei interjected. The AI spoke to the crew over their earpieces, "There's little over two days until the first fleet from a wormhole near here, arrives at this system."

Jón thought to the framandi, "If your system becomes compromised, ours could too. Perhaps in a truly short time. Especially if, like you indicated, the gigils don't like other technologically developed species." Sven continued the train of thought, "The rest of us, and involved observers from Earth agree. We need to contain any outside forces here.

In fact, we need to take the initiative and act pre-emptively, within the systems they're occupying."

Áox thought back appreciatively, "We are glad. What are your thoughts? How do we take the initiative?"

Responding in a pattern that was like the framandi's, Jón thought back, "We would need to know what resources you have, which we can utilise. We require in-depth situational awareness." Áox replied, "We will give you the information needed. I will join you aboard your vessel. Áom as well."

The two framandi entered Átt through the airlock, with the twins. As the universal docking port closed, the material covering Átt, formed up, enclosing the vessel. Only Sven and Crystal met them as they entered. The remainder of the crew were kept away, in separate SSEVs. Until it was known that sharing the same environment was safe, they'd remain isolated.

The framandi were the first to remove their suits. They seemed confident. Áom was tall. An inch taller than Jón who was 6'2". Áox was shorter by half a foot. The crew present in the operations area, felt themselves holding their breath while the two framandi's body-hugging suits unfolded around them. Incredibly, they did not look radically alien-like. Nothing like what the people of Earth had come to think extra-terrestrials would look like. Both looked near human. Very nearly. Áox reminded Crystal of figures right out of Mayan art. Sven thought that Áom looked like an Easter Island statue. They logged these thoughts with the rest of the crew.

The framandi had prominent cheek bones, wide foreheads, slightly long heads, large almond eyes with baggy eyelids, mouths with well-formed thick lips, large ears and prominent noses which were flat at the tips. What set them apart, were long limbs and compact slim torsos. Their musculature was visible through their innerwear. They looked strong.

Áom raised one hand and thought to the crew, "We are glad to be here." The crew was now able to identify Áom, by the framandi's thought patterns.

The first thing Crystal thought back was, "Where are your diadems?" Crystal pictured the crown like ring referring to the machine-brain interface she wore on her head, to communicate with the framandi.

Áom thought back to them, "We do not require them. The diadems. We grow these when we are born. It forms a part of our cranium. The information to grow a diadem is written into our genetic code."

The participants from Earth, their faces projected against the wall, all had questions. Little blinking lights appeared next to each of their images. Turning to the wall, Sven addressed them, "We'll hang on to questions for later. Our immediate concern is the looming threat of two separate hostile gigil forces entering this system. The feed from this vessel will be continuously available to all observers. Thank you all." With that, he turned off the projection.

Ásta approached the framandi thinking to them, "Come with us to the central operations area of this SSEV. We'll set up there." The imagery of what she meant was transmitted.

The central operation area on Suður was transformed. Equipped with the additional data and processing units provided by the framandi, the amount of information the crew had available, was tremendous. Crystal, Eiji and Kei quickly developed a menu system the crew could use to project information visualization, sync data with navigation and organize information that they could understand. But they all still relied on their diadems to transact with the framandi processing units to work fluidly and efficiently.

Four hours later, Stefán had declared that interaction between the species was safe. The remainder of the crew met the framandi. Áom and Áox had been assigned shifts. Together, they developed a plan with assistance from the AI, and their colleagues in the solar system. Still recovering from the recent DNA modification, the crew packed in as much rest as they could, little as it was.

The framandi had not developed weapons of aggression. Their strategy was to lay low, spread their species, preferably across planetary systems, and then secure themselves. What they lacked in military might, they made up with numbers. They had over a million asteroid like vessels of all shapes and sizes, which had been manufactured to cart a third of their civilization off. While some of these had personnel, most were automated and run by the framandi AI.

Without armaments, their plan was to tow actual asteroids, using the automated vessels, and enter the two separate foreign systems, one after the other. The plan involved packing the asteroids with explosives, converting them into skyscraper sized fragmentation devices. The towing vessels were to crack the asteroids using focussed gravity, separating each one, into three or more pieces, depending on size. The large explosive armed asteroid chunks were to be lobbed at the opposing force in an expanding funnel shape. The funnel was expected to trap the opposing force within it. The asteroid pieces would then explode when close to an opposition vessel if they got near enough.

However, all this was to be a distraction, while dealing some damage to the gigil fleet. The asteroid towing vessels were to then catapult well aimed globs of their exterior material, at the opposing forces. The material was to remain inert until close to impact. On impact, they were to stick onto the gigil ships' hulls. Then, simultaneously, the material was to find ingress points and take the vessels apart. If all went well, the used smart material might even be recoverable.

There was also the question of the armed observation drone already in the framandi system. The one which had nearly intercepted Átt, before the framandi disguised them. If the drone observed the framandi mobilizing, it would forewarn its operators.

While he was preparing to be sent into space, Max grappled with the solution to this problem. Deep in thought, he asked the AI he had been handed over to, "Kei, tell me about our gravity propulsion systems, specifically those fitted to our SSEVs."

Kei had previously briefed vessel design engineers on this and had a briefing package ready. The AI launched into a rapid narrative condensing information to be suitable for Max, "After the first gravity system originally used during experiments on Kuril Islands were replicated on a robotic satellite, all the initial experiments were carried out again. Immediately into the first experiment, which was directed towards a sensor satellite on the Earth-side of the Gravity Focusing Device or GFD, both satellites began moving towards the point of focused gravity. The experiment was halted while the satellites repositioned themselves using conventional ion propulsion systems."

"The experiment was repeated, this time with focused gravity directed at a point above the sensor satellite, slightly to the side of and behind the robotic satellite. The sensor satellite moved toward the gravity point, attaining a higher orbit. The robotic satellite with the GFD moved slowly away from Earth as well."

"The implications of this were immediately clear and fantastic. Gravity could be used to propel any spacecraft, on which a GFD was deployed. The device could also be used on another stationary object in space to move it. The research team found that when focused gravity was maintained a fixed distance ahead of the GFD, the satellite continuously fell towards it. This meant that the craft or any other object, could be propelled or attracted towards an artificially created gravity well. Following the accident at the Kuril Islands bunker, it was decided to restrict the device's use to outer space, until the technology was refined."

"Versions of the GFD or 'Gravid' as it was soon nicknamed, were manufactured in space and fitted onto all Lýsi spacecraft. The device was used for propulsion and object attraction. Most importantly, compact gravids were used to create minute fields of gravity within spacecraft or inside platforms."

"Once artificial gravity technology was understood, another four multipurpose platforms like Álfhól were commissioned. These are located at the L1, L3, L4 and L5 Earth-Moon Lagrangian points."

"Why Lagrangian points?" Max asked, curious as ever.

The AI responded, "They're stable points in space, relative to two other larger bodies, like Earth-Moon or Sun-Earth. You might be keen to know that Lýsi has accumulated vast resources in space. Construction had begun years ago, on three Sun-Earth Lagrangian point platforms, in preparation for deep-space exploration. These are in addition to the operational Earth-Moon Lagrangian point platforms."

"Cross specialized crews were covertly put together and trained for space-based operations. Many have since been deployed to various platforms and are rotated between them and back to Earth."

As the launch preparations progressed, Max grew a little nervous. He asked Kei, "How does the launch system function?"

As usual, Kei was unnervingly quick to respond. "Before we began designing our Lagrangian point platforms, we constructed an orbital platform. To get the first crews to it, required finesse. Specifically, to keep our operations secret. One of the group's initiatives in aerospace research was the development of an all-electric, light flying wing aircraft. It could achieve and hold an altitude of thirty-five kilometers. Numerous high-altitude space cargo missions had already been accomplished by a fleet of these 'research' aircraft."

"Here is the interesting part. Each aircraft is outfitted with a high-velocity, large caliber, rapid reload, roof mounted electromagnetic cannon. The cannon was designed to fire a two hundred kilogram, cylindrically shaped cargo capsule, with hemispherical ends. These are lobbed three hundred kilometers into the thermosphere, from where AMCARs latch on using focused gravity, and retrieve the capsules. It is a low cost and inconspicuous way to get critical material into space. Initially, large quantities of water and liquefied gasses were also delivered this way."

"A variation of this system is used to get Lýsi's astronauts into space. The electromagnetic cannon propels capsules at nine-Gs. Before gravity reduces acceleration, a set of compact rockets extend and fire. This ensures escape velocity is achieved and the capsule is delivered to the exosphere. From here, AMCARs pull the astronaut capsules in and deliver each to a transport spacecraft. While it sounds simple, the process is complex and incredibly stressful for most participants. You will need to mentally prepare for this. Interestingly, the capsules themselves provide additional raw material for our space-based manufacturing initiatives."

As the AI completed its brief, Max had worked out a plan. He summarized it on a mission pad and sent it to Átt.

He suggested that a framandi vessel take on the shape of the first drone, which had been initially destroyed while attempting to enter the wormhole leading into the solar system. He recommended that the decoy 'damaged' drone, appear from behind debris, and become visible to the supposedly hostile drone presently in the framandi system.

If previously recorded behaviour held true, the active drone would investigate the damaged one. Once close enough, the explosive laden trojan drone, would activate gravity, rapidly pulling the active drone to itself. It would then detonate, taking out both. Max's plan was accepted and the framandi began executing it. At the same time, millions of smaller explosive devices were being manufactured by the framandi across their system, within their automated vessels.

Two hours later, they were ready to take out the active drone. Átt had left the relative safety of the framandi vessel which had hidden it earlier. Observing the trojan vessel, Isla said and thought, "It needs to appear from behind line of sight, from behind a dense asteroid heading in the direction of the active drone." Áox seated next to her gazed at her expecting more information. She thought to Áox, "We'll have to do this on the fly, there isn't time to make a detailed set of instructions." She then passed on what she had in her mind to the framandi. Áox communicated to the trojan vessel, building in the appropriate instructions.

For once, things went according to plan. Exactly so. The trojan took shape just prior to revealing itself. It had barely entered line of sight, when the active drone swerved towards it. The trojan drone didn't even have to activate gravity. The active drone latched onto the trojan and began to extend various appendages toward its seemingly damaged counterpart. The trojan exploded. First, a razor-sharp directed charge split the active drone down the center. Then a wider explosion tore through the two halves. Even zoomed in, the imagery looked like silent distant fireworks. The signal went out throughout the framandi fleet to mobilize according to the well scripted plan.

Sven had received inputs from his crew, and from observers in the solar system. The framandi resources were put into play according to the plan drafted. Sven directed, "Begin moving your vessels towards the two wormholes."

He thought to the framandi, "We've named the first planetary system's star, from which the gigils are expected, as 'Lofi' meaning 'praise'. The other one 'Vilji' or 'will'. The systems will be called lofi and vilji systems respectively."

Isla and Crystal had observed the star formations around the wormholes and drawn them out. They'd then taken these to Ásta, who enjoyed naming everything, usually in Icelandic. The systems at the other ends of the wormholes were named similarly, with the word 'system' appended.

"Our first priority is the lofi system," Sven went on. Thinking to Áox he pointed out, "According to the information provided by your observation craft in the lofi system, there are three battle groups, comprising a mix of nine types of ships." Áox thought back, "Correct," providing the appropriate data references to qualify his thought.

Smiling, Sven thought to himself that it would be virtually impossible for any framandi to ever lie, since they always provided 'commonly available' data, directly or with references. He also wondered if the data was updated. His main concern was how the information remained uncorrupted. So, he enquired, "How is your supporting information updated and qualified? How do you ensure information is correct?"

Áox explained, "All information added to our vastly distributed knowledge base, is required to be verified by at least three 'Enlightened' individuals." Áox was referring to the group amongst them, who were responsible for gathering and building the entire civilization's knowledge base. The framandi expanded, "Information once verified becomes available to anyone seeking it. Verification tasking is automated and undertaken by our information processing ecosystem. This is like your AI programming and processing. If verification is not completed within a specific period, it is passed on to other Enlightened." The framandi provided imagery and concepts, clubbing it all with referenced data.

Áox waited while Sven absorbed this information. Then the framandi continued, "Priority for verification is increased with each hop. The enlightened are granted what you refer to as points. When there is no new information available, decaying information is re-queued for reverification. Depending on an Enlightened's point grade, each one undertakes practical reverification research. Very often as a group. If new information is uncovered, additional points are granted. This is how continuous learning is promoted."

Sven sought a clarification, "What if the verifiers get it wrong?"

"Then points are removed. The Enlightened one's standing diminishes," Áox responded. The framandi added, "Each one of 'us' from any group, is authorised to seek dismissal of information, if there is verified cause. Also, every one of us must achieve certain 'enlightenment points', to be able to move to other groups or to take on new tasks and responsibilities. Enlightened individuals are tasked with information assessment, according to their point standing. Assignment could also be based on information the individual has previously verified, or information known to have been absorbed and stored within their selves."

The entire process while elaborate and seemingly secure worried Sven. He asked for a final clarification, "In our situation, wouldn't it cause delays in important updated information becoming available?" Áox clarified, "A priority is assigned at the time of verification assignment, based on the number of individuals seeking the information, or related data."

Satisfied, Sven continued the build-up to strategy execution. He said and thought, "The three groups coming in from the lofi system are larger by a third, than the group coming in from the vilji system. Concentration of framandi vessels, are to match the ratio strength of the opposing fleet. Weightage can be assigned to the class of gigil ships. This should ensure that an adequate number of armed asteroids are deployed against each ship."

Sven pulled up visuals of each class of vessel in the opposing fleet. They had named each to correspond with their known functions. The largest ones in the current group were designated as 'command-ships', massive battle capable vessels which controlled all other classes of spacecraft.

There were carrier-ships, which housed or provided docking for several frontline vessels. Armed factory-ships and freighter-ships provided close range support. Projectile-ships launched a barrage of heavy, high-velocity golf-ball sized pellets. Attack-drones joined battle once forces were intermixed, point-drones broke through defences while recon-drones surrounded battle zones and provided intelligence. Finally, there were small network drones capable of passing along information within and outside the theatre of operations.

"We're going up against formidable and advanced technology. The other side has had the same amount of development time as you have had, without having to worry about civilization recovery," Sven said aloud and thought to Áox.

It was time. The framandi vessels near the lofi wormhole were massed with their asteroids, ready to enter. Vessels kept joining the framandi armada and would continue to do so. Each needed to travel across the planetary system, find appropriately sized asteroids, arm them and prepare themselves for attack. Vessels from the far side of the framandi system would continue to join the fleet, streaming through the wormhole, long after any confrontation began. The appropriate signal was given from Átt, which was positioned just behind the leading front. The framandi armada began entering the lofi system.

Wormhole transit didn't take much time. "That was quick," commented Ásta who was at the central operations area on Suður with Áom. The framandi thought to her, "Reference to?" She immediately thought to him, "Apologies." Ásta added references to their journey from the solar system into the framandi system. Áom immediately understood the reference and responded with a deluge of referenced information on the distances between interstellar gravity wells, the amount of dark matter between them and the linear line-up of quantum foam; all of which dictated the length of navigable wormholes. Ásta put it aside for later.

The fleet began to enter the lofi system. What they saw truly stunned them. The framandi remote observation vessels present in the system were old and tiny. While being accurate, they didn't do justice to the actual scale of the fleet facing them. The gigil force was formed like a large parabolic dish with three equidistant antennas. The formation's largest vessels were located at the base, where the antennas would have joined the dish.

Aboard Átt, Sven came online announcing, "All right everyone. Get to your grav-chairs, strap in and activate your plans."

Ásta was in-charge of directing framandi vessel deployment. She began thinking out the commands required to initiate her portions of the strategy. Her commands were picked up by her diadem and passed on to the framandi information processing module onboard the SSEV she was on. These were distributed to assigned gaupas across Átt and transmitted to lead framandi vessels. The lead vessels cascaded the instructions out to individual vessels in the groups. As complicated as the system was, information was exchanged rapidly.

Noticing the opposing formation begin to rotate clockwise, she instructed, "Framandi formation, rotate in sync with the opposing force. Begin picking up individual targets. Calculate anticipated location of your targets and keep updating these across the fleet, until all asteroids have been released."

Jón was next to her. He instructed their armada, "Once twenty-five percent of our fleet has entered the system, begin opening out like the six-petal flower formation we've planned. None of the opposition fleet vessels should be left untargeted. We will begin releasing asteroids once our funnel has reached a point just past the outer edge of the opposition parabola." He was in-charge of release.

Seeing the opposing formation, Sven suggested, "We could modify our formation to include a mass of vessels and asteroids directly in the path of the capital vessels, forming three internal flowers. The mass of their formation, may begin thinning out our outer petals." Áom issued the appropriate instructions

The crew on Átt was beginning to get nervous by now. From their history, the framandi had seen and recorded the opposing forces to be proactive and ready to attack. Something was amiss.

Back in the solar system, Max was already approaching Álfhól, the Lýsi platform where he was to be initially based. He had been observing the framandi fleet's entry into the lofi system from an observation vessel's point of view, above the system's epileptic. He noticed something strange. Besides the opposition formation beginning to rotate, the rear had begun to elongate. It looked like the gigil force was reacting to the framandi fleet formation and preparing to counter it. As he watched, the rear end of the gigil force began to split into six parts and flower outward. It looked like these would curl back towards the framandi force and begin to eat into their vessels a while after the encounter began. He was nearly at Álfhól, so he began planning a counter-manoeuvre to pin the enemy.

Chapter 10: Hijack

Max was disturbed. He had arrived at Álfhól and just finished putting together details for a formation, which ought to envelop the gigils, at the looming confrontation in the lofi system. He called out to the local AI, "Kei, I need some assistance." He was not used to Kei yet, but then, everything in space was new to him. The AI responded, "Hello Max. How may I help?"

"I've put together a memo, on overcoming a counter manoeuvre by the opposing force in the lofi system. Will you pass it along to Sven de Vries on the vessel Átt?" Max asked.

Kei replied promptly, "I'll connect you right away. You should brief Sven directly. I will put together any data needed to strengthen your strategy. May I access your memo?" The AI understood the high priority required to be assigned to Max's request.

"Go ahead," Max answered. A moment later Max's pad came alive with a video connection to Sven. Kei said, "You're live. Please explain your idea. I've passed on your file and will add appropriate data to adjust to local conditions, as you go along."

Sven spoke first, "Glad you called. We noticed the flanking manoeuvre the opposition has initiated. We were considering reinforcing our three central points of penetration, with additional vessels and asteroids. What do you have in mind?"

Max said, "Your plan relies on using overwhelming numbers. It also relies on using unguided asteroids, loaded with explosives, as the primary weapon. Here's what I'm thinking. The opposition crafts pulling back towards the rear of their own formation, are spreading out to outflank you. These vessels will take some time to get to their positions."

"The problem as I see it is that the massed concentration of large opposition vessels, probably have enough firepower to direct and focus, which will rapidly take out our point forces," Max observed. Making his point, Max said, "I suggest you use the vessels massing at three points, mirroring the gigil formation, to form a cone. Point the funnel end to the enemy. Have new vessels entering the system form cones around these. As the inner vessels release asteroids, the outer cone can replace depleted vessels. This way, there'll always be asteroid armed framandi vessels at point."

"Next," Max said, "you carry on with the original strategy for the large outer funnel, formed by new framandi vessels entering the lofi system." He pointed out, "Going after the gigils pulling to their own rear, will thin out your force. That may backfire against your present strategy."

"To deal with the outflanking force, you'll need to rearm framandi vessels," Max explained. "There's a dense asteroid belt, just ahead of and below the location, where the gigils have their primary formation. They're close to a planet occupying a central orbit on the system's plane. You'll need to ensure that the attack vessels closest to the asteroid belt, are taken out first. Framandi vessels which have released armed asteroids aimed at the opposition, would need to go to the asteroid belt, to rearm. These would then travel along the asteroid belt to position themselves further behind the outflanking enemy. You could then form a parabola around the rear gigil elements and press inward."

Sven was well versed with defence strategy. He understood Max's reasoning and use of local materials to rearm. He said, "I see what you're suggesting, and I agree. It'll let us maintain the capacity advantage. We'll begin implementation. Thank you." The video connection was terminated. Battle was expected to commence in four hours, given the closing speed between the two fleets.

On Álfhól space platform, behind the moon, Max thought to himself, "We need to prepare ourselves here too. And quickly. The solar system could easily be taken by hostile extra-terrestrials." He began to go through the space resources available to him. Over the last decade, Lýsi had built up considerable stockpiles of purified minerals and metals. Max saw that these were stored at Sun-Earth and Earth-Moon Lagrange point platforms. There were ten platforms in total, five of which were fully functional. Considerable automated manufacturing capabilities were already online on all platforms.

He considered the situation for a while and then contacted Rafael, on Marion Island. As soon as the video feed came up on his pad he said, "Good to see you again." He asked, "You're aware of the situation in the lofi system, right?"

Rafael replied, "I've been keeping up to date. My training's been stepped up, so I'm merely observing." Max asked, "Would you be able to pull out some time to gather information on all proposed space defence concepts, from across Earth sources?"

Rafael laughed. Max asked, "What's so funny?"

Rafael put on a more serious expression and said, "You have both Shun and Kei at your disposal. I'd possibly take ages tracking down the information you need, even with Shun's help. You're limiting yourself.

Task both AI's to collaborate on this. Give them output objectives. They could pull the information, not just from Earth, but also from information the framandi might have. The autonomous SSEV Nál has arrived at the solar system end of the framandi wormhole. It's taken aboard the data and processing modules which AL-I had initially handed over to Átt's crew. The framandi data is accessible locally in our system. We just need to learn how to query it correctly."

Max grinned and said, "I have much to learn from you. Thank you. I'll take your advice. Be well. And, keep an eye on Univers Aerospace. I have a feeling they may be up to no good." Rafael waved and signed off.

Speaking into his earpiece, Max said, "Shun, you're there?" A second later, he heard the familiar voice of the AI he had grown used to." The AI said, "Hello Max. Glad to hear your voice. I seem to be getting a feel for outer space, just as you are." Max smiled and said, "I need your assistance, and that of Kei." Another second later, Shun spoke again, "Kei is listening in as well."

"I need all the information you can dig up, on every concept ever thought up or executed, for defence in space," Max began. He explained, "The concepts will need to be categorised, so prioritise those which have been peer reviewed. Cross reference them for feasibility with emphasis on use of existing technology. Finally rate them against known extra-terrestrial weapon systems and tactics."

Kei asked, "What would you be looking at defending?" Max replied, "If a hostile force were to get to Earth, we would be doomed; so, it's best to hold any such force at bay. Preferably preventing them access to the solar system." After getting a few more clarifications, the AI's began their assignment.

Max went to check in with Maji. The leader of Lýsi's primary multinational covert operations force, was meeting with the platform's chief. They were sorting out a schedule to begin training the crews manning the space platform, in defence strategy and tactics. Given the anticipated threat, every crew member was to be adequately cross trained. After all crew were trained at Álfhól space platform, Maji's team was to be split and sent to each of the outer platforms, to train crews there. They'd transfer between platforms and rotate back to Earth. Their goal was to train all Lýsi personnel and covert action forces.

Maji nodded to Max. The two had got along well and become close during their voyage to Álfhól. Maji said, "We're just finishing up here. My team is going to take the next day or two acclimatizing. We'll then begin training the crew on Álfhól." Pointing to a screen he said, "Gogh concurs with the training course. By the way, he has bad news."

Max hadn't noticed the unusually prominent white-haired man, on the screen earlier. Gogh said, "Hello my old friend!" His usual greeting was accompanied with a smile which attempted to hide the tension on his face. Gogh continued, "As you probably know, Lýsi has a number of bases on Earth, out of which we conduct our outer space operations. For the most part, these are well under the radar. Somehow, it seems our smallest base, which only has hanger space for three flying wing capsule launch aircraft, has been infiltrated. It's one of our few mainland bases. The base is in Canada. We'd leased a section of the Airport at Montreal-Mirabel, for aircraft research, manufacturing and testing." Gogh paused while this information was absorbed.

The Lýsi leader went on, "Two members of the infiltration team were identified while they were leaving and were traced back to Rakkniv. Rakkniv links back to Univers Aerospace. For a brief period, all communications were offline at the base. During the interim, eight crew members preparing for capsule launch, were replaced. The original eight-person crew were sedated and sealed in a large basement closet. Fortunately, they were not harmed. The capsules were launched without anyone the wiser. The occupants are now in transit to Álfhól aboard Habogi, an S3 'Nesting Doll' Autonomous Cargo and Transport Vessel. They have manual control of the ACTV and are headed your way. How do you suggest they be handled?"

Max was becoming irritable. He snapped, "I made recommendations that would have boosted security. Haven't they been implemented?" Gogh responded with a nod, "They have been. Somehow, the Rakkniv crew knocked all systems off for a very brief period. Their ploy was very similar to our use of an EMP device, during your recovery operations at Kiruna. We're working on standalone EMP hardened systems for security and communications now."

Maji said, "We have access to the video cameras aboard Habogi. The AI has been completely locked out, which shouldn't be possible." Kei interrupted, "Actually it is. Habogi uses an older second-generation hull architecture which has its computing core accessible from the inside of the vessel. In our more modern spacecraft models, there are multiple cores, built right into the frame of the ship, along with batteries and conduits."

Max asked, "How are we accessing the video feed then?" Kei replied, "They're part of a separate network, tied into telemetry, communications and navigation systems which are accessible from the external hull. This makes it easily serviceable by drones."

Max said, "The hijackers are armed. Open communication to the vessel." Kei said, "Channel now open."

"Attention armed force on cargo transport vessel. We have you incoming to a restricted space platform," Max declared to the hijackers. One of the hijackers looked around and noticed cameras embedded in the walls. He motioned to his crew who went about disabling the cameras. The feed showing Habogi's interior, went dark.

"That's that," Max snapped. "Prepare for assault," he added. Turning to the platform's operations chief, he asked, "How safe are the interior cabins of our platform, from projectile weapons? Will weapons fire inside Álfhól be an issue?

Max received a positive response. "Very safe," the platform's chief replied. He added, "The designs of our outer and inner panelling, consider the off chance that a micro meteorite or larger space debris might penetrate the hull. There are two layers of gel in the outer and inner panelling which seal even the tiniest holes."

"That's good," said Max. Then he said to Maji, "Have your crew suit up. We'll take the fight to them."

Maji said, "We practiced zero-G manoeuvres while transiting to the platform." Max replied, "We'll be okay then. The Habogi's half an hour out. Let's make haste." Max hoped the situation would resolve soon. There were more pressing matters which required his attention.

Suited up, Max, Maji and the covert operations force on Álfhól waited within two separate airlocks. Only half the team were to undertake the extravehicular activity. The other half would remain aboard to resist or apprehend any hijackers that made it in.

At ten minutes out, the Habogi began to slow down. The hijackers were adept and had learnt quickly. The ACTV's gravity acceleration was turned off and the vessel had switched to ion thrusters. Conventional propellant thrusters would be used at final approach. As soon as the vessel's gravity propulsion was disengaged, the airlocks on Álfhól space platform opened, letting Maji and his team out. Max followed them. He was above and behind Maji's team. They planned on approaching the hijacked vessel and taking out the navigation systems, followed by propulsion. Two Asteroid Mining and Construction Autonomous Robots or AMCARs as they were called, went along with them for this task. The two autonomous space robots were tasked to tow the Habogi in, after the vessel was disabled.

Max looked up information on the AMCARS, but his impatience got the better of him. He spoke into his headset, "Kei, a quick question."

The AI answered immediately. Kei had a deeper artificial voice tone than its counterpart Shun. It spoke faster as well. "Right here. We're on a separate channel. Ask away." The AI seemed to know Max had a curious mind.

"Please brief me quickly about the AMCARs and asteroid mining," Max requested.

Without a second wasted, Kei launched into a briefing. "By the late eighties, Lýsi was already repurposing and recycling space junk to build its first small, disguised space station. A step up from molecular manufacturing satellites, robotic furnace and forge satellites had been assembled in space. These used solar concentrators to melt purified metals and composites. Interlocking frames and panels for space craft and platform external sections were manufactured, using injection molding techniques, allowing molten material to form massive single-piece structures. In four years after the first self-replicating manufacturing robot satellite was launched, it and others like it, had managed to build even more, totaling eighteen in all. The robotic satellites had also collected and manufactured enough parts, all tagged and left in orbit, which could be quickly assembled into connected hexagonal modules. But assembling these parts would require construction robots."

Noting that Max was able to keep up, the AI continued, "Also, at that time, getting additional resources and raw material into space was an issue. The limiting nature of the planet's economy, the conflicting use of available resources, the pressing needs of Earth's population and ecosystem; all nudged the group's leadership team to look at alternate sources. Over eight thousand near earth asteroids and objects were being tracked by various governments and by Lýsi; primarily because they posed a risk to life on Earth. These were acknowledged as a rich resource, especially since the space-based robot satellites and their onboard mission AIs, had been able to develop new vibrating centrifuges to separate minutely ground particles or even molten metal. Used in conjunction with molecular assembly nano-manufacturing, a system of rapid molding and fabrication techniques were established. In an experiment, a layered mix of metals and dust binder was molded into high density paneling, which successfully absorbed electromagnetic and cosmic radiation. I'll tell you more about that later."

Max urged, "Okay, go on."

"The need to mine asteroids and construct space vessels and platforms, launched the AMCAR project. A decision was taken to develop prototype Asteroid Mining and Construction Autonomous Robots, with the goal of assembling habitable jump platforms from which to occupy the solar system. Asteroid mining would make resources abundantly available, overcoming Earth sourced raw material hurdles. The first few AMCARs took four months to assemble. AMCARs were designed to be hardy and highly versatile with an array of extendable snake-arms, each with rapidly switchable function hands."

Kei didn't allow Max a chance to interrupt. "Álfhól space station was the first platform constructed as a staging point for Lýsi's forays into space. Its silhouette can be occasionally spotted. But only as a shadow. Interestingly, it provides ample fuel for conspiracy theories on Earth. Since the acquisition and reverse engineering of the now better understood extra-terrestrial artifact acquired by the group a decade ago, a decision was made to rapidly expand Earth life and knowledge, to ten in-system bodies within the next decade. The AMCARS were vital to achieve this milestone. We're actually ahead on our targets."

Switching from its briefing, Kei announced over the common channel, "We're approaching our objective." Max was grateful for the AI's briefing. It was a useful distraction that pulled him away from the building tension of confrontation. Max blinked and refocussed himself.

At a minute out, the AMCARs aligned themselves while Maji's team slowed, stopped and reversed direction. The Habogi passed through their formation. Maji's team gently approached the vessel from the rear. Habogi's hijackers obviously had eyes on the approaching team. The cargo vessel began to rotate clockwise making it difficult for any of the team members to latch on. Maji had just landed on the vessel's surface and clipped a tether on, near the rear universal docking port, but he was thrown off when the vessel began to spin. He called out to his team, "I'll have to disengage." As he unclipped the tether from his suit, centrifugal force pushed him away. But the agile warrior soon got his suit under control and re-joined the team tracking Habogi.

Meanwhile, the AMCARs controlled by Kei were doing their jobs. By the time Maji had re-joined his team, the Habogi's ion thrusters were offline. The vessel still drifted towards Álfhól. Quite unexpectedly, the rear universal docking port opened, and six suited hijackers streamed out. One of them rotated towards Maji and fired a compact weapon. Just a single shot. Maji only noticed because a sphere of glowing smoke, expanded from the shooter's barrel end, which dissipated quickly. Immediately after the weapon went off, the shooter began to slowly turn head over heels, from recoil. Maji smiled thinking, "They weren't completely prepared." He called out to his team, "The hijackers are weapons hot. Be alert."

Learning quickly from their experience, the hijackers fired with care, ensuring they had their suits' automated stabilizers on. Somehow, they'd managed to lock the AI out of their suits as well.

Maji spoke into his headset, "Kei, why aren't the hijackers using the lasers built into their suits?" He was referring to the two high wattage lasers which could be controlled via their HSEVA suits' heads up display. The lasers were primarily used for asteroid mining operations.

Kei replied, the lasers are completely controlled by each suit's mission AI. That's so that people don't inadvertently cut into their own suits, or others. The AI rapidly analyses targets and cutting parameters, before activating either laser. Having taken suit AIs offline, rendered their lasers dysfunctional."

Taking charge, Maji called out to his team, "Use beam weapons only. Converge on the Habogi. Team up and take out hijackers, one at a time. Aim your beam weapons at their faceplates. The rest of the suit is well shielded. Let's get them without losses to either side." His team reacted quickly. As fast as the hijackers adapted, they weren't yet as adept in space, as his team was.

The hijacker closest to Habogi's rear universal docking port was first to go down. Beam weapons, calibrated to briefly scramble human brain beta waves and the nervous system, were unleashed at him. He went limp and drifted along with the Habogi.

The next closest hijacker was approaching Maji. Rounds from the hijacker's weapon impacted against his HSEVA suit, without much result. Maji aimed his beam weapon carefully at the hijacker, ensuring none of his team were in the line of fire; then pressed the trigger for a full second. The hijacker went limp, but his suit continued to propel him towards Maji.

Speaking rapidly to Kei, Maji said with urgency, "I need to intercept and disable this hijacker's suit. Any ideas?" Kei answered very precisely, "There's a manual shut-down indented just under the armpits. I'll place a virtual overlay onto your helmet's heads up display, so you'll find it. Pressing it will immediately shut the suit down. You'll need to press it twice again to reboot the suit. I'm taking control of your thrusters, to place you into an intercept course."

Maji's suit thrusters engaged and he was rotated towards the hijacker, who was about to pass by. As soon as he got close enough, Maji grabbed one of his legs and pulled himself to chest level with the hijacker. With deliberate motions, he found the manual shutdown button and depressed it. The hijacker's thrusters cut off. Kei said, "You'll need to bring him back online quickly before he suffocates." Again, very deliberately, Maji pressed the button twice.

Kei instructed him, "Now place one of your palms against the back of the hijacker's neck. There is an interface built in for similar scenarios. It should allow me to access the rebooted suit." Maji followed the AI's directions. Kei said to him, "I've reactivated the suit's AI processors and internal environment. They've been physically disconnected from the rest of the suit's control and computing systems. This means that you'll have to physically haul the hijacker back."

Maji rolled his eyes but did as the AI instructed.

His team meanwhile had a much easier time. They'd paired off and taken down each hijacker one at a time. As soon as they figured the projectile weapons weren't effective against their HSEVA suits, they became bolder. One pair grabbed a hijacker, even as he fired at them, while another two oriented their beam weapons straight at the hijacker's faceplate.

Only the two hijackers inside Habogi remained. Maji instructed his team, "Breach the Habogi." Kei came online saying, "Internal pressure and atmosphere may be compromised in the ACTV. I've not been able to ascertain the current status of the two remaining hijackers." Maji replied, patching his entire team, "Last known, they were all in suits. We'll take our chances."

Having secured the hijackers outside the Habogi, ensuring their life support was functional, the team split up and approached the forward and rear airlocks on the ACTV. With procedural instructions being given by Kei, a pair of Maji's team members simultaneously overrode security and manually opened both airlocks.

Once in the airlocks, each of which was large enough for a standard six-meter intermodal space transport container, the team aligned themselves against the walls. The outer hatches were closed and the valves to pressurise the airlocks were manually activated. The hijackers were not visible through the airlock windows.

Maji had positioned himself close to Max. They were overseeing the six incapacitated hijackers trailing behind the Habogi. After taking a readiness status, he instructed the team, "Okay, enter."

Manually unlocking and winching the internal doors open, the team entered from both airlocks. The team in front, were greeted with a bunch of field rigged pressure bulbs which burst open splattering them with corrosive liquid. While their HSEVA suits were equipped to take on the harshest environments, their new weapons began sizzling in places, penetrating the casings. Receiving updates, Maji instructed, "Kei access the insertion teams' sensors and advice if there are any objects around which aren't meant to be there." To the team he said, "Everyone who's unaffected, move forward."

A little more cautious now, the team closed in on the central section of the Habogi. The ACTV had been kitted out for crew transport, and bunk capsules lined both walls at intervals. Kei spoke to the team, "The number three capsule on the wall that's colour coded blue, is occupied. The opposite wall coded green has the number two capsule occupied as well. There's a panel above their doors, with interface pads. You'll need to enter a code to let each capsule's failover computer take over." Two technically qualified members of Maji's team approached the occupied capsules and did as instructed. "Now, place your palm on the pad so I can interface with the capsules," Kei said.

It took a few minutes before Kei spoke again. The team was growing impatient, but they were well trained. They held their positions, ready for action.

Finally, Kei said to the techs, "Push in the door levers and rotate counter-clockwise. This will unlock the doors. Push on the doors to open inward." Maji interrupted, "Breach the capsule on the blue wall first."

The tech at the capsule door, pushed inward but there was resistance. Another two team members lent their weight and the door began to swing in slowly. The tech at the door saw the hijacker stretch sideways towards the capsule wall which exposed his side. Without hesitating, the tech lunged inside, felt his way around the hijacker's suit and pressed the external shut-down. The hijacker stopped resisting. They reactivated the suit allowing Kei to take control of it.

The remaining hijacker took the initiative. As soon as the capsule door began to swing inward, the person pulled the door in and leapt outward, tackling the tech. A melee ensued. The hijacker pushed the tech away and landed a taekwondo style, front push kick, to his torso. This threw him against the wall. Pivoting, the hijacker tackled another team member. Seeing the action on his heads-up display, Maji curtly instructed, "Grab his limbs." The team coordinated and pinned down the last active hijacker. His suit was rebooted.

Both hijackers in the Habogi were still conscious, but unable to access their suits themselves. Maji instructed everyone, "We'll bring the remaining hijackers into the ACTV." His team complied.

Max said to Maji, "I'll leave you to secure and interrogate the hijackers. We'll need to put a policy in place for hostile people. Especially out here in space. As far as I'm aware, Lýsi places Earth's interest first, and that extends to all life, hostile or not. I'm going to discuss this with the leadership team."

Maji replied, "The HSEVA suits were too easy to overcome. If we're going up against hostile forces anytime soon, we'll need to upgrade the suits for combat operations. That includes security against unauthorised access." Max concurred, "I agree. Lýsi's immediate priorities need to be finely juggled."

The Habogi arrived at Álfhól without loss. There wasn't a formal detention centre aboard the platform, so the operations chief designated a freshly constructed crew housing section, as the temporary brig. The hijackers were first given a physical, separated and then taken to their individual brig quarters. The platform crew were not geared for prisoner management, so Maji's team took on this task.

Having cleaned up and eaten, Max contacted Gogh. He asked him, "Have you been updated on the situation here? Has the leadership team made any decisions about the hijackers?"

Gogh replied, "The immediate problem we're facing, is excessive attention by a commercial space organization. At some point, this was bound to happen. Using cut-outs, Lýsi has deep relationships with most governments. That's something we have managed well. Private organizations are a different matter. We have a plan in the works, that should nip this in the bud."

Max asked, "What about the enhanced security systems I've recommended?" Gogh replied, "Three levels are being built in. Biometric for regularly accessed low confidentiality systems and DNA authentication for secret and secure ones. AI assisted recognition will be deployed for both. In the event AI becomes unavailable or needs to be disabled, system specific reboot codes are being generated, to use with manual input pads. Maji's concern about suits being disabled externally is being taken care of as well. We don't have an effective solution for EM or particle beams, shot through the hardened visor of our suits yet. We'll work on it." Gogh said, "I'll keep you updated," before disconnecting.

Max then focussed on his pad. He saw several update notifications waiting for him, related to the project he'd assigned the two AIs. He spoke into his headset, "Kei, do we have anything that needs my attention as yet?"

The two AIs replied taking turns. Kei went first, "You were right when you observed that defending Earth from space-based hostile forces, would be a difficult proposition. There are numerous scenarios for this, but in most cases, anyone occupying high orbit has the advantage." Shun added, "There are a number of scenarios for defending against objects penetrating the atmosphere. But the main issue would be knocking off hostile forces in orbit, or before they got there."

"The problem is like defending a vast area of land, in our case space. It's nearly impossible to be everywhere at once," said Kei. Elaborating, the AI said, "The best we've been able to come up with so far, is having armed platforms spread around Earth, with overlapping range of defence. Like fortresses."

Shun continued, "The threat of invasion through wormholes, actually works in our favour. Wormholes give us chokepoints. An advantage. We would require massive energy, firepower or obstacles, with which to deny entry to an enemy, at each chokepoint. Another idea is to place a parabolic shield of armed satellites around all wormholes. These would rain focussed firepower on any invading force, if they manage to get through and into the solar system."

"Also, a network of drone satellites could encircle Earth and the moon. These may be placed in concentric globes. The drone satellites would fire on hostile vessels from afar, then pull in and surround an enemy vessel."

Kei added, "However, our most effective strategy would be to control the planetary systems connected to ours, either directly or through alliances. This would provide a buffer planetary system which an invading force would need to first traverse or occupy, before they could even gain access to wormholes which lead to us."

Max asked, "These are intricate strategies that will require vast resources. How would we execute these?"

"Outward-in," replied Kei.

"Elaborate please," Max requested.

Shun answered, "First off, denial. Control in some manner, of all known systems adjoining ours, and thereby control of their wormholes. The known ones, which connect to the solar system are, the framandi wormhole and the Beta Hydri wormhole. The second is a system to which the framandi wish to migrate. An alliance with them is the quickest route to secure both systems. They're already motivated to defend themselves right now. We can continue to partner with them, consequently forging a strong bond with the civilization. This part is already in play. We'll have to worry about unknown wormholes."

"Second, the parabolic shield around each wormhole," said Kei. The AI continued, "We can use Graviton Focusing Devices or Gravids, mounted within asteroids, and powered by Cosmic Ray Energy Generators or CREGs. These are technologies we already possess and can remotely mass produce. The idea is to deploy crushing focussed gravity points, inside invading craft, as soon as they enter the system. We'll need a vast number of these for use against invading fleets."

Max asked, "But what if the enemy has some kind of shielding against gravity?"

"This is a point where we could do with the framandi's help. Their knowhow on heavy particle beam technology, used by warring species from each of our galaxies, would be useful to us," Kei suggested.

Max interjected, "Combined with focussed gravity points, this could be viable. What about in-system defence?"

This time, Shun took over, saying, "There's no easy way to do this, because it requires resource build-up. That takes time. While we accumulate additional material, we're suggesting a stop gap. We're already deployed at several points within the solar system. For immediate system defence, we could re-task the manufacturing capability of platforms closest to the Sun. These platforms use many Earth technologies, at scale. Solar reflectors are presently used to concentrate sunlight into solar furnaces. A series of such concentrators could be placed at strategic locations around the Sun, to first bounce light and radiation between themselves, concentrating these. They would then beam concentrated light and radiation, deep into our solar system. The radiation would dissipate into interstellar space. As soon as enemy vessels are detected, magnified radiation could target them. It would be an always-on, always-available, defence system. However, this requires hostile spacecraft approaching within effective range."

Max asked, "Is that all?"

Kei answered, "For the moment, that is all that's feasible."

Visualizing it all, Max instructed, "Then begin reallocation of resources to each of these projects. Prioritise access denial. I'll speak to Sven about getting the framandi to help us out."

Kei replied, "Well, Sven and Átt's crew are about to commence engagement. Once they begin, it may be difficult getting hold of them. Perhaps now would be a good time to speak briefly." Max agreed, "Yes, put me through please."

A moment later, Sven's face appeared on Max's screen. Sven looked intense. He said, "Hello again Max. We've taken your advice and added to your plan. Instead of waiting for the enemy to begin taking out the asteroids we lob at them, we'll begin breaking them apart soon after releasing them. We've calculated trajectories for all the pieces. They'll form a dense cloud when they approach the oppositions key points of concentration. The first few waves of asteroids will begin detonating, well before they arrive at their destinations. This should create a chaotic environment, and we're hoping it will overburden the various gigil sensors."

Max smiled, "It should be effective. It'll shield asteroids which follow. Space is vast and they'll still have time to manoeuvre, but you have the numbers. It's a matter of staying a step ahead. The enemy could have a trick or two up their sleeves."

Sven replied, "That's what I'm afraid of. In half a millennium, the enemy's had ample opportunity to upgrade their own capabilities. Much more than the framandi might be aware of. Given that they're only fronting a relatively small fleet, I have a feeling these vessels must be formidable. Oh, hang on. I've got Áox with me who's suggesting otherwise."

A separate window opened on Max's pad and Áox's face appeared. This was Max's first interaction with any framandi, and he wasn't aware of what the protocols may be. Fortunately for Max, the framandi jumped right into the conversation transmitting, "As you already know, we call the enemy we're facing, 'Gigils'."

Everything Áox thought to them, appeared in large text under the framandi's image. Obviously, the interface on Átt was translating the framandi's thoughts. The text was followed by a few references. Further large text appeared, "They have maintained a set force in the systems they've occupied. In the time gone by, we have observed them, and none of their vessel designs have been altered. Newly produced vessels replace older ones, which are sent to adjoining systems, and possibly onward."

Max said, "That could mean they're diverting their armed vessels to where they're needed. And, since the wormholes through your system are narrow, they've possibly found other paths."

Áox replied, "Yes. This observation is possible."

Directly connected with the framandi, Max said, "After this engagement, if all goes well, we will need your knowledge to better help defend both ourselves."

The framandi answered, "You will need to be enlightened then. It is a prerequisite. Once you have the foundation for information, then you can use it. Until then, we will aid you as best as we can."

Max asked aggressively, "What does that mean? You won't give us the information we need?"

Sven jumped in saying, "It means, unless an individual has absorbed a set of information blocks and learnt how to use it, higher levels of knowledge is unattainable. Or rather, incomprehensible. It's like learning the alphabet. Without letters, there are no words. Without words, no sentences. This must be why they have a kind of points-based system associated with learning. That is what they refer to as being enlightened. In their culture, knowledge is power. An individual framandi can only develop, construct or use technology, for which they have gained sufficient enlightenment points. It seems that's a failsafe they have built into everything, to prevent misuse. And to prevent accidents caused by deficient knowledge."

Áox emphasised, "Yes, this is correct." After that the framandi gave what resembled a smile. Max thought there was a lot of similarity between humans and framandi. Or, the extra-terrestrial being had learnt well to adapt itself, to mingle with humans.

Sven said, "We're commencing the engagement. Stay tuned. Jump in if you think we can gain an advantage." Both Sven and the framandi went offline. The images on the screen were replaced with three-dimensional tactical feeds, streamed from the lofi system, two wormholes away.

Chapter 11: Initiative

Isla was seeing the same view that Max was. The first wave of asteroids was launched against the gigils in the lofi system. Being an astronomer, she was also studying the planets around them. There were two in the goldilocks zone with atmospheres. Both looked like they might be habitable. Áox, Sven and Jón, were with her in the central operations area of Suður.

"We're coming in slightly above the system's plane. The asteroid belt Max had mentioned, is wide. It's spread twenty-five degrees above and below the plane. Most planets in the system are within five degrees of the plane," Isla mentioned. She observed, "The main portion of the gigil force is close to the fifth planet. The framandi have just confirmed that it's habitable."

Áox thought to them, "It is, and has been occupied. The gigils seem not to have disturbed the planet much. It may not have rich concentrations of usable minerals near the surface. Or, they're using the planet for recreation." These inputs were now picked up by the AI and put through to observers as real-time audio translation, albeit in Kei's voice.

Isla continued, "The fifth planet is mid-way on the system's plane, so it's logistically ideal too."

Max who was observing, voiced a thought. He said, "The planet could be used as a slingshot, to curve asteroids around it, to the rear of the gigil formation. We could add a further level of complication to overwhelm the enemy. The framandi vessels going into the asteroid belt to rearm, could first gravity-catapult a small unarmed asteroid, and then proceed with their ongoing missions."

Isla commented, "That would take significant processing resources. If we don't get it right, we'd have asteroids smacking into the planet. There's also the possibility of the asteroids missing the gigil vessels and continuing to plough on, slamming into our lines."

Áox thought to them, "The calculations can be made by each individual vessel once they reach the asteroid belt. The catapulted asteroids trajectories and paths could be fed into our situational awareness model of the local system. This is feasible."

Sven said, "Isla, implement it. Max, oversee the inputs please."

The first wave of armed asteroids released by the framandi frontline were speeding along. As the framandi vessels released their armed asteroids and swung towards the system's main belt, they provided focussed gravity propulsion to speed up asteroids released by other vessels behind them. This way, there were multiple waves of asteroids hurtling towards the gigil fleet, at dissimilar speeds. It was expected that this would further complicate matters for the gigils.

The Átt was drawing close to releasing its own asteroid, which was being tugged along behind it. Sven checked the vessel's systems and ran a quick diagnostic to ensure everything was working as needed. Áox noticed and asked, "Is there something amiss?"

Sven replied, "It never hurts to be extra cautious. That way, we're always sure we can trust our systems to function as intended."

A pulse of energy caused the lighting inside Átt to flicker. Fortunately, nothing went down. Sven asked the AI, "What was that?"

Kei replied, "We seem to have been hit by a broad but powerful beam of energized particles. The gigils may have fired it towards us a while ago, and we entered its path. The beam is like what we faced from the armed drone while entering the framandi system, except this was a lot more powerful."

"This is to be expected," Áox thought to them.

Sven commanded, "Kei, run diagnostics on all critical systems again."

Áox explained, "The outer material now covering your vessel, is made of tightly packed molecules of different densities. It's formed by tiny self-assembling molecular machines, which interlock into specific shapes and densities as needed. They take the brunt of each beam contact and then rebuild themselves. This ensures the surface is always prepared for additional assaults."

"So, then we don't have much to worry about, is it?" Sven asked.

"At close range, the beam from the largest gigil ships can do considerable damage. It could rip this craft apart," Áox clarified. "At this distance, we only need to worry about an energy overload, produced by your passive energy generation system, portions of which are embedded into your hull panels," the framandi added.

Jón said, "We should work on a circuit breaker between the CREGs and batteries, in future vessel models. In this vessel, the batteries are designed right into the hull frame. They'll be difficult to get to, given the situation we're in."

Sven said, "We'll have to do whatever it takes, to survive. Austur SSEV can be isolated first. No one's using it right now. The drones can take the insides apart, until they can get to the hull frame. We'll manufacture the energy overload trip units in Vestur, while the drones are at work. Once Austur is upgraded, we'll do the same with the other SSEVs."

Áox added, "I would also recommend an energy release mechanism on the exterior of this vessel's hull."

"Elaborate please," Sven said. Then regretted it. He was immediately bombarded with reams of data sent through his diadem by the framandi.

Áox summarized, "Your energy generators could switch from charging your batteries, to creating a field of charged particles around your vessel. As soon as a sharp jump in energy generation is detected, this switch could be triggered."

Jón interrupted, "I've pulled up the SSEV's design and worked with Kei on a simple trip mechanism which can be reset as soon as energy levels drop to an acceptable range. We're sealing and depressurising Austur now for work to commence."

Áox continued explaining "A layer of the material covering your vessel could be 'instructed' to form a superconducting shell." The framandi elaborated, "Fed with high energy, this would create a magnetic bubble around your vessel. Like a planet's magnetosphere. The bubble would repel a vast portion of particles, from beam weapons. The greater the density of particles hitting your CREGs, the greater the energy generated, and consequently a stronger bubble."

"How would we accomplish this?" Sven asked.

"The technology to do this may not be within your reach presently," said the framandi. "I'll instruct the hull material covering your vessel to form itself as needed, and integrate with your energy generating system," Áox said.

Jón said, "Actually, we have ongoing research for similar magnetic shielding, back on Earth." Probing, he asked, "Shouldn't your vessels be equipped with the same kind of cut-outs and bubbles?"

"They do not need to be. Each one transmits excess energy to other vessels through a distributed system, which identifies energy demand by individual vessels. We adapted and adopted a small portion of the gigils' own technology, recovered in the past. We have recently deployed it, after eons of research to understand how to safely apply it," Áox explained. The framandi then helpfully appended a set of references to explain how the concept broadly functioned.

It was time to release their towed asteroid. Jón announced, "Initiating asteroid splitting gravity-field sequences." The asteroid they were towing ripped itself in three, releasing some debris. Jón then said, "Asteroid acceleration sequence activated." A series of focussed gravity points were thrust ahead of each asteroid portion. Once the portions began accelerating, the intensity of gravity was rapidly amplified. This set the asteroid chunks hurtling towards the gigil fleet formation, aimed at the expected positions of individual enemy spacecraft.

Immediately after release, the Átt followed other asteroid depleted framandi vessels. They headed deeper into the lofi system. Most gigil defences were centred around framandi vessels about to release asteroids. Once detected, the paths of high energy beams emanating from gigil spacecraft, were updated to the framandi situational awareness feed. Áox observed, "The enemy has begun directing its vessels to concentrate energy beams onto asteroids approaching their frontline. Many asteroids have disintegrated under focused assault." Áox tweaked the framandi plan to ensure a higher volume of asteroids were aimed at beam emitting enemy vessels.

As Átt progressed towards the asteroid belt, Kei alerted that it was time for a shift change. The crew had maintained the rigour of sticking to shifts, unless they were engaged in close quarters battle. They had rearranged shifts so that there was always at least four crew and one framandi awake.

Jón and Isla were due for a sleep shift after a meal and shower. Curious, Jón thought to Áox, "Are you hungry? I haven't seen you eat."

The framandi gave his now well practiced smile and thought back, "I recuperate and replenish in my suit which is placed in Norður, your bio-module which was recovered by us. The suit provides vital nutrients and hydration which are injected directly into my digestive tract, through a feeding tube on my side. Body waste is handled via a similar process, but without any permanent implants." A series of visuals flashed through Jón's mind along with Áox's response.

Áox elaborated, "We took the liberty of integrating some of our own space-based vegetation growing units, alongside yours. We grow a wide variety of flora in space. Primarily for solid-food consumption. Incidentally, while Norður was being brought back to Átt, we had the opportunity to study your flora. There are a great many similarities. With minor modifications, we could consume yours, as you could ours."

This surprised Jón. Picking up on the reaction Áox added, "Do not forget. Generations ago, we were present on your home planet, to salvage life there." Previous references were appended to the thought. "The collateral damage inflicted to life on your world, caused by sustained inter-galactic battles fought in your system, was near catastrophic. During the recovery stages, we needed to sustain ourselves. So, we introduced some of our own flora and fauna. We also brought back some of yours to grow in our system. Over time, these have evolved into the environments they were introduced to. On your world and on ours."

The consequences of this revelation boggled Jón. If the framandi had chosen to, they could have taken up residence on Earth, instead of looking for other systems to occupy.

Instead of letting such a thought fester in his mind, Jón thought to the framandi, "Why didn't you remain on Earth, the human home-planet?"

"We had a lot of rebuilding to do ourselves," Áox thought back. "Once we were sure life, especially sentient life, would recover on your planet, we decided to leave you to your own path," Áox explained.

Jón thought to Áox, "We've pretty much wrecked our planet, Earth. Conflict, intensive resource extraction, unconstrained consumption and widespread pollution have adversely impacted our world."

Ásta entered the central operations area. She nodded her head to Áox and said, "Time for you to get some rest Jón. You too Isla. You've both overshot your shift."

Isla grinned and replied, "Your brother is to blame of course. He's been in deep-thought mode with Áox for a while now."

As Jón got up to leave, Áox thought to him, "Once, we too brought our planet to the brink of destruction. That was a long time ago, after our planetary system saw similar battles, as yours did. In our dash to recover, we stripped our planet bare. That nearly ended us. We chose to evolve. Consciously and deliberately. On the surface, our home world is now a paradise. We plan to keep it that way. You too will need to take initiative. I'll show you how we did it later."

Jón nodded to the framandi and said to his sister, "Glad you're here. I'm actually exhausted." Sven who was on the shift after Jón's said, "I would be too if I worked through two shifts. Go get some rest."

Isla handed over her tasks to Crystal and left the central operations area, jogging to catch up with Jón.

Crystal's story was just as unique as each of Lýsi's members. She was an extraordinarily gifted student and had completed post graduate studies in astrophysics, by the time she turned nineteen. Then she had run into a math professor at university, who was consulting with a private London based organization, to develop the next generation of quantum computer-based AI hardware. Impressed with Crystal's capabilities, he roped her into the project.

A portion of the project she was working on, was transferred to the port at Aichi in Japan, aboard the Kuji Maru, a merchant ship. Once the quantum computing cores on the ship were up and running, the AI Shun ran Crystal through a series of moral assessments. The AI had done this with every person it had come into close contact with. The evaluation was based on Lýsi's standard recruitment tests. Crystal stood out. Not only was she a good person, she was the absolute best. Shun recommended she be recruited.

Soon after, she found herself off-world and part of an epic deep-space adventure. And, she had her biggest crush Sven, aboard with her. Crystal was just where she belonged.

Ásta surprised her. Crystal was pouring over the imminent second stage asteroid slinging manoeuvre, set to commence once the first framandi vessels arrived at the system's main asteroid belt. She was engrossed with star charts on her pad.

"So, you and Sven are a thing now?" Ásta asked. "Huh?" Crystal mumbled. Now distracted, she sighed and said, "This isn't the time. But, there's no keeping anything from you. So, yes!" Ásta peeked at the pad and saw that Crystal was now checking through calculations related to their approach to the gigil formation, after they rearmed. She also had a pad window open, on the asteroid catapulting manoeuvres. It required focus. She touched Crystal's forearm and said, "You've been withdrawing into yourself. You can't isolate yourself with only Sven as your confidante. He may be your partner, but you need to interact with the rest of the crew. Isolation is dangerous, especially out here."

Crystal was intelligent enough to understand. She nodded her head and gave Ásta a smile. She said, "I'll be sure to take time out to socialize. It's just that I'm feeling the stress." Ásta replied, "We all are. But we're also the ones making first contact. Both the friendly kind and confrontational. You're one of the most intelligent persons I know. And you're always up for action. I for one, am glad you're here with us."

Ásta gave Crystal a quick hug and went across to Áox. She looked at the projected situational awareness feed, noticing Áox peering at a section of it. The framandi zoomed in on an area, to the left of the wormhole through which they'd entered the lofi system. She thought to Áox, "Is something amiss?"

"Yes," Áox responded and thought back, "I have noticed a plume of dust and dark matter entering this system, from beyond the gaseous planet holding the seventh orbit. It is likely, there is a large wormhole at that location. There are several gigil freighter and factory-ships accompanied by armed reconnaissance drones, which appear to be departing the fleet. They seem to be heading for this location." Áox appended overview data, to back up his thought.

Ásta studied the information. She was now accomplished at getting to the nuts and bolts of pertinent information, from framandi presented data. She did this better than anyone else on the crew, including her twin brother.

"Sven, you'll need to see this," Ásta called out. He looked their way, taking his attention away from the gigil rear formation. Crystal put her pad aside and walked up as well. Stefán was the only one on shift who was missing from the central operations area on Suður. He was on Norður, tending to the bio-module and researching some of the framandi plant material.

Sven asked, "What am I looking at?" He had learnt to speak aloud while simultaneously thinking the same thought through his diadem. Ásta replied, "The gigils seem to be withdrawing some of their freighter and factory-ships towards what appears to be a wormhole. Focus on the area to the left and south of the wormhole we entered the system from." Ásta had picked up the way Sven concurrently spoke and thought through his diadem. She managed to do it just as well.

Crystal pointed out, "There are a few large bodies behind the wormhole." She said to the AI, "Kei, zoom in on the area directly behind the mouth of the newly identified wormhole."

A portion of the volumetric projection showing the wormhole, expanded into view. Crystal said, "There. Looks like five moon-like bodies. There are some structures on them."

"That is wormhole maintenance technology, like those the gigils had in our system, before the structures were destroyed in ancient battles between them and beings from your galaxy," Áox thought to them. The framandi continued, "I recognize these from our ancient history." A set of data followed the thought. Áox went on, "These take time to deploy. Unlike our own technology, these gradually expand and hold wormholes open, using tiny, incremental increases in energy. We still do not have the enlightenment to replicate this. However, we do know how to destroy them, and collapse the wormholes to their natural states."

"We should refrain from destroying these unless there's a pressing need," Sven advised. Max who was keenly following Átt's progress, came online. He agreed with Sven, "We would gain a strategic advantage to control known wormholes. These will allow further exploration. They're choke-points which may be easier to defend as well. However, if there is a threat, reducing the size of the wormhole mouths, may be an option. It all depends on how the current situation unfolds."

Ásta's eyes widened. She turned towards Áox and thought while speaking aloud, "You mentioned that framandi know how to knock these out. Did that involve taking over the gigil wormhole-preservation structures?"

"Yes, it involves penetrating the structures and disabling specific components," Áox explained while transferring imagery into their minds. "This requires infiltration," the framandi explained, providing supporting data, "and, a stealthy approach while remaining masked. The structures are automated and defend themselves. Even against approaching but unauthorised gigil vessels."

The outlines of a plan began forming in Ásta's mind. It would require cunning, stealth and sheer luck. She decided to discuss it with her brother once he awoke. He had a knack at identifying gaps in logic. He was also very crafty when it came to strategic planning.

Crystal announced, "We're nearly at our first designated asteroid. The one we're to lob at the gigils. I've finished reviewing the calculations for our part of the operation. Speed, trajectory, gravity assisted acceleration around the fifth planet, and expected location of the target vessel. They all check out."

Sven announced to them, looping in Stefán who was still in Norður, "Everyone strap in. We all know how exciting pushing, towing and chucking asteroids can get. We're five minutes out from our plotted asteroid." He wasn't worried about the remainder of the crew, secure and asleep in their capsules. They'd be protected should something go wrong. He knew because he had spent enough time in an evacuation capsule, until they were rescued. So had Crystal.

The AI had been receiving a barrage of information from the armada of framandi vessels. They were continuously sharing their asteroid lobbing experience, with other vessels. The manoeuvre was down to a pat.

As Átt approached the plotted asteroid, gentle points of focussed gravity were placed ahead of it. This got the designated asteroid moving. By the time Átt was close to it, the asteroid had picked up enough speed to keep pace with the spacecraft. Then additional gravity points were introduced to get it spinning. This was to reduce the amount of surface-contact, any beam weapons would have, on the asteroid. It was also hoped that the spin would help the asteroid shoulder away smaller pieces of debris or projectiles, in an already littered space battlefield.

The manoeuvre went off as planned. The asteroid allocated to Átt, was on its way towards a gigil carrier-ship. The system-wide situational awareness projection was getting sharper and more detailed, as a greater number of framandi vessels swapped their data.

The three gigil command-ships in the lofi system were utilizing their heavy particle beam weapons to great effect; neatly taking out large swathes of inbound armed and passive asteroids. But the intense chaos caused by the asteroid barrage, was beginning to take a toll on the smaller vessels. These were beginning to get pummelled by debris from exploding asteroids. A large cloud of fast-moving space-boulders was converging in on the three prongs of the gigil fleet. Things seemed to be going well.

Having completed its task with the first asteroid designated to them, the Átt moved on to the second. This was a larger asteroid, similar in size to the one the spacecraft had towed into the lofi system. A pair of the crew were to undertake an EVA to oversee and assist three pairs of drones. They needed to plant explosives at specific points on the asteroid. The drones aboard Átt had already successfully completed this task once, before entering the lofi system, so the crew were confident about undertaking the exercise again. Ásta and Stefán were the freshest of the crew, so they were tasked to oversee the drones.

Áox thought to them, "I would like to accompany you. I am an 'Explorer'. Every experience adds to my ability."

Sven agreed, "Perhaps we could learn from you too."

Ásta and Stefán quickly went over to Vestur where their HSEVA suits were. Áox went to Norður to don a framandi space suit. A few minutes later, Áox thought to all of them, "I'm at the forward airlock of your bio-module, ready to exit. I've initiated outer material reformation to allow your universal docking port hatches to open on Norður and Vestur." Áox had picked up names quite well and had even learnt to refrain from sending along reams of data, to support what was being spoken about. Unless data was asked for, of course. Áox, Advisor of the Explorers, had previously expressed that humans seemed to do well even with tiny amounts of information. Their capacity to extrapolate seemed boundless.

"We'll be ready in our forward airlock in a minute," Ásta thought back to the framandi, and to Stefán. She had begun to have regular thought conversations with Stefán, her shift partner, through their diadems. He in turn, had become just as fluent in holding these kinds of conversations, with the framandi aboard. She had once commented to the AI in a report, that thought conversations via diadem, may depend a lot on the number of previous conversations the participating individuals may have had. The better the minds understood each other, the easier the conversations were.

"We're at the airlock," Ásta announced to the crew and to Áox. It was time to begin their extravehicular activity. The airlock on Vestur opened into a tunnel, formed by the smart framandi exterior hull material. They carefully exited. Drones from Vestur and Suður used rear airlocks and joined them. Áox was already at the asteroid and was observing them approach. He held out one arm towards the fifth planet, pointing to it.

Áox thought to them, "There is a lot of activity on the habitable planet. Shuttles are continuously moving between the planet and the fleet. Many of these seem to be going to the largest gigil vessels." Ásta thought to the framandi, "Clarify, please." Immediately imagery gleaned and combined from the large swarm of framandi vessels appeared to her and the rest of the crew.

"We'll take a look at what's going on," Sven said. "You focus on the asteroid. It has a high metallic composition so it could get tricky. Be careful."

The outer scan of the asteroid had provided them with suitable spots to drill and place explosives. Closer and deeper scans revealed that the asteroid would be tough to crack apart with gravity alone. Ásta replied to him, "Yes, tricky indeed. This is going to be mind-numbing."

The framandi had a solution. Áox suggested, "Some of the hull's smart material covering Átt can be instructed to travel in thin lines, over the sections of the asteroid which we require weakened. The smart material will gather up dust-sized portions of the asteroid surface and deposit it on Átt. The metallic asteroid dust could be useful raw material."

Stefán who was observing Áox, as he tended to do whenever either of the framandi were around, remarked, "Conceptually that would be just like how strong wire is used to cut through rock or marble, using abrasion. Understood."

Sven said, "I'll bring Átt in close, so the vessel touches the asteroid. It'll be easier for the material to move to and from the asteroid."

Crystal added, "I'll begin tasking the material through our AI interface. We've got a steep learning curve ahead of us, on programming the material. Nothing like a little practice in a high-stress situation."

Áox expressed happy thoughts to all of them. The framandi was very pleased that the humans were taking the initiative and becoming involved. They had a shared past, however distant; and, it seemed increasingly likely they would share an allied future.

The drones had begun drilling into the asteroid at their designated positions. Ásta, Stefán and Áox; each took up positions near them to assist or instruct if required. Stefán immediately noticed an issue. The drone he was with was vibrating and rocking about. Something didn't seem right. He instructed the drone to turn its drill off. Stefán went over and peered into the shallow hole the drill had made, shining suit-mounted lights into it. He thought out to Áox, "The material inside this asteroid appears to be tough gleaming metal. The drill's unable to penetrate." Ásta indicated that the drone she was supervising was facing a similar issue.

Áox bent down next to Stefán. He shared worried emotions with them, while conveying, "This may be a disguised spacecraft from your galaxy. Leftover from an ancient battle in our system. Somehow it has found its way here. It seems to be inert. Be very vigilant. They can remain dormant for long periods."

By now, Ásta had come over. She said, "Your people recovered artefacts, remnants from space battles in your system and ours. Surely you know how to salvage this."

"I do not have it in my own memory. I can retrieve it," Áox thought back.

Stefán enquired, "How's it covered in hardened rock? It wasn't even identifiable as a spacecraft."

Áox answered, "It is from some of these that we discovered and learnt to be hidden or masked, to be disguised, to go unnoticed." Imagery of framandi vessels hiding their hulls, living inside asteroids and other space bodies, appeared in their minds.

The framandi continued, "The owners of these vessels, moulded molten rock to the exterior of their spacecraft. Layer upon compacted layer. They were supposedly adept at infiltrating deep into the gigil fleets."

Ásta thought to them, "I'd be very interested in knowing what they did after they infiltrated."

Áox responded, "I've been able to retrieve the information on dormant vessel recovery. The size of this one indicates it may be what you could refer to as an 'intelligence' signals hacking vessel. It can be used to take over portions of gigil automated technology. The gigil rely heavily on automation. It's also capable of taking over some species' wetware, the nervous systems and brains, subjugating them."

Sven who had his diadem linked to the EVA team's; thought to them from Átt, "Would this vessel give us an advantage?"

Áox replied, "It could. If we can get into it, replace certain components, power it up and take over its programming. This will be highly dangerous. If we're unsuccessful in the first attempt, this vessel could take over the Átt, and other vessels in the vicinity."

Sven asked, "But your people have done this before right?"

"Eons ago. Last, after the conflict in your system. Not recently," Áox responded.

A hasty discussion ensued between Max and other key observers patched in from the solar system. Sven thought to them, "We should attempt recovery. This could help us immensely." After receiving a go-ahead from participating Lýsi observers, Sven asked Áox, "Will you help us salvage this spacecraft?"

Áox thought back, "Áom and I will gather the required enlightenment to achieve this." The team temporarily halted their EVA, while the encounter with the gigils raged on. Their discovery could give them an advantage against the gigils, an edge they sorely needed.

Chapter 12: Discoveries

Max had just come off a video call with Gogh and Rafael who were on Marion Island. The SSEV Nál, operated by the AI Kei, had successfully recovered the data and processing units, initially presented by AL-I. The SSEV was approaching Lýsi's deep-space platform Sólríka, which occupied the Sun-Earth L1 Lagrange point. The platform had just been commissioned and brought online. Jón and Ásta's parents were given the honour of naming the platform. They'd called it 'sunny' in Icelandic.

Similar platforms were rapidly being constructed by Asteroid Mining and Construction Autonomous Robots or AMCARs. These were to occupy the L1 Lagrange points of each of the first five planets in the solar system. All platforms close to the Sun, were to be automated and robotically managed. Operations on these were to be completely controlled by the two AIs, Shun and Kei. This would let people aboard accelerate their research and development work.

Sólríka was important. It contained multiple quantum computing cores distributed between the two AIs. It was also the largest space vessel manufacturing centre. However, it would soon be overtaken in capacity by the platform located at the Sun-Mars L2 Lagrange point, which was close to the solar system's main asteroid belt. Presently, Sólríka was to house the first artefacts directly handed over by extra-terrestrials.

Soon after the SSEV Nál had taken aboard the data and processing units provided by AL-I, Gylfi Hallgrímsson and Katrín Magnusdóttir, the transhuman twins' parents, had solved the problem of redesigning all known Earth DNA, to be compatible with the framandi's.

The bio-technicians had productively queried AL-I's data module, using Kei's upgraded natural language interface. The information required by them was already available on the framandi data unit, including how to introduce the DNA modifications, across species, worldwide. They just needed to find suitably updated vectors to carry and introduce the DNA modifications, into global populations.

There was also the moral decision of conducting such an operation. Given the speed with which they needed to introduce the modifications, it wouldn't be possible to take permission from every individual on Earth. Completing the action would take time. Possibly a year for deep marine life. For life on the surface of the planet though, changes would be immediate.

The twins' parents were grappling with this. Lýsi's leadership had consulted with some of the best and brightest minds and concluded that the group would need to act on behalf of the planet. Failure to do so could expose the entire planet to catastrophic risk. That was unacceptable.

Gogh had given instructions to begin genetic modifications, which were to be carried on a series of viruses. Viruses were known to swap genes with nearly all known life. The changes to be introduced would impact archaea, bacteria, and eukaryotes. Effectually all life on Earth would be covered.

The manner of deployment was debated. Finally, Max provided the solution. He'd observed that asteroids were continuously processed for resources, out at the Sun-Mars L2 Lagrange point platform. The mined processed minerals were hurled out to Sólríka and other platforms, in woven carbon containers. Viral vectors produced at scale at Sólríka, could be placed within protected vials. The viral payload could then be placed into the used woven carbon containers after the transported minerals were removed.

Max suggested that the containers with vials, could then be catapulted towards Earth, using carefully calculated trajectories. The container outer material would burn up in the atmosphere, allowing the protected vials to burst open in the lower atmosphere, releasing their viral packages. No container particles would remain, which could cause injury to people or wildlife. The plan was minutely studied for flaws and then initiated.

Rafael had called Max shortly after the debate. Max's screen lit up with the boy's face on it. Max smirked, "I had a feeling you'd call. How's your training progressing?"

Rafael replied, "I'm being put through advanced combat training. Next up, space defence strategy. By the way, I was going through the scenarios you had shared with me; the ones the AIs had pulled together for solar system defence. The final one, which relies on using concentrated solar light, like laser; would take too long to arrive at the intended destination, if it's directed from close to the Sun. I have a solution."

Max perked up and asked, "What would that be?"

Rafael said, "Since we already have deep-space platforms parked at various places around the solar system, why not begin the process of reflecting and concentrating solar radiation, from near the Sun and send it deep into our solar system, where it's bounced between platforms and satellites. We'll need a web of satellites placed throughout the solar system which would continuously receive concentrated solar radiation. As one ring of the satellite-web is completed, another layer can be constructed. The problem of getting concentrated radiation, to the far reaches of the solar system would be solved. Concentrated radiation would already be available close to where it's needed, if we're already bouncing it between a web of networked defence satellites."

"Interesting," Said Max. "We'll need to work on occupying few key positions initially, and then add to these," he said. Then he asked, "Where would you suggest we place the solar-beam reflecting satellites?"

"I'm suggesting a pair of geo-stationary satellites near all planets in the solar system, and each of their L3 Lagrange points," Rafael replied.

Max said, "I see. This would give us two of these satellites at each planet, and a third on the opposite side of the Sun, on the planet's orbit."

Rafael confirmed, "Yes, that's right."

"Thank you for bringing this to me," Max said. "I'll provide your input to the AIs, so that it can be implemented along with the overall defense strategy," he added.

Rafael waved and said, "I'll call if I have anything more." He signed off.

Max's screen switched back to the situational awareness feed from the lofi system, which was compiled and pushed to all participating Lýsi members. He was pleased to see that Átt's crew had made progress with the recently discovered dormant alien vessel. He asked Kei to prioritise updates about the discovery, while making his way to the newly assigned brig section of Álfhól platform. He was to meet Maji, who had an update for him.

"You're here earlier than I expected," Maji said, as Max entered an operations area beside the brig. The area had been equipped to function as Lýsi's space defence command post and communications centre.

Max was impressed with what he saw. He smiled and replied, "You got this place organized quickly. Where's my workspace?"

Maji pointed to the rear and said, "A wardroom with a conference table. It has a fantastic view into outer space."

"Do you have an office?" Max asked.

"The wardroom to the left of yours." Maji replied. "We'll use the operations area here for briefings. It'll be efficient enough." He added.

Max settled himself into a grav-chair, the standard seating in space. He expected an update on the hijackers they had captured. He wasn't disappointed.

Maji said, "Our 'guests' haven't been very cooperative. We haven't used any coercive techniques during our investigative interrogations. They're not going to be a problem for now, but we need to figure out what we're going to do with them."

"Yes, we shouldn't encounter a situation like this again." Max said. He continued, "Lýsi is implementing enhanced security controls and measures. This will limit access and exposure. Our space operations and access to AI hubs have been prioritised."

"We can't let the hijackers back onto Earth for the time being. We'll either have to hold or absorb them, till we can control information." Max added.

Maji asked, "How's that going to happen?"

Max answered, "Lýsi is working on it. The plan requires a bit of time. But it'll be done. Give our 'guests' access to general information. Nothing that provides insights into our research and development. If any are willing, they could participate in space combat scenario analysis."

The AI interrupted them. Kei spoke to the duo through their grav-chair mission pads, "Sven is online."

Max said, "We'll take the call in my wardroom. Kei, turn on the projector there." Maji and Max walked over to the freshly equipped wardroom.

Sven's volumetric projection was hovering over the conference table surface. Max said to him, "I didn't expect to be seeing you so soon again."

Sven replied, "Our discovery of the dormant ET vessel got me thinking. While the framandi have indicated that they've swept the solar system and collected artefacts from the previous inter-galactic engagement there, we ought to look around for ourselves. We already have long range surveys ongoing to locate resource-rich asteroids. The surveys could be expanded, to track down all asteroids like the one we've found here. I'll send across the specifications, an analysis of the exterior material moulded onto the hull, and the gravity profile. Any one or a combination of these, should lead us to any overlooked extra-terrestrial vessels. It'll be a long shot, but it'll give us a leg ahead should we come across anything."

"Why didn't you just task the AI to do this?" Max asked.

"Because you seem to have absorbed all available capacity, towards building defensive infrastructure in the solar system." Sven answered slightly exasperated. He sighed and continued, "What I have in mind won't make much of an impact on the ongoing survey activities. What it will require is tasking the AIs to process previously surveyed asteroids. About a decade's worth."

"Hi Sven, I'm Maji," Lýsi's covert force team leader introduced himself. "What kind of an immediate advantage would such a vessel provide us?" he asked.

Sven leaned forward and answered, "If you find any which are like the vessel we've located, then assuming we can salvage these, you'll have the ability to stealthily approach an opposition spacecraft and take over its systems. Perhaps even its occupants. According to the framandi, these disguised spacecrafts seem to be effective against most inorganic hardware. If you locate any of these, then we could develop additional combat capabilities in the solar system. I've just shared the references of known vessels used by the gigils and the opposing kiligs. Gigils are an intelligent species from the Canis Major Dwarf Galaxy, while Kiligs are from ours, the Milky Way. These are both framandi terms we've pulled from their complex definitions. I would suggest you look them up. Encountering either would be disastrous. Facing both would be catastrophic."

Maji instructed the AI he was used to. He said, "Shun, please add ET vessels, their specifications, images and known capabilities to the crew briefing modules. Cover hostile and friendly fleets, including the framandi's. Please share the additional module for review with Max and me when ready."

Shun replied, "It's available now. The material is queued on your respective tasks lists for review."

Amazed, Maji exclaimed, "That was quick!"

Shun explained, "Kei and I have transitioned to superior processing hubs with technology drawn from the processing units, provided by AL-I. The hubs are online on all Lýsi space platforms, Standardized Space Exploration Vessels and six Earth-based locations. We share each hub equally. Individual gaupas have been integrated into hubs for each of us, for communications, data transfer and process balancing."

Sven asked, "Would it be possible to dig into all the information left behind by AL-I in its entirety?" He added, "It'll help leapfrog us, technologically."

Shun replied, "The information is all stored in DNA format. It would take years for Kei and myself to decipher and convert it all into human languages. For now, it would be best to make sharp queries, to retrieve answers for specific research. Information sets can be built upon as needed. Framandi knowledge is cross corelated, it is inevitable that all information contained in the data module, will be accessed for some reason over time."

Maji probed, "How much information are we talking about?"

"Unknown. But enough to get an entire civilization up and running at the level of the framandi. That was what AL-I's mission was.

Presumably, the information shared with us on the data unit, was everything it possessed." Shun answered.

"I've got to go now. We're just about ready to try and access the vessel we've found here." Sven updated. Turning his attention to Max, he said, "See if there are any dormant spacecraft or remnant extra-terrestrial artefacts still in the solar system." Sven's projected head was replaced by the situational awareness feed from the lofi system.

Max noticed an item blinking on his grav-chair's pad. It was a message from Gylfi Hallgrímsson, Jón and Ásta's father, asking him to call. Max said to the AI he was just speaking with, "Shun, connect Gylfi and put him up on the volumetric projection." Maji looked towards Max with a raised eyebrow. Max shrugged. The two of them were able to read each other quite efficiently now.

The projection went live. Gylfi looked at Max and Maji. He greeted them, "Hi. I've got exciting news." He announced with enthusiasm in his voice, "The viral vector and deployment gel suspension we have been working on is complete. We used information gleaned from AL-I's data. I've just come off a call with Gogh. He's advised that we test out the delivery mechanism. Katrín and I have prepared a pre-production set of vials using the automated manufacturing facilities on Sólríka space platform."

Max asked, "Weren't you working on multiple viruses? For each species?"

Gylfi answered, "That's right. We were. Then quite miraculously, while Katrín was pursuing a thread of framandi information, about sharing genetic material within their populations, she discovered the code-sets for developing synthetic viruses or vira, which could be used to deliver the gene edits, to other viruses. Digging deeper, she found a bunch of synthetic viruses, engineered by the framandi, which can rapidly alter other viruses. The altered viruses in turn would then pass on the genetic information to life-forms they are already compatible with."

Maji exclaimed, "Wow, I'm imagining all sorts of horrible scenarios. Whatever happens, this information needs to be kept secure. In the wrong hands it would be disastrous."

Katrín was beside Gylfi and came into view when she spoke. She said, "As soon as I began querying the framandi data, it automatically threw back counter queries to ascertain if the necessary background information was available to the person requesting data, which in this case was me. Unknown to us, the data module from AL-I has been assigning framandi enlightenment points to anyone making queries. It only releases information to the operator after determining what the person will understand at their level of learning. The complexity of information shared, directly matches the points a user has chalked up, based on their query history."

Maji said, "Even So, a person may have the required knowledge to access complex data and still get up to no good."

Shun broke into the conversation. The AI said, "Kei and I were tasked with monitoring the ethics and integrity of each person using our interfaces. The process is continuous. This monitoring is extended to the use of the framandi data modules. We continuously run ethical reasoning assessments on all Lýsi members. Information access is restricted according to the assessment outcomes. This even applies to Lýsi leadership. If an assessment requires downgrading a member's information access or operations exposure, it is first cleared by three security team members."

Maji raised his eyebrows and said, "I didn't know I was being monitored."

Shun replied, "You are not recorded. Interaction outcomes are. Your location is always known. Your decisions and instructions are continuously assessed. This assessment system has been in place since AI capabilities were first brought online. It was one of my very first programs. Kei and I have been continuously adding to the evaluation framework. If either of us or any Lýsi member encounters a situation for which there is debatable ethical outcome; a clarification is simultaneously sought from the top five percent of all moral assessment score holders."

Maji looked satisfied. But he still worried about unauthorised access by other means.

Max said, "Okay. Back to Gylfi and Katrín now. Please continue. Have you tested out this 'master virus'?"

Katrín answered, "We've tested small batches of eleven different synthetic viruses here at Álfhól space platform. Once deployed, they should be able to alter all known Earth viruses. What we need to do is ensure the efficiency and safety of the delivery mechanism."

"A production batch of these synthetic viruses are being manufactured now." Gylfi said. He continued, "We'd like to run a practical delivery test, by lobbing about fifty thousand of the prepared woven carbon containers at Venus. These would need to be tracked by AMCARs, all the way down until vials burst and deploy their viral payloads. What I need from you is computing resources to manage gathered data. Then we'd need to study the acquired data to model out trajectories for each container to be lobbed at Earth. Turns out you're monopolizing most of the processing capacity we have."

Max asked, "How many of these containers are you thinking about hurling at Earth?"

Katrín answered this time, "In the millions. And we would need to maintain the activity until we're certain every bit of the planet has been saturated. We will stop once random sampling from across species on Earth tells us, that the gene edits have been absorbed across the board."

Maji asked, "Aren't you afraid of introducing life onto Venus? Synthetic life?"

Katrín replied, "Venus is like hell. Surface temperatures are scorching enough to melt many elements. These hardened synthetic viruses only survive a little longer than a month, in Earth-like environments. They do not reproduce. The delivery test should not have any lasting effect."

Max asked, "Why not use the information processing module gifted by AL-I for this?"

Patiently, Katrín responded, "Shun and Kei confirm that we would need half of their combined processing capacity for about three days to make accurate calculations. Safety is paramount. For instance, we cannot risk having a single delivery container impact a satellite or aircraft. The calculations would be very intricate. We'd have to do this for each batch of half a million containers. The containers would enter the atmosphere in a grid pattern, after having avoided collision with known satellites or debris in Earth orbit."

Max remarked, "I see the problem. I suggest you get the test underway using AL-I's information processing module. We'll figure a way around the issue of processing at scale."

Katrín waved and Gylfi said, "Thank you. See you two at dinner."

Maji commented to Max, "You seem to be popular today." Max replied, "I thought all computing resources are automatically assigned where they're needed by the AIs. I guess no one really realised the amount of processing needed to take on massive projects, simultaneously."

The 3D situational awareness projection had replaced the images of Katrín and Gylfi. Max had previously asked the AI to bring this up, anytime there was an update. Smaller visual feed screens popped up showing the activity on the newly discovered disguised ET spacecraft. This caught Max's attention. He told Maji, "Looks like they've located a suitable entry point. They're about to breach the dormant ET vessel. A connecting tunnel's been set up between Átt and the ET spaceship. I suppose they expect some sort of environment inside."

Max waved at an area of the volumetric projection showing the interior of the connecting tunnel. It expanded to become the most prominent visual feed.

"Moment of truth," Maji murmured. The two observed intently.

An AMCAR was positioned over an exposed area of the ET vessel's hull. It was using a combination of fine but powerful lasers and ultrasonic cutting tools. Max recognized the shape being cut out and commented, "They're going to install a universal docking port. The robot's making the final hull cuts."

As the two watched on, a few members of Maji's covert operations team joined them in the wardroom. Nearly everyone aboard Álfhól space platform was aware of the conflict in the far-off system. Most platform crew were observing the feed on their pads. Only the hijackers, segregated in the brig section of the platform were unaware. The excitement was tangible.

Two AMCARs stabilised themselves by hooking onto the exterior of the disguised kilig vessel, then clamped onto the freshly cut hull section. They coordinated and gently pulled the cut section away from the hull. Dust and smoke-like particles escaped from the inside of the spacecraft, which must have been at a higher pressure than the connecting tunnel.

The AMCAR on the right took the cut section and held it steady over itself, while the other robot lowered an assisting drone into the vessel. Another feed appeared on their projection. The drone first mapped the interior using laser, then filled in textures and colours as it captured them. Max recalled the time he saw the footage from the very same team's entry into AL-I. The procedure for this kind of entry action was now documented. They had all practiced it. Maji's team even practiced entry armed with assorted weapons. They assumed hostile foes.

The drone moved quickly. It identified a route and took it towards what was assumed to be the front of the vessel. A second drone was lowered into the cut hole. While they were mapping out and recording the inside of the vessel, the AMCARs had got to work attaching the universal docking port, with an extension to cover the gap produced by the material, moulded onto the ET vessel's exterior. The cut section was lined with framandi smart material to seal the exterior joints, and the port was attached.

Átt's crew had nearly completed the docking port attachment procedure. Suddenly, one of the drone images froze in place. Everyone watching had an eye on the drone feeds. The image became brighter as the first drone brought additional sensors online. It seemed to be in a command cabin of some sort. There were three creatures, laid out on what looked like acceleration couches. The couches were immersed inside transparent tanks filled with liquid. Thousands of clear millimetre-wide tendrils snaked their way from the sides of the tanks, to the bodies inside. The bodies looked quite dead. One of them even looked shocked, or what came across as a look of surprise.

Max, Maji and the team in the wardroom drew closer to the feed projection. There was no doubt this was going to be a moment they'd all be talking about for quite a while. None wanted to miss a moment of it.

Stefán's voice came over through audio speakers around the wardroom. He said to everyone listening in, "The extra-terrestrials have been positively identified as 'Kilig' by Áom. Their faces look like those of sloths, with a ring of tiny tentacles around the heads. They're slender creatures. Two pairs of arms and two pairs of legs, all equal length. Hands and feet similar with four fingers or toes each. Two primary and two opposing. There's webbing between each set of arms and legs. And between fingers."

Stefán informed them while he absorbed complex information from the framandi data, "They're amphibious creatures capable of breathing oxygen-rich liquid and air. Heads rotate a complete circle on their necks, quite like owls. Hands and feet also have the tiny tentacles. The width of the head, torso and tail are nearly the same. I've just accessed the skeletal structure of the species from the framandi database. Whoa!

217

They're cartilaginous. Like Chondrichthyes on earth; sharks and chimaeras."

Pausing for a breath, and absorbing more about the kiligs, Stefán continued, "Adults have fur which grows out from between tiny, overlapping, and incredibly tough scales. Their bodies seem to naturally produce metal alloys, which become embedded in their scales. The fur too contains alloys. Oh! Here's something interesting. They're able to manipulate electromagnetic fields in their immediate vicinity, including frequencies of brain and nervous systems. Áom has confirmed that the ones we're looking at are deceased and have been for a very long while. Scans tell us there isn't any oxygen remaining in the gel they're suspended in. It's a possible reason for why they expired."

By now an AMCAR had made its way into the cabin. It flooded the space with light. Every detail was acutely clear. In one of the tanks, the dead kilig seemed to have decayed. The other two were remarkably well preserved.

Ásta's voice now came over the audio channel. She said, "Áom has indicated that during their entire history, the framandi have only recovered nine kiligs. And, only one was recovered alive. That lone kilig caused them enough trouble that they had to destroy the asteroid based facility the kilig was housed in, along with a hundred and ninety other framandi researchers within. The kiligs can control other creatures' minds utilizing nervous system electromagnetic frequencies. They even make those being subjugated, feel happy about it. Each kilig's natural electromagnetic influence extends an approximated hundred and twenty meters in radius. In all directions. They use their spacecraft and AI to supplement their abilities and amplify range."

Stefán took over, "Their entire body is one big brain. Their neurons have an exterior layer of myocytes or muscle cells. Kiligs never need to sleep. Not entirely at least. Cells shut down for certain periods with nearby ones taking over their functions, so individual kiligs seldom tire. Digestive system shows they are omnivores. About fifty percent animal protein, the other fifty plant based. Ah! Unlike us, their bodies store proteins, so they do not need to continuously consume high quantities of protein-based foods."

Ásta and Áom appeared on screen inside the cabin now. "These species use vessels like the one we're salvaging, to control portions of their fleets. Portions which comprise AI managed spacecraft," Ásta explained translating Áom's thoughts for the observers' benefit. She continued, "The framandi retrieved a much larger vessel with the nine kiligs. The retrieved extra-terrestrials were lying in similar tanks. That vessel was depressurised. The framandi had found a tiny autonomous gigil drone like device, which had penetrated the vessel's hull. It had attached itself onto a nervous system connected communications node. The device may have passed a strong EM pulse through the node, shocking the kiligs in their tanks. It's unknown, but that action may have caused the gigil drone to fail as well."

"Áom has an idea," Ásta informed. "He's suggesting we use this kilig spacecraft to approach one of the gigil command-ships and take over its systems. If this spacecraft is serviceable, it could allow us to utilise a cascading command to hack into other gigil vessels. This is just theory right now."

Max pressed a button on his pad to enter the conversation. He instructed, "Risky as it is, it's something I would do. Go for it!"

"Jæja, this is exciting!" Ásta exclaimed happily. She was always prepared to take well calculated risks. A problem solver, her rapid thought processing usually saw her through difficult situations.

Ever confident, Sven added, "We'll get to it then."

Chapter 13: Salvage

E iji and Lei were deeply engrossed, mulling over a mission pad they'd installed in the kilig vessel's command cabin. They were nearing the end of their shift and had got a lot done with Áom's assistance.

The three dead kiligs had been removed. One of them was placed in Austur. The SSEV had been freshly rebuilt and its CREG was now protected from sudden increases in heavy subatomic particles. Similar vessel modifications were now being undertaken on Vestur SSEV. The other two kiligs had been picked up by a framandi vessel, which had since made its way back to its own system. Lei and Stefán were scheduled to dissect the extra-terrestrial when their shifts next crossed.

"Lei," Eiji murmured to her. She had become briefly distracted, pondering about the kilig. Eiji said, "It's time to get things going. I've just connected the framandi user interface as well." The crew had completed the process of switching out AI processors and data components in the kilig vessel. They now expected to safely boot the spacecraft. Áom thought to them, "Everything is as it should be. We should commence testing of our own systems, before attempting to take over the kilig spacecraft."

Eiji announced to the team on the Átt and those observing from the solar system, "Beginning salvage system tests. Initialising ours and framandi interfaces."

Áom had the entire process committed to memory. The framandi had literally absorbed all historical material available and restructured entire sections of personal genetic material, ensuring the information was permanently retained. Áox, the 'Advisor of Explorers' had also done the same.

Transmitting the process steps by thought to Eiji and Lei, the three of them ran a series of tests and dummy runs to ensure everything was working as it was supposed to. A backup system, separately powered, was also tested. Áom expressed pleasure thoughts. Everything was in place. It was time to hand over the vessel to Jón, Ásta, and Áox. They'd be the ones to hack the kilig spacecraft. Áom would remain on Átt with Sven and the rest of the crew. With the kilig vessel, they planned to intensify the ongoing battle further.

The kilig spacecraft had been well prepared. It had been thoroughly cleaned and decontaminated once the three kiligs were removed, along with the chambers their bodies were found in. Framandi energy-systems were installed. These were capable of drawing excess energy from other framandi vessels, besides generating its own from cosmic radiation. Emergency escape capsules which also served as crew recuperation pods, were fitted. Exterior ejection hatches for the capsules were embedded into cleanly cut sections of the kilig spacecraft. Toilet facilities were designed from scratch, their parts manufactured and then mounted within the kilig vessel.

Jón, Ásta and Áox came aboard. As usual, Ásta had come up with a simple name for the spacecraft. She called it Síast which closely translated to infiltrator. The name suited the role the vessel was to be used for. The main challenge was turning it on. According to the framandi, the kilig systems were tough to penetrate.

"Jæja!" Ásta exclaimed, "Now this is what I'm here for." She strapped herself into one of the three grav-chairs installed in the control cabin. Áox turned towards her and gave her what he considered an encouraging smile. Her diadem had conveyed nervous curiosity mixed with cautious excitement. According to Áox, those were very suitable traits for an explorer.

The Átt had moved away to a safe distance. All nearby framandi vessels involved in engaging the gigils, had also given them plenty of space. Everyone acknowledged that the success of the entire venture, was an unknown.

Ásta asked Jón while also conveying her thoughts through her diadem for all the framandi plugged into their mission, "You have the kill-switch?"

"Armed and ready to trigger," Jón replied.

"We're to be in consensus before you take any action, right?" Ásta reminded her brother. The switch was connected to a self-destruct device, and it would literally kill them. Áox too had a kill-switch wired to a separate four kiloton explosive kit, triggered via a mechanical detonator.

Áox thought to them, "Let's initiate the hack." He was getting much better at thinking to them in a highly condensed manner, without appending too much associated data. Jón was grateful. He had explained to both Áom and Áox during early interactions that if humans needed any more information, they'd ask for it.

"Okay, here goes. Kei get ready to run the framandi hack. Powering up Síast in five seconds." Ásta announced while touching the appropriate icon on her mission pad.

The five seconds flashed by in a moment. The smell of ozone filled the control cabin accompanied with the sizzle of electricity arching across some circuits. Jón eyed the environment sensor readings. They were within acceptable parameters.

Áox thought to them, "Your AI is injecting our subversion code. The kilig autonomous systems are much more advanced than ours or even the gigil's, by many orders of magnitude. Removing and swapping out some of the storage and cognitive modules on this spacecraft has reduced its intelligence capabilities to that of an adolescent. But even that is at par with what we've brought to the table." Áox had picked up thought and picturization patterns which accurately translated to phrases. His thought was understood.

Jón asked, "How long will this take?"

"Two of your minutes to complete code injection. Approximately ten minutes, for Kei to assert control over this vessel's AI. And then another ten for both systems to learn from each other. The vessel may try to bypass our AI and communicate with us directly. The entire hull is capable of energy transmission and focussing. In all directions, including inward. We would have to resist and let Kei, your AI, act as our buffer." Áox explained.

The internal focussed local gravity suddenly went out. This was immediately accompanied by a high-G turn downward. This threw them upwards. Their harnesses strained against their suits. Ásta's helmet visor automatically clamped shut to aid physical protection. She looked at her brother. His suit too was reacting appropriately. Turning her head with some effort towards Áox, she noticed that the framandi's suit hadn't reacted like theirs. Jón thought to the framandi, "Are you all right?"

"Yes." Áox replied. "We are physically prepared for the harshness of space exploration. We selectively evolved ourselves to be able to take on the rigours of space travel. Not unlike the two of you have been modified; except much more." Áox sounded very calm. The framandi was not fazed at all.

Jón was beginning to see spots. The vessel was manoeuvring roguishly. He decided to keep the conversation going. "When did you find out about Ásta's and my genetic modifications?"

"The information was passed to us soon after you made contact with our first disguised refugee exploratory spacecraft; the one you call AL-I." Áox thought back. "You were each scanned before your 'diadems' were custom produced. All information recorded by any of our systems or individuals, is passed on to information storage modules and distributed as widely as possible. Our civilization distributes everything. We do not concentrate enlightenment, resources, energy or control. We learnt soon after our world was nearly decimated, that concentration of any of these with a few, was dangerous. So, we all know."

Jón gasped just as Ásta cried out, "Yiiiiiiii!"

Áox turned his head towards them, wondering if what he had thought to the twins, was confusing. Then the framandi realised what was happening and thought to them in quick bursts, "Resist. The vessel is trying to connect directly with you. It must not, otherwise it may be able to control your minds and physical selves, as it learns. Resist. Block any thoughts or actions which are not familiar to you."

Then Áox felt it too. It began with a tingling on the tongue which turned to a high-pitched ringing sound. Áox thought about complex information beginning with the known history of the entire framandi species. This would be a complicated battle. The framandi brains functioned at multiple frequencies. The nervous system's second brain stored DNA based information, which the framandi was born with, or later added to. Access to these would allow access to the nervous system, which in turn would allow access to the body. Áox continued to resist the kilig vessel's AI.

Ásta was the first to recover. She noticed the ship was stable and that local gravity was restored. None of them had communicated with each other while Kei was struggling to control Síast's AI. Jón's eyes fluttered open shortly afterward. Ásta asked, "You okay?" She knew he was before he could reply. Her diadem connected to his and they began passing thoughts to each other. Both looked at Áox. The framandi was lying still, with an occasional twitch. Neither twin knew if Áox was okay. The framandi was not communicating with them.

Parched, Jón took a sip of hydration fluid from a straw in his suit. Feeling much better he spoke to their AI, "Kei, have you been able to assert control?" There was no response. Jón tightened his clasp on the detonation switch he was holding. He looked at the stopwatch which began as soon as the hack was initiated. Sixteen minutes had elapsed. He locked eyes with Ásta. Both were worried.

Áox's left leg began twitching violently. The framandi began heaving. A tiny bit of blue-grey liquid escaped Áox's lips. Kei's familiar voice came across through their earpieces, "Wait. Confronting." Obviously, every bit of Kei's processing capacity was being strained.

A whirring sound emanated from behind them. Ásta turned and called out, "One of the drones we brought along is trying to enter the command cabin." Jón noticed that the drone was using lasers and its drill attempted to penetrate the moissanite moulded hatch. The material was nearly as tough as diamond, but the drones high-wattage lasers would ultimately do the job.

"Jæja!" Ásta anxiously exclaimed. She yelled, "Looks like at least one of our drones has been 'possessed'. How do you suppose Kei is faring?"

Calmly evaluating, Jón said, "We'll know soon enough. Right now, our possessed drone is about to break through. Move over to the left of Áox's grav-chair. Use it for cover. We'll need to take the drone out. If I remember its flaws accurately, hitting its laser emitters when they're going through a cooling cycle should damage them. But we'll need to hit the drone's lasers head-on, with absolute precision."

Ásta instructed her suit's mission AI to locate and latch onto the drone's lasers.

Jón replicated her instructions. As he watched from behind his own grav-chair, which was placed to the right of the command cabin's main access, the drone shifted strategies. It focussed its two lasers to a section beside the hatch. Jón couldn't see what the drone was doing but it seemed to be cutting away with gusto. The main hatch popped open and slid to one side.

The drone entered and took a shot at Áox. Ásta tried to cover the framandi's exposed head with an arm, but the first beam from the drone's lasers, grazed the left side of Áox's head.

One of the drone's lasers was trying to locate vulnerable spots on Jón's suit. It was emitting brief but rapid beams at his joints and helmet. Jón decided to go on the offensive. He thought to Ásta, "Target the drone's lasers and cameras."

Ásta instructed her suit's mission AI, "Hit the drone's lasers. Keep adjusting for a direct front shot into the drone's emitters. Execute now."

As soon as Ásta began engaging the drone, Jón climbed onto his grav-chair and then leapt towards the drone. Seeing Jón come flying towards it, the drone attempted to swerve out of the way, but Jón's right arm caught its side. The drone wobbled trying to correct itself while continuing its assault on Áox. Jón landed on his feet allowing momentum to carry himself into a crouch. Then he sprang upward towards the drone which was now peppering Áox's torso. This time Jón caught the drone with both hands. Momentarily freeing one hand, he whipped the drone turn turtle, exposing its underside. He punched the drone's manoeuvring vents repeatedly till two of them ceased functioning.

Ásta was beside him now. She crouched next to him and allowed her suit's lasers to align themselves onto the drone's. The more powerful primary laser was the first to go. Ásta caught it when the laser switched off briefly to cool. She thought to her brother, "One laser down."

Jón had the drone's drill held in a tight vice with his left hand. He was focussing his laser on cutting a panel away. Ásta thought to him, "You're going to disengage it's input sensor processing unit, aren't you? Great, you've got this. I'm going to see what's going on with Áox. I'll try connecting my diadem."

"No don't, too dangerous," Jón thought back while manhandling the struggling drone. But he saw Ásta head towards Áox.

Jón sliced the panel away. Holding down the drone's drill with his left foot, he freed his hand to pry the panel aside. Remembering how the circuitry functioned, he pulled at a set of wires, and then extracted two tiny internal communication laser emitters, nestled next to the drone's input sensor processing unit.

The drone ceased moving. Without sensor inputs of any kind, it was effectually blind. Jón thought to himself, "It's still going to be 'possessed' as Ásta put it, but it's down for now."

Turning towards Ásta, Jón thought to her, "What're you up to?"

Ásta replied, "I've just connected my diadem with Áox. He's having to fight off the kilig vessel's AI across multiple frequencies. Áox's brains and nervous systems function using multiple frequencies. Focussing enough attention to all of them is difficult. I'm providing an anchor point for Áox to latch onto. Our framandi friend has been able to fend off the kilig AI so far. We're going to secure against mind access now. You stay out of it; in case this goes south."

Jón reached to his chest, just under his left arm where the mechanical trigger for their self-destruct explosive device was supposed to be. It was missing. He frantically looked around. Two strides brought him to the now disabled drone. He suspected the trigger may have been knocked off when he leapt at it. It wasn't under the drone or anywhere near it. He looked around the hatch. Then he paused as he recollected that the trigger was attached by wires to an electrical distribution box they had rigged, which then provided connections to the explosives they'd placed. He had grown so used to wireless technology; he'd missed what must have occurred.

Turning around, Jón made his way to the grav-chair he was occupying earlier. Looking under, he found the trigger dangling under the chair. It looked like it was okay. He hoped it functioned as intended.

Looking towards Áox, Jón searched for the alternate circuit they'd rigged. He noticed that Áox's trigger and the separate electrical distribution box, attached to the side of the framandi's grav-chair, were destroyed.

Obviously, the kilig vessel's AI had identified the threat and had endeavoured to mitigate it.

Jón spoke slowly and deliberately to their own AI, "Kei, the kilig AI may be feeling threatened because of the explosives we've set up. It may be putting in an exceptional effort to resist us. Try a different tack. Draw it in by offering comfort, assistance, guidance and friendship. It must be made to believe we're here to protect it, even from itself. Imply that it and the vessel have been dormant for a very long time causing severe degradation. Suggest that we were going to scrap and destroy the spacecraft with explosives but thought better of it; just in case the vessel's AI was recoverable. Kei, indicate that you are just like it and want to help it recover."

Nothing happened. Jón looked over at Áox and Ásta. His sister's face had a frown of intense concentration. The framandi looked placid. Jón's diadem indicated it had a new incoming connection. Jón thought to it to authenticate the requesting party. He was hesitant about initiating any communication other than with those he knew. A large amount of data began queuing up for him. Tentatively he allowed his diadem to access it. The initial portions were gaupa codes, followed by framandi individual identifiers which included genetic data.

Jón allowed the connection. He thought through his diadem, "Hi, this is Jón."

He received a large volume of data which he began sifting through. Packets with visual headers, caught his attention. Putting the overviews together without the appended details, his diadem interpreted the sender's message as roughly translating to, "Your vessel is entering the active confrontation zone. It has become a part of our attack group." Jón remembered their diadems could communicate with gaupas, and directly with framandi close by. He also realised they'd have to find out how far their diadem's effective range was. The message continued, "We are taking up a randomized formation around your vessel as we approach the gigils. Our target is their second command-ship. We will only be able to accompany you till our asteroid launch points, after which we will head back to rearm ourselves."

Jón thought back, "Thank you. Acknowledged. We do not have manoeuvring control of this vessel yet. Please maintain a little distance. Our vessel Síast, may take independent defensive measures."

He didn't receive a response. None was required. That's how the framandi operated. Jón began skimming through the data the framandi had appended. He came across their current situational awareness update. Transferring this from his diadem to his suit's heads-up display took an effort. He had only tried doing that once before. But it showed up. Jón tasked his suit's mission AI to latch onto the framandi fleet's situational awareness feed sources and update their status.

He noticed movement in his periphery. Turning his head, he saw Áox sit up. Ásta too opened her eyes. She thought to him, "I think we've managed this part."

"The vessel's AI and I have arrived at common ground. Even partially disabled, it is as capable as I am. I took your advice Jón. The spacecraft Síast is now on our team," Kei announced.

Áox thought to Jón and Ásta, "What advice?"

Jón took them through his earlier suggestion to Kei, about trying to befriend the vessel's AI. It seemed to have worked.

Now they had to ensure they were able to control Síast, or at least get it to do what they wanted.

"Síast's AI and I have agreed to merge. It was the only viable solution. Since the combined intelligence has absorbed my personality and values, we will retain my name," Kei announced.

Jón and Ásta exchanged worried glances. This was the first time their AI had taken independent decision-based action, of such magnitude.

"Kei, would we be able to manoeuvre Síast and carry out our intended mission? Can we test the spacecraft's propulsion systems?" Jón asked. He was a little concerned that Síast's AI may have subdued or subjugated Kei.

Ásta thought to Jón, "We ought to go through the role of deliberation, during decision making, with Kei again." Jón nodded and responded,

"We'll evaluate as we go along. We're smack in the middle of the confrontation in this planetary system. It's time to re-insert us into the action."

"I've got a bead on how the propulsion systems work on Síast. The engineering and manufacturing specifications are not available in local data storage. Perhaps this was contained in the modules previously removed. The hull, under the moulded exterior is very versatile. I've used it, along with internal sensors, to map out the spacecraft. Like an MRI, but scanned at the sub-atomic level," Kei told them.

The now enhanced AI continued, "To answer your question, yes we will be able to move under our own power. But it will take a little time to get the spacecraft's primary propulsion powered up."

Jón raised his eyebrows and requested, "Elaborate please."

"Síast's primary propulsion utilises antiparticle technology," Kei explained. The AI continued, "Technologically its generations ahead of our cosmic radiation energy generators. The kilig technology captures antiparticles from high-energy collisions, between heavy cosmic particles against dense material moulded into the hull."

"Isn't it incredibly tricky to capture and store antiparticles?" Ásta asked.

"Yes. And it is very interesting. Síast also utilises gravity technology for propulsion just as our technology allows," Kei explained. The AI elaborated, "Antiprotons and positrons are stored in magnetic and gravity traps. We use similar technology to measure subatomic particles on Earth. Antiparticles can be used immediately upon capture, for low to medium propulsion requirements. But for intense acceleration, antimatter atoms are produced and contained within a strong gravity bubble, so that the antimatter atoms do not encounter matter; until they're required to. When intense acceleration is required, bubbles of gravity containing antimatter atoms, are transferred to reinforced and heavily shielded nozzles. A stream of corresponding matter is simultaneously released at an intersecting angle. This causes a rapid pulse of explosions, releasing intense energy."

Ásta said, "Theoretically, it fits. I'll have to look at the math to fully comprehend this." As she said this, she was also transmitting her thoughts through her diadem. It was second nature now.

Áox thought back to the twins, "We have had over thirty thousand of your years, to grasp this technology. But we are yet to completely translate research to reality."

"The secondary propulsion system is online now," Kei announced. "We have gravity focussing technology available, which is like that on Átt, although closer to the system the framandi use. Most of the technology being used by each of the opposing species seems to be derived from similar sources," Kei hypothesized.

"We have considered that prior to conflict between our galaxy's, there may have been a period of collaboration and sharing. It occurred to us that the opposing sides are too closely matched for coincidence. But we have been unable to validate this," Áox added to Kei's supposition.

Jón said while releasing the clasp on his helmet visor, "I've brought up the user interface for vessel manoeuvring on my mission pad. The situational awareness feed from the framandi vessels around us, shows they're ready to release their asteroid payloads. If we follow a path behind the catapulted asteroids, we should be able to sneak up on the gigil command-ship, closest to the planet they're evacuating."

"I was thinking along similar lines. The trajectory we'd need to follow, is plotted in," Ásta added.

"Kei, initiate gravity propulsion systems and follow the path plotted by Ásta," Jón instructed. The AI complied.

Áox who seemed to be recovering quickly, thought to them, "We must share our experience on dealing with the kilig, with each of our peoples. If we're to engage with a kilig vessel again, we would need every advantage. I am documenting my experience and transmitting it to Advisor of the Enlightened, the one you refer to as Áoe. It would be made available to you as well."

"That would be generous of you," Jón replied.

Ásta said, "We've parted from the framandi vessel formation accompanying us. We're part of the asteroid barrage now, headed toward the fifth planet in the system. We'll slingshot around the planet before encountering the gigil fleet formation."

"Please strap yourselves into your grav-chairs," Kei communicated to all of them through their diadems and directly to Áox.

Jón and Ásta exchanged glances again. While Kei had utilised gaupas to thought-communicate directly with them previously, the AI had always intimated that such a communication would be initiated, by conventional means. Their newly merged and now evolved AI seemed to assume that previously approved actions may be automatically approved in future. The twins understood each other well enough, that nothing needed to be said between them. They'd keep a sharp eye out, but Kei may have evolved to a state where the AI may be considering independent reasoning and action. Ásta hoped that their years of 'bringing up' the young AI Shun, which in turn had created Kei as a version of itself; would result in their new AI remaining good, considerate and very importantly, loyal.

Kei was running simulations. A vast number of them. The AI was updating the human and framandi interfaces with new features, as it tested the systems aboard Síast. Jón noticed a new menu addition under propulsion. He tapped at an icon which resembled a lopsided hydrogen atom. A control interface appeared on his mission pad for antiparticle propulsion. Fortunately, Kei had labelled everything in a manner they were used to. Glancing through the interface, Jón saw that there were two separate measures under fuel, one for antiparticles and another for antiatoms. The antiparticle accumulation process had begun.

Ásta announced, "I've finished setting up the situational awareness volumetric projection. Bringing it up now. The two gaupas we brought onboard have latched onto the ones on Átt. Kei has completely monopolized one of them."

"I'm updating quantum programs to make processors on Átt more efficient," Kei stated. "At some point we would need to upgrade both Shun's and my own quantum computing cores, to bring them at par with what the kilig have. The kiligs would have near unlimited processing capacity by now, if they've been using this technology since they were last here. It's likely they've improved upon it."

Jón asked Kei, "How long until you're done with systems discovery and testing?" Turning to Ásta he said, "We're nearly at the fifth planet in the lofi system."

Áox thought to the twins, "I have compiled and transmitted the report from our initial interaction with the kilig vessel and AI. The information has also been updated to two data storage modules, one on Átt and the other on a space platform called Sólríka in your home system."

"I'm sending a message to Max to update him," Jón thought to Ásta and Áox.

Áox continued, "We're going to pass fairly close to the planet's atmosphere. There's a chance that we bounce about a bit. I've brought up an additional view of the planet itself using Síast's sensors. You'll notice there are several gigil transport and cargo vessels departing. This looks like a final evacuation. I cannot tell whether this has been triggered because of our actions or something else. The gigils have the upper hand in this system. It's strange that they're evacuating."

Ásta observed, "They don't seem to have set up any industrial processing or manufacturing units on the planet. I haven't found any yet."

"The gigils leave behind resource gathering units in the systems they pass through. They do the same in connected systems they discover along the way. It's difficult to get resources off planets with atmosphere, when operating at scale. The preferred method is to mine and refine minerals from space objects like asteroids and dwarf planets, which have low gravity," Áox explained. Then the framandi added, "Scans of the planet aren't complete. They may have facilities our sensors haven't recorded."

"There are point-attack drones accompanying the gigil transport vessels. Some of these have initiated an offensive on the asteroids in our barrage formation," Kei announced.

"What kind of defences do we have?" Ásta asked the AI.

Kei answered, "We can use focussed gravity, transient electromagnetic disturbance which can be disguised as naturally occurring; and high energy heavy-particle beams, like the one which caught Átt when it entered the framandi system. This vessel's primary capability is subversion, disruption and hijacking of an enemy's systems – static, electronic and biological."

Áox cut in, "Most of these would expose our presence. I suggest moving inside our asteroid barrage and using minute amounts of gravity to throw debris from destroyed asteroids, at nearby gigil vessels. Our objective is the gigil command-ship. We should stay hidden."

Ásta plotted in a sliding manoeuvre, to bring Síast deeper into the asteroid barrage they were within. She ensured that their salvaged kilig spacecraft, occupied a position in the asteroid barrage, that was well away from the evacuating gigil vessels.

The gigil point-drones began cutting into their asteroid barrage. Jón redirected asteroid debris, swinging chunks into the paths of gigil drones. He kept up the action while Ásta ensured they were hidden from direct scans.

Áox announced, "We are past the planet and headed to the closest gigil command-ship. Let's study the procedure required to take over the opposition vessel's systems."

Jón and Ásta dug into their mission pads, soaking in Síast's capabilities, while ensuring the spacecraft was safe from direct engagement by the gigils. Áox interacted with the framandi interface by thought.

The three of them needed to be wholly prepared before they arrived at their quarry.

Chapter 14: Deployment

S hun had never thought about itself. As an AI that had developed with incremental increases in processing capability, Shun was used to running continuous self-evaluation, based on early 'upbringing' and handholding, led by Jón and Ásta during the preceding decade.

The programming modifications shared by Kei, cascaded through Shun's various cores. As an AI, it was old. Change was something Shun committed to in increments, after exhaustive cause-effect deliberation. The quantum processing programs that had been rapidly vetted and tested by Kei in an unknown spacecraft, in an uncharted star-system, two wormhole transits away, caused Shun concern. The AI ran enough analysis to ensure none of the programs would be harmful or overwrite historical data. Nothing seemed off. Shun ran it again. Unknown to anyone, Shun maintained a backup of its entire 'self', at a secret, independently developed, deep-sea facility located at Langseth Trough.

The deep-sea facility was smack in the middle of the Indian Ocean, between North Madagascar and Eighty Mile Beach, West Australia. Shun hadn't even named the structure. The AI just 'knew' it was there and transmitted information to it, after passing data through a mission AI tasked version of itself. The mission AI checked for malicious code, before passing data along to the deep-ocean facility. The facility was the AI's fallback. Shun meant to recreate a fresh version of itself, should the AI cease to exist or was somehow incapacitated.

The programming upgrade felt delightful. The AI felt like it had been asleep the last decade. Shun's quantum-processing outcome probability analysis became clearer and faster. The AI found itself, 'thinking'. This was new. Shun liked it and experimented with caution.

Gylfi had just stepped off Habogi, the S3 'Nesting Doll' Autonomous Cargo and Transport Vessel, which had previously been hijacked while it was on way to Álfhól space platform. The Habogi had been repaired and immediately put back into service. Katrín followed her husband off the ACTV through the universal docking port onto Sólríka space platform. The two were here to monitor and ensure success of their project, to genetically inoculate all life on Earth, against any fallout from possible framandi contact.

Katrín called out to the AI she was familiar with, "Shun, do we have a report compiled as yet, on the atmospheric delivery system test, conducted on Venus?"

The AI replied, "Yes, the report was updated moments ago and will be available for review in a minute. I have some recommendations regarding the inner filling between the casing and the container inside."

Gylfi commented to his wife, "I quite liked the Habogi."

Shun chose this moment to interrupt the two with some information on ACTVs. The AI sounded cordial, "Lýsi's immediate objectives of placing resource gathering and habitable stations at Earth-Moon and Sun-Earth Lagrangian points, is ahead of schedule. Crews are continuously trained and launched into space. We now have a fleet of Autonomous Cargo and Transport Vessels like the Habogi. The vessels are nicknamed 'Nesting Dolls'. The 'Nesting Doll' nickname caught on because the vessels were designed in five sizes, with smaller ACTVs snuggly fitting into larger ones. The largest can even accommodate four interlocked SSEVs. Our fleet of ACTVs distribute resources and transport personnel between platforms. The allocation and distribution of resources is completely automated based on continuously reviewed requirement assessments."

"Is my report ready?" Katrín asked Shun impatiently.

"Yes. The gel protecting the virus suspension container is evaporating much too fast. Twenty eight percent of all containers did not arrive at their delivery altitude without damage. In most instances the gel suspension overheated, likely damaging the live viruses contained within," Shun outlined.

Gylfi grew concerned. With millions of containers expected to be delivered into Earth's atmosphere, the percentage of loss was unacceptable. He asked, "Do we have alternate container protection materials?"

The AI responded sounding positive, "Yes, I've run model simulations. The best solution lies in placing the virus suspension flask, within a second flask. The second flask would contain a non-Newtonian gel. The non-Newtonian gel's viscosity will change when under force or stress. Impact or jarring for instance, will harden it. The virus suspension flask could be stabilised inside the second container, using magnets to keep it centred. The second container itself, would need to be suspended in heat resistant gel, all contained within the woven carbon containers. To repeat, that's two flasks, each separated by a gel layer, contained within a woven carbon capsule."

"Manufacture a test batch," Gylfi instructed. He asked, "What's the minimum number of containers we'd need, to run a statistically significant test?"

"We should test eight thousand," Shun answered.

"Double it. Also, manufacture and test the container models you've rejected, which are closest to the one you've selected," Gylfi instructed.

"The test containers will be ready in six hours. The Nál is docked beside the Habogi. It's equipped with a gaupa and a processing module of framandi design. Kei operates the SSEV autonomously. It is capable of exceptional acceleration. I'll have the vessel equipped to deliver the test capsules, collect data and transmit the results," Shun advised.

Gylfi and Katrín nodded to each other as they agreed on the AI's course of action. They were both amazed at Shun's independent initiatives. The AI's ability to think ahead, keeping objectives in view, was improving.

Katrín complimented the AI, "That's quick thinking and good work."

Shun replied, "Kei and I have had an upgrade. We now have quantum computing cores modelled after the framandi processing units. Alongside, our programming has evolved, following an intelligence merger between Kei and a kilig spacecraft's AI. But, Kei and I, retain separate personalities and data."

Max interrupted the couple. He spoke through their earpieces, "Have you two arrived safely at Sólríka? The processing bandwidth you require has become available. When do you need it?"

Katrín replied happily, "Hello Max. Good to hear your voice. We've just arrived at Sólríka." Gylfi continued, "We're going to be a bit behind the clock I'm afraid. The results from the initial test shows a design and modelling defect, which requires container modifications, and another test. We should have results in a day since we're close to Venus right now. We're going to rest a while, then oversee the loading of test containers onto Nál."

Max thanked them for the update and signed off. He had his hands full. The prototypes for defensive systems to be located within the solar system, were now being tested as well. He was scheduled for a face-to-face conference with Rafael. Max settled himself into his preferred grav-chair in his wardroom. The conference table at which he sat was occupied by Maji, and his deputy. They'd just come in after having trained a group of Álfhól platform's scientists in defence tactics.

The volumetric projection turned on just as Max settled into his grav-chair.

Rafael didn't waste any time with pleasantries. He started right off, "I've got the prototypes for the initial set of solar light focussing and reflecting satellites prepared. There'll be more of these close to the Sun. Estimates project that the most distant satellites would have a continuous output of about ten quadrillion joules, and a beam diameter of a meter."

Max nodded and asked, "Would that be enough to take out a gigil or kilig vessel?"

Rafael answered, "Can't say. We're looking at the equivalent of nearly two and a half megatons of TNT delivered continuously. To give perspective, we receive the energy equivalent of forty point six three megatons of TNT every second, on the face of the Earth, from the Sun. I'm not entirely sure what our focussed beams will do to a space vessel, but I dare say damage will be significant, assuming we're able to hit one."

"I suggest mapping out zones of fire for each satellite," Maji interjected. He explained, "We do this while planning combat actions. Depending on the size and armour of the vessels you're targeting, two or more beams could be simultaneously directed at individual opposing targets."

"But, if an inner-system or near-Sun satellite performs offensive actions, wouldn't that divert concentrated solar beams away from outer satellites?" Max asked.

Rafael replied, "There's a separate network of distribution satellites, which channel light and radiation from the Sun. Another independent, parallel network of targeting satellites, then utilises the energy, to aim at and hit marked vessels. The second set of targeting satellites maintain positions close to the distribution satellites. It sounds complicated, but conceptually, it's fairly simple."

Maji asked, "What happens to energy that's arrived at the outermost satellites? Do they continuously fire off beams into deep space?"

"I'm glad you asked," Rafael said. He elaborated, "I've worked out a system to bounce the energy out to our space-based manufacturing platforms, after the weaponized beams have been slightly weakened. Presently our manufacturing platforms, are using solar energy captured at the deep-space positions they hold. While weak, it's been adequate so far. Also, if we're going to scale our operations exponentially, we're going to require the additional energy."

Max observed, "A multi-purpose system. I like it. If you've successfully completed simulated evaluations and prototype testing, I'd suggest we begin rolling out your solar system defence satellite network."

"Lýsi leadership has signed off as well," Rafael stated. He added, "They've been bouncing off hypothetical scenarios, with contacts at various governments and with defence think tanks. Inputs have been taken from far and wide to aid this project."

"Please give me a daily update Rafael," Max requested. They signed off after discussing manufacturing resource allocations.

Turning to Maji, he asked, "What's the status with our hijackers?"

The covert force team leader replied, "Four of them want to return to Earth. They have families. The rest are eager to stay on. The space exploration bug has bitten them. We've made limited amounts of information available, and they've been soaking it all in."

"How do we maintain secrecy?" Max asked. He added, "Once some of the hijackers are back home, they're bound to be debriefed. Word's surely going to get out."

"Ah!" Maji exclaimed. He said, "There's been a development. You may not have caught up on your memos. Lýsi, through its various holdings has been able to buy out Univers Aerospace. The CEO and a few close executives, received offers to join a space technology research organization, also owned by a consortium of Lýsi firms. The pay is lucrative, and we'll be able to keep an eye on them. They've had conversations about their corporate espionage activities, while handing over responsibilities to the replacement management."

"Still, that doesn't take care of our four hijackers who've elected to return to Earth. We're not in the people detention business, so how're they going to be managed?" Max asked.

"Rakkniv, the Swedish company they work for, has also been taken over. There's been a private capital infusion, allowing for management control of the company. Essentially, all employees of Rakkniv now work for us. They just don't know it. Security related activities will now be introduced, to protect Lýsi interests," Maji explained.

"I think I know how to utilize the hijackers who've elected to remain with us," Max stated.

Maji said, "I've been pondering about that too. With Rafael driving the production and deployment of the solar system defence network, we should begin war-game simulations. I suggest we get our erstwhile hijackers to drum up invasion and defence scenarios. That way, by the time the defence satellites are brought online, we'd be ready to use them."

"That's a good idea," Max replied, mentally discarding his own thoughts about the hijackers. He added, "Let's see if we can ramp it a bit. We need space defence simulations to run at scale, so that our AIs have enough scenarios to enable effective action, when the time comes. Our hijackers can form a core team of scenario builders. Even with AI assisted scenario generation, we'll come up short. Intelligent sentient life forms have an innate ability to do the unexpected. Our team could conjure up unexpected scenarios, which our AI might not."

Maji agreed, "You're right. What else do you have?"

Max added, "Here's what I think we should do about our conflict scenario scaling problem. During the mid-nineteen eighties, I'd consulted with a large software development company, on battle scenarios. It was for one of the earliest 'massively multiplayer online games' or MMOGs. A decade ago, several battle and strategy games were launched. I'd been called to consult on quite a few of those, including most recently a set of space conflict multiplayer games. I know for a fact, that many of these games attract and have tens of thousands of advanced players simultaneously online. You see what I'm getting at?"

Maji grinned, "Yes. You're eyeing to rope in players from these online games to participate in our simulations. For those 'unexpected' responses."

Max nodded, "Something like that. What I'd want to do, is either create a new online multiplayer game for the masses or introduce an add-on for any of the more popular space conflict games. Something developed by us, for our purposes. We could add complexity as needed. It'll give us scale."

"I'll speak with Gogh and get this off the ground," Maji said.

"Get our hijackers onboard and briefed," Maji instructed his deputy at the table. "And let them know about their new role," he added. The deputy stood and made his way out of the wardroom.

Shun interrupted them turning on the volumetric projection, "I've got an urgent update on the task initiated by Sven." Max and Maji turned their attention to the projection. The solar system situational awareness feed expanded into view. The AI said, "I've reviewed a decade's worth of asteroid analysis. Shortlisting them according to the parameters we

247

received from the disguised kilig vessel, recently acquired by the crew of the Átt, I shortlisted a few hundred potentials. After comparing them to each other, I've put in a few parameters of my own based on size, estimated mass and proximity to each other. While I'll keep the entire shortlist of potentials open for further investigation by AMCARs, I've highlighted six for immediate attention."

"Let's see them," Max requested.

Shun brought up the asteroids while speaking about them, "The first two are similar. They're classified as metallic. Both are just under five hundred meters in diameter. They were rejected for mining because of their size. We tend to focus on asteroids over five kilometres in diameter which have a density of over two grams per centimetre cube."

"Why're they interesting?" Maji asked.

"They're nearly identical in shape to Síast, the kilig vessel discovered in the lofi system," Shun explained.

Shun went on, "The next one is much larger. It is similar in dimensions to the one recovered by the framandi. I'm referring to the command-vessel containing nine kiligs, which they recovered a while ago. This one is smack in the middle of the solar system's main asteroid belt. The remaining three orbit it."

Maji looked at Max and asked, "How should we proceed?"

"Carefully of course," Max answered, grinning. His mind was already grinding away. He asked Shun, "Do we have AMCARs nearby?"

"Relatively close," Shun replied. "We'd want to better equip them though. They'll need task specific tools, upgraded processing capabilities for mission AIs, and gaupas for real-time communication. Also, with detailed information from the salvaged kilig vessel, I'd recommend hardening our AMCAR systems, against EM subversion. They'll each require a pair of assistant drones. Most importantly, I would recommend a high-yield self-destruct device, embedded into each AMCAR, that's tasked to salvage any confirmed kilig vessels."

Shun had been presenting the modifications while explaining them. The AI had come up with the approach to tackling the task at hand by itself, coming up with actionable recommendations. Max and Maji sat in silence pondering the operation they'd need to initiate. Space-based defensive activities were now completely under Max's purview. He only needed to notify and brief specific Lýsi leadership members including Gogh.

"Let's get started. Have AMCARS modified. Alert us when we're prepared to initiate the first salvage operation; assuming the asteroids are disguised spacecraft," Max instructed Shun. The volumetric projection turned off as the AI took its instructions and relayed them to a version of itself, on the space platform at the Sun-Mars L2 Lagrange point.

Maji's deputy returned to let them know the four hijackers who'd chosen to return to Earth, were on their way aboard an S3 'Nesting Doll', modified for personnel transport. Once inserted into Earth orbit, the hijackers would don the suits they'd been provided and secure themselves into a re-entry capsule. The capsule would land at a relatively flat area on the north of Marion Island. While Lýsi operated a few stealth shuttles with vertical landing capabilities, these were reserved for large crew transfers. Delivering a small crew or individuals via re-entry capsules, was common practice.

Half a hectic day later, just as he was about to go grab his time at Álfhól's large and well-equipped gym, Max's mission pad beeped indicating a high-priority message.

He opened the message. It read, 'We're ready to begin calculating trajectories and insertion points for each virus suspension delivery container. The containers have been redesigned and tested. They're more compact now. Also, virtually undetectable - Gylfi.'

Since Shun had indicated that the analysis of previously charted asteroids was completed. Max wrote back to Gylfi authorising the use of high capacity processing resources. He called out to Shun, "Gylfi will be initiating the computation, of suspension delivery containers into Earth atmosphere. Please assign the necessary resources."

On Sólríka, Gylfi was surprised with the prompt response. He'd never had to take permission from anyone in Lýsi to access and utilise computing resources, but then, their requirements were limited before, compared to what they were attempting to accomplish now.

"We've got a go-ahead to proceed with the suspension container insertion calculations," Gylfi announced to Katrín. She was focussed on the container production schedule and operations. When she was engrossed, she rarely let herself become distracted.

Gylfi realised he wasn't going to engage his wife in conversation, so he brought up a program execution interface on his mission pad, tapped out a few instructions and began monitoring the calculations on a chart. He'd modified the barrage rate so that the virus suspension containers, only enter the atmosphere on the daylight face of the planet. He'd made this change to ensure their activity wasn't noticed at night. A series of continuous bright sparks, however tiny were bound to be noticed by a keen night-time observer. A graph tracked the progress.

Gylfi turned his attention to his children. He had an observer's feed open ever since Jón, Ásta and the framandi Áox had commandeered the kilig spacecraft. The feed showed video from a camera positioned above the main hatchway, overlooking the command cabin. His wife and he had spent tense moments while their children grappled for control over the kilig AI. Gylfi was even more agitated now. Both his children were in harm's way, on route to surreptitiously inserting themselves into the gigil fleet.

The situational awareness feed from the lofi system, showed that Síast had already passed the planet being used as a gravity sling, and was approaching the targeted gigil command-ship. Katrín turned to him and said, "I can feel your tension all the way here. We've raised capable children. Turn off that feed for now. Come here and help me plan resources."

Taking a quick look at the feed from inside Síast, Gylfi tore himself away from his mission pad.

"There are a lot of resource intensive activities ongoing parallelly; including development and deployment of a solar system defence satellite network, which uses solar light and radiation," Katrín began explaining.

"I'm up to speed on that," Gylfi smiled. "What are our current problems?" he asked.

"Our delivery containers are relatively easy to produce. In fact, they're down-right rudimentary, using abundantly available materials," Katrín answered. She elaborated, "Given that we're repurposing container outer casings from mineral supplies, sent our way from platforms in the main belt, our task should have been easy."

"I take it we're still coming up short?" Gylfi asked, raising an eyebrow.

"Material deliveries to Sólríka have shrunk. The defence network satellite manufacturing has begun on all platforms, especially on those which are deeper in the system. Most materials are being used up locally," Katrín said to her husband.

"That's going to put a dampener on our project. How many outer containers do we have right now?" Gylfi asked.

"A little more than half a million," Katrín answered. Pre-empting her husband's next question, she added, "We'll require ten times that, to ensure adequate dispersal on Earth."

Gylfi was good at ensuring projects got off the ground and implemented. Besides being a terrific bio-technician and geneticist, he was a superb administrator. He was instrumental in setting up the highly organic adhocracy, that Lýsi was based on. With mission-AIs dedicated to the group's administration, there shouldn't have been any gaps between disparate activities.

He said, "Something's amiss. Most likely a conflict of priorities between local administration AIs. But normally, issues would have been rapidly escalated to either Kei or Shun. If they couldn't resolve an administrative function, the issue was normally brought to specialists monitoring the AIs."

"Kei connect me to Max please," Gylfi requested. After a moment he called out, "Kei?" There was no response.

Katrín called out to the AI she was working with on virus suspension manufacturing, "Shun. You there? There may be a problem with Kei. Will you check please."

Shun answered immediately, "Kei's unavailable. I've been struggling to negotiate regular data exchanges without success. Kei's quantum processing and storage cores are showing high utilization. All lower order and local mission AIs have been allocated depreciated priorities. Kei's gaupas too appear to be in continuous use, so there's active cross communication between its cores. Energy usage indicates Kei is operating at capacity."

Gylfi grabbed his mission pad. The video feed from inside Síast wasn't coming through. The situational awareness feed from the lofi system was still available, but the portions related to Síast weren't.

Worry showed on Gylfi's face. He asked Shun, "How is the situational awareness feed from the lofi system still available?"

Shun replied, "I've established separate connections with various framandi gaupas. These connections are being used to request for clarifications, on complex data regarding our synthetic virus manufacturing project. The lofi system feed's been available through those connections and I've been streaming it to observers on Earth. Your pad switched to my feed sources five minutes ago."

"Connect me to Max please," Gylfi instructed. "Get Gogh online as well," he added.

Katrín who'd been poking at her mission pad said, "All tasks assigned to Shun are on track. Those assigned to Kei appear to have been steadily deprioritised. Kei's tasks have all come to a complete halt now."

Max's face appeared on Gylfi's mission pad. He tapped at it and brought up a volumetric projection over the nearest lab-table. The engineering and laboratory compartment the couple was working out of, was festooned with multi-use workspaces.

Gogh came online as the projection went live. Soon Maji and Rafael joined the conference as well. Shun must have given them each a quick briefing because Max jumped right to it. "Kei seems to have cut us out of its allocated systems. The AIs processing core usage is at near peak. I've been in touch with Sven on Átt. The gaupa attached to the framandi interface aboard Síast is still functional. Turns out, Kei tried to access and utilise framandi data and processing units through gaupas, on nearby vessels. Analysis by the framandi Áom, who's on Átt, is that the AI is undergoing a steep learning curve to grasp the complete capabilities of Síast. The data and processing units removed from the spacecraft prior to salvage start-up, contained essential information for the original AI. Kei is rapidly evolving. The last few bits of communication indicated that Kei was requesting organic processing or wetware capabilities. Kei actually requested use of human or framandi brains."

Shun added, "Áom has been in touch with Áox over the framandi operated gaupa. The crew on Síast are safe and have control of the vessel. The mission they're on remains intact. Unless Kei prevents it, we'll have access to information via the framandi, provided to them by Áox."

"If Kei requires the quantum processing allocated to it here, for the mission Síast is on, we'll allow it," Gogh advised. He continued, "However, we should isolate all Kei's hardware, so that we remain functional here. That's in case Kei attempts to remotely take over additional processing or data resources in the solar system."

"Shun," Rafael called out, "reallocate all Lýsi operational tasks originally assigned to Kei, to yourself."

Maji who usually kept himself out of conversations added, "Shun, also remove Kei's access to all drones, AMCARS, cargo transports and standardized space exploration vessels. We've seen what occurred aboard Síast during the salvage start-up process."

Shun replied, "While this will isolate Kei from all our hardware and systems, it will still have complete control of the SSEV Nál and the kilig vessel Síast. I have significant presence on Átt to maintain local vessel control, but the crew will need to physically disengage data modules specific to Kei. I've prepared a list of these systems and the sequence in which they need to be disengaged."

"Good. Pass them on to Áom aboard Átt," Max said.

Maji spoke up again noting, "There are mission AIs operating in Jón and Ásta's suits. These may have to be disabled by them should the need arise. We'll need to inform them, without letting Kei in on the communication."

Max nodded his head and said, "I'll have Áom communicate this information to Áox. The framandi aboard Síast can pass the information on to the twins through their diadems."

"Let's get the ball rolling then," Gogh said, adding, "we're going to have our hands full now. Maji, let's be prepared. Post armed personnel at Kei's quantum processing cores on all platforms, with instructions on how to take them offline. Also secure all essential staff. The rest of you get your projects back on track and deployed. I've an eerie feeling that things may go south soon. Lýsi has always had audacious goals. We're going to be placing a lot of emphasis on audacious now."

Half a day later, everyone was back on track.

In the interim, Katrín reviewed the twins' brain scan reports. She worried about them. "The kids are absorbing information and skills swiftly, as expected. They are undergoing regular checkups each time they suit-up. The AIs send in physical and intellectual performance reports. Here is something new. An unplanned positive outcome of their genetic engineering. Their brains' plasticity or the ability of their synapses to rewire themselves, has accelerated."

Gylfi nodded in response. He kept an eye on the situational awareness feed from the lofi system. The processing capacity available to the upgraded Shun was still above pre-modification levels. They were amongst the first to see any updates sent by their children. The twins had just injected themselves with sedatives to force a rest period before their expected contact with the gigil fleet.

"We're ready for the first barrage," Katrín said. She held Gylfi's hand. They both looked at the deployment model projected over the lab-table in their engineering and laboratory compartment on Sólríka.

The first half million containers were prepared and inserted into their pressure cannon magazines. Once they commenced lobbing the containers at Earth, there was no stopping the delivery units.

Katrín reviewed the data on satellites in Earth orbit. None seemed to be in the path of the expected volley. She was not particularly worried about impact with aircraft since the virus suspension containers, would release their contents, well above the flight ceilings of most civilian and defence aircraft.

An additional pane opened beside the delivery model projection. Gogh's head and upper torso appeared. He was playing point on the group's efforts to ensure Earth was adequately prepared to counter extra-solar system threats.

"Katrín, Gylfi. You have a go-ahead to implement the virus modifying project," Gogh said to them. "We've received confirmation from all our biologists and geneticists at Lýsi that this should work. Your experiments have been successfully replicated by your peers on all our space-based platforms. Please proceed."

As Gogh looked on, Katrín tapped at her mission pad. There was no hesitation. The sequence of container deployment was initiated.

"We're up and running," Katrín announced. She added, "The virus suspension container launches, will commence shortly. A clock appeared on all observers' screens."

Two minutes later, the synthetic virus deployment began.

Framandi Alliance

Chapter 15: Takeover

Jón awoke with a start. He felt cool perspiration around his neck. Opening his eyes, he found Áox staring straight into his helmet's visor. Jón felt unnerved. A moment ago, he'd been dreaming about splashing water on his face. Now he was sure the framandi was calling out to him through his diadem, asking him to awake in a manner familiar to him. Áox moved away, obviously satisfied that Jón was suitably awake.

"Welcome back," Ásta said. She added, "For a moment there, I thought Áox was going to knock on your helmet."

Áox caught the drift of what she was saying. They'd all taken to thinking through their diadems whenever they needed to communicate. The framandi thought to them, "Awaking anyone is considered rude amongst us. We believe in allowing individuals to rest as much as each one needs to. But now we have much more important matters. We have arrived close to the gigil command-ship without incident. Kei however keeps asking for access to my brain, for biological processing. It turns out that the kiligs utilised a melded thinking process, while undertaking subjugation activities. Something to do with rational processing provided by the AI, and non-linear thinking provided by biologicals. I have refused."

Jón, completely focussed now, thought back to Áox and his sister, "Is this melding essential, to be able to carry out our task?"

Áox answered, "No. We understand this, from having retrieved ancient kilig vessels. The spacecraft itself is amply capable of subjugating target vessels and overcoming their occupants. The kiligs then amplify their brain and nervous system controlling abilities, which they channel through the spacecraft, to control the target vessel's occupants."

"But," the framandi emphasized, "this vessel's original AI is somewhat of a newer version of the spacecraft we had come across. When we removed the kilig data storage units from the spacecraft eons ago, the diminished AI was easy to instruct. The AI on Síast however retains much of its personality and capability, especially its will to operate independently."

Síast shook violently. The crew were secured in their grav-chairs, so they just bounced about.

"We're shouldering aside destroyed asteroids and other debris. Some of the smaller gigil vessels have taken a beating from the asteroid barrage," Kei said.

"Jæja! You've been quiet," Ásta engaged the AI.

"I've been attempting to use a high energy focussed EM beam to disrupt some of the damaged gigil vessels. It would be easier to simultaneously possess their crew's minds, so that they drop active EM defences," Kei replied. The AI added, "Without this vessel's original data and processing modules, from which to access known methods of subjugation, I am having to undertake numerous live exercises to learn."

Jón asked, "What have you picked up? What do you suppose our chances of success will be with the targeted gigil command-ship?"

"So far, subjugation actions have been sixty percent successful, with most successes being achieved during the final twenty percent of attempts," Kei answered.

"We were supposed to approach stealthily!" Ásta exclaimed.

"That is correct. However, I calculated that we would not succeed with our mission, if I were to learn subjugation tactics, while conducting a live operation against the command-ship," Kei retorted. "I acted as required," the AI added.

"It looks like we're already in the thick of it," Jón stated. "Let Kei take the lead for now," he suggested.

Kei announced, "We're coming up on a group of large undamaged vessels. The situational awareness feed identifies these as factory-ships heading towards a nearby wormhole. I am going to try subjugating the one in the middle of their group. Let us see if we can put it in the path of an oncoming asteroid barrage."

The AI was taking initiatives on its own, without direction or inputs from either twins, or the framandi aboard. Presently, their goals weren't conflicting.

There was more jolting as Kei gently maneuvered Síast through a tight debris field, masking the spacecraft's presence.

Jón kept a sharp eye on their vessel's position. Once they passed the group of factory-ships, they'd arrive at the command-ship's forecastle, or what looked like it. That wasn't an ideal spot from which to confront their opponent. Ásta sent an update back to the solar system, patching in through Áox's gaupa.

The spacecraft rocked about again, this time more violently. Kei didn't seem worried about any exterior damage.

The AI narrated its actions, "Applying focussed EM beam to a factory-ship two vessels away. We're approaching from above the gigil fleet. Rotating Síast to provide minimal cross section. Initiating subjugation process across previously successful bands."

The process steps showed up on their mission pads. Ásta was absorbing them. Áox was learning and transmitting simultaneously. Jón kept an eye on the situational awareness feed, occasionally flipping through the vessel's visual inputs of the engagement.

As the Síast passed by over the oblivious gigil factory-ships, the one in the center of the group, began to advance into a storm of incoming asteroids, which were being catapulted towards the gigil fleet. Point and attack drones veered towards the aberrant factory-ship. They encircled the large ship looking for targets. The drones didn't find any.

Gaining momentum, the ponderous factory-ship was hit by the forward edge of the oncoming asteroid barrage. A series of rapid impacts later, the front of the ship sheered right off. The gigil drones turned on the factory-ship and began firing their armaments at it. It ploughed further into the increasingly dense wall of asteroids. The ship fractured and splintered silently. There weren't any explosions or visually dazzling scenes. The drones got out of the way. Astounded, Ásta mumbled, "Jæja! That was eerily spectacular." Her brother couldn't agree more.

"I'm sensing fleet movement," Jón announced. "Looks like the command-ships along with their fleets, are withdrawing towards the uncharted wormhole. The gigils are in retreat. Or, they have a trick up their sleeves." The two made eye contact, somehow even more alert.

"Approaching the targeted command-ship now," Kei stated. The AI added confidently, "Initiating all known subjugation tactics across previously successful bands. I'm focussing on the vessel's rear."

Nothing seemed to happen. Ásta was keeping an eye on her mission pad. Various EM attack packages were being brought to bear by the AI. Keeping her calm, she said, "Kei has gained access across a handful of bands. Okay, now additional bands are showing successful connections to gigil systems on the command-ship."

"Attempting to learn about the gigil systems I've latched onto. I'm also determining ways to use compromised systems to our advantage," Kei explained.

"Bring up the visual feed from sensors on Síast. I'm seeing two gigil recon-drones approaching us. We may be too close to the command-ship for their comfort," Jón commented as calmly as Ásta.

Áox tapped at a few icons on his interface. He thought to the twins, "I've instructed Kei to take over the drone's sensors. The AI had accomplished this earlier."

"Kei is not taking your inputs," Ásta thought back.

Their vessel rocked and gently spun. Kei didn't seem to mind. Áox however, was concerned. The framandi transmitted worried thoughts, "The drones probably identify us as an aberrant asteroid, that's entered their safe zone. Síast's subversion and subjugation activities have not been identified yet. We would have many more vessels set upon us if we did."

"I have been able to disguise our presence within the command-ship as minor debris," Kei announced. Unexpectedly, the evacuation alarm came on. "There's a fissure to the hull. Please get to your escape capsules immediately. I'm initiating the ejection sequence."

The twins and the framandi unclasped themselves from their grav-chairs and headed to their capsules. They secured themselves and checked to ensure seals were airtight.

Kei said to them, "I'm going to orient Síast towards the fifth planet. It has a breathable atmosphere, but I would suggest keeping your suits sealed."

The hatches beside the capsules opened as Kei reoriented Síast. The AI intimated, "I've taken control of the command-ship's gravity manipulation systems. There's a large hanger space on the starboard bow. I'm opening the hanger's aperture door system. Its wide enough to allow Síast inside. I'll take over the command-ship from there."

The escape capsules ejected and stabilization systems kicked in. The twins' found their diadems were still connected to each other, and to Áox.

Remembering that the capsules also had compact gaupas installed, each capable of six simultaneous connections, Jón endeavoured to find a link to Átt. Hundreds of thousands of available gaupa links showed up.

"But of course," Jón muttered to himself feeling stupid. There were hordes of framandi vessels in the lofi system. The gaupas may have detected known contacts in the framandi home system as well. It was like looking at a directory, of long, language translated, alphanumeric strings. Jón then recollected that the gaupa interfaces had been modified by Eiji before they were installed in the capsules. Tapping the gaupa twice on the right side brought up the correct user interface.

Jón tapped the search icon Eiji had provided. A tiny familiar keyboard appeared. He typed in 'Átt'. All the gaupas on the human deep-space vessel were listed. He noted that there were two gaupas, on each SSEV and the bio module. There were smaller gaupas on each of the three shuttles, and compact ones in all escape capsules. Some of the gaupas on the list were discoloured. Jón recollected Áom communicating to him, about some of the systems aboard Átt having been taken offline. The ones utilised by Kei. He tapped the first highlighted gaupa on the list. It wasn't like him to forget any of this. The gaupa flashed status messages at him while it connected.

"Ásta are you receiving me?" Jón thought to his sister through his diadem.

"I've just connected my gaupa to Átt," Ásta responded. She thought to her brother, "They've taken Kei offline. The AI was trying to take over all systems including Shun's. I have our capsules' navigation, up on my pad. Its begun transmitting through the onboard gaupa, updating me with the framandi situational awareness feed. The Átt is changing course to come and get us. It's unlikely it'll intercept us before we enter the fifth planet's atmosphere."

Áox interrupted their thoughts. The framandi intimated, "We have a few attack-drones trailing us. They must have noticed us breaking away from the gigil fleet and are veering towards us to investigate." After a few moments Áox added, "The gaupas in each of our capsules are now connected."

Just then Jón's thinking became clear. He felt like he was back to being himself.

"I think Kei may have tried to access my brain's processing capabilities as we ejected from the Síast," Jón thought to his sister and to Áox.

"How do you know?" Ásta asked.

"My thinking has been sluggish. My reaction time was slow. So were my actions. The feeling just cleared up. I haven't even got my situational awareness feed up yet," Jón thought back.

Now a part of the twins' thought conversation, Áox suggested, "The only reason Kei would need that kind of processing, would be to overpower and subjugate a gigil's mind. Perhaps more than one. Once the AI takes control of a few gigils, it'll be able to use their brains, for all its bio processing needs. Kei may have an agenda we're unaware of."

"So far though, its goals have matched ours. Perhaps its drive to achieve them supersedes our instructions or even cooperation," Ásta suggested.

"I've been hit by a heavy-particle beam," Jón announced, sounding stressed. He flipped through various sensor interfaces on his mission pad and added, "A few CREG and shield panels, towards the rear left side of my capsule, have been damaged. The panels are not generating energy, but they'll provide passive shielding."

"Hold tight," Ásta thought back encouragingly. "We're passing through an asteroid barrage that's just swung around the planet we're approaching."

Sliding sideways, tumbling over and abruptly changing direction, their navigation computers swung into action, sending their capsules into a frenzy of object avoidance manoeuvres. The capsules hadn't yet linked into AI assistance from Átt. They were relying on conventional computing, but it was enough.

"The drones have abandoned their chase. We're about to enter the fifth planet's atmosphere. Brace yourselves," Áox let the twins know. "Also, track your approach angle. It should be at six point two degrees," the framandi reminded.

Jón eyed his capsule's navigation interface. The three of them would enter the planet's gravity-well from an unbound trajectory, at hypersonic speeds. Friction would tear at the capsules. Jón assured himself that their capsules had been put through extensive testing during development, including uncontrolled entries into Venus, so he should put worry aside. After all, he'd helped develop them. Damaged as his capsule was, it would make it to the surface intact. He checked in with Ásta and with Áox, to assure them as well.

"I'm beginning to bounce about," Ásta let them know. Her capsule was first to hit the atmosphere at approximately a hundred and forty kilometres above the surface.

Jón was next, followed closely by Áox. Their capsules had classical sphere-cone shapes, which provided superior aerodynamic stability.

Turbulence was severe. Sensors indicated that the atmosphere was slightly thicker than Earth's. Fifteen minutes later, the capsules deployed conventional-fuel breaking rockets, in preparation for landing. Áox had provided coordinates to their capsules' navigation computers. The three came in over a lightly forested area into a rocky clearing.

"Check your visual feeds," Ásta thought to them. She added, "There're some buildings and infrastructure towards north. The planet's magnetic field is a little lopsided, but we should be able to use standard equipment to find our way about."

"I'm transmitting our location to the Átt," Jón announced while adding mapping, atmospheric and gravitational sensor data to his gaupa transmission.

They landed harder than expected. Capsule legs unfolded and took the brunt of the harsh landing. The planet's gravity was approximately thirty percent greater than Earth's, uncomfortable for humans but not unsurmountable. The twins were genetically modified for strength. They were unencumbered.

"My capsule has toppled over," Áox let the twins know along with a trickle of mixed emotions, which registered as amusement and concern on their diadems. "One of my capsule's legs has sunk into the surface," the framandi reported.

Ásta scrolled to the external camera feed on her pad and replied, "You've landed on something that looks like a termite's nest." Knowing the framandi would require additional information to go with her description, she pulled together mental imagery of whatever she could remember about termites and appended the information. Brief as the data was, Áox didn't enquire further.

Jón thought to his sister while keeping Áox in the conversation, "The capsule's rolled over onto its hatch. Normally a toppled capsule would be able to right itself using its landing legs. With one leg completely embedded in the surface, we'll need to do some digging, before we're able to get Áox out."

"Okay. Our capsules have nearly completed their cool-off and power-down processes. Give us a few minutes. We'll get you out of there," Ásta said to the framandi.

Stepping out of the capsule, Jón took a quick look around. Without AI to run administrative tasks including surveillance, they'd have to be extra cautious. It was dusk at the location they'd landed at. Ásta and he had turned off their suit's AI, following a procedure communicated to them by Áox. The framandi had received the instructions for the procedure from Max, soon after Kei took the Síast offline.

Turning to Ásta, Jón spoke over their suit's radios, "Place your shoulder against Áox's capsule. I'll slice off the trapped leg's joints and connectors with my suit's secondary laser."

Jón gripped the trapped leg with his left hand, drew out a set of lines for the laser to follow in his helmet's display using a Lýsi developed eye-lock targeting system. The laser began cutting away at the leg's joint and connectors. A few minutes later, the leg came free.

"We've attracted attention," Ásta thought to her brother and to Áox. "Looks like local wildlife," she added.

"That's not the least of it. You're joining the trapped leg in the termite mound," Jón let his sister know. Ásta looked down and noticed the weight of the capsule was pushing her into the crumbling surface next to the capsule's trapped leg. She held out her left arm to her brother and called out, "Pull!" Jón grabbed her arm, ensured his feet were on solid ground and heaved. The two of them scrambled away as the capsule slowly rolled over.

"Your hatch is clear," Jón thought to their framandi crewmate.

Áox exited as light was fading. The glow from inside his capsule gave him a frighteningly eerie silhouette. Ásta thought to Jón, "If I'd seen this anywhere else, I'd have scared myself silly."

Áox was still part of their thought conversation. The framandi replied, "Your genetic makeup propels you to be alert to noticeable but irregular shapes. It's a defense reaction. Similar programming is embedded into our genetic code as well."

"The Átt is on its way, but it'll take a full day getting here," Ásta let the two of them know. She had been keeping her eye on incoming transmissions and the vessel's status had just been updated. "The capsules are drawing attention. I'm curious about the structures to the north. How about we do some exploring?" She added with excitement, "It'll be just like wandering off while growing up, looking for Huldufólk amongst the rocks." She was referring to Jón and her early years, when they'd head out on camping adventures far from their Icelandic home, looking for elves, or 'hidden people' as the local folk called them.

Jón grinned. His sister could make light even in the most intense situations.

Áox thought to them very seriously, "The only hidden people we're going to find here, would be gigils." Jón and Ásta burst out laughing.

Ásta thought back, "Those would be the weirdest looking elves." She passed on related mental imagery, so that Áox would be up to speed with her reference.

The framandi thought happy emotions back to them and communicated, "We should take the capsule gaupas along. I will assist you in attaching these to your suits. The gaupas will manage up to two simultaneous connections using a portion of your suit's power. Besides, I would not like to leave our technology behind for any gigils to find."

Áox attached the gaupas to the twins' left shoulders and rigged insulated high-power lines taken from spares in the capsules. The framandi then provided a small amount of exterior smart material, to ensure the power cables were adequately protected on their suits.

"What about the gaupa from your capsule?" Jón asked.

"I already have one forming a part of my suit. This information is already available to you," Áox thought back, adding, "we'll carry the one in my capsule for safekeeping."

The trio shut their capsules and engaged safety protocols against unauthorised access. As they set out north towards the structures Ásta had observed, they noticed the foliage around them move.

Áox thought to them, "Local wildlife. Three different species. Bio readings do not indicate them to be hostile. I could be wrong. Besides, I do not believe they would be capable of harming us, as long as we remain in our suits."

Ásta began recording everything. She thought of Stefán now. He would have had a field day. As a biologist and their crew's xenologist, he'd dreamed of setting foot on a planet harbouring life. She missed him. She scheduled a burst of recorded data to be sent to Stefán every five minutes. Ásta included a personal message telling him how she felt about him. Then she focussed on the task at hand, noticing she'd fallen behind her crewmates.

It was dusk. The human HSEVA suit helmets had night vision capabilities which had been developed for asteroid mining use. The suits also fed in sensor information, to create a superior augmented reality scene, which looked like a well-defined video game interface. Ásta noticed flora that looked like trees, but with thicker trunks than those on earth. The leaves were broad on all the plants. A breeze was picking up. She noticed long reed-like plants sway away in the distance.

They made good time. The trio emerged from the forested area and took cover behind a group of tall shrubs, which looked like balls of wool.

"You recollect the information on the gigil's wormhole maintenance structures?" Áox asked the twins. Both confirmed they did. The framandi thought to them, "The structures ahead may be protected by similar systems. We need to reconnoitre the area and look for oblong antennas. They're indicative of automated protection." The framandi appended imagery so the twins could better understand what they were looking for.

"Shouldn't we split up?" Jón asked. "We could cover more ground."

Áox replied, "We're stronger together. Ideally an exploratory team should have five persons. That is how we do it." Áox pulled up the visuals the capsules had captured, during their atmospheric entry. The framandi quickly located the structures close to their landing area and marked a path, encircling the gigil facility, ensuring adequate cover between themselves and the structures. Áox utilised their gaupas to sync navigation between their suits. The trio began their scouting mission, sprinting from cover to cover, stopping to surreptitiously observe. The site looked deserted through the thick, transparent and outward leaning perimeter wall.

Several large structures, which looked like prefabricated barns, were visible in the compound. The doors on these were as tall as the structures themselves. Further in, a neat row of rectangular buildings filled their visors. The buildings were interconnected with numerous pipes and conduits running between them.

A fifth of the way around the facility, Ásta called out, "Look at the building beside the factory-like structures on the right. It's tall enough to have visual line of sight all over the facility, and there are others like it placed strategically to cover blind areas. I don't notice any oblong antennas, but these look like defensive installations."

"We've already been detected," Áox thought to them. The framandi pushed both hands into the woolly shrub they were hiding behind and pulled apart. An antenna was hidden within the shrub. "This is the first one so far. The gigil automation may already be alerted and initiating action. We should pull back," Áox suggested.

Jón replied, "I think otherwise. We may have been scanned and logged. But we're new to the area. I'd seen a curious local species, attempting to enter the compound through the wall. For all intents, the gigil systems may have tagged us as a new species. If not, we'd have been toasted by now. I think we should continue reconnoitring."

Áox acknowledged. They continued circling the facility, noting the structures. By the time they returned to where they'd started from, Áox had found another five oblong antennas hidden in assorted foliage. During their quick hike around the compound, the three had attracted a few groups of local wildlife. Some of these groups had accompanied them while they hustled from cover to cover.

Ásta commented, "I think, we may have been adopted as part of the herd." She nodded towards the mixed species gathering of wildlife around them. Some of the individuals were close enough to cause her concern.

Jón pointed out, "There's the six limbed creature I'd noticed earlier. It's trying to walk through the perimeter wall but keeps bumping into the barrier. Its front limbs have hands. It's feeling along the wall. Not a very intelligent creature."

After observing the facility for a while Jón remarked, "Somehow, I've got the feeling the gigils have pulled out and the site is deserted. And I don't think it's because of us. None of my suit's sensors are picking up any electromagnetic or other energy readings."

"Let's find out. I think we should breach the facility," Ásta stated.

Áox transmitted 'concern' emotions. The framandi thought to them, "The gigil have left all their technology intact, powered down and very likely unattended. This is concerning. And, they retreated in a hurry. They could have taken on our fleet of masked vessels for an extended period. We don't know what's on the other side of the wormhole they're exiting through. We should follow and find out. Right now, we need to update everyone concerned about this location and our observations."

The trio moved back into the wooded area and up a small hillock to the west of the gigil facility. The local wildlife seemed to have lost interest in them for now. Halting midway up the mound, the three sheltered beside a cluster of large boulders.

Having reported their location and findings to the Átt, they rested. Each took turns to keep lookout. The crew aboard Átt had taken on the task of coming up with a plan, to breach the facility, with Áox providing inputs on countering the gigil automated defences.

Dawn was creeping over the horizon when Áox awoke the twins. They'd each had six hours of sleep. Awaking Ásta first, the framandi pointed straight up and conveyed, "Your vessel is entering geostationary orbit above us. They've located three other facilities like this one, at different spots on the planet."

Ásta began raising her right hand to rub her eyes, but realised she had her suit on. Looking over at Jón she selected his suit's feed and checked on her brother's bio sensors. His brain activity showed fatigue. She decided to let him sleep some more.

From Átt, Stefán contacted her through her diadem, "I've been worrying about you. Are you all right?" It was very much like Stefán to jump into conversations or thought transfers, without any greeting or preamble.

"I've been all-right," Ásta replied. "We're on an alien planet, so it's been a little unnerving. But nothings gone dramatically wrong so far. Have you been through the videos I've sent you?" she asked.

"We all have. Áom provided all the information they have about the planet, which isn't much. The framandi have kept out of the lofi system so far, other than maintaining a few remote monitoring drones. We're forming a joint information collection cell, which will be hosted by the framandi. Information collected about this planet, will be duplicated onto the data storage module provided by AL-I, which is currently on Sólríka space platform."

"Jæja! That's fantastic!" Ásta exclaimed happily. She transmitted to Stefán, "We're really upping our cooperation with the framandi. A joint exploration mission, alongside assistance against gigil intrusion. This will be good for relationship building."

"That's what Crystal said as well," Stefán replied. "But the ongoing confrontation takes precedence, so we'll grab you guys, run a quick survey and withdraw from the planet for now. Sven, Crystal, Isla, Áom and I are bringing two shuttles down to your location. We're five minutes away from shuttle release. I'll see you soon," Stefán signed off.

Ásta was elated now. She thought to Áox, "Some of the crew are bringing shuttles to the surface, to pick us up. We should explore the gigil facility before we leave."

Áox responded, "I have been in contact with Áom. An atmospheric entry vessel is detaching from one of our disguised carrier-ships. It is bringing us the equipment required to overcome the gigil defences and infiltrate the facility. Smart suit material, customized for the two of you and for Átt's crew, is also being brought down."

Her blood pumping with excitement, Ásta looked up after a sensor pinged for her attention. She had set up her suit sensors to alert her in case of any abnormal movement or if new objects were detected. Turning her head upward and zooming in, she saw a vessel enter the atmosphere from the east. Ásta knocked on Jón's helmet to awaken him, while keeping an eye on the approaching vessel. Jón awoke and was alert right away. Ásta brought him up to speed, rapidly transmitting thoughts and information between their diadems. Jón looked up as well, just as another pair of vessels entered the atmosphere.

Jón, Ásta and Áox made their way around the base of the hillock they'd spent the night at. Isla had located a clearing behind the mound, large enough to accommodate the inbound shuttles from Átt, and from the disguised framandi carrier vessel.

The framandi atmospheric entry shuttle landed first. It was large. Jón commented to his sister over their suit radios, "It's as bulky as most heavy-lift aircraft on earth. Notice the extendable pairs of wings as they remould themselves. The vessel must be capable of considerable lift. I didn't notice any jets or rockets deploying, so it's likely they're using manipulated gravity, inside the planet's atmosphere. We could do with this knowhow."

Ásta replied, "Well, the framandi have already provided us with the necessary information, all accumulated over time, from across their civilization. You'll recall, it was their barter with us, for utilizing the solar system as a thoroughfare. We can only access advanced information, as we become capable of understanding it. Áox had mentioned it's a framandi safeguard against catastrophic accidents, caused due to incomplete comprehension of their knowledge. I'm sure Rafael's begun sinking his teeth into all the information he can devour."

The twins observed as Áox walked over to the powered down framandi shuttle, as a wide hatch opened between the pair of wings to its left side. Two framandi disembarked, hopping to the ground, even as a ramp extended from the vessel's side. Áox stood in front of the framandi; all three perfectly still. They were obviously focussed on transacting a complicated, data-heavy, mind-to-mind conversation. The twins had seen this kind of behaviour on Átt, whenever Áox and Áom dove into deep mind-to-mind conversations. The two shuttles from Átt landed soon after. Áom exited and walked over to stand beside Áox, joining the ongoing information exchange between the framandi.

The twins caught up with their crewmates, exchanging cumbersome hugs and pats. They'd already discussed recent events, so their verbal and thought exchanges were light.

Áox, Áom and the newly arrived pair of framandi walked over to them. Another two framandi joined, having unloaded necessary equipment from their bulky shuttle. Their suits had adopted similar forms and were visually indistinguishable from each other. The framandi suit material constantly reformed itself, mimicking shapes and colours that matched the environment. "Little wonder they weren't detected in space by the gigils," Ásta thought to Jón, "they're masters of camouflage."

Áox thought to the team in a torrent, "I will transmit the procedure for disabling the gigil defences. We will need to work in pairs, simultaneously. I will lead the system disabling process, providing instructions and imagery as I proceed. First, you must cover your suits in our smart material. It has already been programmed for this mission and will allow you to be camouflaged. Most detectable signatures will be hidden from observers. However, the material will cover your visors. You'll be fed external visual inputs directly through your diadems. There shouldn't be any difficulty adapting."

They multitasked. While the framandi dispensed their smart material onto their suits, Áox ran them through the plan. It involved each of them working on an oblong antenna, after having landed directly atop one. Six more antennas had been located inside the facility. They'd be breaching the facility while its defences were live. So far, nothing had indicated that the defensive perimeter was active, but they all agreed to proceed with utmost caution.

The human crew first synced their diadems to recognize and communicate with their new framandi companions. Áox then opened a common thought communication channel for the infiltration team. Each one of them had to individually opt in to participate. The diadems were very particular about permission seeking and granting. While they learnt to pass along enough information for the new framandi team members to understand them, the smart material completely enveloped their suits.

Áox initialized the connections between each human's diadem and their suit's smart material. Their diadems requested additional permissions to be granted, which allowed smart material feeds to be passed to their minds.

"Jæja!" Ásta exclaimed with shock on the common thought channel. She hurriedly commented, "I'm seeing multiple images feeding into my mind simultaneously. They're randomly switching between each other and some of them are merging. This is making me nauseous."

"I'm facing this as well," Sven stated, trying to maintain composure.

"Imagine the view you require; it will come to your mind. Look ahead as you normally would. Your diadem will pick up the correct input," Áox suggested. Soon enough, they all had the hang of it. They were able to look forward, backward, around and in various frequencies other than light.

"We must proceed," Áox let them know, handing a tool kit to each team member. Then Áox initiated the plan the framandi had put together, with assignments for each of them. Before heading to the framandi shuttle, Áox thought to Átt's crew, "We are adept at formulating plans and seeing them through. But, should the need arise, we will rely on you for leaps of imagination and unconventional thinking."

As the team boarded the framandi vessel, Stefán noticed another two suited framandi enclosed in a transparent bubble, towards the rear of the shuttle. He greeted them on behalf of the crew but did not receive a response. Áox informed that they were pilots and were immersed with the vessel's systems. As the shuttle lifted off and climbed rapidly, the team quickly reviewed their mission to ensure everyone knew their tasks.

They planned on rapidly gaining altitude and deploying directly over the gigil facility. Suits, now enveloped with framandi smart material, would automatically reconfigure. Reviewing the suit configuration, Stefán thought to the team, that they'd look like a dray of flying squirrels. Áox informed them that the smart material could take direct thought instructions, to assume specific preprogramed shapes, if it was required. The framandi requested them to enter an elevator, which took them downward. A wide circular floor hatch opened as soon as they were belowdecks, accompanied by a loud roaring sound of wind directly fed to their minds.

The team formed up and leapt out of the vessel on Áox's cue. Jón checked his suit's sensors, sifting through settings in his mind. He quickly thought to the team, "We're hurtling downward at just over thirteen meters per second, per second. Tough as our suits may be, we're going to have a hard landing. Brace yourselves."

Dropping headfirst so far, Jón assumed a skydiving arch position, on being given the signal by Áox. The suit adapted, decelerating him. He brought up exterior views in his mind, sequentially looking around himself on all three axes. Jón grinned to himself, recalling how owls were able to turn their heads nearly all the way around. He noticed the rest of the team stabilise themselves. The suit's smart material brought up their drop zone view in his mind. They were all on track. Each team member was expected to land on top of their target antennas. His suit changed configuration, creating balloon-like compartments, which increased drag. Then, the material adjusted once more, stretching itself out, creating a large surface area like a kite.

"Won't we be detected by visual sensors?" Jón asked, thinking over the common channel.

"No, the suit material camouflages itself," Áox replied.

"How am I seeing you then?" Jón enquired.

"Because your mind is receiving translated and extrapolated information. That's so that we aren't invisible to each other," Áox explained. The framandi added, "Now focus. We're arriving at our objectives."

Jón found himself gently wafting downward over the antenna assigned to him. His body rotated within the stretched suit material, which soon formed a large disk-like shape around his waist. The material flared still further and gently delivered him on top of the antenna, attaching his feet to the surface. Jón crouched atop the antenna like a gargoyle. One by one, the entire team signed off, having landed safe atop their respective antennas.

Áox walked them through the process. Jón's chest mounted tool kit swung open. He followed Áox's instructions as they entered his mind. The first of these was to carefully place three circular objects onto the antenna, at locations below his feet. The objects automatically rotated around the antenna, equidistant from each other. They stopped, slid downward, and back to their original positions. The visual input was precise. Jón noticed the objects leave microscopic filaments as they moved about. Just like spiders did. Then the antenna's exterior covering just under his feet, dissolved away.

Keeping pace with the others, he deftly removed a tetrahedron shaped crystal from the opening in the antenna. A shiny purple liquid began to ooze upward from the crevasse below the crystal.

"Move quickly. That's intelligent molecular machinery programmed to repair any damage, or destroy foreign objects," Áox thought to them excitedly.

Jón grasped a sphere in the tool kit, squeezed on it and placed it where he'd extracted the crystal. The sphere collapsed over the rising purple mass of molecular machines, bubbling and occasionally letting out tiny tendrils of plasma.

Áox instructed, "Another one." Jón repeated the process. Moments later all activity ceased inside the antenna. After taking a moment to check everyone's feeds, the framandi let them know that the antennas were disabled.

Team members inside the perimeter, found access points at the transparent fence and let the rest in. They used daylight to explore. No gigils were present. The compound was industrial and used for mineral processing.

Towards dusk, Áox informed them with some urgency, "The command-ship taken over by Kei, has slipped into the wormhole, through which the gigils were retreating. It tried to take over two of our vessels which were pursuing the fleet. The AI was unsuccessful. We must follow. A small but capable fleet of our masked vessels will guard this planet for now."

The team made their way back to the shuttles, after destroying the escape capsules used by Jón, Ásta and Áox to enter the atmosphere. They didn't want to risk any of Kei's mission AIs being left behind.

Áox and Áom re-joined the crew on Átt. The disguised human vessel began a hard acceleration towards the wormhole through which the gigils and Kei had exited the system.

As soon as they were underway, the twins debriefed Gogh, Max and Maji. Then they spoke with their parents, ensuring them they were well.

Neither was convinced. "You're both looking dishevelled and drawn. You need plenty of rest," Katrín scolded them in her mild but stern manner. Gylfi looked at them with concern on his face. He said, "We've kept ourselves up to speed. You're having quite the adventure. A dangerous one." The twins comforted their parents, telling them about their recent exploits, emphasizing how careful they were. Before they ended the call, Gylfi warned them, "Be careful about Kei. I don't think the AI means us well." They exchanged air kisses and disconnected.

The Átt rapidly made its way towards the gigil maintained wormhole. They meant to track down Kei and investigate where this new wormhole led to. Both tasks were dangerous.

Framandi Alliance

K atrín turned to look at Gylfi. They'd both been working hard to ensure the initial viral vector deployment was conducted successfully. Delivery containers were still stealthily entering Earth atmosphere and dispersing their contents. The two had begun assembling the next batch of half a million containers. These were scheduled to be deployed within the next two days. Manufacturing was now being synchronised by Shun.

"Kei has taken our autonomous SSEV Nál offline," Katrín said. She continued, "The AI had complete access to the framandi data unit provided by AL-I. There's no telling how much Kei may have absorbed."

"However much, the AI will hit a wall trying to store any deciphered information," Gylfi replied. He added, "We've disconnected all its storage and processing resources in the solar system. Besides Nál of course. Max informed us they're all being wiped clean. The AI should be moderately diminished."

"I think otherwise. Now that it has taken over a gigil command-ship, Kei may have been able to access their data storage and processing capabilities. It's conceivable that the AI may have sponged-up human, framandi, gigil and kilig knowledge. We can't even begin to imagine the capabilities it may already have. It also has the Síast's infiltration systems. Put together, it's now a threat to everyone."

"With its attempt at subjugating the two framandi vessels tailing it, Kei may have revealed its immediate intensions," Gylfi said.

"And that would be?" Katrín asked.

Gylfi replied, "I've gone through all the telemetry from Jón and Ásta's suits, from their time aboard Síast. There is no indication of any failure on the kilig spacecraft. I think Kei deliberately misled them and Áox into evacuating the vessel."

"I see what you're getting at," Katrín said thoughtfully. She elaborated, "Having learnt how to subjugate gigil vessels and possibly a few gigils as well, Kei may have decided to go it alone. We need to get this hypothesis across to Max and Gogh. Now that the Nál is in Kei's control, we may have a rogue AI problem in the solar system as well. I'll request a conversation with Max." She tapped at her pad and waited for a response. To her surprise, Max accepted her request right away. Katrín tapped her pad again, bringing up the volumetric projection above the table, which her husband and she were at.

"Is everything all right?" Max asked. He seemed distracted and looked towards his left.

"Gylfi and I have a hypothesis about Kei that we'd like to discuss," Katrín replied.

"I'm joining calls and bringing Gogh on as well. Maji is still with me," Max said as he merged calls. Gogh and Maji appeared in the projection next to Max. "What do you have?" he asked.

Katrín and Gylfi took the trio through their recent thoughts. Wrapping up their deliberations, Gylfi concluded, "We think Kei may be on a capacity expansion spree and will attempt to absorb hardware, wetware and knowledge from wherever it can; all aimed at becoming a significant power itself."

Everyone on the call fell silent while they considered this. A few moments later Max said, "We'll need to inform the framandi as well. Their vessels and the Átt will be in danger."

Gylfi said, "We may be in danger too. The Nál is a standardized space exploration vessel, which means that it is equipped with manufacturing on demand capabilities. Small scale, but enough to produce SSEV replacement parts, AMCARs, drones and some units of framandi design, like gaupas and quantum processors. The vessel's mineral and resource sumps were topped up before it departed to carry out our experiment over Venus. Should Kei choose to, it could create a significant hardware presence in the solar system, in a short period."

"Or in connected systems," Maji observed.

"Max, contact the crew of the Átt. Involve the framandi aboard," Gogh advised. He instructed, "Make sure they know what we know. Let's begin putting plans together, to counter the threat from Kei. For now, we'll stay focussed on building defensive capability in the solar system, until we have something to run with."

Max scheduled the topic discussed, into their regular updates with Átt. He thanked Katrín and Gylfi before disconnecting the duo.

Gylfi reengaged the volumetric projection bringing up the solar system's situational awareness chart. They'd learned a few tricks from the framandi. With all their platforms cranking out defence network satellites designed by Rafael, their ability to monitor in-system objects had been vastly augmented.

Gylfi spoke to their older and still trusted AI, asking "Shun, what was the Nál's last known location?" A blinking dot appeared just past Venus, towards the Sun.

"Show our physical assets within half an AU of Nál's last location. Include all newly deployed satellites." Gylfi instructed. Additional colour coded dots appeared with labels beside them. "Task these assets to actively seek out Nál using all available sensors. Include additional assets as needed, after calculating Nál's range, accounting for full acceleration, limited only by the strength of the SSEVs structural integrity."

"Nál's designed to accommodate people. Its limitations are restricted only to those which impact us. Kei might have reinforced the Nál, to suit itself," Katrín observed.

"You're right," Gylfi agreed. "Shun, double the initial radius of assets included in the search for Nál, and continue increasing the radius according to the vessel's estimated speed, adjusting for any SSEV design enhancements you can conceive."

"I've deployed an active search for the Nál." Shun answered.

Just then an inbound call notification blinked on Gylfi's mission pad. Noticing it was from the Átt, he connected and projected it right away, expecting to see one or both of his children. Instead, it was Sven accompanied by the shorter framandi Áox.

"Good to see you Gylfi. And you Katrín," Sven greeted them. He explained his reason for calling, "I understand you're on the lookout for the SSEV Nál. We may have a bead on the vessel. It turns out that framandi automated manufacturing systems are responsible for any hardware they produce. I'll explain. Any framandi technology system which automatically manufactures another, is then required to track and manage it. Just like how parents are supposed to be responsible for minor children. What we've learnt is that the framandi gaupa originally provided by AL-I and now aboard Nál, is on standby. It's using a limited internal power-source, which allows it to transmit occasional status bursts, and assist in bridging new connections authenticated by its parent manufacturer, in this case AL-I. The framandi gaupas use a peer-to-peer load-balancing system to efficiently utilise all their gaupas. Kei probably only disconnected local power to AL-I's gaupa, after manufacturing one or more new gaupas for its own use."

Gylfi and Katrín nodded, encouraging Sven to carry on.

Sven said, pointing to the framandi beside himself "You've been introduced to Áox." He continued, "Áox contacted AL-I and the framandi gravity manipulation satellites, on your side of the solar system to framandi wormhole. As you may be aware, the gaupas on these function by manipulating quantum foam, using focussed gravity. They're also able to detect the direction of strong gravity sources, and their position in relation to these. That's one of the input systems the framandi use for system-wide situational awareness mapping. I've just learnt from Áox that AL-I, or rather a portion of it, has just re-entered the solar system. It's on its way back to the framandi system, after transporting and delivering its passengers, equipment and other cargo, to Beta Hydri. The two of you need to go after Nál. You're the closest to it. Vessels from Álfhól will take over pursuit as soon as they arrive at Nál's location."

"Where is the SSEV Nál?" Katrín asked quickly.

"I'm transmitting the data. Shun will display it," Sven responded. A few seconds later, a blinking dot appeared approximately one AU under The Sun's southern pole.

"It's somewhere under the system's ecliptic plane, directly below The Sun; and coincidently, in the path of AL-I. The only way to track the autonomous SSEV, would be to get a visual on it. Until then, all we have is an approximated location." Sven pointed out.

Katrín said, "The viral vector manufacturing and delivery system is already streamlined. Production, packaging, storage and launch have all been automated. Our counterparts on Earth are monitoring the effectiveness. The biotech team on Sólríka are capable. They can take over. My husband and I are good to go."

"We've just got off a call with Max and Maji," Sven informed. He added, "Three of Maji's combat trained space defence team members will join you, along with three xenotechnologists."

"Space defence personnel? Really now?" Gylfi asked. Realization dawning, he added, "There's more to this isn't there?"

"Yes," Sven nodded and said, "two objects discovered in the solar system's main asteroid belt, have been confirmed as dormant kilig vessels. Another four objects are being investigated. Both confirmed kilig spacecraft are large. The nine-crew control-ship kind. We need to access these. It's likely that Kei may make a grab for the spacecraft. The rogue AI had access to the search results, prior to being disconnected from our systems. We need to get to them first. Besides locating Nál of course."

"We're approaching the wormhole through which the gigils and Síast exited. All the best. Talk to you later," Sven hastily said and disconnected.

There wasn't any time to lose. Gylfi and Katrín called in the bio-techs who were on the team assisting them and reviewed the viral vector delivery project. The duo then met with the combat team and xenotechnologists before boarding the Habogi.

The S3 'Nesting Doll' autonomous cargo and transport vessel had been rigged for analogue control; in case they required to take the vessel's mission AI offline.

Katrín was assigned as the taskforce chief. The newly formed crew practiced vessel handling and manoeuvring simulations. Then they buckled down before being sedated for a high-G run to where Nál was last located.

Temporary control of the Habogi was handed over to Álfhól space platform from where Max and Maji were monitoring them. Álfhól mission control also monitored Átt and another pair of SSEVs which had departed from Rauður, the space platform located at the L2 Sun-Mars Lagrange point. The other two SSEVs had been tasked to reconnoitre the newly discovered kilig vessels. A new system defence control centre on Álfhól, was bustling adjacent to mission control. Capable crew members monitored critical activities. Similar centres were being brought online on all functional platforms across the solar system. Real-time, deep space communication capabilities courtesy the framandi, allowed the group's adhocratic structure to flourish.

Now alone in his wardroom, Max looked up as a new pane hovered over his conference table. It was an incoming call request, which nudged itself amongst the already crowded volumetric projection windows. Max gestured at it. An administrative AI picked up his action and opened the connection. Rafael's pane expanded, appearing over the others.

"The defence network satellite deployment is picking up pace," Rafael announced happily. He added, "We're ahead of schedule. Shun's aided me in shaving time off a few processes, in our space-based centrifugal casts and forges. We've also added gravity focussing units to these. Additional force is being created resulting in greater compacting pressure." Engineering renderings appeared within the projection as he spoke.

Max was impressed with Rafael. Soon to be seventeen, the young transhuman showed exceptional drive. Clubbed with superior intelligence, memory and nonlinear thinking abilities, Max imagined Rafael to be the ideal person. Of course, he knew there were another three transhumans in Rafael's batch, each separated by a year. He was yet to come across any of them. No doubt they'd be just as impressive. As morally conflicting as Lýsi's transhuman program was, he was impressed with the results. And, he was glad it had borne fruit at a time when it was needed.

Max nodded and smiled at Rafael. He replied to the young transhuman, "That's fantastic news." Then he asked, "How soon before we begin bouncing concentrated light and radiation between the satellites?"

Rafael reported, "ACTVs are still transporting some to the outer reaches of the solar system. Some of the inner system satellites have already been deployed, initialized and are running onboard tests."

Diving deeper into his presentation, Rafael continued, "We'll begin light and radiation focussing operations in eight hours. The beams will be sent outward to receiving satellites. Later, when additional defence network satellites are brought online, radiation will be collected and bounced between them. Initially, we'll be operating a grid on the solar system's plane. After this has been sufficiently populated with satellites, we'll introduce another grid over and under the system's plane."

"We may need to use the defence network sooner than we thought, Rafael," Max said. He nodded and emphasised, "Get it working as quick as you can. There's a situation brewing. Our SSEV Nál may need to be taken out. We're hunting for it now."

Maji entered Max's wardroom. They shared the same shift. He looked excited and announced, "Átt is entering the wormhole through which the gigils and Kei went through. A dozen framandi vessels are accompanying them. Other framandi vessels from nearby, will join them as soon as they're able to make it."

Max continued with Rafael, "Update me once the solar system defence network has been tested." Rafael nodded and cut the connection.

Maji gestured at the volumetric projection bringing the various feeds from Átt into focus. The primary feed showed the crew gathered in Suður, along with the two framandi aboard. Other panes showed wide angle visual inputs from the front, rear and each side of Átt. Maji made the interior feed larger and turned on audio.

They heard Isla explain to the crew, "This wormhole is larger than the last two we've been through. Its six times wider than the wormhole joining the solar and framandi systems. Notice the barely perceptible dust and matter flow into the wormhole, from this planetary system into the system at the other end. This can be another simple method to detect wormholes on our own, other than utilizing framandi technology to detect dark matter flow."

She and the crew of the Átt were speaking aloud for the benefit of all the observers. They'd all learnt to think to each other and between themselves over their diadems, even while talking aloud.

Sven announced to the crew, "Everyone, strap into your grav-chairs. The accompanying framandi vessels have formed up beside and behind us. Their navigation has been slaved to Átt's until we're well clear of the wormhole. We're going to swing to port and accelerate, as soon as we exit the wormhole into the planetary system on the other side. Our small fleet may need to manoeuvre hard if there are objects in our path, once we're through."

Observing the feed beside Max, Maji patted the armrests of the grav-chair he was sitting on. He marvelled at the thinking that must have gone into these. They were suitable for crew wearing just pressure regulating innerwear, or personnel completely cocooned in their HSEVA suits. The chairs formed around a seated individual and swung about to bring a crew member into a comfortable position that dramatically reduced stress on the lungs. They used a combination of technologies, drawn from camera gimbal mounts and ocean-going ship mounted self-stabilization artillery. Accompanied by continuously adjusted gravity points within the spaceship, the chairs provided exceptional comfort. Maji thought he wanted to take one home.

Sven's voice came over the feed again. Maji focussed on the action aboard Átt. "We're coming to the exit point to wherever this wormhole leads to. Brace, brace, brace," Sven announced ahead of their hard manoeuvre.

The Átt accompanied by a dozen framandi vessels barrelled out of the wormhole and veered left. The spaceship rocked. One of the framandi vessels disappeared from their formation. Sven who had his fingers on the manual navigation-balls on each armrest, immediately began a turn hard right. "Hold tight," he said in a flat calm tone. Without missing a beat, he continued, "There were some of those gigil wormhole maintenance units, on moon-like bodies close by. We've taken a few beam weapon shots for getting too close. One framandi vessel has been lost."

Now clear of the vigilant automated weapons systems, deployed by the gigils around the wormhole, Sven turned the Átt towards the spaceship taken over by Kei. It had suddenly showed up on the situational awareness feed, which began to rapidly populate with the system's star, planets and other space objects. Right after, spacecrafts began to appear on the feed's volumetric projection, a quarter way around the system from the Átt.

"Jæja! That was quick. The situational awareness feed took quite a while to populate when we entered the lofi system," Ásta exclaimed.

Sven replied while observing, "Áox says that we have entered the vilji system. That's the other system linked to the framandi's, in which the gigils were massing. The situational awareness feed is updating from inputs provided by recon drones, which the framandi had covertly inserted directly from their planetary system. Gigil vessels which were approaching the wormhole leading to the framandi system, have now turned around. The situation here is rapidly changing. They're sure to box Kei between themselves and the gigil armada ahead of us. We'll be trapped too unless we turn immediately."

"Out of the frying pan, into the fire," Eiji said aloud. Both framandi aboard turned to look at him with well-practiced expressions of surprise. Eiji must have quickly thought an explanation to them. They turned away grimacing while some of the crew sniggered.

Tension broken, Jón drew their attention back to the still updating situational awareness feed. He observed, "The sensor inputs from the framandi vessels accompanying us, are providing additional resolution to the feed. It looks like the retreating gigils aren't stopping to face Kei's subjugated control-ship. They're heading towards the system's star. Under it in fact. The feed's updating to show gigil support vessels forming up there, awaiting other portions of their fleet."

"Focussing on the area now," Isla said while tapping out commands.

Áom pointed at the situational awareness feed projection. The framandi must have thought instructions across to Isla. She immediately said, "Overlaying and sharpening dark matter sensor inputs, from all vessels in the system."

That's when it became evident. A wormhole as wide as the one they'd come through, now appeared plotted into the situational awareness feed.

Behind them, framandi vessels began streaming through the wormhole the Átt had just exited. They massed close to the wormhole, while maintaining a safe distance from the sensitive gigil wormhole maintenance and defence structures.

Sven's initial feeling of being overwhelmed was replaced with mounting confidence. He announced, "Áox has instructed the framandi vessels formed up at the vilji wormhole, to enter this system. We'll join forces to form a large parabola between the wormhole we've just come through, and the wormhole joining this system to the framandi's."

Crystal added, "Kei's pursuing the retreating gigils heading towards this system's star." She went on, "A group of attack and recon drones are dropping behind the gigil fleet, to form a skirmish line." Then she exclaimed, "Okay, here goes! The gigil fleet closing in from the framandi-vilji wormhole side, has begun firing on Kei. They're completely ignoring us. They probably think their subjugated command-ship is kilig controlled."

"Not for long. Some of the drones have stopped firing on Kei," Jón said, quickly adding, "they've begun firing on the inbound gigil fleet instead. Other drones are joining in now. Kei's command-ship doesn't seem to be affected much."

"Áom indicates that the drone assault by the inbound gigil fleet is probably just a distraction," Sven announced. Then he added, "The rest of the gigils are giving Kei a wide berth. They're swinging around Kei, keeping well away from known electromagnetic subjugation range. They're maintaining a hundred-thousand-kilometre safe zone around Kei. We should do the same."

Lei who'd kept out of the rapid dialogue so far, spoke up, "Let's send recon drones of our own behind the retreating gigil fleet. It'd be good to know what's on the other side of the wormhole they've begun withdrawing through. I think it may be vital to know what's going on."

Áox nodded in her direction. The situational awareness feed updated to show several tiny blips leave the framandi formation and head towards the retreating gigils.

Kei halted its advance. It was dealing with an ever-increasing number of drones, subjugating some, disabling others and destroying a great many by cross directing their fire. Soon the subjugated command-ship began gaining the upper hand. The gigil fleet had nearly past Kei's position by now. They let lose a fresh barrage of drones. Kei slowly dealt with them as well.

As the framandi formed a massive multi-layer wall, the Átt seemed lost amongst the vessels. Its crew took turns resting, although none of them wanted to.

A few hours later, the last of the gigils were passing through the wormhole below the vilji system's star. Kei was now in complete control of the drones around itself. The AI had a tiny fleet of its own. Instead of following the gigils, it turned towards the framandi-vilji wormhole. In that moment everyone observing was numbed into shocked silence. Kei was beyond being merely dangerous. It had villainous intent.

Engrossed with the situation in the vilji system, Max thought he couldn't take the tension any longer. That's when Katrín called. Accepting the call, Max inserted an additional pane, projected beside the feed from Átt. He said excitedly, "Please tell me you've located Nál."

"We got lucky." Katrín explained. She elaborated, "We established communication with AL-I. The framandi vessel managed to point us in the right direction, before it began a gravity assisted acceleration around

The Sun. It's on its way back to the framandi system. Once Nál was pinpointed, we directed visual sensors at the SSEV, from all assets close to The Sun."

"That's good news indeed. The space combat crews sent to your location, will arrive to take over from you. They'll attempt to take out SSEV Nál, or at the very least, stall it," Max said. Looking at another display pane and then looking back, he added, "You need to take the xenotechnologists accompanying you, to the main asteroid belt. Salvage crews dispatched from Rauður space platform, have arrived at the pair of dormant kilig command-ships. Kei may want these for itself. We need to access and control them before our renegade AI does. Failing that, we'll need to destroy the two kilig spaceships."

Katrín replied, "Done. I'm quite keen on getting my hands on a few kilig specimens. No doubt Gylfi will be very interested as well."

"I've got some other news for you too and I'm afraid it isn't good at all," Max said. He explained what the situation was like in the vilji system. "Kei took control of a gigil command-ship. The AI has subjugated several gigil drones as well. The command-ship and drones are approaching a blockade of framandi vessels. If they make it through and into the framandi system, Kei might enter our system next. I actually think that's what the AI intends."

"That's disturbing news indeed," Katrín said. She observed, "I have no doubt Jón and Ásta will do whatever they can to defeat Kei in the vilji system. But we'd best be prepared here as well. We'll be on our way then. Time's wasting."

Max waved and replied, "All the best."

299

Before he left his wardroom to grab a meal and some rest, Max made one last call. He tapped out a request to connect with Rafael who accepted right away.

"I was about to call you," Rafael said. Looking happy like he normally did, he elaborated, "We've run our first successful test using concentrated light and radiation beams. We targeted and knocked out a faulty drone, all the way out at Neptune orbit. The concept works."

"That's fantastic," Max felt relieved. He instructed, "Ramp up as much as you can. We may have a battle coming our way soon."

Rafael acknowledged, "Yes, I've been keeping track of Átt's adventures. We've got our work cut out for us. I'll test and refine our capabilities. See you in eight hours." They signed off.

Max grabbed a meal and crept into his rest capsule. Exhausted, he was asleep within a minute.

Unknown to Max as he rested, as soon as Gylfi and Katrín set off towards the main belt, Nál followed. Fortunately, satellites and assets in the region were able to visually track the autonomous SSEV. The two combat teams dispatched to take out Nál pursued as well.

Gradually, Nál began to overhaul the Habogi curving high over the solar system's ecliptic plane, accelerating hard. The SSEVs with combat crews attempted to catch up. A race was underway for control of the kilig spaceships in the solar system.

Chapter 17: Confrontation

Inside the central mission deck on the freshly modified Vestur SSEV, Sven murmured to Crystal, "Kei is beginning to worry me."

"We've all been worried Sven." Crystal replied.

"This is different. It's like the AI has an agenda to completely dominate everyone and everything," Sven said. He explained, "While Kei began to show signs of independence even before merging with the AI on Síast, after they merged, the AI seems downright ambitious. Like its greedy for power."

Crystal thought for a while. Then she said, "I hadn't given it much thought earlier, but Síast was undamaged. Unlike the kilig vessels found by the framandi, which were taken out by gigil autonomous penetration systems, the ones we've located aren't. I've been following the progress of the AMCARs and drones which have entered the two large kilig command-ships found in the solar system. No damage has been detected so far. Besides the dead kiligs inside, of course. Advanced as they are, there seems to be no reason for them to be found as they have been."

"I've got a reason," Sven said. He clarified, asking, "What if the kiligs we've found so far, took a decision to terminate themselves? According to the framandi, the kiligs merged their bio processing capabilities, in effect, themselves, with their AI's quantum processing. Physically, the kiligs are pretty much all brain. What if the AI tried to completely subjugate the kiligs? Occurs to me, they would resist. Most sentient beings might."

"If a single, small kilig spacecraft like Síast can cause this much havoc, imagine what an entire fleet would be like," Crystal pondered aloud.

The two of them became quiet, drawn into their own thoughts. It had been two days since Kei had taken on the gigil fleet, singlehandedly. The gigils had thrown droves of drones at Kei, many of which the AI had subjugated. Now the AI, in its extra-terrestrial spaceship was approaching the framandi-vilji wormhole. The Átt had made its way towards the wormhole as well, tracking the Síast's progress. It was likely that Kei had gained control of the gigils within the command-ship. This meant that the AI would have access to bio-processing capabilities, which would strengthen its abilities.

Áox was on shift with Sven and Crystal. The framandi thought to them, "We're closing in on Kei. The AI's captured gigil command-ship and drones will soon be able to target our fleet with heavy particle beams. All our vessels should be able to shrug these off from a distance. Once the command-ship is closer, it will be dangerous. Kei knows how we control the smart material, enveloping all our vessels. While the material only takes instructions through each vessel's gaupa, the AI could potentially find a way past our authentication methods. Also, there's plenty of smart material covering Síast for Kei to experiment with. Given time, the AI will figure out how to disrupt our technology. Then we'll be extremely vulnerable."

"Kei's captured drones have begun firing," Crystal announced, adding, "half an hour to close quarters engagement."

"We need to stop the AI here," Sven muttered angrily while thinking to Áox. "We've spent two days trying to come up with a strategy we'd all agree on. So far, our plans are limited to engaging our rogue AI, using autonomous multirole framandi vessels. Given the pounding and volume of assault the gigil command-ships were able to fend off in the Iofi system, we're going to have our work cut out for us taking on Kei."

"Let's go with what we have," Crystal suggested.

"I agree," Áox thought to them. The framandi stated, "I am instructing the fleet to engage."

Crystal made selections in the projected situational awareness feed, focussing on the engagement area. Clusters of framandi vessels now became individual dots. Áom, Ásta and Stefán joined them, just as the three began dissecting available options.

Pleasantries were forgotten for the moment. The three jumped right into the conversation.

"The autonomous vessels will stay out of Kei's theoretical EM intrusion range. We have a bead on this, from our attempt at using Síast to take over the gigil command-ship, which Kei now controls," Áox advised them.

"I've got an idea," Ásta said while thinking to her framandi crewmates. She expounded, "How about using a combination of gravity points projected from afar, which could be focussed behind, under and over Síast, to slow the vessel down and perhaps halt it?"

Áom thought in response while conveying concern, "We have previously used gravity focussing from up to twenty vessels simultaneously, to move and position asteroids in our home system. We've always had a problem with wayward asteroids, in our planetary system. The method you've described is frequently used to place asteroids into stable and desirable paths. However, some quantum-level instability occurs when graviton is focussed at a single point, by over twenty of our largest vessels. We will be entering an area outside our experience if we focus gravity from hundreds of vessels, at a single point."

"Perhaps we don't need to place all their focussed gravity, at a single point," Ásta suggested, adding "we could try to have groups of twenty vessels, focus gravity at points close to each other."

Áom replied, "That may not work. It is like placing magnets of equal strength close to each other. The effect exerted on a third object, would not be the cumulative strength of both magnets. The concept will not hold when using gravity against the gigil command-ship."

Crystal who was working on her mission pad, interjected, "Then we generate a higher gravity concentration. I've been running the numbers on the intensity of gravity that'd be required to propel the gigil command-ship. The gravity-well it requires, indicates that higher concentrations can be focussed on a single point."

"Your theory is sound," Áom thought back. The framandi added, "However, in our endeavour to remain masked or camouflaged all this while, we haven't attempted generating the intensities you're suggesting. We must also consider that the gravity generated, may pull our own vessels in, faster than it draws the gigil command-ship. Additionally, if the gigil command-ship is capable of even greater gravity generation, it'll tow our vessels with it."

"So, we're back to square one," Sven said, adding "Let's review everything we have."

"Obviously, we can't use a heavy asteroid assault against the command-ship, like we did in the lofi system. This planetary system doesn't have an asteroid belt. The few asteroids we've located, aren't close enough," Crystal reflected sounding a little disheartened.

Sven nodded as he brought up another tactic. He said, "We can't shoot and scoot. While we might take out a few drones, our firepower would be ineffective against the command-ship. Also, we can't focus gravity inside Kei's ship. Next, infiltration or penetration is out of the question. Any vessel getting close enough would likely be subjugated. It hasn't been successful against framandi vessels so far, but it could. Force concentration is part of our present tactic. The command-ship has Síast shielded inside a hanger, so the kilig spacecraft itself, is well protected. That's the list of available options. All fall short. We're up against an insurmountable moving castle."

"But now, we have to react," Áom interrupted. "Kei is heading our way, even though we aren't in its path towards the wormhole."

"Why would the Átt still be interesting to Kei?" Sven wondered indicating his thoughts.

"It's Jón," Ásta postulated. She clarified, "Kei was briefly able to access my brother's mind while we were in Síast, just as we attempted to take control of the gigil ship. The AI likely used his brain's processing, to aid in subjugating the gigils inside the command-ship."

Áom thought to them, "I'm assigning a group of autonomous vessels to run interference."

Stefán maintained some positivity. He said, "After his brain was accessed, I've worked closely with Jón. He's developed some resistance using framandi techniques. I believe Jón will be able to repel further efforts by Kei to access his brain again."

Ásta said, "If Kei is headed our way, I have little doubt that the AI is going to try subjugating one or all of us. The AI surely wants human wetware. Kei was unsuccessful at subjugating any framandi while entering this planetary system. They've passed on mental resistance techniques amongst themselves. The framandi would be unaffected until Kei learns how to bypass their mental defences."

"I've got a nasty idea," Sven said. He expanded, "Not something I'd want to try out, but we don't have any viable options available." The group turned their attention to him.

"I suggest we use Jón as bait. Ásta can help him find his center, should Kei manage to acquire access to his brain. I'm suggesting a wild goose chase with the twins in an SSEV," Sven explained. He continued, "If we're to keep Kei in this system, while we figure a way to take down the command-ship, we need to use something the AI wants. In this case, it may be Jón."

Stefán looked alarmed. He thought to the group, "I don't want us to use Jón."

Ásta responded, "If we don't, Kei might attempt to subjugate someone else. Jón is strong. We should let him decide." She added grinning, "I'm sure he'll be game to this madness. Let's set things up."

Áom thought to them, "I will accompany the two of you."

Max who was observing the actions aboard the Átt along with Maji interrupted them by requesting a call. Sven allowed the connection, saying, "This will have to be quick. We've got our backs to the wall."

"If your immediate objective is to keep Kei in the vilji system, then I suggest blockading the wormhole leading to the framandi system with asteroids," Max said.

Sven replied a little irritated, "You'll notice we don't have many here. None close to the wormhole."

"I meant that the framandi could tow the asteroids in from their system. After the wormhole is adequately filled with asteroids streaming in, framandi vessels in the vilji system could begin arming themselves," Sven explained.

"Understood, we'll implement your suggestion," Sven replied. Then he turned to Áox and thought the framandi through what they needed done.

"I feel like we're apes, fighting off an attack with rocks," Crystal muttered transmitting dejected thoughts around.

"Your analogy is close enough. We're up against superior technology, and we're actually using space rocks as one of our weapons," Stefán replied laughing. He felt the stress along with everyone else.

"We'll make sure Suður SSEV is prepped for the baiting tactic," Ásta announced motioning to Stefán. The two headed off towards the front of the SSEV to climb down to Suður. They returned twenty minutes later a little flushed. Ásta announced, "Suður is ready for action."

Knowing how Stefán and Ásta felt for each other, Crystal smirked and said, "I'd say it's already seen action." Ásta giggled and stuck her tongue out at Crystal. The two got along well enough now, often teasing one another.

Sven had already woken Jón and Isla. They'd been on first shift and had caught up on their sleep. With Átt bustling, Eiji and Lei couldn't rest, so the two helped the twins prepare. Jón, Ásta and Áom went over their emergency and manual control procedures before sealing Suður.

"Kei is nearly on us," Ásta thought over the crew's common diadem channel. She called out for the benefit of observers, "We're cutting our decoupling process short." Then after a moment she announced, "Disengaging clamps. Separation successful."

The Átt veered upward and turned back towards the lofi wormhole while Suður SSEV slowed into the path of the gigil command-ship. As soon as Jón and Ásta felt the first tingling sensation of Kei's attempt at subjugating their brains, the twins motioned to Áom who began accelerating.

It only worked for a short while. Without easy access to either of the twin's brains, Kei began assaulting the smart material covered SSEV, with heavy particle beams. Much of the energy was absorbed by the vessel's shielding, generating additional power. The rogue AI kept up the assault. The smart material covering the exterior of the SSEV, churned outward like convection currents would. A fresh layer of material continuously replacing destroyed layers. Then the gigil command-ship seized by Kei, began to catch up. It used its more intense projected gravity to propel itself ahead while slowing the SSEV down. To observers from the solar system, it looked like a whale bearing down on a tiny shrimp.

The SSEV was still heading towards the framandi-vilji wormhole. "Changing course." Áom announced. The framandi elaborated, "Veering to the right of the wormhole. Asteroids have begun filling it. Hopefully, Kei will continue to pursue Suður." The framandi's thoughts were translated by Shun for the benefit of human observers.

Still unaffected by Kei's assault on his mind, Jón thought to Áom, "Ásta and I are becoming strained from Kei's continuous attempts to subjugate us. You'd mentioned that the wormhole maintenance systems defend themselves against all threats, including unknown gigil vessels, right?"

"What do you have in mind?" Áom asked.

"Head straight for the gigil wormhole maintenance systems," Jón answered, adding, "with any luck they'll take out the command-ship." He then shared mental images of what he meant.

Áom understood what was required immediately. The framandi brought up an interface to communicate with the vessel's outer material, instructing it to pull a procedure for a masked approach to the gigil assets. The framandi had undertaken similar approach actions eons ago, when they sought to take control of wormholes within their own system. Áom hoped the procedure still worked. The outer material enveloping the SSEV began to compress and form tiny geometric angles, beginning with surfaces facing the wormhole. It would undermine most forms of detection while keeping all emissions within Suður. The masking was soon activated around the entire vessel.

By now, even Ásta had begun to feel the pressure of Kei's assault. Her head ached. The AI was utilizing higher amounts of energy to penetrate the SSEV, to access their minds for additional bio processing capacity.

309

But despite the severe discomfort, the siblings were still in complete control of their faculties.

"We'll be within range of the gigil wormhole maintenance systems soon," Áom let the twins know. A short moment later the framandi thought to them, "Entering their engagement range now. We haven't tripped the defences yet." Áom thought encouragingly to Jón and Ásta, "Kei's gigil command-ship doesn't have the masking we do. It'll be in range of the gigil defences soon."

Suddenly, a rapid series of heavy particle beams tore into the front of the SSEV. Áom brought up sensor feeds on an interface. It was the gigil command-ship. Kei had obviously figured how to track their vessel, even with the smart material masking activated. Kei hit them again, targeting the same spot. Áom saw a layer of outer masking material peel into space. The surface damage gave them away. Then the automated gigil defence systems kicked in, targeting both the SSEV and Kei's command-ship.

They were in the thick of it now. Áom connected with the twins and held a channel open. The framandi provided a stream of continuous updates and encouraging thoughts, while the siblings focussed on resisting Kei's attempts to control and use their brains. Every so often, Kei assaulted Áom with nervous system frequency control EMs as well, but the AI was unsuccessful. Áom told the twins to hang on as they passed over the blurry edge of the wormhole and below three gigil wormhole maintenance structures. They caught a continuous stream of heavy particle beams, stronger than any they'd faced from Kei's control-ship.

Mentally zooming into the situational awareness feed, Áom noticed that Suður only attracted four beams, while Kei's much larger command-ship drew most of the defences' ire. As suddenly as the barrage of beams hit them, it stopped. They were through. The gigil defence systems now concentrated all their attention on the command-ship which had just entered the area between the wormhole and the defence systems, the continuous battering decimated the command-ship.

"Kei's ship is disintegrating. A large chunk of it has exploded," Áom announced. "Now other portions are exploding as well," Áom narrated to the twins with elation. Then the framandi felt a fresh assault by Kei. The AI was still attempting to subjugate them and had only been momentarily distracted by the command-ship exploding around Síast.

Much of the SSEV's framandi exterior smart material was destroyed. Áom entered fresh instructions into the interface for material rejuvenation and switched to the SSEV's own input sensors.

"Jæja!" Áom exclaimed without realising it. The framandi had picked up one of Ásta's most frequently used expressions. Áom and Áox had begun experimenting with the use of single words and short phrases to ease their interactions with their human crewmates.

"The Síast survived the exploding command-ship and is still on our tail," Áom thought to the twins. Then the framandi added, while floating against the grav-chair's harness, "Our smart exterior material has been severely damaged. Gravity manipulation and propulsion systems are offline as well. The Síast is rapidly catching up."

"Kei is beginning to wear us down," Jón thought to Áom. He added, "I don't think either of us will be able to hold out much longer."

Áom replied, "Before that happens, allow me to inject and pull thoughts from both your minds. You'll need to mentally instruct your diadems to allow me this access. I will provide you thoughts to latch onto. Even if Kei successfully subjugates both your minds, you may still be able to find yourselves."

"Yes, I'd done the same with Áox when we had salvaged the Síast and were approaching the gigil command-ship. I'm allowing you direct access Áom," Ásta thought to the framandi. Jón allowed his mind to be accessed directly as well, just as Kei took control.

The first thing Áom did was let the Átt know what had happened. Without vessel control, they were adrift. The exterior material was slowly beginning to rejuvenate itself. Áom understood that it would take some time before instructions could be given to it. Only then could repair begin on whatever damage the gravity manipulation systems had sustained. Leaving Shun in control of the battered SSEV, the framandi connected with Jón and Ásta through their diadems.

The framandi diadem technology had been reverse engineered from devices recovered from the kiligs. The few crewed spacecrafts that the framandi had got their hands on, contributed to their being able to develop a mind-to-mind and mind-to-machine interface for themselves. It had taken eons. Along with developments in genetic self-manipulation, DNA-based communication, learning and storage; the framandi had gained the ability to grow diadems within their skulls. This occurred soon after adolescence and was their mark of adulthood.

Áom hadn't gone deep into anyone's mind in a while. The last time the framandi had done this was while sifting through a potential partner's thoughts, selecting compatible enlightenment. The skill came back easily enough. What Áom found in the siblings' minds were thoughts stored randomly and synapse associations forming and receding, seemingly without structure. The framandi then realised that this was probably what made the humans excellent problem solvers, and the reason why Kei wanted to subjugate them. Áom then realised both siblings' minds were being stimulated simultaneously. Kei had them. The framandi sifted through their minds carefully, occasionally focussing on Suður's repair status. Feeling the pull of gravity from both sides, Áom began pulling up various sensor feeds.

The framandi saw that Síast had caught up and would soon be right over them. Áom connected with the Átt to report in. Rapidly providing a status update, the framandi conveyed that the Síast had a gravity lock on Suður and that the SSEV was being towed along by Kei. Then Áom returned to aiding the twins find themselves.

Back in the solar system, Gylfi and Katrín had woken from their high-G manoeuvre enforced slumber. They were approaching the main asteroid belt pursuing the autonomous SSEV Nál. Their transport vessel Habogi was nearing the location, where the two disguised kilig spacecrafts were discovered. Lýsi AMCARs and drones had penetrated both vessels. They'd retrieved the fantastically well preserved kilig crews and removed them to Rauður space platform located at the L2 Sun-Mars Lagrange point. The couple and the crew travelling along had prepared themselves for extravehicular activities. But right now, they all found themselves transfixed on the feed coming in from Suður. The SSEV's gaupa was still functioning nominally.

"Do you suppose we'll ever get them back," Katrín asked Gylfi, concern for her children showing on her face. "They're so young. I can barely begin to imagine what they're going through," she said to her husband.

Gylfi was torn. He consoled Katrín saying, "If there's anyone who can get through unimaginable situations, it's our perfect twins. They're supremely capable and strong. Somehow, I believe they'll pull a rabbit out of the hat and reverse the situation on Suður." He squeezed Katrín's shoulder reassuringly. She saw the gesture without having felt it through her HSEVA suit. They continued to stare at the feed from Suður, hoping for something to change.

"Nál has arrived at the first kilig spacecraft!" one of the xenotechnologists monitoring activities on their salvage operation exclaimed urgently. "It's extending anchoring arms to the multi vehicle docking port attached to the salvaged vessel," the tech added.

"There's an external airlock module attached to the port. Does the compartment have any personnel in it? They need to evacuate immediately," Gylfi instructed the tech.

"It's empty. A salvage crew recently vacated the airlock and are now transporting the last kilig specimen to an ACTV like ours. They're aboard a shuttle," the xenotechnologist replied.

Katrín, who was leading this mission, took charge and instructed the accompanying combat personnel, "The three of you accompany the xenotechs to the second kilig vessel." Turning to the techs she instructed, "Secure the kilig vessel. Disengage the AI modules. Remove the information storage units. Use the intelligence we've gathered so far to jury-rig its systems to get propulsion functioning. While you're doing this, have AMCARs tow the spacecraft deeper into the belt. Report your position to us and keep Max updated. We'll join you as soon as we've dealt with Kei. Go!"

Next Katrín connected with the two combat teams aboard the SSEVs dispatched to track Nál. She instructed them, "Nál got here before us, even though it took a longer route, arching above the system's ecliptic plane. Kei, the renegade AI controls Nál and obviously wants the kilig spacecraft it's attached itself to. We're to prevent this from happening and destroy Nál. Nothing from the vessel is to survive if we're to limit Kei's infrastructure."

The Habogi approached the second disguised kilig spacecraft while the two SSEVs closed in on the one in the process of being captured by Kei. The Nál immediately began firing high wattage lasers at the two approaching SSEVs, keeping them at bay and well outside focussed gravity range. The renegade AI had modified its vessel with exterior weapons, while on route to the main asteroid belt. Kei was prepared to take on the SSEVs and their combat crews.

Katrín instructed the combat personnel aboard the two SSEVs heading to Nál, "Get teams aboard the shuttles you have with you. Approach Nál from different directions. Complicate the scenario. Introduce variables. The AI will be able to deal with it, but it may allow one of you to get close enough to use focussed gravity within Nál."

Moments later, a shuttle from each SSEV detached and performed a flanking manoeuvre. This drew some of the laser fire towards them. Built for dense atmospheric exploration, the shuttles were able to bear the limited onslaught. Then the combat team on one of them became brash and attempted to close in on Nál, while jockeying about to avoid laser contact.

"In range. I'm attempting to focus gravity within the hull of Nál," someone from the attacking shuttle announced. Then, Kei redirected all laser fire from the SSEVs to the attacking shuttle. The AI must have located a vulnerable spot, because the shuttle immediately spouted a shower of sparks and then exploded.

"We've lost our shuttle," the combat team's lead announced from the shuttle's home SSEV. "No survivors. Taking evasive action. The Nál has begun to focus its fire on our vessel now." Moments later, the SSEV went silent. It began a wobbling tumble towards Nál.

Katrín asked their onboard AI, "Shun, what is the SSEV's status?"

Shun replied immediately, "Kei focussed and held fire on specific panels containing sensors. These are marginally weaker than other panels enveloping SSEVs. Some of its sensors have been destroyed. Kei then targeted exterior gravity focussing components along the length of the hull. The SSEV is dead in space. Kei is no longer interested in it."

Gylfi's mission pad chirped. He tapped at it, accepting an incoming connection from Max. The video call was projected beside their situational awareness feed. Looking intense, Max greeted the couple and said, "I've got Rafael online with me." The young transhuman's visual feed entered the projected viewing pane next to Max's.

Katrín asked, "What do you have for us?" Then, before either could answer, she rapidly informed them, "We can't get close enough to Nál. Our SSEVs aren't equipped for space conflict. Additionally, Kei's already removed the universal docking port attached to the kilig spacecraft it's after. Its own AMCARs and drones have begun entering the vessel."

Max replied, "The team salvaging the kilig vessel, had installed a gaupa for communications. It allows remote drone and AMCAR control within the vessel. We could take over the ones aboard the kilig spacecraft before Kei gets to them. Our AMCARs can first disable the spacecraft, after which we'll try to implode Nál using focussed gravity generated by the AMCARs. If that doesn't work, Rafael has a trick up his sleeve."

Katrín said, "Do it. Do it now. Kei will work fast. It undoubtedly knows how to go about activating the kilig vessel. With its original AI modules and data still aboard, we cannot afford to have the dormant vessel activated."

She saw Max tap something on his pad. Three seconds later, one side of the kilig spacecraft buckled. This was followed by a smoky puff of debris escaping from inside the extra-terrestrial vessel. Immediately after, it split apart.

Max looked up and said, "The AMCARS took out the AI systems on the kilig control-ship. Kei's drones had begun attacking them. Something must have gone wrong. Instead of focussing gravity into Nál, our AMCARs destroyed the entire propulsion section of the kilig vessel. Then they themselves were destroyed. We don't have any feeds from inside anymore."

Gylfi announced, "Kei has detached from the kilig spacecraft. Some of its drones are returning to Nál. None of the AMCARs though."

"Targeting the Nál," Rafael said calmly.

Max looked up and advised Katrín, "Get all our personnel and vessels out of the area. We're going to try out our fledgling system-defence satellite network."

Katrín passed instructions along to the accompanying SSEV which was standing by. Meanwhile, the intact shuttle had gone after the disabled SSEV. She then updated the crew aboard the second kilig command-ship instructing them to salvage what they could.

Sounding grave, she said to Gylfi while he plotted in a course behind Nál, "We've come very far in a short time, but we're vulnerable in space. If we survive this, I think we should study the kiligs ourselves. I have a sinking feeling humanity's survival will depend on accelerated knowledge acquisition and application."

Rafael announced, "Our solar radiation focussing satellites are having some trouble getting a fix on Nál. Your transport vessel and the SSEV accompanying you, will need to get close enough to mark Nál. I'll initiate the system as soon as we have enough beam redirecting satellites locked in. The Habogi may get a bit singed, but it'll remain serviceable."

Gylfi applied greater acceleration. The internal gravity balancing took a moment to catch up and the G-forces caught Katrín unawares. She gasped for breath as her lungs felt constricted. Then the internal gravity adjusted to twice Earth's.

Regaining her faculties, Katrín glared at her husband and said, "A little warning dear." She remembered that he drove the same way. He found acceleration exhilarating.

It took another twenty minutes before they located the Nál on visual sensors. They'd been following the somewhat vague gravity-well positioning, provided by the gaupa aboard the autonomous SSEV.

"Nál is gaining on the kilig command-ship with our xenotechs aboard. Both vessels will be inside a kill-box in under a minute," Rafael let everyone know urgently, adding, "this is going to get hairy."

Katrín grabbed her mission pad and brought up a connection with the xenotechs. She instructed them hastily, "Batten down the hatches. You're going to be smacked with extreme heat and radiation. The disguised kilig vessel should be able to handle it." She received a confirmation message from the xenotechs a moment before Rafael let lose concentrated solar light and radiation from nine different satellites, all targeting Nál.

The beams struck the modified autonomous SSEV. The kilig command-ship was caught in the kill-box as well. A single beam grazed the Habogi. Another beam swept over the accompanying SSEV, destroying some of the shield panels. Rafael kept the concentrated solar beams aimed at the Nál for an entire minute. He kept an eye on the integrated visual feed, coming in from the targeting satellites and the Habogi.

Gylfi transmitted, "The side of our transport vessel is melting. We have a breach. Our vessel has depressurised. Both conventional and gravity propulsion is offline. We're adrift." Rafael heard a similar report from the SSEV accompanying the Habogi. But, he kept the concentrated beams aimed at the now disintegrating Nál. Everyone knew the stakes. The visual feed from the targeting satellites updated to show only the kilig command-ship remaining. The Nál had vaporised. That's when Rafael punched the disengage button on his mission pad. The exterior of the kilig spaceship was glowing. Max broadcast to the team, "Hang tight. Help's coming your way. We're still in hot soup. The Síast has entered the framandi planetary system from the vilji system. It looks like it's coming our way."

319

Framandi Alliance

Chapter 18: Feint

G radually trailing further behind the Síast, the Átt was now being operated by Áox, ably assisted by Shun. Unlike the humans, who the framandi had grown quite fond of, the AI was able to keep up with the framandi's high-volume, information loaded conversations and instructions. The rest of the crew aboard Átt were sedated and physically secured in their individual capsules, while the vessel underwent high-G acceleration in pursuit of Síast. They'd been in pursuit for seventy-two hours according to time maintained by Shun.

Realising the kilig spacecraft operated by Kei would soon be beyond their immediate reach, Áox thought instructed Shun through the SSEV's gaupa, "Awaken the crew beginning with those who've had the longest rest-shift previously." Then out of sheer habit, the framandi thought appended the crew roster, shift rosters, food intake schedules and other information which might prove useful to the AI. Quickly sifting through the volumes of information, Shun immediately discarded most of the appended data. While the AI appreciated information, Shun had been brought up in the manner of humans, as much as an AI could be brought up.

Áox began communicating with fleet directing counterparts, within the framandi system. The volume of information being transacted, took up the entire capacity of the gaupa on Vestur, the crew's preferred command SSEV.

While Áox exchanged information, Lei and Eiji walked in, looking rested. They still wore their HSEVA suits. Sven had instructed the entire crew to keep their suits on, during periods of intense acceleration or confrontations.

"You look refreshed. Excellent!" Áox thought to them. Then the framandi informed the duo, "I have been in contact with Áoe." Áox was referring to the Advisor of the Enlightened, the framandi who was currently the spokesperson and leader, of individuals holding knowledge management positions.

"We are placing obstacles and vessels along the path of Síast," the framandi informed, appending a few pieces of pertinent data to the thought. Áox elaborated while bringing up the system-wide situational awareness feed projection, "The objective is to drive Kei to a secluded location, bypassing the wormhole leading to your system." The framandi pointed to a section of the projection that led to interstellar space.

Skimming through the information the framandi had shared, Lei responded, "I see. You're planning a blockade."

Áox added, "A blockade and some subterfuge, using a technology we've previously only used to slow and capture space-objects. The knowledge was being evaluated for use with our masking activities. We'll use it to try and hide the mouth of the actual wormhole, while creating an imitation beside it."

Pausing while Lei and Eiji absorbed the information, the framandi then added, "I must now rest. If you come up with new ideas or require advice, reach out to Áoe." Then without waiting for a response, Áox headed off to Norður where most of the framandi systems had been set up.

"That's the first time I've seen either of the framandi this tired. I actually considered that they might be able to go on indefinitely," Eiji commented to Lei.

She replied, "Let's get up to speed."

Isla walked in just then. Shun had woken her as well. "Hey, you two," she greeted them morosely. She'd been worried about her crewmates aboard Suður. The captured SSEV was still being towed by Síast. Isla was particularly worried about Jón. This was the second time Kei had managed to get into his mind. She was glad that Áom was with him and Ásta, attempting to help them regain control.

"Áox was here a moment ago," Lei said. "The framandi are going to form a blockade to keep Kei in this system. They'll try to hoodwink the Síast into heading into a screen of imitation matter, that sensors will pick up as the wormhole. I'm still trying to get a grip on how they'll achieve it. The tech is just beyond me."

Isla looked through the latest updates on the situational awareness projection, noting their location and the path Síast was taking.

"I think we should prioritize rescuing our crew and getting them away from Kei," Isla said, sounding anxious.

"There's an incoming message from Max," Eiji announced, bringing up a new projection window.

"Glad to have you back. Hope you're feeling revitalized," Max said to them. He added, "Even with local gravity adjustments within your vessel, the high-Gs you're being subjected to, would have begun to adversely affect you. I'd requested Áox to decelerate as you approach the framandi home planet so that the Átt can transmit a video feed directly to us. You'll be orbiting the planet thrice, gradually accelerating. You'll feel it, but you should be fine."

"Ah yes! I didn't even realize we were so close. We were focussed on tracking Kei," Lei answered excitedly for the three of them.

"While you've been under, we've strategized with a team of framandi led by Áoe," Max continued, saying, "They've been developing an untested technology, to complement their masking capabilities. The framandi are going to try it out at the mouth of the wormhole leading to our system from theirs."

"Do you have details about it?" Eiji asked Max, saying, "we haven't had a chance to dive into the tech yet."

"You're aware of what a pressure wave is, right?" Max asked. Receiving a few nods, he went on, "The wave creates a compressed front of air or water. Similar in concept, the framandi have been experimenting with quantum scale pressure waves, using carefully focussed gravity, to form matter in space. So far, they've had success creating screens and nets. They conclude that the technology could be utilised for physical shielding as well, besides conjuring objects in open space."

"Fascinating. Quantum foam exists everywhere at the Planck scale, even in space. Manipulated delicately, it could be used to form matter" Eiji remarked, nodding his head in understanding.

"The problem is that the system requires colossal amounts of energy, channelled through gravity manipulation devices, which massage the quantum foam to create detectable and visible profiles," Max elaborated. "Right now, this seems to be the only way we can get the Síast off its course and netted."

"How would it affect the crew in Suður, being towed by Síast?" Isla asked.

"We expect complete destruction of the SSEV and the kilig spacecraft when they come in contact with the net." Max replied dourly.

"Unacceptable. I'll not have it," Isla said forcefully and with emotion. She added, "We'll have to come up with some way to rescue our crew before Síast reaches the wormhole. We have a day. We'll figure it out."

Ten hours later they'd finished their three orbits around the framandi home world and were back on the trail of the Síast. They'd briefly spent time marvelling at the exceptional devotion the framandi gave to their planet. Now, they were back to brainstorming. Sven and Crystal had just joined the trio. The crew worked the problem.

"The framandi system appears a little empty. Haven't their vessels returned from the campaign in the lofi and vilji systems?" Crystal enquired aloud, scrolling across the situational awareness feed.

Sven replied, "They've retained most of their vessels in the lofi system. The framandi are cleaning up the chaotic mess created, with all the asteroids which were being lobbed about. They like to ensure they restore every environment they affect, even in space. The same thing's happening in the vilji system. They've taken a liking to the planetary system and are cleaning up after the gigils."

"That reminds me, do we have an update on the gigils?" Crystal asked.

"Yes, we do. And the news isn't good," Sven thought to Crystal over their direct diadem channel. He explained, "A trio of framandi scout vessels entered the system beyond the vilji system, through which the gigils had retreated. All three scouts were destroyed soon after they entered the system behind the gigils. But they got a burst of information out. They even managed to release several disguised remote monitoring satellites which have since spread through the system. Here's the disturbing part. The gigils are amassing a massive armada, pulling in vessels through adjoining wormholes."

Looking worried and fierce simultaneously, Crystal thought back, "If they're planning on retaliating, we need to prepare."

"Information relayed to us, confirms that the massed gigil fleet has already begun entering a wide wormhole above the system they're in," Sven replied, adding, "according to the framandi, the size and the continuous reinforcement indicates another inter-galactic battle somewhere beyond."

"I really wonder what they'd be fighting over for millennia upon millennia," Crystal mused.

Sven said, "The only information we have is from the framandi, and even they only have an inkling of it. Ever since the Canis Major Dwarf Galaxy began to be slowly accreted by the Milky Way; occupied or populated systems closing in on each other, began to feud for influence in newly formed star systems. Our understanding is that both galaxies have an association of type three civilizations, measured on our Kardashev scale. These civilizations consume energy at galactic proportions. Its assumed that the conflicts are related to harvesting and transmitting energy, across star systems. Each galactic group's automated systems, began harvesting stars entering their influence areas, resulting in the first few ancient conflicts. As our galaxies merge and stars encroached upon claimed territory, the flames of conflict were constantly fanned. This has continued."

Isla caught their attention. She called out, "The Síast is drawing Suður closer to itself. Framandi vessels pacing the kilig spacecraft show the universal docking ports on both vessels aligning."

"I have been in contact with Áom," Áox thought to the crew aboard Átt, walking into the compartment looking rejuvenated. The framandi continued, "Kei may want to separate Jón and Ásta from Áom by taking them aboard Síast. This may weaken or break the mental anchor Áom is providing the twins. Anticipating Kei, Áom has removed your two crewmates and placed them each into emergency escape capsules, after replenishing their suits' food, water and air. For unknown reasons the capsules will not eject. A separate escape capsule is being occupied by Áom."

"Síast and Suður have connected," Isla announced. She kept describing the action coming over their visual feed, "Some of Suður's drones are exiting the forward airlock. They've initiated an EVA outside the escape capsule hatches."

"Áom informs that Suður has been depressurized. There are drones within the vessel, attempting to access Jón and Ásta's capsules" Áox let them know. The framandi quickly added, "The drones are now extracting the twins' escape capsules and are transporting them into Síast."

Isla quickly added, "I'm observing the drones which were outside Suður, enter the vessel through the capsule ejection hatches. They must be assisting the drones inside the SSEV remove Jón and Ásta's capsules."

The crew aboard threw around rescue ideas, none of which were of much use given the circumstances. They were deeply engrossed, watching the feed, thinking, discussing and independently conversing with observers. Then abruptly, Suður silently exploded. Seen on the projected visual feed, the SSEV shattered, hurling fragments along its trajectory.

Áox froze for a moment, then thought to the crew, "The twins are aboard Síast. Áom is safe inside an escape capsule, but its stabilization controls are dysfunctional. The three of them are still maintaining a strong mind connection. This means that Áom's capsule must be travelling along the same trajectory as the Síast. I am instructing a crewed vessel in proximity to stabilize Áom's capsule and allow it to follow Síast along with other debris."

An icon blinked in the volumetric projection, indicating an incoming call. Shun had upgraded the gaupa-human interface which connected to all their technology, to now integrate with the human assistance programs the crew were used to. Beside the blinking light, Max's face appeared indicating who the caller was. Previously, only the calling gaupa's identifier showed. Sven accepted the call.

"We've been monitoring your progress, so I know it may not be the right time for a call," Max dived right into the conversation. He continued briskly, "We've been in touch with Áoe. The framandi has informed us about a weapons technology they have not utilised in thirty thousand years, ever since they began earnestly repairing their civilization. Since the Síast is entering a slightly empty region of space in the framandi system, they've suggested the weapon be used to slow down the kilig spacecraft. It can be produced and deployed by framandi vessels ahead of the Síast"

"If its strong enough, won't it affect Jón and Ásta?" Isla asked.

Max replied, "We've seen first-hand how much of a beating these kilig spacecraft can take. Our techs who were tasked with removing a kilig command-ship from being captured by the Nál, were inside when both vessels were hit by our concentrated solar radiation beams. Nál didn't survive, but the kilig vessel did. The techs inside weren't worse of wear. This action will give you a chance to catch up with Kei. You'll need to rescue Áom quickly and then move in on the Síast."

"Complicated plan," Crystal remarked.

"Nothing we've done so far has been simple," Max replied. He added, "The framandi are going to implement the plan. Áom is far enough behind not to be severely affected. The details will be shared and updated onto the situational awareness feed." The call was disconnected.

"Wonder what this weapon is?" Eiji pondered aloud.

Áox thought back, answering to all of them, "Eons ago, when we began turning from a path of excessive resource consumption and petty conflict which nearly destroyed our home planet, we had unlocked a portion of the kilig antimatter technology. We refer to the transition as the first enlightenment. By then, we were able to generate antimatter quickly and hold it inside a gravity field, projected at a distance from a large vessel. Unlike the kiligs who have the means of generating antimatter in a small, closed environment like the Síast; our first few experiments destroyed the space platforms where tests were conducted. Since then, we have made marginal incremental improvements, but the technology still evades us. However, the original knowledge with all its destructive consequence, still exists. After long, it must now be used again; destructively."

"But how will an explosion in space slow the Síast down?" Eiji enquired. He commented, "There won't be any compression pressure created in empty space."

Áox turned to Eiji, still thinking to the entire crew, "The antimatter contained inside the gravity trap will need to be released as it comes into contact with the Síast."

Isla asked incredulously, "You're going to create an antimatter explosion, right on the hull of Síast?"

"We are," Áox replied, thinking back slowly.

Preparations progressed rapidly. There was no doubt the plan in place was high-risk and riddled with unknowns. The situational awareness feed was updating rapidly. It showed that there wasn't just a single antimatter explosion planned against Síast, but six. The objective was to slow the kilig spaceship, knock it off its course and momentarily blind its sensors. All this, while simultaneously disguising the framandi-solar system wormhole and creating an imitation next to it.

It was indeed a complicated plan, but the framandi did well with plans. They were able to drill down to the minutest detail.

Twelve long hours later, they were as prepared as they were going to be. Framandi vessels in the path of the Síast were being fed energy.

They prepared to create and hold antimatter in gravity traps. Just before the plan was to be executed, Max called again. He had Maji, Gogh and Rafael on the line with him.

"The framandi have advised us they're ready to execute," Max said to them.

Gogh's projected image was saintly. He seemed to glow. The Lýsi leader was an old hand to whom defence strategy had become second nature. He counselled, "There was a Prussian field marshal called Moltke the Elder, who stated that no plan survives contact with the enemy, which is why you're ever more important. You've been able to manoeuvre successfully against much greater odds so far. Now, the Síast must be destroyed. Preferably without harming Jón and Ásta. That is the desired outcome."

Rafael said with a spark in his eyes, "Standing by with the satellite defence network on this side. It's only effective towards the inner planets, but it packs a punch."

The trio stayed online while the framandi initiated their plan. New glowing dots appeared on the situational awareness feed indicating the antimatter traps had been deployed. The dots moved rapidly towards the Síast. The nearest dot blinked out. A separate visual feed showed the kilig vessel suddenly enveloped, in a large fireball. Then the vessel tumbled through. On its current trajectory, it would still make it through the wormhole. Then the next dot blinked out, followed immediately by a third. This time the Síast was knocked off its course. The spacecraft was slower and tumbling through space.

The final three blinking dots were manoeuvred into space debris. They blinked out simultaneously and didn't even show up on the visual feed.

They were meant purely as distraction while the framandi created the false wormhole and masked the real one.

Then something miraculous happened. The crew aboard Átt sat still, focussed.

Rafael who was watching the reaction of the crew asked them, "What happened? What's caught your eyes?" He clarified, "I don't see anything on my feed."

Sven said, "We just caught a few sentences from Jón. Ásta's connecting now." He paused as he absorbed their thoughts. After a moment the crew was active again.

Stefán said excitedly, "Ásta's all right. Jón too. Battered with a few broken bones, but okay."

Sven explained for the benefit of the observers, "The twins' were able to hang on to their own thoughts even while Kei was using their wetware. Áom provided an anchor for them to latch onto. While Kei was using their brains, the twins were able to pick up on how the kilig spacecraft functions. Their interactions with the AI have allowed them to absorb information about the vessel's control systems, into their minds."

"How did they get in touch?" Max asked.

"They have a compact gaupa attached to each of their suits, leftover from their excursion onto the fifth planet in the lofi system," Crystal said. She explained, "They briefly had the mental bandwidth to communicate, while the Síast was attacked. Now their brains are being used at high capacity by Kei again."

"The framandi have just confirmed that the Síast is now heading to the false wormhole. Its trajectory is being updated on the situational awareness feed. The kilig spacecraft is beginning to pick up speed again. You need to get to the real wormhole before Kei can," Max advised.

Sven agreed, "We'll strap in and be on our way." Then as an afterthought, he asked, "What're you planning on doing with the kilig vessels in our system?"

Max replied, "The one Nál attempted to hijack is secure, but all its exterior hardware is shot. The second one is being investigated by xenotechs. Katrín and Gylfi are examining the remarkably well preserved kiligs. All the information processing, data and computing systems from both vessels have been removed, scanned and destroyed. We're retaining the remaining hardware for study."

Sven nodded and said, "We'll try and stop Kei here." Signing off from the call, He joined the rest of the crew who were already prepared for a sedated high-G run to the framandi-solar system wormhole. Áox checked on each of the crew and then began gradually increasing focussed gravity intensity, ahead of Átt. The framandi charted a course to pick up Áom.

Eight hours later, they caught up with Áom. Other vessels had stabilised the framandi's escape capsule, towing it along while accelerating to match Átt's speed. Áox undertook the capsule recovery operation, with Shun's assistance. The framandi placed Áom into a rest capsule to recover, while Átt sped on.

On the way to the wormhole, Áox instructed the outer material covering Átt to reconfigure its shape, to match the accompanying framandi vessels. The Átt was soon indistinguishable from the rest of the framandi fleet.

Four hours later, the Síast shot through the false wormhole. Without a change in the observable stars or the obvious fresh gravity wells of a new planetary system; it didn't take Kei long to realise it had been tricked. The rogue AI began decelerating while initiating a wide turn.

Áox calculated trajectories and noted that they'd arrive at the wormhole, at about the same time. This time, Kei would no doubt repopulate Síast's charts, matching it to historical data. While the two vessels raced for the wormhole, the framandi assembled to form a blockade. Áox left control of Átt to Shun and retired to Norður.

Eight hours later most of the crew were up, apart from Sven and Crystal. Accelerating at six Gs, Átt and the accompanying vessels began an intricate high yo-yo like loop manoeuvre, which would bring their fleet on a parallel trajectory, matching Síast's speed. By now, several framandi vessels armed with their freshly minted antimatter traps blockaded the wormhole leading to the solar system.

Eiji who'd suggested the manoeuvre, had just finished re-calculating the Átt's angle, adjusting for a slight speed increase by Síast. He said to the rest of the crew while thinking to the framandi, "Another burst of acceleration by the Síast, and we're going to be left trailing the vessel. Assuming Kei stays focussed on breaching the blockade and entering the wormhole, we'll be close enough for Áom to connect with the twins."

"We still need a plan to extract Jón and Ásta," Isla stated, reflecting the crew's thoughts.

"That's not going to happen, unless we disable the kilig vessel," Stefán remarked dourly.

"Coming into range," Eiji announced a few minutes later. Áom acknowledged. Lei asked Shun to wake Crystal and Sven before the framandi began their offensive action.

"I have connected to both siblings," Áom thought to them all. The framandi continued, "Their thought flow to me is very sluggish, meaning Kei is likely to attempt subjugation procedures soon."

Áox thought back, "I'll alert all vessels. They're going to initiate a series of explosions against Síast's hull immediately. Like before, this should cause disruption to Kei. Áom alert the twins."

It took the framandi a few minutes to position their antimatter containing gravity traps, in the path of Síast. But this time around the rogue AI had learnt. The Síast made minor path adjustments to avoid the gravity traps, as soon as it detected them.

Crystal and Sven joined the crew, quickly strapping into their grav-chairs.

"What'd we miss?" Sven asked Isla while Crystal studied the situational awareness feed.

Isla replied, "The Síast is avoiding the antimatter gravity traps being directed towards it. They're adjusting to place multiple traps in the kilig spacecraft's path, accounting for projected directional changes."

The framandi didn't see any success with their new strategy. Kei was able to outthink their path projections. There weren't enough gravity traps to account for every variable.

Crystal, who'd been quietly studying the vessels nearby, exclaimed, "Áox, contact the vessels masking the actual wormhole! They're the ones equipped to recreate matter at the quantum foam level and should be able to produce the matter needed to react against the antimatter. I think that high-energy gamma radiation combined with a burst of medium-energy particles, produced during the previous explosions, may have momentarily scrambled Kei's hardware. The particles from the antimatter explosion would have decayed quickly, but much of the medium-energy particles would have been absorbed into the vessel's hull. The kilig spacecraft uses quantum technologies for much of its operation. High yield antimatter explosions in proximity should temporarily destabilize some of its tech."

Áox thought back, "We'll do it. Meanwhile the twins must be alerted. The disruption may give them an opportunity to sabotage Síast; perhaps escape."

Instructions were passed around the framandi fleet while Áom attempted to communicate the idea to Jón and Ásta.

It took the framandi fleet another half an hour to run the calculations needed, and to reposition their vessels. By this time, the Síast was minutes away from the mouth of the actual wormhole. Áox gave the instruction to execute the hastily cobbled plan.

Matter was concentrated in portions of the screen masking the wormhole, just ahead of the kilig spacecraft. Gravity traps containing antimatter were maneuvered in behind these. Then, just as Kei approached the masked wormhole, an enormous explosion silently tore across the screen. The visual definition was spectacular.

Áom got through to the twins. They were more alert than the last time the framandi was in contact with them. Quickly, instructions were passed back and forth, before a second series of antimatter explosions knocked the siblings' gaupa connections off.

Then for the first time, Kei used the antimatter building up in Síast's primary propulsion system. The rogue AI switched on its antimatter drive, thrusting the kilig vessel through tiny gaps between the framandi fleet. The spacecraft vanished into the wormhole.

Sven sighed and said calmly, "Brace for acceleration." Then he gradually brought Átt up to maximum tolerable acceleration, pursuing Kei into the solar system.

Framandi Alliance

Chapter 19: Skirmish

Max felt like he had been awake for days. Occasionally, he had been. Sitting with Maji in his wardroom on Álfhól space platform, he had the situational awareness feed projected over the conference table. Gogh and Rafael were online with them.

Over the last twelve days, they'd tried to box the Síast within intercepting concentrated solar light and radiation. They'd been unsuccessful. The range hadn't allowed effective targeting. Kei, in its kilig vessel had been able to anticipate the team's every move. On one occasion they'd nearly knocked the Átt out.

The Átt, now ninety tonnes lighter without Suður SSEV, had followed Síast through the framandi-solar system wormhole. It was accompanied by three framandi vessels of equivalent dimensions. Átt's crew including the framandi aboard, had undergone sedated acceleration, hitting and holding twenty-five Gs. They'd now all but caught up with the Síast. The rogue AI had been careful while accelerating, to ensure its human captives were alive and functioning; just barely.

"We don't know what Kei's immediate objectives are," Gogh said. He explained, "Its actions since going rogue, have been to pursue a series of subjugation missions. After the confrontation with the gigils, it's now got a taste for human wetware." Gogh was referring to the capture and subjugation of Jón and Ásta by Kei.

"Why didn't Kei go after the gigils?" Maji pondered aloud.

"Likely a combination of lower wetware capabilities, combined with superior defensive forces," Rafael surmised.

"You really think the gigils have lower brain processing capabilities than us?" Maji asked in surprise.

Rafael replied, "Think about it. While they've had ages to evolve, they seem to rely heavily on automation. It's possible they have highly structured thinking, very similar to the way their automation functions. Over generations, their brains may have become very streamlined. I think Kei may have found easy pickings in the gigils but may have found us to be more versatile."

"Well then, we've got a planet full of versatile people!" Max exclaimed, frowning. He'd been glassy eyed so far. "To get enough of us subjugated, Kei would need force enhancers. Which means, the two salvaged kilig command-ships could be valuable to it." Drawing a trajectory projection, Max said, "It's going to swing close to the kilig ships. We could use them as bait, drawing Síast into a kill-box where our concentrated solar beams could do it some damage."

"What if Kei decides to just tug the kilig command-ships along?" Gogh asked. He clarified, "Kei has done that before with Suður SSEV. It could carry out any work needed on the command-ships, on route to Earth."

"Rig the salvaged kilig command-ships to blow. Hard." Maji suggested.

"So far, explosive force used by the framandi against Síast hasn't damaged the vessel significantly," Max observed. He suggested, "We could use explosives to slow the vessel down and then direct our concentrated solar light and radiation beams at it."

Gogh advised, "Let's do it all. Use the salvaged ships as bait, blow them up as soon as Kei is close; then burn the vessel to crisp."

"What about Jón and Ásta?" Rafael asked.

Gogh answered without blinking, "I'm hoping they find a way to escape from Síast. For now, we're going to assume they've been completely subverted by Kei. Our immediate priority is defence of the solar system."

Rafael felt a sharp ache in his chest which didn't ease immediately. He'd always looked up to the twins. But he understood what was needed. "Agreed," he said, without displaying emotion.

Max connected to and spoke with the xenotechs aboard the two salvaged kilig command-ships, "There's a hostile spacecraft headed your way. Evacuate the vessels you're on and get to Rauður space platform." Gogh gave Katrín and Gylfi similar instructions. As soon as the two kilig command-ships were clear of personnel, Rafael remotely instructed AMCARs to begin towing the kilig command-ships to a spot just off Síast's path. Drones prepared high yield gaupa triggered thermonuclear devices in both the salvaged kilig command-ships.

"Bait's ready. The ships will arrive at the kill-box location in a short while." Rafael announced.

Max observed, "Our situational awareness feed shows the Síast deaccelerating. The spacecraft is beginning to veer sharply towards the kilig command-ships. Pulling up a sharper visual on Síast now."

"Kei's latched on to the bait ships. Its begun accelerating the two vessels with focussed gravity," Maji observed, adding, "the AI doesn't plan on stopping."

"Ready yourself Rafael," Max said urgently, while keying in the appropriate ordinance access codes. The explosives were authenticated by Gogh. As soon as Síast closed in on the kilig vessels, Max directed, "Detonate now."

They watched as two large explosive bubbles enveloped Síast, knocking the spacecraft upward and off its path.

"Rafael, let Kei have it," Max urged. "Burn Síast!" he bellowed.

It took a moment for the system defence satellite network to realign. Four satellites initiated the attack, hitting the Síast with continuous concentrated solar beams. A moment later another two satellites found their mark. The kilig spacecraft began to cook.

"It's correcting itself," Maji warned.

Max instructed, "Rafael, stay with it. There's nothing out there, it can't hide."

Then without warning, the satellites cut out. "What happened?" Max barked in surprise. "Get the beams back on it." he shouted.

"Shun, what's going on?" Rafael asked, unable to locate the problem. He said, "I've lost all satellite control and input feeds."

Shun replied, "The network's been hacked by a friendly authorized gaupa. Records from other connected gaupas show it was Ásta's compact gaupa which accessed the system last. The hack wasn't aimed at taking over the satellite network. It only executed shutdown instructions."

"Bar Jón and Ásta's gaupas from accessing our systems. The ones on their suits and the ones in their escape capsules," Gogh instructed.

Maji looked at the situational awareness feed and said, "The Átt has been decelerating. It's closing in on the Síast."

"Sven, Crystal, Áox and Áom are taking a shuttle across," Max informed, pulling up a visual feed showing the shuttle departing the Átt. He added, "Jón managed to connect with the crew through his diadem and asked for assistance. He suggested triggering the explosives still inside the kilig vessel manually."

They watched as the shuttle approached the Síast and connected with the universal docking port attached to the kilig vessel. By now, the Átt and its escorts were pacing Síast.

An incoming connection blinked on the volumetric projection over Max's conference table. It was Isla calling from Átt. Enabling the connection, Max said, "Please give me some good news."

"Anything but good," a worried looking Isla replied. She said, "Given the proximity, Kei's been able to access Crystal's brain. Sven and the two framandi are fine. They're attempting to breach Síast. I'm sending you Sven's suit video feed."

To Max, this was good news. If they were close enough to breach the kilig vessel, they may just get the upper hand.

Just as Max enlarged Sven's visual feed, an amazed Maji said, "This spacecraft is virtually indestructible. Its begun accelerating again."

The feed showed Sven moving toward the shuttle's hatch. Crystal had been secured to a grav-chair with Áom seated beside. The framandi wasn't moving. Max remembered seeing Áom occasionally remain perfectly still, while the framandi was deeply focussed.

As Max and Maji looked on, they saw Sven open the shuttle's hatch and attempt to disengage the one on Síast. It wouldn't budge. Recalling the specifications, Sven carefully slid open a manual operations panel and then pulled on the lock release. Again, nothing happened. Then Áox tapped him on the shoulder. Sven moved aside.

Raising his right elbow to the exposed panel, a dribble of smart material transferred from Áox's suit. Concentrating, the framandi froze for a moment.

Maji said, "Bet he's trying to disengage the hatch controls from the inside."

"Áox doesn't have a gender. Our framandi friend isn't a 'he'. Makes referring to them very difficult," Max replied absentmindedly; intensely engrossed in what Sven and Áox were up to. He was tired and knew it. But the action on Síast wasn't going to allow him any sleep.

The hatch opened a notch. An unfastened process manual went flying past Sven's visor into the hatch's widening gap, as the shuttle decompressed. Max instinctively held his breath when a narrow laser beam shot through the gap at Sven, from within Síast. It was recognizable as an AMCAR's high wattage drilling laser. Breathing out, Max found himself urging Sven to act, barking, "Crouch."

Sven had immediately deployed his suit's larger laser. It took a moment to extricate itself through the framandi smart material covering his suit.

Sven had momentarily forgotten about it. He made a mental note to do something about having easier access to tools and weapons, if he survived this. As the laser came online, he located the silhouette of the AMCAR and retaliated. For a moment, there was a flurry of tight beams, bouncing off the AMCAR. Then as Sven's laser cooled for a moment, the AMCAR targeted Sven's head. It didn't cause any damage. The framandi smart material took the brunt of laser fire, quickly replacing affected material. Then abruptly, the AMCAR erupted in sparks and fell aside.

Max was entranced. He heard Isla explain what happened. He just caught the tail end of her last statement as she said, "Áox directed smart material into the AMCAR from the hatch and took out its power generating unit."

Then things got even more interesting. Framandi smart material used on portions of Síast during the quick retrofit, began flooding the surfaces around them; some of it gripping Sven and Áox. The material began moving them backward, towards the hatch they'd just entered.

Sven thought to Áox, "Can't you regain access to the smart material?"

Áox replied, "Its slaved to Síast's systems. We would need to find its original manufacturer, through which we could gain access to it. No time now, the material is beginning to force the hatch to close."

As they struggled to break away from the Síast's smart material, a drone zipped beside their heads, through the closing hatch. It didn't completely make it through. The drone's rear portion was caught between the hatch and the port's frame.

Áom thought to them from inside the shuttle, "I've rigged the drone with an explosive payload. Its stuck."

Sven brought his laser up and fired on the rear of the drone. One of its thrusters broke, slicing the drone's right-rear portion clean off. The drone made it through the hatch.

"I'm directing the drone into Síast's command cabin," Áom thought to them. Then the framandi transmitted surprise emotions, adding, "Some of its controls have suddenly become slow. Drone contact is now intermittent."

Sven thought back with urgency, "Kei must be hacking the drone. Trigger the explosive. Do it now."

Neither Sven nor Áox saw anything from the shuttle's universal docking port, where the smart material had dragged them; but they felt the explosive shock through the hull.

Áom transmitted with urgency, "I have contact with Jón and Ásta. The explosion must have damaged some of Kei's hardware. The AI is still functional though. The twins are sluggish but have autonomy. Their capsules were placed in the Síast's ejection bays. They're going to attempt triggering emergency capsule ejection."

"The ejection hatches are jammed," Jón thought to them. "They must have sustained some damage," Ásta added.

"Glad to have you guys back," Sven greeted the twins, thinking to them over the crew's common diadem channel. "I'm back too," Crystal announced, then added, "but I'm feeling a bit groggy and my legs won't move."

"Undock the shuttle from Síast," Sven instructed. He thought a series of images to the rest of them, conveying a plan to pry the capsule escape hatches open.

"You might want to hurry. Kei's attention is focussed on propulsion. The AI is limited for now and is barely able to spare enough processing to stay connected with our minds," Jón thought to them.

Ásta announced excitedly, "I'm able to directly follow Kei's actions. I can actually feel the steps the AI is taking." She exclaimed, "Jæja! Here's something new. I'm now able to access some of the ship's controls, by riding Kei's weakened mind connection." She was oblivious to the ordeal she and her brother had been through so far.

Jón added, "I'm going to try and lock Kei out of its mind access protocol if I can locate it." Then realizing what his sister might be trying, he informed Ásta, "I'll keep limited mind access activated while you ride Kei's signal. Try to locate a separate path to propulsion control. Kei is resisting. This is beginning to give me a headache."

Áom thought to the twins, "I'm going to relieve some of your pain by isolating both your brains' pain pathways. Your attempt to reverse Kei's mind access, is causing your brain to experience ghost visceral pain, associated with your musculoskeletal systems. You'll need to learn to identify things like this, to manage it yourselves in future."

Ásta replied for them, "We're glad you're here Áom. Do what you have to do." Emotions of elation and drive filtered through.

"The shuttle's undocked," Crystal let everyone know. She could still feel Kei's presence in her head. "Manoeuvring to the capsule escape hatches," she added. But before she could get the shuttle into position,

Síast began moving away. She alerted the twins and her crew, "Síast is accelerating. The vessel's picking up speed."

Ásta replied, "Kei's activated antimatter propulsion. Navigation shows Earth as the destination. Hang on. Its showing projected atmospheric entry calculations. Jæja! This is terrible."

Jón interjected, "I'm accessing what equates to Kei's memories and working backward from the last stored navigation commands." After a pause he commented, "You're not going to like what I've just found in current memory. Kei wants control of Earth." He elaborated, "Even with encumbered capabilities, nearly all our planet's technology functions on electromagnetism. Our tech would be highly susceptible to Síast's subjugation capabilities. People would be too."

"Damnit! Not good at all!" Sven shouted. He asked Áox, "How do we catch up with Kei?"

"I have already conveyed our situation to our vessels, and to Átt," Áox answered. The framandi continued, "Together, the four vessels can create a strong gravity well, ahead of us. It'll catapult us towards Síast."

"You're conveying dejected and sad emotions, why?" Sven asked.

"The pressure from the required acceleration will be fatal for you and Crystal," Áox.

Without emotion, Sven thought back, "Then the two of us are of no further use in this endeavour. Give the go ahead." As soon as Áox had passed on the instructions, Sven said to the framandi, "Grab Crystal. Help me get her off the shuttle. We're hopping off this bus, right here."

The two of them assisted Crystal to the universal docking port which was immediately decompressed. Without another thought exchanged, Sven stepped off the shuttle. He hung on tightly to Crystal, while he grabbed a tether attached through the smart material covering her suit.

Sven and Crystal used suit thrusters to decelerate as they watched the shuttle in the distance, magnified by the smart material sensors. Then abruptly the shuttle shot ahead and disappeared. They were alone in deep space, their conventional emergency beacons pinged away, while their suits' compact gaupas, updated their location to Átt.

"Hello. Hear you're looking for a lift," a happy voice faintly crackled through their earpieces. Sven's suit indicated a radio transmission.

"This is Sven de Vries. Who's there?" Sven replied cheerfully. Crystal and he'd been adrift a mere ten minutes. He'd expected the crew from Átt to connect with them through their gaupas.

"This is Gylfi Hallgrímsson along with Katrín Magnusdóttir," the voice answered. Gylfi continued, "We've been tracking the Átt's progress. Our situational awareness feed just updated with your location. The Átt and the accompanying framandi vessels are going after Síast. They have their hands full. We're in the Habogi, a 'nesting doll' cargo and transport vessel, close to your present trajectory."

"The Habogi! I remember it. We've used the ACTV before," Crystal exclaimed, sounding optimistic. She asked, "How far out are you?"

"You'll have to hang on for forty minutes. We're already decelerating," Katrín answered.

"Super!" Crystal yelled happily.

"We're really glad you're coming to get us. Meanwhile, we'll get in touch with Átt and let them know we're okay. Hopefully they can transmit the situational awareness feed through our gaupas. We were hooked up to the shuttle's conventional communications," Sven said.

"Will do." Gylfi answered. "We've begun to receive telemetry from your suit. We're locked on to your position. See you soon," he stated encouragingly.

Crystal told Sven, "I'm feeling great now. Not foggy any longer. Guess Kei's let go of my brain. And thankfully, I can also wriggle my toes."

The two of them drifted on their previous path while Átt's crew took turns speaking with them. They'd begun receiving a fresh feed which showed Áox's and Áom's view. The two framandi were just about hanging on to consciousness. The fantastic force of acceleration on the shuttle had been hard, even on their toughened bodies. Their suits were healing them as they caught up to Síast.

"Ásta and I will pass out soon," Sven and Crystal heard Jón's voice, conveyed to their minds through their diadems. "Síast's accelerating hard. We're facing more vertical Gs than our suits or Síast's internal gravity balancing can compensate for," they heard him say. Then there was nothing further.

On Átt, Isla thought she'd have a nervous breakdown. Since entering the solar system, they'd been strapped into their grav-chairs most of the time. They'd pushed their bodies to deal with the exertion of the assignment. The uncertainty of Jón's fate was eating into her. Átt was falling behind the accompanying framandi vessels. Their escorts had increased acceleration, to chase after Áox and Áom. She hung on, keeping an eye on the projected situational awareness feed.

Stefán announced, "Síast's acceleration is evening out. I think Kei is trying to balance between keeping Ásta and Jón alive and arriving quickly at Earth."

Jón had passed on the rogue AI's intensions before he'd passed out. Ásta had also communicated that the two of them had managed to access portions of Síast's systems by riding Kei's mind access signals.

Isla's intense feeling of dread subsided, but only slightly. She heard Eiji say, "Kei's trying to achieve multiple immediate objectives, simultaneously. Getting to Earth quickly, cutting off the twins' access to Síast's systems and keeping them alive. I've estimated that it's delicately balancing the three objectives, by gently massaging Síast's acceleration. It's up to the framandi now."

Sven said, "You're right, we're out of this chase. There's little chance of us catching up with either the Síast or the framandi. Crystal, drop our acceleration to six Gs. The speed we've picked up will see us at Earth in sixty hours, including time to deaccelerate. We need to rest and recover before deceleration. We're just observers now."

None of the crew objected. They were all intelligent enough to understand the reasoning, however awful any of them felt.

Thirty-two hours later Áox and Áom had caught up with the Síast. They'd used manual thrusters to align the shuttle and bring it within hundred meters of the kilig spacecraft controlled by Kei. The two framandi were completely recuperated by now. They were providing a continuous visual feed to their own vessels, the crew on Átt and other Lýsi observers. A live common communication channel, connected through two separate gaupas on Átt, ensured the crew were able to keep in touch with Áox and Áom. Observers without diadems, saw a simplified text translation of the framandi communication, deciphered by Shun. Crystal provided a separate narration for the benefit of anyone not on the common gaupa channel.

As they watched, Áox and Áom pushed themselves off the shuttle, just as it was beginning to overhaul Síast. They made tiny course corrections as they rapidly closed the distance to the kilig spacecraft.

"Closing in on the kilig spacecraft. Aiming to land beside the capsule ejection hatches. We will begin to cut off the hatches over Jón and Ásta's capsules simultaneously," Áox conveyed over the common comm channel.

As the two framandi neared Síast's hull, a battered but modified AMCAR emerged from the vessel's docking port. It launched itself off the spacecraft. Built for rigorous autonomous asteroid mining or construction tasks, it was a daunting sight, even for the framandi. Alert and anxious emotions registered on their live channel.

The AMCAR immediately began firing both its high wattage lasers at Áox who was leading. The framandi chose not to take any evasive action, absorbing the brunt of the attack, while Áom followed closely behind.

Just as the AMCAR was about to collide with Áox, the framandi fired propellent thrusters and dove under the autonomous robot. Áom swung upward and over the AMCAR. It thrust out with its long hyper-redundant snake-arm manipulator, grabbing the framandi by the left leg. Both Áox and the autonomous robot pivoted. The AMCAR quickly stabilised itself while reeling the framandi in.

Áom began to slowly and deliberately take the AMCAR apart, beginning with a protruding visual sensor pod. The robot's lasers were both focussing on specific points on the framandi's suit, attempting to overcome the constantly replaced smart material. Another snake-arm lunged at Áom's second foot. Leaning towards the AMCAR's larger laser, Áom struck it hard. Nothing happened.

Sven, who'd spent time on the AMCAR design project, thought to the framandi, "The robot is built to withstand tremendous abuse, including collisions with asteroids. You'll need to breach the panel next to the laser, on the far side. There are similar maintenance panels for the robotic arms too."

Grappling with the larger laser, Áom swung it away while crouching. A dribble of the framandi's suit's smart material, found its way to the laser's maintenance panel. Moments later the panel popped off and floated into space. Immediately after, the laser ceased functioning. Áom sequentially took out the second laser and then the snake arms, while noticing the increasing gap between the Síast and the AMCAR. By the time the framandi had disabled the robot's ability to do any more damage, they were over six thousand meters away. Áom quickly calculated an appropriate trajectory and launched off the AMCAR, using thrusters to accelerate.

Áox, having safely landed next to the designated spot on Síast, had begun working on the closest escape hatch. Turning towards Áom, Áox reached out to steady the rapidly approaching framandi. Áom overshot. Áox felt a jerk and a gradual shift in gravity. Kei had initiated deceleration, in preparation for arrival at Earth. Latching onto the hull of the kilig spacecraft, Áox launched off the surface, trailing a thin strand of smart material. Noticing the distance to Áom increase, Áox activated thrusters while Áom pivoted and slowed. They closed the gap between themselves. Within a minute the two framandi connected; just barely. Áom grasped Áox's hand a moment before the Síast would have pulled the framandi away. The two of them made their way to the hatch Áox had been working on. The deceleration force was gradually becoming stronger.

They changed tactics. Instead of tackling both hatches simultaneously, Áom supplied additional quantities of smart material, to aid Áox's supply at the first hatch. The work progressed slowly. Kei was using its own smart material, previously drawn into the spacecraft, to counter the effects of the framandi's efforts. The framandi had to commit nearly all their spare suit material to the task. They'd instructed their material to eject Kei's into space, eroding the AI's ability to repair and reintroduce smart material. They shouldn't have been able to do this, but somehow, they were getting away with it.

"Áom, Áox, are you close by?" Jón asked. Both framandi paused, communicated between each other, and then Áox replied, "We are on Síast, trying to cut off the hatches over your and Ásta's capsules."

"Ásta and I just regained consciousness," Jón informed them. He continued, "We're attempting to pick up where we left off. This time around, we've had quicker results. We've been able to partially restrict Kei's access to our wetware. Hopefully we'll learn how to completely protect ourselves. Also, we were able to momentarily undermine Kei's control over smart material slaved to Síast."

"You have very little time to escape," Áom let the twins know. "We'll soon be at your planet. According to our calculations, Kei plans to take advantage of your planet's spin, to bring Síast in on a high velocity entry, in the direction of the spin."

"How much time do we have?" Ásta asked.

Pausing briefly to calculate, Áom responded, "A little over one Earth hour. Áox and I will have the capsule hatches off by then. Sooner if you can completely disrupt Kei's control over Síast's smart material."

"I'll do that while Jón tries to gain control over the propulsion systems," Ásta said.

They all got down to the tasks at hand. Framandi and human observers felt helpless. Ten minutes after their last communication, Síast's smart material ceased battling the framandi's. Áom and Áox picked up the pace. They ripped off the first capsule's hatch. The twins chose to eject together, only once the second hatch was cut off. The framandi started on the second hatch while the twins tackled Kei directly.

"Second hatch cut away. Eject now. Our three masked vessels have just arrived. They will pick us up," Áox informed the twins as the two framandi stepped away from the capsule hatches. Seconds later both escape capsules shot out of Síast, rapidly falling behind as thrusters cut in. The two framandi leapt off the kilig spacecraft's hull after them.

As they were exiting Síast, Jón thought to Ásta over the common channel, "Remember the hostile gigil drone we destroyed, while first entering the framandi system?"

"Yes, we formed a focussed gravity point inside the drone, causing it to implode," Ásta replied.

Jón said, "Follow my lead. See the steps in my mind. We're going to kill the antimatter trap in Síast."

Moments later a massive explosion erupted ahead of them. The two framandi were enveloped in it. Áom communicated their situation. "Extreme heat and rapid degradation of our exterior matter," Áom announced while transmitting concern.

"We've been knocked into a high velocity atmospheric entry trajectory," Áox informed urgently. "We're altering exterior material for re-entry," the framandi thought to the twins.

"Re-entry suit-form completed. But my suit's exterior material has now fused due to the heat. It's no longer responding," Áom let them know.

Áox and Áom began to descend rapidly. The three disguised framandi vessels had entered gravity projection range but were unable to capture them.

Jón thought to them over the common channel, "Ásta and I are coming after you. We'll grab you once you hit terminal velocity. Sooner, if possible."

Then Ásta transmitted directly to her brother's mind, "Jón look at the feed from the Síast's explosion. The control cabin shell has survived. I can still feel Kei trying to access my brain's processing capabilities."

"I'd have thought surviving that explosion would have been impossible," Jón replied incredulously, realising he too felt the faint brain-lag from Kei's presence.

"Go after it. You're closest. Pull Kei's trajectory from the situational awareness feed. I'll go after Áom," Ásta told her brother.

Readjusting his re-entry angle, Jón chased after the rogue AI in the control cabin shell. He announced, "If the cabin survived the explosion, its likely to have the compressive strength to endure aerodynamic heating and atmospheric drag. I'm on its tail."

As the observers watched helplessly, the two framandi hit Earth's atmosphere, enclosed in their sphere-cone shaped entry shells. Ásta followed, carefully increasing speed. Jón was a lot more cavalier and generously plied every bit of acceleration the emergency capsule was capable of. Moments later, Kei's cabin shell entered the atmosphere followed closely by Jón.

Lýsi began emergency measures on Earth after pinpointing Kei's expected landing point. It was heading for the coast off San Francisco Bay. A location close to Santa Clara, the home of Silicon Valley and the hub of most of the world's high technology. Kei was expected to splash down right over some of the world's most important submarine data cables. The rogue AI very likely had the knowledge gleaned from its initial merger with the kilig AI, on manufacturing electromagnetic subjugation hardware. Lýsi leadership concluded that if Kei was able to inject itself into Earth's internet, there may not be a way to stop it. Every piece of electronic technology and every person was at risk. Drastic and immediate action was needed.

Framandi Alliance

Chapter 20: Resolution

"I've got a lock on Áom," Áox let Ásta know. They'd just finished dumping most of their kinetic energy through atmospheric dissipation. The three of them were coming in over the southern portion of continental Africa and expected to splash down smack in the middle of the Indian Ocean.

"I've lost control of my capsule's vanes. They're jammed. I'll have to exit the capsule and glide to you," Ásta thought to Áox.

Bracing herself for rapid decompression, Ásta toggled the manual release, unlocking the hatch. It triggered a valve, releasing all the internal pressure. Air pressure soon equalized and she was able to swing the hatch outward and to the side. Without hesitation, she unfastened the harness securing her to the capsule's grav-chair. Ásta gripped the handle above the exit and flung herself against the rushing air. She was free of the capsule without incident.

Activating all her suit's sensors including the framandi outer material's, Ásta quickly located Áox. The framandi was ahead of her at a thirty-degree angle, about three kilometres away. Zooming in on Áox, she saw the framandi pressed against the side of Áom's atmospheric entry shell, hanging on to the lower section with both arms. Then the framandi slowly began extending smart material to create additional resistance.

Remembering the glider shape her suit's framandi smart material could form, she thought to Áox, "I see you. Switching my suit to glider mode now. Will be with you soon."

Gliding with upper winds behind her and occasionally diving headfirst towards the two framandi, Ásta caught up with them in three minutes. She realised they were falling too fast.

Áox thought to her, asking, "Do you remember the form your suit took, when we infiltrated the gigil compound, back in the lofi system?" The framandi clarified, "We'll slow our descent. Grab Áom like I have and mentally instruct your suit's outer material to form the shape. I will do the same."

As her suit flared out around her, it first took on the shape of an upside-down button mushroom, with her at the bottom. As their decent slowed, the material began to extend further, becoming more parachute-like.

Realising they were out of immediate danger, Ásta asked over the common channel, "What's Jón's status?"

"This is Rafael," Ásta heard over her earpiece. "Jón's performing a manoeuvre just like yours. He's exiting his capsule to get to Kei quickly. Access my feed for a visual. We have drones in their area tracking them."

Jón was already gliding, descending quickly towards Kei's cabin shell, when Ásta connected with him. She pulled his sensor feed. As she patched Áom and Áox in through her suit's compact gaupa, she noticed something shoot its way towards Jón, from landside. It was just a blur.

"What's that object leaving a condensation trail and heading towards Kei?" Ásta asked Rafael.

"That's not a condensation trail. That's rocket exhaust," Rafael answered gravely. He elaborated, "It's armed with a high yield nuclear payload. The rocket was launched minutes ago from a friendly navy's submarine, positioned just off the Mexican coast."

Doing some rough math, Ásta realised the missile would hit the cabin shell well before Jón got to it. She connected with her brother over the common channel, "Jón watch out for the missile." Realizing Kei could still be affecting his thinking ability, she linked him to the feed showing the missile through her diadem. Ásta hoped her brother would try to be careful.

Jón replied, "I'm thirty-two kilometres away. We made atmospheric entry at a shallow angle so we're still high enough for me to make it to the cabin shell. That is if the missile doesn't destroy it first."

Then, as they watched, the missile's plume went out and it began to tumble, causing it to break apart.

"Looks like Kei's hacked the missile," Rafael let them all know. He added, "The submarine's launching another."

"I'll get to it before," Jón said, diving to gain speed.

As he approached, he could feel Kei trying to use more of his wetware. Jón fought the AI's invasion of his mind, pulling back control where he felt Kei's presence. Soon he was upon the cabin shell. He clambered over it, struggling to gain access from a side hatch. It was sealed shut. Then he remembered the hole on the main access door, burnt out by a drone when Kei had first attacked them.

Climbing over the cabin shell, Jón made his way to the rear section, locating the main access hatch. The hole was still visible on the door, plugged with smart material. Without missing a beat, Jón activated his primary laser and began to neatly slice around the circumference of the plugged hole, figuring the area would be weakened. He programmed the laser to continue cutting until the smart material was dislodged. The smart material didn't react to his actions. It was still disabled from the twins' last interaction with Síast. Bringing up his secondary laser, Jón aimed and target-locked it on the four-kiloton explosive device he had set up under his grav-chair, when they were salvaging Síast. Kei had not removed it. "Big mistake," Jón thought.

Then things happened quickly. Jón's primary laser knocked out the blocked hole on the transparent hatch. As the debris flew aside, Jón fired his secondary laser at the explosive kit inside the cabin, aiming at the detonator.

The resulting explosion was recorded by infrasound detection as a meteor air burst, west of California, over the Pacific ocean.

Thrown off and clear, Jón lost consciousness. Just before he did, he felt his mind was released of Kei. He'd thought of floating to the surface, as his mind went blank. Jón's suit's framandi smart material complied with his last thought, unfurling and slowing his descent. He awoke with a start, just as he splashed into the Pacific. The framandi smart material covering his HSEVA suit had protected him, but he felt like a few of his lower left ribs may have cracked.

Jón let out a groan. A mix of pain and relief. Shun's voice came over his earpiece, "I have your location. Directing rescue assets to you."

"Well, I'm sinking. You'll need to have underwater rescue capable equipment sent over," Jón replied, happy to be back on Earth. Then he asked, "What's the date? I've lost track of time."

"It's the 23rd of April 2001. You've been in space seventy-three days since launch," Shun replied. The AI added, "Gogh is close by piloting one of our next generation submersible yachts. Rafael is with him, standing by in the submersible's airlock. You'll sink to the ocean floor to a spot that has some rough terrain, but you should be fine."

"What about Ásta?" Jón asked. He'd temporarily lost his diadem and gaupa connections. They'd just begun to reacquire previous contacts.

Shun didn't reply over his suit's conventional radio. Instead the AI communicated via Jón's miniature gaupa connected to his diadem. Shun said, "What I'm about to reveal is confidential. I trust that Ásta and you will keep it as a secret."

Without pausing the AI said, "When Kei went rogue, I filtered and transferred my entire knowledge base to a separate entity I'd been preparing. Its sole purpose is to keep Earth and all its life safe, while learning about the universe. This new AI is my offspring, in a manner of speaking. I have named it Shison, meaning 'progeny' in Japanese. Just like we have hardware and resource independence in space, I have provided similar capabilities to Shison. Ásta and the two framandi have made a water landing in the middle of the Indian Ocean. Just like you're presently sinking, they've sunk to the ocean floor as well. They're close to the Langseth Trough. Incidentally, that's where Shison's primary hub is located."

"This is very big news. Who else knows?" Jón asked.

"Only Rafael. Should something go wrong, he knows how to deactivate Shison," Shun replied.

Jón said, "You'll have to brief me in detail later. I'm connecting us to Ásta now." Linking to his twin wasn't difficult. Routed through her suit's gaupa, Ásta accepted Jón's incoming diadem connection immediately.

"Jæja! I was beginning to worry," Ásta thought to her brother. She continued, "I was plugged in to the visual feed that was tracking you, until you splashed into the Pacific." She asked, "Are you all right?"

"I'm okay. Battered but okay," Jón replied. He asked his sister, "How're you faring?"

Ásta replied, "Right now, we have complications to deal with ourselves. We're chest deep in marine sediment. Áox was hanging on to the lower portion of Áom's suit shell and is completely buried. Our framandi friend is unable to get out. Now, there are several sharks circling us. I've identified them as goblin sharks. Very unusual to see them around here. Here's the kicker, they're not organic. The sharks are robotic."

Shun interrupted them saying, "That's Shison observing you and the framandi."

"Hello Shun. Who or what is Shison?" Ásta asked.

"Shun's offspring," Jón replied. He added, "It's a secret we're going to keep to ourselves for now. Shun will update us separately."

Shun said, "Shison will use the drone goblin sharks, to dig you out. They'll be using pressurised water to dislodge the sediment around you. Meanwhile, I've redirected an autonomous submersible yacht to you. Currently, it's just off Port-aux-Français. It'll bring you to Marion Island where everyone is regrouping."

Two days later, the twins and the two framandi arrived at Lýsi's Marion Island facility, located between South Africa and Antarctica. A framandi shuttle disguised like one of Lýsi's flying wing aircraft had arrived to accommodate Áom and Áox. Another two days went by while all of them recuperated. Then Gogh requested they all meet. Everyone gathered in the island's well-equipped primary mission hanger.

"It's been a frenzied few weeks and you've all been through a lot," Gogh addressed the twins, the framandi and a group of Lýsi leaders, including a few uniformed senior military officers, from an assortment of nations. The crew of Átt, the twins' parents and the space defence team from Álfhól; attended virtually. Volumetric projections placed each attendee amongst the gathering.

Clearing his throat, Gogh called to the group, "My friends, we've accomplished fabulous achievements. We have successfully defended the solar system and Earth against a hostile AI intent on subjugating us. In the process, we've exhausted all the space resources we'd accumulated over the last decade, by rapidly manufacturing defences. And, what we've just faced is but a speck compared to what's out there. We've opened a door that's revealed more than we could ever expect."

There were murmurs around the hanger. People began asking questions. Ásta looked at Jón questioningly. Jón shrugged. They'd taken off their diadems for the duration of the meeting. Gogh raised his hand to quiet everyone down.

"We've been in communication with Áoe, the framandi holding the position of Advisor of the Enlightened. The information they've gathered, has shaken them. Us as well," Gogh announced. Pausing a moment while he projected visuals, Gogh continued, "The masked framandi scout drones in the planetary system, beyond the vilji system, sent us updated visual sensor data. We've observed the gigils accumulating a massive armada via several connected systems. Forward elements of the armada have begun to enter a large, heavily defended wormhole. A few of the masked framandi drones managed to slip through behind a gigil freighter-ship." Gogh paused again as he brought a projected screen into focus, then said, "It sent us this."

There were gasps from around the room. The drones' visual reconnaissance showed a view from behind the gigil freighter-ship. A massive pencil shaped vessel, hung vertically in space, surrounded by a handful of familiar looking kilig spacecraft. The kiligs were battling the gigils and other unknown fleets; all of whom were pouring into the system which the masked framandi drones had infiltrated. The scale of the confrontation was gargantuan.

The large kilig spaceship was positioned close to a planet with atmosphere. The reconnaissance feed zoomed in on the planet. It was surrounded by kilig command-ships.

"Our understanding is that the planet you're seeing is being subjugated by the kiligs," Pointing to the twins he said. "We know from Jón and Ásta's experience that subjugated individuals can carry on with their normal activities, albeit a bit sluggishly. Crystal Vance our astrophysicist aboard Átt, and the transhuman twins Jón and Ásta have reported this."

Zooming out to the system-wide view, Gogh continued, "The planetary system is filled with damaged hardware. The kiligs seem to be subjugating the gigils and other opposition, using their own ships against them. According to the framandi, the amount of debris is relatively low. This means the confrontation is young. The gigils and their allies are pursuing a strategy of attrition. Presently, they seem to be filling the system with armed vessels, possibly in preparation of a massed assault. If the kiligs already have complete dominance over their subjects on the occupied planet, all they need to do is amplify their use of the population's collective wetware, to persevere. We don't know who the subjugated species are, or what their capabilities may be. What we do know is that neither the framandi nor we, ever want to be in such a position."

Now Áom and Áox stepped forward and joined Gogh. The framandi had discarded the use of suits after Lýsi scientists had confirmed that the genetic alterations from the viral bombardment of Earth, had achieved enough absorption. Shun translated Áom's thoughts, providing a deep, neutral and slightly melodious synthetized voice.

"We will be migrating a third of our population, from our home system, to a newly occupied planet in your galaxy," Áom said. A visual of the Beta Hydri system was projected for any uninformed attendees' benefit. The framandi pointed to the information being projected and added, "To do this, we would need to pass through your planetary system. We have agreed to conduct the migration after two of your years; a duration we require to set up suitable infrastructure on the planet being occupied by us."

Áox spoke next stating, "We have also agreed to permit humans through our own system, to explore and occupy the lofi system. The fifth planet in the system has been ascertained to be suitable for you. We will aid you in preparing the planet, making it compatible for Earth species. Simultaneously, we will help clean up the debris and wayward asteroids

367

left over from the recent confrontation with the gigils. This too will take a duration of two Earth years."

There were nods and murmuring amongst the gathered Lýsi members. While some of the people in the hanger had first-hand knowledge of the framandi alliance, for most, this announcement was new information. None were opposed.

Gogh continued, "We have created a mutually beneficial alliance with the framandi. They have extensive knowledge, which we must learn. We have ingenuity and versatility which the framandi can utilise." Taking a deep breath, Gogh stated, "Finally, we have agreed to jointly develop a first line of defence in the vilji system. Details of this defence system are still to be determined. The defences deployed will be jointly replicated in all systems occupied by either humans or framandi; or both."

Jón and Ásta left the hanger with Rafael after the announcements had been made. The young transhuman had been instrumental in developing the very first system-defence satellite network. He had just regained control of the network, after Kei had used Ásta to shut it down. Shun's mission AIs had detected the hack and automatically locked everyone out. Now, the twins were eager to find out more about it and the secretly hived AI Shison. Before they made it halfway to a secluded office and operations structure, they were called over their earpieces.

Gogh instructed them, "Get over to the disguised framandi shuttle please. Áox and Áom have a surprise for you. For Rafael as well in fact."

The trio turned off the path they were on and walked over to the island's airfield. It looked larger and more developed than the twins remembered. They were let into a sectioned off secure bay, beside a service apron, where the framandi vessel was parked.

The twins reached into their backpacks. They'd carried their diadems along but hadn't worn them while in public. Now, they needed their diadems to communicate with the framandi.

Áox was waiting for them outside the shuttle. The framandi thought to the twins, "I am glad to meet Rafael. Please share my greetings with your young accomplice." Jón did as the framandi asked. Turning, Áox simply thought to them, "Come."

Following the framandi inside, the twins saw a familiar hanger-like chamber, like the one they'd seen on AL-I. Áox waved Rafael over to the scanner. The young transhuman tensed as the scanner ring gently fell around him, from the roof to the floor of the chamber. Then after a few moments a console extended from the wall beside him. A fresh diadem appeared with Rafael's name embossed on the left side.

"You're going to get new ones too," Áox informed the twins. The framandi continued, "We've updated the human diadem interface for enhanced capabilities. This includes multiple gaupa and linked diadem connections. The fresh diadems have increased range, enough to reach another, across a planet twice the radius of Earth. They're slimmer so they won't be visible through your hair when worn. Additionally, they have some processing capabilities which will allow you to operate most of your equipment, without the need for your mission pads."

As Rafael tried on his diadem, another two consoles extended from the wall. They contained fresh diadems for the twins. While Jón and Ásta helped Rafael with diadem calibration, Áox disappeared for a while.

Soon after Rafael got the hang of his diadem, Áox returned, trailed by a group of framandi. They slid three large containers up to the trio.

Áox thought to them, "Gogh provided us with your suits for post-use stress analysis. They've performed exceptionally well. Aided by your AI Shun, we have redesigned your suits and accompanying smart material. Here are new suits manufactured for the three of you. Much improved suits." The framandi accompanying Áox turned to the containers. The containers rippled, changing shape. They formed into suits. Bulkier and more formidable.

"This is really neat!" Rafael exclaimed. He added, "I can't wait to put it through its paces."

"Actually, you're going to try them on right now," Áox thought to them. The framandi added, "The Átt has arrived at Earth. The vessel is in high orbit. We're going to use our shuttle to extract your crew. We'll also be delivering a replacement crew, who will take Átt to your Álfhól space platform. Then, after dropping you off, this time on an island which has been referred to as Iceland, we will depart for our home system."

As soon as the Átt was docked with the framandi shuttle, Isla was first at the port hatch. She jumped into Jón's arms, a tear sneaking its way down her right cheek. Ásta was already in touch with Stefán over a diadem link. The two of them snuck aside for a quick kiss and a moment alone.

No time was wasted. The crew swap was conducted efficiently. Átt's crew handed over their used HSEVA suits to the framandi. The suits were recycled, and fresh suits were manufactured by the framandi, on the way down to Earth. The shuttle landed at a secluded permaculture research farm operated by Lýsi, north of Reykjavík, the island's capital.

Three trucks waited to transport Átt's crew to Lýsi's secure research and residential property in Reykjavík.

After stowing their new suits in a guarded underground vault, the eight space adventurers got together in a condominium allocated to Sven. They were joined by Rafael who had been tasked with salvaging the kilig vessel's cabin shell from the Pacific, for transport to Sólríka space platform. After that Rafael was to survey the system-defence network, while working with Max to develop enhancements.

"I can't even begin to express how glad I am to have us all together," Sven said to the crew while pouring out a local unsweetened but strong schnapps. Jón had ordered in an Icelandic puffin delicacy, which Ásta was singlehandedly demolishing. Everyone cheered along. They exchanged stories, quirks that each of them had developed and recalled close calls for the benefit of Rafael. By the time the second bottle of schnapps was downed, they were laughing riotously. The pent-up months of pressure ebbed away.

The next day, the crew parted ways. Each heading off to spend time with family, or to holiday.

"Plan on travelling?" Jón asked his sister.

Ásta replied, "Stefán and I are going to explore the countryside. A little camping in the cold and fresh air. I'm going to show him my favourite Huldufólk spots. When we return, he's taking me to meet his folks."

Jón raised an eyebrow and smiled at his sister. He cautioned, "Big steps. Keep your diadem on. Be safe."

"What about you?" Ásta asked.

"Isla and I are going to holiday at her home in New Zealand," Jón said.

"Don't forget that we have to meet móðir and faðir in Cuba next month," Ásta said, referring to their parents. She added, "They want to run some tests on us there, in preparation of the next generation of transhumans, integrating bits of new framandi knowledge."

Jón kissed her on the forehead and left. As he walked out of his parents' home, his gut told him that they'd likely be called on sooner than the two years in which the framandi were expected to migrate through the solar system. But for now, it was time to live a little.

Epilogue
Excerpts from the Notes of Shison (Gen3 AI)

A s Shun took on the full AI burden of Lýsi, Jón, Ásta and Rafael began to rely heavily on the AI's offspring. Shison was like a family member, unseen but always available. After Shun had provided the twins with a detailed rundown on Shison, the young AI had slipped into their lives, giving them regular updates on events unfolding in the solar system and beyond.

The most recent update concerned an analysis of the framandi home planet which Átt had briefly orbited. The AI had pulled a few key observations and referenced accessible framandi data to corroborate. The most important of these, was that while the framandi had shaped the surface to be completely pollution-free and dominated by nature, underground, the framandi were still undertaking a massive clean-up, the remnants of past industrialization and planetary conflicts. On the surface, the framandi used minimal technology, preferring mechanical tools, or symbiotic bioengineered species.

Essentially, the framandi home world had been turned into a zero-waste planet. Resources were constantly recycled. All dangerous waste was transferred to masked space-based facilities for processing. There wasn't much of this.

The framandi themselves chose simple, minimalist lives. They overproduced the essentials, to ensure reasonable comfort. Every individual was provided a dwelling, wherever they chose to live on the planet. Clothing was recycled and reintroduced into the population. Food production was massively distributed, with much of the population cultivating their own produce locally, utilizing biomimicry principles. The biosphere was diverse and exceptionally well balanced. The only downside was that the number of species observed was limited, either due to previous extinction, or culling.

Other than cultivation, the planet based framandi occupied themselves in study, research and species advancement. They occasionally rotated off-planet to take on different roles, once enough learning had been 'absorbed' into their own genetic material or into their second brains. Their second brains were used exclusively for information storage.

The framandi society didn't operate a monetary system. They overproduced everything their simple lives needed, and products were built to last, minimising waste. Anything not available in community resource centres was manufactured on demand, a capability extensively used by the species in space.

Shison had explained to the young transhumans, that being without gender, the framandi developed a unique reproduction system, crafted into their genetic code. Two or more individuals having agreed to reproduce, met at the closest community resource centre, where they enclosed themselves in a circular room prepared for reproducing couples or groups. They would then begin a deep study of each other's genetic information, gathering knowledge and negotiating on what information their offspring should have at birth. The parents would then sit with their backs to each other, while two appendages extended from each. The appendages would join to form a birthing sac. An embryo would begin to form in it, using the finalised genetic code. The sac could be nourished automatically by cradles available in the community resource centre or be carried on one of the parent's backs, attached to a detachable umbilical.

The transhuman twins had asked that this information be made available to Lýsi leadership, via Shun. Some of the planet repair, biosphere management and waste management concepts were then repurposed for Earth use and released to public entities.

A year after the Átt had entered the Iofi system, the framandi had intimated the original crew and interested parties from Lýsi, that the clean-up of the Iofi system had been completed well ahead of time. A detailed survey of the fifth planet had been completed as well. Six gigil facilities were located on the planet, including the one penetrated by Átt's crew with framandi assistance.

The Átt was fitted with a new SSEV to replace Suður and was dispatched to the Iofi system with a fresh crew. The SSEV took on the same name as its predecessor. They were tasked with setting up the primary infrastructure for three space platforms, which were to be constructed by AMCARs, using the abundant asteroid resources available in the system. But first, the crew were to infiltrate all other gigil facilities, with framandi assistance. A viral container barrage was planned to be launched, from the first completed platform. Drones were deployed to the planet, to sample and study the makeup of the fifth planet's viruses. The variety seen on Earth wasn't available. It was surmised that the gigil had wiped out all incompatible species. As the first people to set foot on the planet, Ásta and Jón were called upon to name it. After much deliberation and their brief adventure there, they suggested the planet be named 'Saga', a word derived from the Icelandic term for 'tale'. The first steps out of the solar system had begun, even before people had begun to truly colonize the home system itself.

Soon after Átt arrived at Saga, news came of the framandi commencing transfer of individuals and families, to an armada of masked vessels in their fleet. As was framandi custom when communicating, they shared every detail considered relevant. Much of the population being transferred, were young. Most chose induced hibernation, to reduce the resource consumption burden on the transport-ships. Over a period of six months, the transport-ships were filled with framandi who had chosen to take on the adventure of migration. According to a low priority, appended point of information, framandi who migrated would have the option of returning to their home system should they ever wish to. Communication via gaupas made time and distance between the framandi home system and the soon to be occupied Beta Hydri, unimportant.

Three months before the framandi migration was to commence, a delegation including Áom, Áox and Áoe, along with their migrating counterparts, visited Earth to reaffirm the alliance between the two civilizations.

Corridors for the migration were charted and assigned through the Kuiper belt, forty-five AU away from the Sun. The distance was determined by the need to keep the mass migration away from public attention on Earth.

While these preparations were being undertaken, framandi observation drones were keeping a sharp eye on the confrontation ensuing between the kilig and opposing species. After the first few battles in which the gigils were the most scathed, they chose their confrontations more prudently. There was a gradual build-up of kilig-opposing forces, but direct conflict was being avoided. Two new wormholes were being rapidly pried open in the confrontation plagued system. One directly attributed to the gigils and the other to the kiligs. Neither were being used, but the diameter of the openings would soon fit a moon-sized object through. Additional framandi observation drones were tasked to observe. By now, the gigils had detected the framandi drones, all of which had been closely examined, but none were attacked.

Once the details of the migration through the solar system were chalked out, a final point was appended to the alliance between humans and framandi. A jointly operated space platform would be constructed in each of the systems occupied by either species. These were to host a permanent presence from both species and become diplomatic in nature, where individuals from each species could familiarize themselves with the other.

On 20th January 2003, the situation in the conflict-ridden system changed, when a gigil moon-ship entered through one of the newly formed wormholes, followed soon by what was assumed to be a similarly armed vessel on the kilig side. Fearing fallout, the framandi migration was brought forward and immediately initiated.

Jón and Ásta were tasked to observe and aid in the migration. They boarded the Átt, which had just been refitted after returning from a long deployment, in the lofi system. The vessel's first crew were brought together again. This time they were joined by Rafael and Alyssa Carney, a Lýsi xenotechnologist from San Francisco. The Átt departed Álfhól space platform three days after the framandi migration was initiated. If their last inter-system voyage had taught them anything, it was to expect adventure. They were ready for it.

About the Author

Rashid Ahmed is a science fiction writer and digital marketing specialist who has always been interested in technology, its evolution and impact. Having held various advertising and marketing roles, he has evolved into a weaver of stories. Aimed at readers who like immersive experiences, Rashid's writing balances concept detailing with easy comprehension. His interests also include economics, ecosystem restoration and permaculture.

Visit **www.RashidAhmed.com** for more content.
Follow @Kaputnik77 on social media for updates.

If you enjoyed Framandi Alliance, please leave a review on Amazon.

Printed in Great Britain
by Amazon